Making
Waves

Making Waves

A NOVEL

LORNA SEILSTAD

Revell

a division of Baker Publishing Group
Grand Rapids, Michigan

Published by Revell
a division of Baker Publishing Group
P.O. Box 6287, Grand Rapids, MI 49516-6287
www.revellbooks.com

Printed in the United States of America

Library of Congress Cataloging-in-Publication Data
Seilstad, Lorna.
    Making waves : a novel / Lorna Seilstad.
      p.   cm. — (Lake Manawa summers ; bk. 1)
    ISBN 978-0-8007-3445-9 (pbk.)
    1. Mate selection—Fiction. 2. Manawa, Lake (Iowa)—Fiction. I. Title.
PS3619.E425M35 2010
813'.6—dc22   2010015515

Scripture is taken from the King James Version of the Bible.

This book is a work of fiction. Names, characters, places, and incidents are the product of the author's imagination or are used fictitiously. Any resemblance to actual events, locales, or persons, living or dead, is coincidental.

Published in association with the literary agency Books & Such, 52 Mission Circle #122 PMB 170, Santa Rosa, California 95409.

10   11   12   13   14   15   16   7   6   5   4   3   2   1

To my mother
And all those who loved her

My little children, let us not love in word, neither in tongue; but in deed and in truth.

1 John 3:18

1

If forced to endure Roger Gordon for five more minutes, Marguerite Westing would die. Dead. Gone. Buried. Six feet under Greenlawn Cemetery.

Her parents would need to purchase a large headstone to fit all the words of the epitaph, but they could do it. Money wasn't an issue, and after bearing this unbelievable torture, she deserved an enormous marble marker complete with a plethora of flowery engravings. She could see the words now:

> Here lies Marguerite Westing.
> Only nineteen, but now she's resting.
> Strolling through the park with Roger Gordon,
> Once full of life, she died of boredom.

Marguerite giggled.

Roger stopped on the cobblestone path of the park and frowned at her. "I don't see anything funny about my uncle Myron's carbuncle, Marguerite."

"I'm sorry. My mind wandered for a minute."

"You do seem prone to that. Perhaps you should work on your self-control." He patted her hand, lodged in the crook of his arm, like a parent would an errant child.

And perhaps you should work on making yourself more interesting than milk toast. She bit her lip hard to keep the words from escaping. Good grief. What did he expect when he was talking to her about a boil?

"Now, as I was saying, Uncle Myron . . ." He droned on, his dark mustache twitching like a wriggling fuzzy caterpillar on his upper lip. "Marguerite, are you listening?"

She forced a smile. "Of course I am. How terrible for your dear uncle."

This whole ordeal was her mother's fault. If her mother hadn't insisted she accept Roger's attentions, she could be home enjoying her newest book about the stars.

After the tedious monotony killed her this afternoon, she hoped her parents would make sure her final resting place would have a view of the Iowa bluffs, and that they wouldn't let Roger know where they'd buried her. After all, he'd insist on bringing flowers to her grave and would probably stay for a long, carbuncle-filled visit. No. They mustn't tell him where she was. She couldn't spend all of eternity listening to him. This afternoon was long enough.

Around the park, crab-apple trees exploded with crimson blossoms and lilacs perfumed the air. How could one man ruin such a spectacular summer day?

The clang of the streetcar's bell drew her attention, and she turned to see it clickety-clack past the two-story brick-and-frame storefronts. Horse-drawn carriages and busy patrons bustled out of the car's way. It snaked its way down Main Street and made an easy turn onto Broadway, disappearing into the business district. Marguerite sighed. If only she could go with it.

Then she spotted the striped awning of the ice cream parlor on the corner directly across from the park. Salvation.

She squeezed her escort's arm. "Roger, let's get a soda."

He gaped at her, his spectacles sliding down his nose. "But it's still morning!"

"Oh, fiddle-faddle. For the life of me, I can't see what harm there is to drink a soda before lunch."

"Marguerite."

She wanted to swat the caterpillar off his scowling face. "Can't we at least get that new ice cream with the syrup on top? The sundae?"

"Very well. I suppose you are used to being indulged." He drew his hand over his mustache, smoothing the sides, and pushed up his spectacles.

His flippant words stung. *And what about you, Roger Gordon, son of one of the wealthiest men in the state? "Indulged" should be your middle name.*

She clamped down on her lip so hard she tasted blood. Glancing heavenward, she sent up a silent message. *If You want the world to end right now, God, it's fine with me.*

Upon entering the ice cream parlor, Marguerite disentangled her hand from Roger's arm. She selected a wood-topped round table out in the open before he could lead her to one of the darkened booths where the courting fellows often took their girls. Roger ordered two bowls of vanilla ice cream—no syrup, no nuts, no berries—without consulting her tastes.

Bland. Plain. Boring. Just like him.

He carried the scalloped bowls to the table and presented hers as if it were pure ambrosia.

After waiting until he sat in the heart-shaped iron dining chair, she picked up her spoon and dove into the treat. She scooped a spoonful into her mouth, and the creamy sweetness melted on her tongue, almost making up for the agony of the late morning stroll.

"For what these cost, we could have purchased a chair for our first home."

She dropped her spoon and it clattered against the bowl, the blissful taste replaced by a bitter one. Coughing, she waved her hand in front of her face. "Roger, please don't jest like that."

"I wasn't jesting."

Marguerite cringed as he covered her hand with his own. *Please, Lord, strike him with muteness. Strike him with lightning. Strike him with anything. I don't care what. You choose the pestilence. Have fun. Be creative. Enjoy Yourself. Just don't let him say another word.*

With a tug, she tried to pull her hand away, but he held fast.

"Surely, Marguerite, you've been able to see where our courting has been leading."

She could almost hear God's laughter. He must take great enjoyment in watching her squirm. It was punishment for the ungodly thoughts that ran rampant through her mind. Right now, for instance, she was seriously contemplating a murder—that of her mother.

❦

Seeking the solace of the piano, Marguerite stomped into the parlor only to find her mother already in the room. Ignoring her, she sat on the bench and began to play an angry aria, pouring her frustration into the polished ivory keys.

"That's enough of that," her mother snapped minutes later, closing her leather-bound volume with a thud. "I take it things did not go well with Roger."

"I simply cannot endure one more outing with that man."

Her mother set the book on the marble-topped table beside

her. "Theatrics are not becoming, Marguerite, and it can't be that bad. Roger Gordon is from an excellent family."

"But he's a miserable man to be with. He bores me to tears."

"Then you must engage him in more interesting topics. Please tell me that you did not let your lack of enthusiasm show."

"He talked about his uncle Myron's carbuncle for fifteen minutes!"

Her mother appeared to stifle a smile. "Still, he's a good catch. You'd be well taken care of."

"Taken care of? It's 1895, and more and more women are taking care of themselves. Besides, I could never love him."

"Love is highly overrated." She waved her hand in the air, pausing as one of the household servants delivered a tea tray. Waiting while the young woman poured a steaming cup, she kept her gaze on Marguerite. "Why can't you be like your older sister? She is well matched."

Marguerite rolled her eyes. "Being well matched is highly overrated."

Her mother shot her a stern look and touched her coiffed chignon to make sure all her golden hairs remained in place. Of course they were. They wouldn't dare defy Camille Westing and come loose.

War was imminent. Marguerite had thrown down the gauntlet. Steeling herself, she met her mother's hard blue eyes. "I don't want him to call again."

"What you want isn't the issue here. We're your parents, and we must see to your future—a future that should consist of you being cared for in the manner to which you're accustomed. If you are lucky, Roger will ask for your hand soon."

"If I'm lucky," Marguerite murmured, "Roger Gordon will be attacked by a pack of wolves on his way home."

"Marguerite! That's incorrigible. You should be ashamed."

"You didn't suffer through hours of boredom. I have to speak to Daddy about this. He won't give my hand to a man whose idea of adventure is choosing a patterned vest over a solid. I'd wither and die in a matter of months if I married him."

"Don't exaggerate." Her mother poured a second cup of tea and nodded toward the empty seat beside her. "Do come have tea with me and calm yourself. I have an additional item to discuss with you."

Discuss? Marguerite's stomach cinched. Whenever her mother began a talk in that way, it meant she intended to address something Marguerite would dislike, and there would be no *discussion* whatsoever. Marguerite's fingers clutched the lid of the piano to keep her from bolting from the room. This whole day had felt like one prison after another, and now her mother's worrisome comment slammed the jail door shut with an ominous clang.

"What is it?" she asked, refusing to join her mother on the settee.

Her mother set the teapot down on the tray. "I'm going to dismiss Lilly."

The news robbed Marguerite of her breath. Dropping the piano lid with a clunk, she jumped to her feet. "Mother, you can't send her away just like that! I won't let you!"

"You'd better control your tongue, young lady. And I will do as I wish with those in our employ." She reached for her needlework.

"Employ? Is that what you call it?"

14

"I believe you've made your position on our help quite clear." She pinned Marguerite with her steely blue gaze. "Your father may allow you to speak your opinions so openly, but I do not. Besides, you know we have always paid the Dawsons well."

"You pay enough for them to survive, but never leave. Her family came to Iowa with dreams of going West."

Her mother fired another warning look in her direction. "That was years ago, and before Alice lost her husband. She's lucky we took her in to cook and let her bring Lilly along. And now it's time for Lilly to find her own place of employment and make friends with those of her own station."

Hot coals of anger burned deep inside Marguerite. *I know, I know—be slow to speak. Slow to become angry. But do You have to make it so hard?* She inhaled a steadying breath. "Mother, how can you send her, of all people, away? She's like my sister."

Her mother took a sip from her teacup and released an exasperated sigh. "Must you always make waves, Marguerite? Lilly is not your sister. She's your chambermaid. I admit you are obviously fond of her—overly so." She paused, giving her words weight. "But dear, you need to realize your position in society and understand her place is not beside you."

A man cleared his throat in the parlor's doorway.

"Daddy!" Marguerite launched herself into his arms.

He swung her in a circle and lowered her to the floor. "What's all this? I thought I heard raised voices."

"Mother is going to dismiss Lilly."

Her father looked at his wife and raised an eyebrow. "Our Lilly?"

"Our staff is too large, and it needs to be trimmed. Marguerite doesn't need a constant companion any longer. She's nineteen and will be marrying soon."

Irritated, Marguerite wrinkled her nose.

Her father appeared to bite back a chuckle and stroked his beard. "Well, I think we may need Lilly after all." He dropped his long frame into a wing chair.

"Edward, you can't keep babying her." Her mother puckered her lips.

He held up his hand. "Hear me out, Camille. I've secured a camping site for us at Lake Manawa. Marguerite will not want to be in a tent by herself."

Face ashen, her mother reached for her tea, the cup shaking in her hands. "We're going to spend the summer outdoors?"

"Yes, isn't it splendid? You know, all of the best families are doing it. I know the Grahams, the Deardons, the Longleys, and the Kelloggs have already set up campsites near the Grand Plaza. I was lucky to get one for us there at this late date. The season is already in full swing."

"The whole season at the lake?" Marguerite squealed with delight.

"All summer long."

"In tents?" Her mother's lips thinned to a tight line.

"Yes, but we'll take many of our things from the house." Her father reached for the newspaper and shook it open.

Her mother cleared her throat. "But Edward, dear, what about your work?"

"I'll take the streetcar into town every morning, but that shouldn't keep my son and the two beautiful women in my life from enjoying the greatest entertainment mecca of the West."

"And Lilly?" Marguerite dared to ask.

Her father grinned. "Well, I do believe you'll need your

personal maid to keep all your party dresses in order. Don't you think? Now, go tell your brother the news."

⚜

Mosquitoes swarmed around Marguerite's head, tangling themselves in the netting of her new summer hat. She swatted them away with a gloved hand and smiled, refusing to let one minute of what her mother insisted on calling her "last summer of freedom" to be wasted on something as petty as insects.

The camping area her father had arranged was at the end of one of the long rows of tents. Well-established oak trees offered shade, and with neighbors only on their right side, they would have more privacy than most of the families. In front of their tents, a path led from the camp to the Grand Plaza. In the rear, a tree-lined service road provided access to area farms for fresh produce.

"Edward, can't you hurry them along? I think the whole lot must be dawdling." Cheeks flushed, her mother waved a fan in front of her face. She used the lacy instrument to point toward the area where their household servants struggled to erect the last of the four tents that would make up the Westing family summer home. Her parents would have the large tent like hers and Lilly's. The cook's tent and her brother's tent, which he would share with Isaiah, one of the male servants, were each considerably smaller.

Two weeks had passed since her father's announcement, and her mother had needed every moment to organize supplies and furniture for the lake home. A wagon loaded with their belongings sat a few yards away. Although Marguerite kept insisting they didn't need a silver tea service at the lake, a blanket lay on her mother's precious server, and a bit of the shiny surface reflected the bright sun. That, along with pots, pans, brass beds, feather mattresses, and Wedgwood china, would bring all the comforts of home into their tiny tents—even if home was only a few miles away.

The two male servants, Clay and Lewis, stretched a large sheet of heavy canvas over the two center poles and then covered the four corner poles in record time, but Camille grumbled about how slowly the two men worked. At least they would be returning to the main house in town.

Marguerite glanced at her mother and noticed a shimmer of perspiration beading her face. She touched her mother's arm. "They should be done soon. Why don't we go sit in the shade?"

"That's a wonderful idea." Without hesitation, her father scooped up two folding camp stools and carried them to the nearest tree. He snapped them open, patted one of the canvas seats, took his wife's hand, and seated her. "There, darling. I told you that you'd enjoy camping."

"Humph." Her mother settled on the stool and smoothed her green traveling dress until it appeared wrinkle free. "I'll have to watch over the staff like a hawk. All these diversions will have them dallying constantly. And Marguerite, don't you think for a minute that I won't have time to keep an eye on you as well."

"What about Mark?" She turned to see her twelve-year-old brother attempting to help Clay but getting shooed from the area.

"Mark's a boy. Exploring is what boys do."

Marguerite sighed and watched as the two burly servants each took a diagonal corner of the canvas and pulled it tight. Almost in unison, they drove in stakes to secure the tent in place.

"Are you listening to me?" her mother said.

"Yes, Mother, I heard you, and I assure you that I don't need to be watched like some child."

Her father patted Camille's arm. "She's right, darling. Our little girl is a young woman, and by next summer she'll be setting up a camp of her own." He winked at Marguerite.

She grimaced. Mosquitoes might not ruin this day, but a reminder that her mother expected acceptance of any proposal Roger Gordon might offer, even in jest, certainly would.

Feeling smothered by more than the late June heat, she rose from her chair. "If you'll both excuse me, I think I'll go look around. I believe I saw the Grahams' camp on the way in, and I'd like to say hello to Emily."

"Don't wander too far off," her mother said as if the effort to speak had drained her. "We're expected for dinner at Louie's French Restaurant with the Underwoods promptly at 6:30."

"Mother, we're at the lake. It's in vogue to be late."

A deep scowl marred her mother's perfect complexion. "As Westings, we are always prompt. It would serve you well to remember that."

❧

Willowy Emily Graham, who was a couple years younger than Marguerite, jumped from her camp chair and ran to greet Marguerite. "When did you arrive? Is that your camp that's being set up down the way?"

"Yes, it was Daddy's idea to summer here at the lake."

"We arrived three weeks ago. Let me go grab my hat and parasol and I'll show you around."

She rushed off before Marguerite could even answer, then returned just as quickly. Linking her arm in Marguerite's,

Emily directed her down the pebbled path. "Now, where should we go first? Oh, I know. The Grand Plaza."

Soon they were walking beside the lake on the paved, tree-lined walkway leading to the social center of the resort on the northeast side. They passed the main pavilion with its red-tiled roof and crisp white veranda.

"Inside there's a restaurant, a refreshment bar, a dance floor, and several meeting areas." Emily squeezed Marguerite's arm. "Did you know they even have a telephone? If you pay the fee, you can call as far as New York!"

Progressing further, Marguerite noticed that besides the various vendors around the Grand Plaza, there were several additional larger structures on the shore. When questioned, Emily named each of them: the Yacht Club, a boat shop, and two icehouses. Across the lake, on the south side, fewer buildings dotted the area. "Emily, how big is this lake?"

"My father says it's about six miles around, but it's more crescent-shaped than circular." She pointed to the center of the lake. "The big island in the middle is Coney Island and the smaller one is Turtle Island. See those rowboats? You can rent them from the Yacht Club."

Before long, Emily had paraded them through the Grand Plaza, headed toward the sandy beach to show Marguerite the dive tower and toboggan runs, and given her a history of the lake, which was formed in 1881 after a flood. Emily explained that the south side was called Manhattan Beach, as the developer, Mr. O'Dell, wanted it to have an Eastern feel.

Marguerite and Emily sat down at a park bench as the wind carried a cool breeze over the water. Marguerite released a slow breath. "It's so peaceful here."

Emily giggled. "It should be. *Manawa* is an Indian word meaning 'peace.'"

"I sure hope it lives up to its name. I could use a little peace." Away from humdrum Roger Gordon.

As they returned to Emily's camp, thoughts of Roger suddenly spurred Marguerite's memory. "Good heavens. I'm going to be late. Emily, please forgive me. I have to leave. I'm supposed to be meeting my parents for dinner at 6:30."

"Hurry. I can only imagine what your mother is like when you're late. Do you remember the way back to the pavilion?"

Marguerite nodded and rushed down the path. If she didn't stop at her own camp to freshen up, she might make it.

Skirting the deck chairs lining the pier, Marguerite held on to her hat and ran as fast as she dared toward the enormous pavilion. Her mother would be furious. She shouldn't have spent so much time wandering around the lake with Emily.

But it had been delightful, and it had confirmed her hopes. Her heart skipped like a child's on Christmas Eve just thinking about a summer full of excitement.

She came to a halt in front of a young man sweeping the boardwalk and pressed a hand to her stomach, attempting to catch her breath. "Excuse me. Would you by chance know the time?"

He checked his pocket watch. "It's 6:30, miss."

"Oh no. Which door of the pavilion do I enter to reach Louie's French Restaurant?"

"Louie's is on the other side of the lake, miss, not inside the pavilion. If you hurry, you can catch the steamboat over there. She's headed across the lake."

"Thank you," she called over her shoulder as she hurried toward the end of the dock where passengers boarded the steamboat *Liberty*.

"Miss," the attendant shouted, "I wouldn't rush if I were you. The planking gets pretty slick this time of night."

The warning registered a fraction of a second too late as she skidded on the dock. Her arms flailing, her feet flew out from under her, and she fell headlong into the lake, the murky water swallowing her. Frantic, she searched in vain for something—anything—to hold on to. Kicking with all her might, she resurfaced, only to have her dress entangle her legs. Then, without warning, the lake claimed her again.

2

Breaking through the surface of the water, Marguerite thrashed about wildly. A thick arm encircled her jaw and held her tight against a solid chest. Panicked, she made contact with the man's unyielding arm and sank her nails deep into his flesh. The rescuer held firm.

"Settle down," he commanded, his deep voice solid and unrelenting, his hold tightening. "I'm just going to pull you to the edge of the pier. Relax."

She coughed at the fishy taste of the lake water and willed her body to do as he said, but she could not stop the trembling. "I—I can't."

"Try."

With three more strong strokes, he reached the pier. The dock assistant hoisted her up, led her to a deck chair, and draped a blanket around her shoulders. He crouched in front of her. His mouth was moving, so she knew he was speaking to her, but she couldn't tear her eyes from her rescuer, whom she could see rising from the water over the assistant's shoulder.

Standing at least six feet tall, the rescuer walked directly toward her. His white shirt clung to his broad chest and his dark trousers dripped on the planks. With a flip of his wrist, he shooed the gawkers away, admonishing them to hurry or they'd miss their boat.

The assistant stood up when the man approached. "She must have cracked her skull, Mr. Andrews. She isn't answering any of my questions."

The dock assistant reached for her head, but she pushed him away. "My head is perfectly fine."

The rescuer smiled, revealing a dimpled grin that took her breath away. "What about the rest of you?"

Well, what do you think? I love meeting handsome men when I look like a drowned rat.

Her cheeks warmed, and she squeezed her eyes shut to block out the view. "I'm fine. I'll just go back to my tent and—" She stood and wobbled on her feet.

He caught her arm and pressed her back into the chair. "Whoa, there. Why don't you rest a few more minutes, miss?"

"Mr. Andrews, if you've got her, do you mind if I get back to work?" the assistant asked.

"Go ahead, Pauly. I'll see to her." He squatted before her. "Miss, I need to know the truth. Do you need a doctor?"

"No!"

The man rose. "Then at least let me escort you to wherever you came from. Hotel or camp?"

"No, that's not necessary. I'm really all right now." Marguerite stood again, grateful to find her rubbery legs didn't betray her this time. "I need to hurry. I was already late for a dinner date with my family."

"So I noticed." He gave her another dimpled, mind-spinning grin.

"What's that supposed to mean?"

"In the future, I wouldn't recommend running on the dock."

"I wasn't running. I was . . . stepping lively."

"Then I wouldn't step . . . so lively."

She suppressed a smile that ached to get out. "Thank you for your concern and aid. I'll see to it that your efforts are duly compensated if you'll give me your name."

He frowned. "My name is Trip Andrews. I'm glad you're okay, but no other thanks are needed."

Strange name—Trip. Unlike me, he doesn't seem to have any coordination problems. She studied him. Warm hazel eyes, well-built, probably midtwenties, and the assistant obviously knew him. Was he another guest at the lake? A local? Perhaps he stayed in town at one of the fancy hotels?

Before she could ask, Marguerite spotted a familiar round-shouldered form approaching and moaned. "Would you mind throwing me back in the lake now, Mr. Andrews?"

"What?" His brows drew together.

"Marguerite!" Roger ran the last few feet toward her. "What happened to you?"

"I slipped on the pier."

"You fell in the lake? How could you be so careless?"

"I'm fine, but thank you for asking."

He pushed up his spectacles. "Forgive me. I'm concerned because we were supposed to meet your parents at 6:30. I missed my streetcar and had to wait for the next one. Don't you realize how upset they'll be with our tardiness? You really should have been more careful, Marguerite."

Trip cleared his throat. "I don't believe the lady anticipated how slick the boards can become in the evening."

Roger turned to him and eyed the dripping man from head to toe. "And you are?"

"Trip Andrews, sir." He offered his hand. "I pulled her out of the water."

Roger gripped his hand, simultaneously snaking a protective arm around Marguerite's waist. "In that case, I owe you a debt of gratitude for saving my intended's life."

Her stomach roiled and she attempted to step free. "Roger, I am perfectly capable of walking home on my own."

"None of that, Marguerite." He yanked her close. "You will let me assist you back to your camp, and then I will send for a doctor and notify your parents as to your whereabouts."

Catching a final sympathetic look from her rescuer, Marguerite let Roger lead her down the pier. She sighed. Suffering the indignity of being caught in such a sorry state in public, and, even worse, having to do so on the arm of Roger Gordon in front of the dimpled stranger, simply wasn't fair.

❧

While the walk back to the camp had eliminated the worst of the dripping, Marguerite still felt like a bowl of cold, mushy oatmeal. As soon as she entered her tent, Lilly began peeling off the sodden layers.

"This is as bad as skinning an onion." Lilly draped the wet dress over the humpback trunk, smoothing out all of the wrinkles. She turned to Marguerite, propped tiny hands on her hips, and shook her head. Her lips formed a perfect, upside-down *u*.

Marguerite caught a glimpse of herself in the washstand mirror and knew why. She was clad only in her lace-trimmed corset cover, and her blonde curls hung loosely around her heart-shaped face. Her lips sported a bluish tint, almost matching her deep-set, cornflower blue eyes. Gooseflesh pimpled her skin, and she shivered in the cool evening air.

Lilly clicked her tongue. "Look at you, Miss Marguerite. You are a sorry sight."

26

"Oh, and I thought I was ready for the ball."

"Sorry, princess, but I'm not your fairy godmother." Lilly handed her a soft cotton towel. "We'd better hurry. Mr. Gordon said he'd be back with a doctor soon."

"I don't need a doctor. I need some supper. I'm starving. And maybe a warm bath."

Lilly cocked an eye. "Haven't you had enough water for one day?" Moving behind Marguerite, she released the bindings on Marguerite's corset and tossed it in a pile beside the trunk. She then began to untie the wet drawstrings holding up her crinoline.

"Can't you hurry? I'm freezing."

Lilly snagged a quilt off the brass bed they'd brought from home and offered it to her. "This will take a good long while. Untying a wet string is hard."

"Just cut it."

"And ruin a perfectly good petticoat because you decided to go for a dip? I don't think so. Your mama would chew my hide."

"I suppose you're right." Teeth chattering, Marguerite tried to remain still while her maid finished. Finally the last of the garments gave way and heaped at her feet. "Thank you, Lilly."

Lilly dropped a nightgown over Marguerite's head. "Now, hop on in that bed and get warm and toasty before the doctor comes."

"I don't need—"

"I know. You don't need no doctor. Maybe you should've told that to that beau of yours and not to me."

"He's not my beau." Unpinning her hair, Marguerite stuck the pins in her mouth and blotted her damp hair with the towel.

"He sure thinks he is." Grinning, Lilly folded down the blankets on the bed and motioned Marguerite toward it.

Marguerite rolled her eyes. Withdrawing the pins from between her lips, she set them on the nightstand. "That's the problem." She drew the quilt up to her neck and moaned. From the way Roger had swooped in and taken charge, her dimpled rescuer would think him to be her beau as well.

Lilly picked up the wet undergarments and paused to study Marguerite's face. She raised an eyebrow. "So, was he handsome?"

"Who?"

"The man who pulled you out of the water."

"Very." Marguerite's lips curled into a smile. Lilly knew her so well. "Broad shoulders, strong arms, kind hazel eyes, and the most heartwarming grin."

"Too bad."

"Why?"

Lilly flicked a damp curl. "Because you, Miss Marguerite, look like a dishrag."

❦

Head pounding, Marguerite forced her eyes open and squinted at the sunlight filtering through the tent opening.

"Mornin', Miss Sunshine." Lilly held up two dresses—a peach chiffon with tight sleeves and an enormous bustle, and a white cotton gored skirt with a rose-colored tailored jacket. "Which one do you fancy today?"

Marguerite moaned. "Mother wants to have breakfast, doesn't she?"

"A little friendly chitchat over scrambled eggs won't hurt you."

"Nothing like a helping of guilt to go with my splitting headache. Did you hear her last night? You would have thought I intentionally fell in the lake and missed a dinner engagement just to upset her."

"The doctor warned you about that headache—the one in your head, not your mama—and you were the one who said you'd be fine and didn't need to stay in bed today."

Marguerite propped herself up on one elbow, wincing at the sudden spike of pain in her head. "Can I change my mind?"

"You'd do better to spend your time trying to change hers. I heard her talking to your daddy again about your impending nuptials to Mr. Exciting."

"And?"

"Your daddy said they'd discuss it if and when the time came. He told her it was your decision."

Marguerite pinched the bridge of her nose. "Did she just accept it?"

"What do you think?"

"Daddy won't give my hand to a man like that. He'll take care of me. He always does."

"I sure hope so—for your sake." Lilly held out the two dresses again.

Marguerite swung her legs out of bed and pointed to the white shirtwaist, matching skirt, and jacket. She liked how modern it looked. Besides, no one wore bustles anymore.

Lilly chuckled. "You know your mama would have picked the other one."

"She likes me to look like an old woman, and she thinks ladies' jackets are too masculine. She says I'll never make a good catch in one of them." Sliding to the floor, Marguerite knelt at the side of her bed.

"What are you doing now?"

Marguerite laced her fingers together before glancing at her maid. "I thought I'd better start this day with prayer, because between my mother and Roger, it sure looks like I'm going to need it."

3

Extending her parasol, Marguerite felt a breeze kiss her cheek, and she inhaled the fresh air. Her gaze drifted from the puffs of white clouds against an azure sky to the Grand Plaza packed with strolling throngs gathered to see and be seen. A brassy, patriotic tune filled the air, and Marguerite headed toward the sound. She glanced at Lilly, whom she'd persuaded to accompany her on her promenade along the boardwalk. Lilly kept her eyes focused on the path ahead of them.

Familiar well-to-do families nodded in greeting as they ambled along in front of the bandstand. A few gave Lilly's modest gray dress a once-over and scowled.

How could people be so cruel? This was a park. God's creation. How could they think certain areas should be reserved for only the wealthy?

"I should've stayed back at camp, Miss Marguerite. I don't think these fine people like me being here."

Marguerite shot Mrs. Winnifred Long a defiant stare. "I don't care what they think. You're my friend, and I want you with me. Besides, people from all over the city come to the lake every day."

"Not to this part. Maybe you should see if your sister will come for a visit from town. She'd be a more suitable companion."

"I'd love for Mary to come, but it's hard with a four-year-old. And as much as I love spending time with her, I happen to enjoy your company even more."

"But . . ."

Understanding Lilly's discomfort, Marguerite led the way past the crowd watching a juggler tossing five balls in the air toward a grove of shade trees off to the side. She settled in the grass. "This better?"

Lilly gracefully slipped into place beside her. "Much, but I should've brought my mending."

"Can't you simply enjoy yourself?" Marguerite took a deep breath, rejoicing in the fresh, lake-scented air.

"I could mend and still enjoy myself." Lilly fussed with the folds of her skirt.

"Look around, Lilly." Marguerite stood and twirled in the grass. "Those trees are swaying to God's music, and see all these planters filled with flowers? I'm sure they're as beautiful here as anything they have back East."

Marguerite plucked a blossom and handed it to her friend. She pulled Lilly to her feet and turned her toward the lake. "And those sailboats! Aren't they splendid? Look how they glide across the water like they're floating. Can you imagine what it would be like to be on one of them? It would almost be like flying on your own magic carpet." She leaned against the tree trunk and sighed. "If only I could . . ."

Lilly turned, brows scrunched together. "I know what you're thinking, and you'd best get that thought right out of your mind."

"Why shouldn't I learn to sail?"

"Because ladies don't sail boats. Because your mama would have a fit. Because you don't know the first thing about being on a boat. Because you can't swim worth a lick."

"But I'm a quick study." Marguerite opened the frilly layers of her white parasol. "I've even had a year at the university."

"Oh, you're smart enough. It just isn't done."

"That isn't fair. A woman could sail as well as any man."

"Maybe so, but it isn't gonna happen, so don't go setting your heart on something you can't have." Lilly brushed a wisp of chestnut hair from her eyes. "You'll just get disappointed like you always do."

Marguerite swung the parasol down. "If we don't have dreams, Lilly, what do we have? Besides, aren't you the one who always says to delight myself in the Lord and He will give me the desires of my heart?"

Lilly shook her head. "Only you can twist the Scriptures to get what you want. Seems to me the only thing you're delighting in is the idea of doing something that would make your mama have a conniption."

❧

Gliding across Lake Manawa, the *Endeavor* sliced through the water with ease. Trip motioned to his crewmate and best friend, Harry Fellows, to adjust the mainsail. Although he usually sailed the thirty-two-foot *Endeavor* with a crew of five, today he and Harry decided to take her out alone. With the perfect breeze, sailing took little thought, so each of them methodically set to work.

"Can you sheet in the jib?" Trip asked.

Harry moved toward the smaller sail and tugged on a line. "All set, Trip. You know, she's one fine ship. I never asked you what your dad said about her."

"You know him. Nothing I do is ever as good as it is when he does it."

33

"He'll change his tune when we win the regatta." Harry tipped his head to the side and raised a single eyebrow.

"Glad to see you're as confident as ever. I guess we do have over two weeks to prepare. By the way, did you see the boat the Hendersons brought down from Spirit Lake?"

Harry laughed. "Those pretty boys? They don't know a rudder from a centerboard."

"And you do?" Trip tossed a rag at his friend's mass of dark curls.

Lightning quick, Harry caught the towel and threw it back, but it fell short of its target.

"Ready to tack." Trip glanced at his mate to make sure he'd heard his announcement.

With one hand Harry secured a firm grip on the coarse lifeline surrounding the deck and grabbed the jib sheet with his other hand.

"Tacking." Trip turned the tiller to the right, and Harry let the jib sheet free. Soon the edge of the sails began to flap wildly. They were in the no-sail zone, and a beginner would have stopped turning at this point. But Trip had been on the water most of his life and knew he had to keep the tiller pressed hard to the opposite side. He looked at Harry and shouted, "Boom coming across!"

They both ducked as the boom swung over their heads, and Harry set to trimming the headsail while Trip adjusted the tension on the mainsail. Trip moved the tiller back toward the boat's center and slowed down his turn as the sails began to fill with air on the new tack. Now, heading straight, the boat picked up speed. With water spraying against his face, Trip nodded toward Harry. The turn had gone as smoothly as glass.

Even though they were not in full race mode, they were making good time. If they could keep this up, they might have a chance at winning the Manawa Regatta, and he might have a chance at finally impressing his father. It was a good thing too.

He had to win.

It was a matter of life and death.

⟨≈⟩

"Isn't she beautiful, Daddy?"

Edward Westing watched Marguerite lean over the white railing in front of the pavilion as if she couldn't get close enough to the sailboats. Wispy, honey gold curls danced across her forehead. The gauzy snow-colored skirt billowed around her ankles, swirling in the breeze, and the rose jacket hugged her narrow waist, the color making her cheeks blossom. His daughter, the spitting image of his wife as a young woman, never looked more beautiful.

"So this is what you dragged me out to see?"

Marguerite nodded. "I've been enjoying the view all afternoon. Can you imagine what it must be like out on one of those?"

"I don't think I've ever thought of it." He leaned his hip against the rail.

"I told Lilly that it must be like flying." She glanced at her father. "Daddy, I want to learn to sail."

Edward laughed. His youngest daughter had never been one to adhere to the confines that society dictated. To her mother's horror, she insisted on attending the university, rode a bicycle, wrote for the suffrage paper, read everything she could get her hands on, and spent hours studying the stars instead of practicing the piano. While he admired her spirit, he walked a fine line between Camille's desires for Marguerite and Marguerite's desires for herself.

He filled his lungs with the tangy lake air. "Darling, you know that ladies do not sail. Rarely, you might see one as a passenger, but it's much too grueling a sport for ladies to participate in."

"Then, can I go as a passenger?" Her eyes, blue as the water in the afternoon sun, sparkled. "Please, Daddy."

"I don't know, Marguerite. It could be dangerous."

She waved off the comment. "I've been watching them all day. It doesn't look one bit dangerous."

"I haven't heard of any of those pond yachts taking on passengers."

"But we haven't really tried to find out, either."

"No, I guess we haven't." He chuckled. "You know, you get me in a lot of trouble, young lady. I'm not making any promises, but I'll see what I can do. Now, we'd better hurry or you'll be late for dinner—again."

The smile slid from her face.

"What's wrong?"

"One more night of enduring Roger. Mother invited him to come in from town to join us for dinner."

"Sweetheart, does he really make you that miserable?" He offered her his arm, and the two of them started back toward their camp, steps crunching on the pebbled path.

"It's not that Roger doesn't have admirable qualities. He's basically thoughtful, and he's well-mannered to distraction. I'm sure some girl will find him wonderful."

"But you don't."

She sighed. "No. He is impossibly tiresome. You know, it's like spending the afternoon at one of those long meetings you complain about. I've honestly tried to find things that I could like about him, but he doesn't make me feel special."

"I kept telling your mother that he wouldn't. I knew

he wasn't right for you from the start." He squeezed her hand.

"How?"

"He's a selfish chap. He likes the sound of his own voice far more than he could ever like anyone else."

"So you won't make me marry him?"

"Have I ever been able to make you do anything?" Edward stopped and plucked a petunia from an overflowing planter. He tucked it behind her ear. "When you decide to marry, I want it to be to someone who holds your heart and not just a large pocketbook. You deserve that, sweetheart. You deserve to know the kind of love that takes your breath away. Now, let's get to dinner before your mother has us both hung by the yardarm."

She kissed his cheek and slipped her hand into the crook of his arm. "Thank you, Daddy, for everything."

4

Rigging the mainsail, Trip readied the *Argo* for passengers. Much larger than the *Endeavor*, the keelboat had been built by his father to impress the wealthy lake patrons. For a fee, he allowed them to enjoy the lake from aboard a sailboat. Sure, two small steamboats ferried guests across the lake, but the steady chug of a steamboat felt nothing like gliding over the water in a sailboat. More than one lake patron had fallen hook, line, and sinker for the sport of sailing, and if they were fortunate, the wealthiest then asked Trip's father to build them their own boat.

"Lloyd, where's Harry?" Trip glanced around the *Argo*.

The lanky sailor shrugged. "Must be running late."

"Just don't let Dad know."

Stepping from belowdecks, his father scanned the ship. "Don't let me know what?"

"Nothing, Dad."

"Where's Harry?" Weathered wrinkles deepened across his father's brow.

"He'll be along any minute."

"I told you if he was late again that he was done here."

Trip tensed and checked the rigging on the mainsail. "Dad, we need him. He's a great sailor."

"Great sailors are made. They aren't born." Captain Andrews slapped his captain's hat against his leg, then jammed it back on his head. "Just train a new one."

As if it were that easy. Trip had taught sailing to several young men during the summer for the last two years, and so far only a few seemed to have a feel for the sport. They couldn't afford to lose Harry, especially with the regatta so close.

"Dad, I'm sure he has a good reason. He always does." At least he did now. There was a time when that certainly had not been the case.

Harry ran down the dock and hopped aboard with practiced ease. "Sorry I'm late. I got stopped by someone who wants to sail with us today."

Trip cast an I-told-you-so look at his father. "Who did you meet?"

"A local businessman." Harry immediately began coiling a rope. "Said he and his daughter want a ride."

"Did you tell him we don't allow children?" Trip's father scowled at the young man.

"He said she was a young lady of age." Harry draped the rope on a peg. "He said he'd pay double if we let her on." He pulled out the cash and waved it in the air. "Paid in advance."

"Must be ugly as sin," Lloyd piped up, slugging Mel.

Harry shrugged. "I wouldn't know. I didn't see her."

By the time they were ready to cast off, three men had appeared, but not the young woman or her father. Trip cast a quick glance at the crowd on the pier and spotted a flurry of commotion. A young woman darted out of the crowd, dressed in a pearly shirtwaist and matching skirt, and ran along the dock. She held her wide-brimmed white hat in place with her gloved left hand and hiked her skirt with her right. The satin ribbon tails on her hat trailed behind her as she rushed. Oblivious to the aghast looks from the ladies watching her, she pulled an older man along—presumably her father. She stopped at the back of the boat and waved.

"Ahoy there!" she called.

Captain Andrews shot Harry a stern look, but the curly-haired young man held up a shiny fifty-cent piece. With a grunt, the skipper turned to his son. "Oh, good grief. Trip, go get her before she falls flat on her face running on the dock like that."

Hopping over the lifeline, Trip met the two on the dock. He stared in disbelief. Could this be the same girl he'd rescued the other night? Then her drenched hair had seemed dark, and now it shone like spun gold in the sun.

"You?" Her azure eyes grew wide.

"Running on the dock again? No, wait, I remember, you step lively."

She smiled, revealing a dangerously impish grin. "I do just that. We came for our sailing excursion."

"We were expecting you." Trip offered his hand to her father. "Hello, sir. I'm Trip Andrews, first mate of the *Argo* and son of her captain."

The man extended a beefy hand. "Edward Westing, and this is my daughter Marguerite, but it appears you have already met."

"Actually, we haven't officially met. I pulled her out of the lake the other night."

"That was you? I don't know how I could ever repay you."

"I'm just glad she's all right. Ready to come aboard?"

Marguerite nodded and stood on her toes as if the anticipation alone would make her explode. Trip chuckled. He led her to the transom at the back of the boat and hopped onto the *Argo*. "Give me your hand and I'll help you get on. Take one big step up."

Though most unladylike, Marguerite didn't hesitate for a second. She bounced on the deck, unable to contain her excitement. "Now what do I do? Trim a sail? Swab a deck?"

Trip heard Harry and Lloyd laugh heartily, and a smile tugged at his lips. He managed to keep it from breaking free. "Have a seat over there with the others, Miss Westing, Mr. Westing. My father, Deuce Andrews, is captaining the ship. We'll be under way in no time."

"Isn't there anything we need to know?" Marguerite asked.

"Oh, yeah, there's one thing. When someone yells, 'Duck!' do it."

"Duck?"

He dropped his head down to demonstrate. "You got it?"

"That's it?"

"That's it."

She flashed him a smile. "I think I can handle ducking."

"Make sure you do. I'd hate to haul you out of the lake twice."

❧

Wishing she had some way to record every minute on the sailboat, Marguerite tried to memorize each man's movements as they prepared to set sail. It took little time to learn each of the crew's names. The curly-haired man, Harry, liked to tease Lloyd, who was skinny as a stick. Mel and Max, twin brothers, were hard to tell apart except for Max being a good five inches taller than his brother. Trip swung around the mast with ease and landed on the deck like a cat.

Even if Trip hadn't told her, she'd have known the skipper

was Trip's father. Tall and muscular, the two men appeared to be cut from the same cloth. She smiled. *Cut from the same sail. I have to start thinking nautically.* Both father and son sported dimples, but the father used his infrequently. He seemed to smile only when he poked fun at someone. His current target appeared to be Mel, the shortest of the crew, who struggled with securing a sail they called the "spinnaker."

A middle-aged passenger removed his bowler and rubbed his balding head. "Captain Andrews, are you sure it won't bring bad luck to have this young lady aboard? I thought a woman on board a ship will make the sea angry."

"Ah, but a naked woman on board will calm the sea." Max elbowed his brother in the side.

Marguerite's cheeks warmed.

Captain Andrews silenced Max with a stern look. "We'll take our chances since this is a lake and not the sea." He made his way around the ship, inspecting the crew's preparations and barking orders at a few of them to secure more ropes. Finally he told his son to "set her free."

For a moment Marguerite feared he'd changed his mind and meant to set her ashore. Instead, Trip vaulted over the side and unwound the thick rope holding the cruiser's bow. After the current carried the bow clear of the dock, he released the next set of ropes and then jumped aboard the back.

Pulse pounding, Marguerite held on to the edge of the bench she'd been assigned to. Questions filled her mind. What were the different sails for? Why did the ship lean so far to the side when the sail filled with air? But she swallowed the questions. Since they were still so close to the shore, it would be too easy for them to take the "unlucky" lady back.

"Your first time on the water?" the balding passenger beside her asked.

"Yes, is it obvious?"

"Well, I doubt most young women in Iowa have been aboard sailboats. I don't know if I'd want my daughter risking the rigors of sailing."

"Rigors?"

"There's the wind and the sun, and of course the spray. You do realize you'll probably get damp."

She smiled and glanced at Trip. "It wouldn't be the first time. Are you a sailor?"

"No, but my son is taking sailing lessons from the gentleman over there, and he thinks we should have our own vessel built, so I'm here to discover for myself what my son calls the 'thrill of the sea.'"

The mainsail filled and the *Argo* suddenly picked up speed. With one hand holding her hat in place, Marguerite turned her face to the wind and watched Lloyd attach a second smaller sail up front.

"Thrill" hardly described her wildly beating heart and volcanic excitement as the ship began to cruise along. Only when she'd raced her horse when no one was looking had this kind of exhilaration surged through her. She closed her eyes and imagined floating on the breeze.

The man harrumphed, wiping the thin mist from his face with a linen handkerchief. "I don't see what my boy is talking about. More chill than thrill."

Didn't he feel the freedom the wind carried? Out here, the only rules were dictated by the skipper and the water. Maybe four wood-paneled walls of an office suited this man, but it wouldn't her. She could never get enough of this.

And in that moment, she made a decision.

She would find a way to learn to sail.

5

Flopping across the bed in her tent, Marguerite closed her eyes, trying to recall the motion of the water rolling beneath her. "Oh, Lilly, it was the most wonderful experience I've ever had."

"From that grin on your face, I thought as much." Perched in the rocking chair beside the bed, Lilly clicked her tongue. "Well, at least you got it out of your system."

Marguerite sat up and put a knuckle to her lips.

"I know that look, and I know it means trouble. It's like you're doing your best to keep those words stuck in your mouth."

"I just have to do it again, Lilly. Once could never be enough. I'm going to learn to sail."

"And I'm going to be the queen of England."

"Well, good, you can commission a ship for me to sail around the world, Your Majesty." Marguerite curtsied with a flourish.

Lilly dropped her darning into the basket beside the chair. "You're planning something, aren't you?"

"Please, Lilly, you've got to understand. I need this. If I have this one summer where I really feel alive, then maybe I can endure years as the wife of a boring man."

"Is that your way of tryin' to convince me to help you?"

"I'm not like all the other girls who are happy to be social-ites. I need more adventure and excitement."

"And you think you need to tell me that?"

"I knew you'd understand."

"What I understand is you're making some wild plan up in that head of yours, and you're planning on me helping you get it done, when what you should be doing is telling that man the truth about how you feel."

"Mother would have a conniption if I did that." Marguerite poured water into the washbasin, dipped her hands in, and splashed the water over her face. "So, you'll help me?"

"Do I really have a choice?" Lilly passed her a towel.

"Of course you do."

Lilly cocked an eyebrow at her.

"I guess you could refuse, but . . ."

"Put me out of my misery and just tell me what I have to do."

With a grin on her face, Marguerite pulled a list from her pocket. "Besides covering for me with my mother, I need you to pick up a few things for me in town."

An hour later, Marguerite asked Isaiah to take Lilly to town in the wagon to obtain the needed items. Marguerite hurried to meet her mother for lunch at one of the local restaurants. A waiter dressed in a double-breasted white jacket held the door for her as she entered. She paused to scan the room: fine linen tablecloths, lovely view of the lake's rippling waters, fresh flowers on the tables, a host of dapper young waiters—and Roger Gordon. Her mother's dream. Her worst nightmare.

Her mother waved her over. Taking a solidifying breath, Marguerite made her way to the table.

"Roger, what a surprise." She allowed him to pull out her chair.

"The good kind, I hope."

Not unless you intend to tell me you're entering the priest-hood. She forced a weak smile.

"I came to meet with my investment partners. We have big plans for the Midway, and perhaps some other financially beneficial endeavors." He slid the chair beneath her. "Then I ran into your mother, and she was kind enough to ask me to join you both." Before returning to his seat, he bent and kissed Marguerite's cheek. The thick mustache tickled, and she cringed.

"Isn't it a treat, darling?" Unfolding her napkin, her mother smoothed out its wrinkles in her lap. "Marguerite, how did your cheeks become so pink? Have you been out without a parasol?"

"A little sun won't hurt me, Mother. I intend to go wading this afternoon."

"In the lake?"

"No, Mother, in a bathtub."

"Don't be petulant."

"Yes, in the lake." Marguerite snapped her napkin to the side and laid it on her lap, deliberately leaving a few wrinkles. Her mother's turned-down mouth sent a silent thrill through her. "Haven't you noticed swimming is a regular pastime here? Remember the new bathing costume I purchased in town? I'm dying to try it out."

"Perhaps Roger would care to join you."

She turned to him and raised her eyebrows. This could liven things up. "Do you swim?"

"No. I don't care for the water, and I'm not sure I approve of you carousing with the commoners in such a manner." His spectacles slid to the end of his nose.

"Excuse me?" Even wading? Did he want to suck every last bit of fun from her life?

"Marguerite, you're young and naive." Her mother graced Roger with a practiced social smile. "All sorts of people swimming together is hardly proper. I'm sure you can entertain yourself with more acceptable things to do."

"Yes, that's it." Roger pushed up his spectacles. "Something befitting a young woman of your position."

She gaped at them. For several seasons now, the lake had entertained hundreds of people. Young and old, rich and poor, men and women, enjoyed the water. There had been a time when genders remained separated, but it was 1895. Times had changed. At least, they had here at the lake. What did her mother expect her to do? Be content with milling about with the socialites, displaying their season's finery like plumage?

Her mother's frown deepened. "I agree with Roger. I think I shall have to forbid this foray."

"What would be more acceptable, Mother? Sailing?"

"Don't be ridiculous. Ladies do not sail."

"I did." She cocked an eyebrow, lifting her chin in defiance and fighting the smirk trying to come to the surface. "Today. On the *Argo*. Father took me."

Her mother's face paled while Roger's colored a vivid shade of crimson.

"H-h-how could you?" he asked. "What will people say?"

"No one will say anything, and I don't care if they do. I found it to be most exhilarating."

Roger scowled. "Mrs. Westing, what are you going to do with her?"

Her mother lifted a water goblet to her lips with shaky fingers and sipped from it. "I simply don't believe you. You're saying this to shock us so we'll approve of your intentions to swim in the lake. A greater evil to make a lesser one look more appealing. I know for certain that no man would let a lady sail on his vessel."

"Of course. I should have realized your ploy, my dear." Roger laughed. "Never enough to keep you entertained, is there? That will change soon enough."

Although she'd enjoyed watching them both squirm—much more than she should have—the effect was short-lived. Her mother's ability to shroud her emotions in a veil of propriety never ceased to amaze Marguerite. She ached for a genuine reaction—a mother's honest concern, a shared moment of laughter, even anger. Any of it would fill the empty space in her heart.

The conversation effectively dismissed, Camille and Roger began to discuss the unseasonably warm weather.

Marguerite released a long sigh. She would share no more about the day. Roger would not hear about the thrill that had surged through her on the water. She would keep the yearning to repeat the experience a secret. Her secret. Roger would call it a childish whim, and her mother would be mortified at the thought. Neither of them cared about what made her happy, so neither deserved to know the desires of her heart.

Fresh pain seared her. Perhaps it was better that her mother didn't believe her, because that way she wouldn't question her comings and goings. Besides, keeping the truth hidden was the Westing family motto, and no one did it better than her mother. Whenever anything occurred that her mother thought might tarnish the Westing image, no matter how insignificant, she was quick to admonish Marguerite and her siblings to keep the event a secret. It simply wouldn't do for Camille Westing to be seen in an unflattering light.

The sound of laughter from the entryway drew Marguerite's attention. She spotted Trip Andrews and his crew entering the dining room. Harry appeared to tease Trip and then rough up his sun-kissed sandy brown hair. Trip caught her gaze and gave her a broad, dimpled grin. Quickly she averted her eyes. The last thing she needed right now was for Trip to saunter to their table and greet her.

The waiter arrived and Roger ordered for all three of them. Fried beefsteak, mashed potatoes drenched in white gravy, and egg custard. Colorless. Bland. Ordinary.

She moaned inwardly.

Lord, I can't live in his mashed potato world. I need my tubers scalloped and diced and baked and fried and different every time. I need excitement and change as much as I need air. I know what I'm planning is deceptive, but You understand. After all, You made me this way. Right?

⤜∾⤏

Hurrying around the corner of the tent, Marguerite nearly toppled Alice into her washtub. She grabbed the cook's ample arm and steadied her.

"Alice, I'm so sorry. I wasn't looking where I was going. I'm afraid my mind was on my own affairs."

"Ain't it always?" Alice chuckled and rubbed a bar of lye soap on a jelly stain on one of Edward's cotton shirts. She briskly scrubbed it between her sausage-shaped fingers. "Where's my Lilly?"

"I-Isaiah took her to town for some things I needed."

"I see."

How did Alice always make Marguerite feel transparent? Unlike her own mother, Lilly's mother wasn't condemning, just mildly omniscient. She had been with the Westings for years, and she had practically raised Marguerite alongside Lilly. Little that happened went unnoticed by the housekeeper

49

and cook. And she seemed to have a keen sense about anything related to Marguerite.

Alice glanced at Marguerite and held her gaze.

Marguerite tried not to flinch. *Stay calm. Look her in the eye.*

"Hmmm. It might've been nice to know you sent Lilly off on your errands since it's wash day." Alice dropped another shirt into the cloudy water.

"I'm sorry. She should be back soon. I could help if you like."

The heavyset woman laughed. "Your mama would sure like that. Can you picture her face if she found you up to your elbows in wash water?"

They both smiled. "I really wouldn't mind," Marguerite said.

"I know you wouldn't, missy." She eyed Marguerite from head to toe again. "You been carrying your parasol?"

Marguerite touched her pink cheeks. "I forgot it this morning."

"The pink looks good on you. Gives you some color." She swished the shirts with the wash stick and displayed a gap-toothed smile. "I suppose my Lilly can use a break now and then. Every girl needs a little fun."

"I believe my mother would disagree."

"Probably, but that's never stopped you before."

Marguerite started to walk away. Her heart stopped when Alice called out to her.

"And missy, you be careful with whatever you're planning, you understand?"

❧

Marguerite felt exposed.

Made of soft, light-blue striped serge, the bathing suit hugged her waist and then flared out with a bouncy skirt that barely brushed her knees. She adjusted the wide sailor collar, running her fingers along the white braided edge. She took a second look in the long mirror her mother had insisted on bringing to the lake. The trim on the capped sleeves matched that on the collar. The pantaloons beneath exposed her stocking-clad calves and ankles much more than any of her cycling costumes did.

Her mother would probably call it scandalous, but Marguerite preferred to think of it as daring, bold, fun.

She slipped into her shoes just as Lilly arrived.

"What do you think?" Marguerite spun to show off the attire.

"It's a fine costume."

She tugged on the skirt. "I wish you could join me. You swim much better than I."

"You hardly swim at all."

"I'm not that bad." Marguerite paused. "On second thought, maybe you should come along just to keep me afloat."

"I don't think your mother would approve." Lilly picked up Marguerite's discarded dress and folded it. "Just remember what I taught you when we were kids."

Marguerite recalled the afternoons Alice had taken both girls to a pond outside of town and let them swim in their chemises and drawers. Lilly dove and swam like a mermaid, while Marguerite found it a struggle just to dog-paddle across the pond.

"How'd you convince your mother to let you go?"

"I didn't." Marguerite scooped up her overdress and slipped her arms into the sleeves. "It was Mark. He needs someone to watch him, and you know she can't tell him no. I, on the other hand . . ."

Lilly snickered. "So are you going to talk to him about your plan? What if he doesn't want to learn?"

"What twelve-year-old boy would turn down the chance to learn to sail?"

Lilly handed her the wrapped bundle of items she'd secured in town. "Better give him this stuff to stow. I still can't believe you made me part of this."

"It's the only way." Marguerite accepted the parcel filled with new boots for each of them and a new sailing cap for Mark.

"That's what you keep saying. Now, when you get to that lake, you need to work on your stroke, 'cause I doubt it would do for a sailor to not know how to swim."

Marguerite's nerves tingled. If a sailor had to know how to swim, she was in trouble, and even if she did practice today, one day at the lake couldn't remedy her inability. Maybe she should reconsider.

I need to stop fretting. If I fall in the water, surely I know enough to stay afloat. After all, how hard can it be if I'm not wearing all those petticoats?

The lacy fan in her manicured hand did little to disperse the humid Midwest air, but Camille Westing refused to look bothered by it. Instead she sipped the lemonade Alice had prepared for her, keeping her eye trained on the path leading to their camp.

Their camp. She recalled the day of their arrival when Mark announced he wanted to call it "Camp Dew Drop Inn." Sweet Mark didn't grasp why a name like that would appear to be an open invitation to every ne'er-do-well on the lake. No, she'd explained, if they had to summer amid the bugs, they should at least have a proper-sounding name. Always the most creative of her children, Marguerite suggested "Camp Andromeda," and Camille admitted it sounded quite regal. By the next day, Marguerite had arranged for Isaiah to carve a sign for them, and it was now mounted on a post at their camp's entrance.

Camille glanced at her surroundings and sighed. Besides the four tents, only the new set of Heywood Brothers rattan furniture she'd insisted on bringing spoke of any culture. Two chaise lounges, a settee, and four chairs with a matching table were arranged in the center of their camp on which to dine, relax, and of course entertain. All the serpentine, rolled-back pieces sported beadwork and curlicues. She'd ordered the pricey rattan months ago for their sunporch back home. The fortuitous purchase made life here bearable. If the wicker furniture suffered because of the elements, then so be it. When the time came for Roger Gordon's mother to join them one evening, all would be in perfect order.

Camille ran her hand along the solid surface of the rolltop travel desk sitting on the wicker table before her. The desk, perfect for use on her train trips to visit her sister, had been a gift from Edward last Christmas. Now, as she sat waiting for her husband to return home, she rolled the top of the desk up, revealing the stoppered inkwells. She unlocked the hidden storage drawer beneath the angled writing surface and withdrew the letter she'd placed there.

The handwriting on the envelope, full of lovely flourishes, echoed the fine breeding of the author—Mrs. Richard Gordon, Roger's mother. Camille traced the lettering with her finger. No one would ever question her parenting skills once Marguerite wedded Roger. No one.

With careful precision, she set the envelope in the upper left corner. Reaching into the drawer again, she withdrew a piece of fine linen stationery. Then, after checking the nib, she dipped her Warren quill pen in the inkwell, ready to write an overdue thank-you for last month's ladies' tea to the woman who would become Marguerite's mother-in-law. At least, she would if Camille had anything to do with it.

The corners of Camille's lips lifted. If the look of adoration in Roger's eyes was any indication, even Marguerite couldn't stop this now.

Just as she wrote "sincerely yours" at the letter's close, Edward appeared at the edge of the camp. She blotted the letter and folded it before he drew close enough to kiss her cheek.

"I see my gift has come in handy."

"Did you have this summer at the lake planned in December?" She rolled the desk's drawer down. "Is that why you gave it to me?"

He chuckled. "No, sweetheart. I just saw the travel desk and thought of you. A beautiful woman should surround herself with beautiful things."

Her cheeks heated. "How was your day?"

Edward sat down on the settee. "The prospectus for the new streetcar company is coming together. I should be able to go over it with Roger later."

Alice ambled to the table with a glass of lemonade for Edward. He took a long swig. "Alice, you always know just what I need. Thank you."

"Mr. Westing, you tryin' to get yourself an extra slice of pie by flatterin' me?"

"I'm certainly hoping. Is it working?" He grinned and raised his eyebrows.

"Humph. We'll just have to see." She waddled off.

"You're as bad as Marguerite. Treating the help like they're friends."

"We've lived in the same house with her for almost twenty years. I think she deserves a kind word every now and then."

Camille picked up the fan and waved it before her flushed cheeks. "There's something of greater importance I wish to discuss with you."

"Oh? Has something happened?"

"Only what you have allowed to happen." She stilled the fan and met her husband's curious gaze. "Do the words 'Marguerite' and 'sailing' ring any bells?"

His lips curled. "I take it she told you about our adventure."

"What were you thinking? Don't you realize how difficult it is to negotiate a suitable match for her already? When Roger learned of her adventure, he was appalled."

He took another sip of the lemonade. "Then perhaps Roger isn't the one for our daughter."

"Nonsense. He is quite smitten with her and will provide for her admirably."

"Camille, the decision is ultimately Marguerite's, just as marrying me was yours."

Edward's wink sent a familiar thrill through her. How well she remembered their courting days, and not once had she regretted her decision to marry the man beside her. "Has it become warmer, or is it just me?" She fanned her heated cheeks. "The fact remains that you are making my job much more difficult than it need be."

"*Your* job?"

So they'd come to this place again—their greatest source

of disagreement. Why did Edward always have to force her to be the strict parent? Didn't he see that Marguerite played them against one another?

"I'm her mother, Edward, and I truly want what's best for her. She's only a girl. She can't possibly know what is best for her, but as her parents we *are* supposed to know."

He rubbed his hand over his bearded chin. "You're probably right."

"That shouldn't surprise you." She smiled and inclined her head in his direction. "And if you continue to indulge her unorthodox tendencies, Roger may begin to see her as unmanageable."

"If he thinks he can manage Marguerite, he is in for a surprise." He crossed his arms over his chest, making no attempt to hide his delight in that fact.

"That's exactly what I'm talking about." She frowned. "We need to take her in hand."

Leaning forward, he clasped her hand in his. Drinking in the softness in his eyes, she felt her heart warm. This charismatic charmer had been her undoing from the start.

"Camille, dear, she doesn't love him."

She cupped his cheek, feeling the bristly whiskers on her sensitive hand. "Once Marguerite discovers the truth about Roger—how he can give her so many things and make her feel secure—she'll be as happy in her marriage as I am in mine."

"And as I am in mine." His eyes sparkled, and he winked again.

"That won't get you out of this. Why did you let her go sailing, of all things?"

"Her heart was so set on it."

"And of course you couldn't tell her no."

"I didn't feel I needed to." He brought the back of her hand to his lips. "It was simply a boat trip around the lake."

"Edward, please try to understand. It's imperative that Marguerite present herself as a suitable wife."

He released a long breath. "All right, my dear, I admit it's difficult for me to disappoint her. Can you fault me if I like to make the women in my life happy?"

"I suppose that's true. So unless you want her to be an old maid, in the future perhaps you should defer to me in matters concerning Marguerite."

Lifting her fingers to his lips, he kissed them. "I place her in your capable hands, darling. Will you forgive me?"

"I'll think about it."

He placed another kiss in her palm. "Then perhaps you'll allow me to persuade you."

❧

Wearing his red Union-style bathing suit, Mark dove off the stern of the sunken steamer and resurfaced seconds later. Marguerite watched from her spot in the sand, trying to decide how to best approach the topic of Mark taking sailing lessons.

Somehow she had to make her brother believe he'd come up with the idea on his own. If he thought she wanted him to do it, he'd never willingly participate. And while she had a sufficient pile of blackmail material for everyday use, she didn't have enough to persuade him that far.

"Come on in the water, Marguerite," Mark called. "You can't learn to swim on the beach."

She glanced at the cool water and pressed her hands to her sun-warmed cheeks. Mark jogged toward her, and at the last second he bent and sent a shower of water in her direction.

Marguerite sputtered and wiped the water from her eyes. "Mark! Why did you do that?"

"Now you're already wet, so you don't have no excuse not to come in."

"*Any* excuse," she corrected. As she stepped toward him, the water seeped through her wool stockings and her legs instantly felt weighted. Mark, possibly sensing her intention, moved farther into the lake. The desire to retaliate ran deep, and she moved farther into the water until it reached her waist.

"Well, well, well, what are you going to do now, sis?" Mark darted around her.

"You know exactly what I plan to do." She lunged at him and water flew in the air.

Mark easily sidestepped the barrage. "You were saying?"

"Mark Westing, so help me—"

He made a perfect surface dive. Suddenly something gripped her ankle. She screamed.

Mark popped up in front of her, laughing. "Gotcha!"

"I'm going to ring your scrawny little neck, Mark Westing!"

Half an hour later, they sat side by side on the beach, sopping wet. She still hadn't managed to douse him, but she had been thoroughly initiated into Lake Manawa.

"Isn't this place grand?" Mark lay back in the sand and stretched his arms above his head.

Marguerite, arms wrapped around her knees, saw an opening. "And there's so much to do."

"And explore."

Perfect. Just the direction she wanted him to go. "What would you like to explore?"

"Caves. Think there are any caves around here?"

"There aren't a lot of caves in Iowa, Mark. What else?"

"Indian trails. There are lots of those. I already found two arrowheads. Do you want to see them? One was little but the other was a big one. Isaiah said it might have even been a spearhead. I'll show them to you when we get back."

She smiled. "I'd like that. Is there anything else you'd like to do while you're here at the lake?"

"Not really."

Marguerite hit her head against her knees. Didn't Mark see the whole exciting world stretched before him? She needed a new approach.

"Mark, did I tell you what I was able to do this morning?"

"What?" He stood and skipped a stone across the water. It bounced—once, twice, three times—before sinking into the lake.

"Daddy took me sailing on the *Argo*."

He whirled to face her. "Why you? Why not me?"

She shrugged. "Maybe you're not old enough to sail."

"I am too. I could sail if I wanted to."

She sucked in the sides of her cheeks to keep from grinning. Like taking candy from a baby. "I don't know about that. They don't usually let boys take sailing lessons."

"I'm hardly a boy. I'm almost thirteen."

"You'll be thirteen in eight months." She paused, seeing him fidget beside her. "So you really want to learn to sail?"

"Yeah." He stood and brushed the sand from his behind. "I do."

"So, when are you going to ask Daddy?"

"Me?" His voice cracked. "I was thinking maybe you'd ask him for me, seeing as how you know all about sailing now, that is."

Marguerite swallowed a giggle and stood up. "I guess I do

know what it's like to be told I can't do something. I suppose I could try to talk to Daddy for you. I could tell him how responsible you're becoming."

"And what a good swimmer I am."

"Yes, that too." She gathered her overdress and shoes. "But only if you're certain it's what you want to do."

"Absolutely." He crossed his arms over his puffed-out chest. "Captain Mark Westing. It has a ring to it, doesn't it? This is my best adventure idea yet."

She tipped her head back and laughed. "Sure, Mark. Whatever you say."

6

"But Daddy, he truly wants to learn to sail." Marguerite slipped into the seat beside her father on the streetcar.

"Of course he does. What boy wouldn't want to be on the water? But he's young and impetuous, Marguerite. Some of his stunts have made yours look like catnaps." He chuckled. "Remember when he decided he wanted to be a snake charmer?"

Marguerite moaned. "I thought poor Alice was going to fall over dead when she opened that basket."

"And what about when he decided he could have honey all the time if he kept bees in his bedroom?"

"I didn't know that Mother could run that fast." Marguerite giggled.

"So you see why I can't trust Mark out on a boat alone?"

Biting her lip, Marguerite took a deep breath. It was now or never. "I have an idea of how Mark could learn to sail and, at the same time, be chaperoned sufficiently."

Her father shook open the morning newspaper, absently telling her to go on.

"I'll oversee his lessons."

He looked at her over the top of the paper. "You? Your mother would have my hide."

"She wouldn't have to know." Placing a hand on his arm,

she hurried to continue. "Daddy, if we just let Mark try this, he will probably have it out of his system by the end of the week and be off on some other tangent. But if you forbid it, I'm afraid he'll sneak around and get himself in all kinds of trouble."

"Hmmm. You have a point." His crystal blue eyes bore into hers. "But if Roger was unhappy with you taking one trip on a boat, what would he say if he found out you were supervising your brother's lessons?"

"I don't care what he says."

Her father's eyes narrowed. "Your mother certainly does."

"Then I won't let him know."

"So, you're willing to sneak around on both your mother and the man you're courting in order to do this. You must love your brother even more than I realized."

He knows. I know he knows. He sees right through me. Any minute he's going to let me have it. Double-barrel. Marguerite diverted her eyes to the window and watched the oak trees pass. *Now what am I going to do?*

"So," he continued, "if I let Mark do this and I allow you to supervise his studies, then how exactly will I keep this little experiment from your mother?"

Marguerite coughed into her handkerchief. Was he playing with her? "Well, I thought perhaps Mark and I could go cycling each morning. After all, it is good for one's lungs."

"It is indeed." He lifted an eyebrow. "And you would need to wear appropriate clothes for cycling."

"Yes, sir. I guess I would."

"And your one cycling outfit will hardly do, so that would be why you are going to town with me today—to purchase additional cycling clothes."

She nodded.

"And I'm sure you'd both be home before lunch every day."

"We would." A smile split her face.

"And how much will this little venture cost me?"

"I'm not sure. I haven't spoken to Mr. Andrews about it yet."

"Your rescuer? Good choice. Tell Mr. Andrews that I'm willing to pay double if he'll let you oversee Mark's lessons—from on board the boat, of course."

"Daddy, how can I thank—"

His lips curled and his eyes twinkled. "I hope Mark has a good time."

⁂

Wearing boys' leather Wellington boots beneath her russet divided skirt, Marguerite pedaled her bicycle down the wide, dirt-packed path toward the boathouse. The boots, along with a matching pair for Mark, who rode beside her, were part of the errand she'd sent Lilly on two days before. Moving around on the deck of a sailboat in her regular heeled shoes could be fatal.

The sun blinked at them through the canopy of trees as they rode. Even this early in the morning, the park was beginning to come to life, and excitement bubbled in her like a bathtub filled with too much soap.

Lord, thank You for this perfect day. It has Your seal of approval stamped on it.

"You lied to Mother," Mark said in his all-too-familiar I'm-going-to-use-this-later voice.

"Do you want to learn to sail or not?" Marguerite negotiated a turn in the path and Mark followed. A prick of guilt stabbed her. "Besides, it was just a little white lie. No harm done."

"I could have asked her. I bet she would have told me yes." Mark pulled beside her.

His emphasis on the word *me* chafed. "Oh, I'm sure she would have let you do it since she lets you do anything you want. However, she wouldn't have agreed to let me supervise you, and if you recall, that was Father's stipulation."

"But it's dumb. I don't need a nanny." He leaned back on the seat and let go of the handlebars.

"Just like you don't need anyone to tell you to put your hands back on the bicycle before you fall off and crack your head open?"

She didn't have to see his face to know he'd rolled his eyes at her. She shook her head but noticed he'd returned his hands to their proper position. Did he always have to be so obstinate?

"Mark, you don't have a nanny. You have an older sister who wants you to have a pleasant adventure and to keep safe in the process." *And if I happen to learn to sail while you're at it, then so be it.* Her heart quickened at the thought, and she picked up her speed.

Ahead of them loomed the redbrick Manawa Yacht Club wrapped in white trim. Beside it stood a humble wooden structure.

"That's the boat shop. Now, when we get inside, you let me do the talking." Marguerite slowed her bicycle as they drew near.

Suddenly Mark darted in front of her. She swerved to avoid a collision, but unable to stop, she slammed into a park bench. The bicycle's rear tire lifted, throwing her over the handlebars.

Somersaulting, she rolled to a stop in the grass and then sat up, shaking her rattled head. She pressed the palm of her hand to her forehead. Though her hat was askew and her skirt was torn, a quick inventory told her nothing was broken. She poked her finger through the hole in her new cycling outfit. *Here I thought You were on my side today, Lord.*

A shadow passed overhead, and Marguerite looked up. "Mr. Andrews!"

"Miss Westing." A lopsided, dimpled grin reached his hazel eyes. "Nice of you to drop in. You're not injured, are you?"

"I'm fine." She puffed the hair from her eyes and flicked a piece of grass from her cropped jacket.

"Good." He offered his hand and pulled her to her feet.

Only then did she notice Mark's peals of laughter. She glared at him, but it did little to squash his chuckling. "Hey, you can't blame me. That was better than a vaudeville act."

"Excuse him, Mr. Andrews. He's normally much more polite." She smoothed her divided skirt and then caught the twinkle in the sailing instructor's hazel eyes. "And for your information, we didn't drop in. Well, perhaps I did, but that isn't why we're here. We—my brother and I—came for sailing lessons. I don't mean we, I mean my brother wants to take them, and I'm to supervise. That's why we're here. To arrange for the lessons. When can we—I mean Mark—begin?" Fireflies flitted in her stomach. What had turned her into a babbling idiot?

Trip righted her bicycle and propped it against the park bench located only yards from the front door of the boat shop. "Miss Westing, I don't think I understood a word of that after 'We came for sailing lessons.'"

"Me." Mark dismounted and stood beside her with his

bike still in hand. He jabbed a thumb into his chest. "I came for lessons, but my dad won't let me take them unless she gets to be on the boat too."

"This is your brother?" he asked Marguerite.

"Yes, this is Mark. Mark, say hello to Mr. Andrews."

Mark stuck out his hand and Trip shook it.

"And why won't your father let him take lessons alone?" Trip eyed the boy suspiciously.

Marguerite straightened Mark's collar. "He's a bit impetuous."

"I can watch out for that. No need for you to come along."

"That's what I said." Mark looked up at her. "I don't need a nursemaid."

"Mark." Her voice dropped in warning, and she tucked an errant strand of wispy hair behind her ear. "My father forbids him from taking lessons unless I'm on board as well to oversee his instruction."

"In that case, the answer's no." Trip turned on his heel and started inside.

"Wait!" Marguerite called. "My father will pay double."

Trip stopped and frowned. "My decisions can't be bought."

"I apologize. I didn't mean to imply differently. Can you at least give us a reason?"

"First of all," he said, stepping closer and holding up his hand to tick off the count, "I don't teach ladies how to sail."

"But she's not the student, I am," Mark insisted.

He turned toward Mark. "Okay, second, if you're that much of a troublemaker, I don't want any part of it. A boat is no place for a kid to play."

"He'll take his lessons seriously. I'll see to that." She laid her hand on her brother's shoulder.

"And third, can you swim?"

Mark tried to shrug off her hand, to no avail. "Sure, I can swim like a fish."

"Not you—her. And before you answer, remember, I've seen your abilities firsthand." He crossed his arms over his chest, revealing solid muscles beneath rolled-up shirtsleeves.

Mouth suddenly dry, Marguerite licked her lips. What difference would one more white lie make? God understood. Besides, he didn't ask how well she could swim. She could dog-paddle with the best of breeds.

A long time ago, she'd learned that when lying, it was best to stick as close to the facts as possible. That way she could state the facts convincingly.

She forced a smile. "Yes, Mr. Andrews, I can take care of myself. The other day I was caught off guard and my skirt wrapped around my legs."

Mark opened his mouth to protest, but Marguerite dug her fingers into his shoulder, and he clamped it shut.

"Are you sure?" Trip's eyes bore into her. "'Cause I don't let anyone on my boat who can't swim. It's just too dangerous."

Was he softening? Marguerite pressed on. "Mr. Andrews, we've already assured you that we can. What else do you need to know?"

"How does your mother feel about this?" Trip kept his gaze nailed to her face.

Great. In for a penny . . . Marguerite took a deep breath. This one she could handle. "Suffice it to say that my mother fully supports any of Mark's endeavors."

Mark elbowed her side. "Please, Mr. Andrews. Don't let my dad's dumb ideas keep me from learning to sail."

One side of Trip's mouth lifted. "Fathers usually have a reason for doing what they do."

"He has a point, Mark."

"But, Mr. Andrews, can't I learn even if she has to tag along?"

"I am not tagging along. I am supervising your lessons."

"Only if I say there'll be any lessons." Trip sighed. "I know I am going to regret this, but you can start Monday. We'll give it a try."

Marguerite opened the chatelaine purse clipped to her belt and removed a wad of bills. "How much do we owe you for the lessons?"

"They'll be a dollar a day."

Her mouth dropped open, but she quickly snapped it shut. "But the ride the other day was only fifty cents for both my father and me, and that was double the price."

"Rides are cheaper than lessons. Besides, you said you'd pay double for the lessons too. If it's too steep . . ."

She peeled off a five-dollar bill. "For five lessons."

He reached into her hand and tugged a one-dollar bill from her stack. "One lesson. One dollar. After that, we'll see if there will even be a second lesson."

<figure>❧</figure>

Good grief, his voice hasn't even changed.

Trip kept the brother and sister in view until they'd ridden their bicycles out of sight. He doubted the boy would be able to do the work that sailing required, but it didn't really matter. Mark Westing wasn't the first boy to come knocking at his door with sailing ambitions. Long ago, Trip had worked out a system for eliminating the starry-eyed rich boys from the serious students before they even hit the water.

Now, figuring out the Westing girl's story might take a bit longer. She intrigued him. How many sisters would accompany their brother day after day to sailing lessons? Then again, on the boat the other day, her face had glowed almost as much as her honey gold hair. He'd never seen anyone fall in love with the water like she had. It would be a pleasure to watch her cornflower blue eyes light up like that again.

Stop right there. I don't need to go fancying a woman right now. Regatta. Regatta. Regatta.

Her trim form disappeared around the bend in the path. He sighed. Maybe just a little looking wouldn't hurt. Besides, it would be days before either of them boarded a boat—if the boy lasted that long. Monday he'd see what Mark was made of. He only hoped that Miss Westing knew how to keep out of the way.

For some reason, he figured she didn't.

The portrait of his father, Richard Mason Gordon, stared accusingly at Roger. Every morning his father's cold eyes reminded him of the hard lessons he'd learned under the man's strict tutelage. Even in death, his father's words haunted him. "What Darwin said in *The Origin of Species* goes for business and life too," the rock-hard businessman had repeatedly told him. "Survival of the fittest. No mercy. See what you want and take it. Only the strong survive."

Roger pushed back from the heavy walnut desk, stood, and approached his newest framed acquisition angled against the mantel. He untied the burlap cloth wrapped around the artwork and let it slide onto the Turkish rug. As he ran his hand along the gilded frame, a slow smile spread across his face.

He straightened and removed his father's portrait from the wall. How weak and simpering the once strong man had become in the end. Pitiful. Lifting the new portrait of himself into place, a deep sense of satisfaction filled Roger.

"Who's the strongest now, Father? Who survived?"

7

Marguerite glanced at the watch tucked beneath her belt. She didn't want to be late. Not on the first day of Mark's lessons. The last thing she wanted was to give Trip Andrews a reason to cancel them.

"Mark, don't dawdle. We want to be early."

Mark propped his bicycle against a tree, then balanced on his left foot while propping his right foot over his knee. He tugged at the shoe. "These new boots hurt my feet. You should have let me wear my old ones."

"Those are scuffed. I want you to look your best."

"I don't think Mr. Andrews cares what my boots look like."

When he stepped back onto the path, Marguerite adjusted his pin-striped vest and tapped on the bill of his new cap. "This is going to be fun, Mark. Don't mess it up."

"What's the big deal? It's just something to do."

"It's the adventure of your life. I won't let you ruin this." She smoothed a tuft of his hair sticking out near his ear. "Now, let's go."

They found the boat shop door already ajar when they arrived. Marguerite eased through the door and wrinkled her nose at the acrid stench. She covered her face with a handkerchief. "What's that smell?"

Trip walked through the door and wiped his hands on a rag. "Varnish. The boats have to have several coats of it. Or you might be smelling the glue. It's just as bad. Depends on which one you dislike more." He gave Mark a once-over. "Hang your coat on that hook, Mark, and I hope those new boots don't make it impossible for you to work."

"Work?"

"Come on. Let's get started."

The odor became stronger as they followed Trip through what appeared to be an office, down a hallway, and to the back workshop. "Wait here."

Stopping in the center of the massive room, she watched Trip go to a workbench lining the wall. From her boat excursion the other day, she recognized the man he spoke to as his father. The elder Mr. Andrews glanced at her, scowled, and grunted.

Good morning to you too, Mr. Andrews.

She quickly diverted her eyes to the workshop. Various tools hung on one wall. She tried to recall their names: awls, planes, chisels. As a child, she'd often snuck into her grandpa's workshop to watch him work. With infinite patience, he'd explained each step in his deep bass voice. He had even helped her make a jewelry case once.

If she closed her eyes, she could still sense his rough hands on top of her own, showing her how you had to "feel" the wood to see if it was smooth enough. Her mother, she recalled, had scolded her when she ran her hand along his casket at the funeral. Her grandfather would have been honored.

Mark fidgeted from foot to foot beside her.

She nudged him. "Hold still."

"Look at that." He pointed to another area of the workshop, which held the bare bones of a new craft hanging upside down. "It looks like a giant skeleton."

Harry, one of the young men from the boat ride, dipped a brush in a tin can and then glided the liquid over the hull of another nearly finished upturned boat. Marguerite figured it must be the varnish. The steady swish of his hand over the bent boards mesmerized her.

"Miss Westing!"

She spun around to see Mark and Trip walking away. "Sorry, I wasn't listening."

Trip strode over to her. With a good five inches of height on her, he glared down. "Don't let it happen again. In sailing, not listening can get you knocked plumb off the boat."

"Yes, sir." She cast a glance through the wide-open doors toward the docked boats. One of them, the *Endeavor*, caught her eye with its gold lettering on the hull. "Which boat will we be taking out?"

"We won't be sailing today. Mark has to learn about boats from the ground up. I decide when and if he's ready to set sail. Understand?"

She nodded.

"Wait a minute," Mark protested. "What do you mean I don't get on a boat today?"

"Mr. Andrews wants you to learn about how boats are constructed, Mark."

Trip strode across the room to two large pieces of wood atop a set of sawhorses and explained that this would be the mast of a new sailboat. "This is Sitka spruce. You're going to make a mast from it." He picked up a paint brush and a jar and passed them to Mark. "Brush this glue on the first piece, and then I'll help you set the other on top of it."

"And this is teaching me how to sail?"

"Nope." He started to walk away. "It's telling me if you know how to learn."

Mark turned to Marguerite and murmured, "This is your fault."

"Hey, you wanted to do this. Don't blame me."

"Well, maybe I'm un-wanting to do it."

A surge of panic made her heart race. "Mark, you don't want to quit. You're just getting started."

"I'm telling you, if he tells me to mop the floor . . ."

She leaned close to his ear and hissed, "Then you'll do it with a smile on your face. You want to learn to sail, right?"

Marguerite glanced at Trip, who had begun work on the skeleton of a vessel, and sighed. He might have tousled, sun-kissed sandy hair, warm hazel eyes, and to-die-for dimples, but he didn't know a thing about teaching a twelve-year-old boy.

Mark dipped the brush in and slathered a thin layer of the acrid glue over the flat surface.

"Not like that." She took the brush and meticulously applied it to the sides of the mast, keeping the layer thick and even.

"What do you think you're doing?" Trip marched across the room toward them. "I told your brother to do this." He pulled the brush from her hand and gave it back to Mark. "Take about half that glue off."

"Off?" she squeaked.

"When we clamp the pieces together, all that extra glue will seep out." Ignoring her, he spoke only to Mark. "Lesson one. If you don't know something, ask."

And if you want him to know something, tell him.

Trip watched Mark remove the excess glue, then pointed to the far end of the mast. "Now, we're going to put one half of the mast on top of the other. Whatever you do, Mark, don't drop it. If it cracks, we can't use it. I'll lift my end and you lift yours, on three."

Trip counted aloud and the two of them lifted the heavy piece of wood. Mark strained beneath the weight.

"Do we need to put it back down?" Trip asked.

Mark shook his head, but as they reached the other half of the mast, his step faltered. The board slipped from his fingers and landed in place with a thud. Trip's brow creased in a scowl.

"I'm sorry. I couldn't hold it any longer. It was too heavy."

Trip laid a hand on his shoulder. "Lesson two. If you can't do something, then say so. There are no heroes on the water." Moving to a barrel, he reached inside, pulled out a set of wet leather straps, and tossed them in Mark's direction. He wiped his hands on his white cotton shirt, leaving a smear of water. "Now, tie these on the mast every two feet. As they dry, they'll clamp the wood together. And don't let your sister help you. Tomorrow, when the mast dries, the real fun begins."

"And until then?" Marguerite asked.

"You go home."

He had to be joking. They'd been there only an hour. What about sailing? "Home? But I thought . . ."

The corners of his mouth curved. "Lesson three. Here, I do the thinking."

Marguerite whirled and stomped away, afraid to say another word. Outside the boat shop, raw fury burned inside her. How dare he take their money, use Mark in the shop like a hired hand, shout at her for helping him, and then send them off after only an hour with no boat instruction whatsoever.

She climbed on her bicycle and pedaled away, vaguely aware of Mark calling to her. Maybe she'd been wrong about Trip

Andrews. There had to be other instructors on the lake. *Ones better suited to work with me—I mean Mark.*

❧

Legs pumping like a freight train, Marguerite rode off into the distance. Trip chuckled from the doorway. Her brother would never catch her now. Maybe the work wasn't what they had expected, but he figured they'd be back. At least, she would. Fierce determination shone in those crystal blue eyes, and the spark he saw in them, as she ran her hand along the mast just before she left, had said it all.

Trip shook his head. He had to remember she wasn't the student.

Poor brother. Mark didn't stand a chance with a sister like that. Although young and a bit impulsive, the boy appeared teachable so far. Trip walked back inside the boat shop and headed for the workshop area. Checking the first of the leather straps on the mast, he nodded. At least the boy hadn't argued, even when Trip deliberately provoked him. But Mark appeared to give up easily, and that worried him.

"Hey, Trip, what do you think of your new student? Pretty wet behind the ears, isn't he?" Harry set down his varnish can and brush and crossed the work area.

"Yeah, but not any younger than you or me when we first started out."

"Eons ago." He clapped his friend on the shoulder. "But I think it's the girl you gotta worry about. Did you notice how moony-eyed she got when she just looked at your *Endeavor*?"

Trip checked the tightness of the rest of the leather thongs around the mast. "Can't blame a lady for recognizing quality."

"Do you think the boy will be able to stick with it?" Harry took a seat on a barrel, picked up a splintered piece of wood, and chewed on it like a toothpick. "Those rich boys aren't used to hard labor."

"We'll see. If he survives tomorrow, then maybe—just maybe—I'll take him out before the end of the week."

Harry laughed. "You're getting soft. Used to be you'd wait two weeks."

"I don't know. This one seems different."

"And you wouldn't mind getting in good with his sister."

Trip feigned ignorance. "Who?"

"You aren't fooling me. I saw the way you looked at her, but hey, like you said, you can't fault someone for recognizing quality. Never saw anyone take to sailing like she did the other day either. You'd have thought she was born on a boat."

"Harry!" Captain Andrews bellowed. "What's this mess?"

Harry hopped to his feet. "All I ask is that you find out if she has a sister."

⌘

Roger arrived at the Westing camp in search of Marguerite. His business meeting with the other investors developing Lake Manawa's Midway ended much earlier than he'd anticipated, and one of the benefits of being a wealthy man was not having to return to the office right away. Noticing her bicycle gone, he rubbed his chin. Last night, she'd said that she and Mark would ride this morning, but since it was almost 2:00, she should have returned long ago.

Perhaps he could hunt her down. Once they were married, these impulsive wanderings would stop. He'd watched his own father handle his mother's assertiveness, and he knew that Marguerite's, too, could be eliminated in time. It was almost a shame. He admired her spunk, but it wouldn't do in a wife.

The nursery rhyme "Peter, Peter, Pumpkin Eater" popped into his head. When Marguerite was secured in his pumpkin shell, he would certainly keep her very well. And all the while, he'd be free to enjoy her beauty every day.

She might never love him, but she would learn to respect him.

That he could guarantee.

❧

In asking around for the names of other sailing instructors, Marguerite learned two things. No one else would take her and her brother on as students. And Trip Andrews was considered the best.

Marguerite also discovered that wandering around with Mark in tow did have its benefits. As long as her brother walked beside her, she could investigate the docks and no one seemed to notice. Even when she perched on one of the railings to watch Trip Andrews's *Endeavor* raise its pristine sail and cross the seven-hundred-acre lake, no one said a word. Had she been alone, all sorts of sensibilities would have been ruffled.

Two small, regal sailboats raced one another across the lake, leaning heavily to the side and skimming lightly across the surface. A few days ago on the boat, a thrill had shot through her. How long would it be before she felt it again? It wasn't fair. Why did men keep this incredible world of beautiful vessels closed to her and all women?

And as a woman, I'm not supposed to care.

Mark kicked the earth and muttered words against Trip

Andrews that no lady would say. She'd never felt free to express herself like that, but men were free to do it all the time. They could say anything they pleased, and they didn't have to care how they walked or how they sat or if their hat was pinned at just the right angle.

She made a mental note to jot down the idea in her journal. It would make a good topic at the next suffrage meeting: the unexpected joys of manhood.

After wandering the dock, they remounted their bicycles and pedaled along the path to their campsite. She came to a sudden stop just outside the tents.

"What are you doing?" Mark asked.

"Look who's coming." She moved off the path, behind a clump of trees. Disappointment swept over her. Roger was here again. She'd hoped summering at the lake would set her free of having to constantly see him. Why did he have to keep showing up at the most inopportune times?

"Why do you care if Roger sees us?"

"If he sees me in my cycling outfit, he'll ask where we've been. He knew we were supposed to ride this morning, not all day long." She dismounted. "I'm going to hide my bicycle behind the camp. You can go get it for me when the coast is clear."

"And what are you going to do?"

"Figure out a way to sneak into my tent and change."

"What difference does it make if he knows the truth?"

"You know Roger. He'll probably tell Mother and ruin our fun."

"So far I haven't had a lot of fun."

Reluctantly, Mark agreed to fetch her bicycle. She eased down the dirt road behind the campsite. Even from the back of the camp, she could see Roger sitting on the wicker rocking chair in full view of her tent. What was she going to do now?

A fresh idea made her pulse quicken when she glanced toward the Grahams' camp near their own, where clothes hung out to dry on lines. Emily Graham was about the same size as her. But stealing clothes? Lying about her whereabouts was bad enough, but taking something that didn't belong to her? She just didn't think she could do it. Then again, she wouldn't exactly be stealing a skirt. She'd be borrowing it and would return it before its absence was noticed.

She scanned the camp to see if anyone was watching, then darted to the clothesline before she lost her nerve. Yanking the plainest skirt free, she raced back into a grove of trees. She leaned against a large tree trunk, skirt pressed to her chest, and caught her breath.

A dog barked, and she jumped.

Lord, You're enjoying yourself now, aren't You?

She slid the skirt on over her Turkish pants and buttoned it in place. Removing her hat, she pulled the pins free, shook out her hair, and let it fall about her shoulders. Not perfect, but it would do as long as she didn't run into her mother.

Worrying her lip between her teeth, she slipped out of the dense trees and into the clearing behind their camp. After she spotted Isaiah head toward the water pump, she eased behind the men's tent and walked up the center of the camp.

"Marguerite, I've been looking for you," Roger said, rising to his feet. "A new skirt?"

"Sort of." She sat on the settee. "I'm sorry I didn't see you come in. What brings you to the lake this early in the afternoon?"

"Remember, I'm working with some other men on further

developing the Midway. We're trying to arrange the addition of a carousel. I wanted to surprise you."

"You certainly did." She squeezed out a smile.

He dropped his gaze to her skirt, then looked into her eyes. "So I've been here at the lake most of the day."

"Oh?" Her heart pounded. Had he seen her and Mark? Of course not. The Midway was the other direction.

"Yes, I thought I might run into you." His voice gave no indication either way. He motioned to her approaching father. "You should probably rest after your busy day—cycling. Your father and I have some personal business. If you'll excuse us."

She gave him a weak smile. "Gladly."

Making it into the haven of her tent, she dropped on the bed and heaved a sigh.

The tent flaps flew open and Lilly breezed in.

Marguerite jolted and pressed her hand to her chest. "You scared the life out of me."

"Expecting someone else in your tent?"

"Heavens no!"

Lilly giggled, then paused and eyed the skirt. "Where did you get that?"

"It's a long story, and right now I just want a nap." She flopped back on the bed and closed her eyes.

"Uh-uh-uh."

Marguerite moaned and opened one eye.

Lilly waved her finger in the air. "No rest for you. Mr. Roger called on your parents while you were out playing and asked for you to join him at a dance at the pavilion tonight."

"Tonight? But I just saw him. He didn't say anything."

"He didn't need to." Lilly lifted Marguerite's foot and began to untie her boot. "Your mother accepted on your

81

behalf. Then she ordered me to get your pink ball gown ready."

Marguerite moaned. "I hate that dress almost as much as I do the idea of dancing with him."

"It's a perfectly fine dress. You just don't like it because she does." She dropped the boot to the floor with a thud. "So, how'd your first day go?"

Marguerite threw her arm over her face. "You wouldn't believe me if I told you."

"That bad?"

She sat up and rubbed her brow with her palm. "It's complicated. We were in the workshop all morning. Trip says Mark has to learn about boats before he can sail."

"Makes sense to me."

"It would."

"Now, don't go getting sore with me." Lilly gathered the frilly pink dress from the chair. "Are you both gonna go back?"

Marguerite stood and slid out of the borrowed skirt, then shucked the Turkish pants and the shirt. "You don't understand, Lilly. I have to go back. I want this more than anything."

"Right now you'd better want a washbasin. You're starting to smell like Mark." She gave Marguerite a shove in the general direction of the washbasin and picked up the discarded skirt. "So, are you gonna tell me where this skirt came from?"

Heat rushed up Marguerite's neck. "I sort of borrowed it."

"You stole it!"

"I just needed something to cover up my cycling outfit before Roger saw me." She glanced at the skirt. "Can you take it over to the Grahams' camp and ask them if it blew off their line?"

Shaking her head, Lilly sighed. "I hope the Lord's already telling you He expects you on the front pew this Sunday, Miss Marguerite, 'cause I know I do."

⁓

Preparing for the evening took over an hour and a half. While Lilly returned the skirt, Marguerite dressed in the overly lacy, high-necked pink gown before securing her hair in a topknot.

"Ooooh, I can't get this to look right." Marguerite relinquished the tortoiseshell comb to Lilly, who'd arrived in time to get the tresses to cooperate.

"It looks fine. Now stop fidgeting." Lilly placed a hand on Marguerite's shoulder as she tucked the jeweled comb in place. She added a few more pins to the twist and adjusted the springy curls at the nape of Marguerite's neck before declaring her mistress ready.

Marguerite stood and tugged at the cap sleeves on the gown. "These sleeves just don't lay right. Maybe I should put on the blue dress."

"Why do you care? You don't want to impress Mr. Gordon anyway."

"Lilly, hush. He might hear you." She drew on a white kidskin opera glove and attempted to do up the tiny pearl buttons.

Lilly gently nudged her hand out of the way and hooked the buttons through the hoops with ease. "And it would be a good thing if he did. You should have told him the truth ages ago."

"But Mother . . ."

Lilly shook her head. "She's not the one he's boring to tears."

"Marguerite," her mother called from the doorway. "Roger is here."

Marguerite rolled her eyes. "Coming." She hugged Lilly goodbye. "Pray for me. I'm going to need it."

"I always do."

⬥

Soaking up the atmosphere at the Pelican Bay restaurant, complete with gas chandeliers, fresco paintings, and glistening place settings, Marguerite made a decision to enjoy the evening.

With the dance following in the great pavilion's ballroom, the well-dressed diners quickly finished their food. She recognized many guests, including Penelope Worth and Emily Graham. A stab of guilt surged through her at the thought of poor Lilly returning the skirt. At least Emily was a good friend.

Marguerite hurried through the meal's courses, anticipating the dance. After having an obligatory dance with Roger because he'd brought her, she would be free to dance with others. In fact, she would have to in order to avoid any appearance of impropriety. For once the social rules worked in her favor.

Roger, however, ate painfully slowly. Every time she looked up from her steak and mashed potatoes, she found his gaze locked on her. "What is it? Do I have something on my lips?" She dabbed her napkin against them.

"Your lips are lovely as usual. I was just admiring how truly beautiful you are. Like a priceless painting."

She smiled. "Thank you, but I'd rather not be hung on any walls."

Roger set his fork down and sipped the red wine he'd insisted on ordering. He licked his lips and the bushy mustache wriggled. "Your father and I are working on a complex business deal," he said. "Has he spoken to you about it?"

Marguerite laid her spoon beside the raspberry ice. "Me? I wish he would, but Father doesn't confide in me about business matters."

"Odd. I thought the two of you were close."

"We are. He just doesn't talk to me about his work. I guess I haven't shown much curiosity."

"What does interest you, Marguerite?"

Marguerite stared at him. In three months of outings, not once had Roger ever inquired about her personal hobbies, her likes and dislikes. The glint in his eye made her uneasy. Was his interest genuine, or did he suspect her sailing excursion? Had he somehow learned what she was up to?

No, he couldn't possibly know about the sailing lessons. She forced a smile. "As a matter of fact, I enjoy stargazing."

An ugly, halfhearted laugh erupted from his mouth. "Why doesn't that surprise me? My Marguerite wishing on stars."

She cringed. *My Marguerite?* Tonight Roger didn't just seem boring, he seemed almost possessive.

The sweet raspberry ice puddled in her compote. Trying to ease the mounting tension between them, she folded her napkin and set it beside her plate. "We should get going. After all, we don't want to miss the first dance."

He lifted her hand to his lips and pressed a kiss to it. "No, we certainly wouldn't want to do that."

⤜⤛⤜

Roger danced with every step perfectly timed and joylessly performed. Prior to this evening, Marguerite had danced with him only a few times. She found it amazing that anyone could approach something so enjoyable with so little excitement. Then again, it was Roger.

When she misstepped, he frowned. "Concentrate, Marguerite. People are watching."

She threw her head back and laughed. "So? What does that matter?"

He pressed his hand hard to her waist and held her in place. "It matters."

"Roger, relax. This is a dance. It's supposed to be fun."

"Life isn't the game you make it, Marguerite."

When the four-piece orchestra concluded the lively waltz, she sighed with relief. "Would you be so kind as to get me a glass of lemonade?"

"And where will you be?" Behind his spectacles, his dark eyes chilled her.

"Right here."

"Then I shall return directly."

She sat on a bench and tried to make sense of Roger's actions. Maybe he'd overheard Lilly or maybe he'd sensed her discomfort concerning the secret morning outings. Whatever the reason, she almost wished boring, predictable Roger would return. This Roger frightened her.

She shook her head. That was ridiculous. Roger Gordon wasn't to be feared. Maybe his caterpillar mustache was, but the man certainly was not.

"Hello, Miss Westing."

Marguerite's head shot up. Before her stood Trip Andrews, hair still tousled and dimples still dangerous, wearing a fine black tailcoat, white vest, and tie. He seemed as at ease in the wealthy crowd as he did on a sailboat.

"What's a lovely lady like you doing sitting out on one

of my favorite dances?" He held out his hand, apparently expecting her to take it.

But that was not going to happen. Not after how he'd treated her and Mark today. "I'm sorry. I'm waiting for my escort to return with refreshments."

"I see." He didn't appear disheartened. In fact, his fire-flecked eyes seemed to sparkle at the challenge. "Then I will catch you in a few dances."

He moved off, and a bit later his friend Harry asked her to dance. Since Roger had yet to return, she accepted his offer.

Harry, who immediately admitted he was a horrible dancer, made her laugh the entire time, telling stories of the various gents and ladies in attendance. When the dance ended, another young man stood ready to whisk her away.

As the last notes closed on the fast waltz, Roger appeared.

He grabbed her elbow and drew her to the side. "What do you think you're doing?"

"Dancing."

"But you're with me." He thrust the lemonade at her and it splashed on the awful pink dress. He whipped out a handkerchief and held it out to her. "I apologize. How clumsy of me."

Taking the handkerchief, she dabbed at the stain.

Roger cleared his throat. "I guess you'll want to go now."

"No, this little spot will dry."

He took hold of her elbow. "Actually, I think we'll leave."

Marguerite jerked her arm away. "What has gotten into you? You aren't yourself at all."

"I'm sorry. I guess I'm just more tired than I realized."

She studied him. He seemed sincere. "Do you honestly want to go?"

"No, we can stay awhile longer. Let me get you another lemonade."

He quickly departed, and Marguerite shook her head. Lately, his personality changed more than the shifting sands on the beach.

✆

Trip Andrews didn't like what he saw. The man accompanying Marguerite Westing appeared anything but gentlemanly. Who was this cad? Trip knew most of the regulars at the lake by now, and other than the night he'd pulled Marguerite from the water, he'd never seen this man. Holding his breath, he watched the situation, ready to intervene if necessary, but as he expected, she handled it admirably. He expelled his breath when her escort left her.

She took a few wobbly steps toward a chair and sat down. Whatever had happened, it had shaken her, and a frown marred her beautiful face. Even a few minutes ago, when she'd danced with Harry, he'd glimpsed the same lightheartedness in her that he'd seen on the *Argo* the other day. Now, from the sag of her shoulders, it was apparent something wore heavy on her.

Determined to bring back her glowing smile, he crossed the room and held out his hand. "I believe you owe me a dance." When she lifted her eyes to his, he flashed a broad grin. "Or do you just need a friend?"

Where did that come from? Smooth, Trip. She's likely to make a beeline for the door after an offer like that.

But to his surprise, her face bloomed and she rose. "I believe I'll take both, if I may."

❧

Up until five minutes ago, Marguerite had thought Trip Andrews was the most arrogant man at the ball.

Things could change a lot in five minutes.

As they waltzed to the strains of Muller's "Evening Star," he asked her if she had enjoyed her sailing adventure on the *Argo*. She sensed something she'd never felt around a man before—a genuine interest in her. An unexpected tingle of joy shot through her. Was this the spark that was missing with Roger?

She couldn't keep a smile from curling her lips. "Sailing was an invigorating experience."

"Your brother Mark seems bright." He swung her in a wide circle. "But I'm not sure he's ready for all of the work involved."

"He really wants to learn."

"If so, then he will. You must care about him a great deal in order to help him achieve his dreams. Few sisters would go to such lengths," Trip said. "You know, you two look a lot alike. Same blue eyes. Same golden hair. Same bright smile."

She laughed, and her face warmed at his words. "Promise me you won't tell him that. Mark would die if he thought he resembled me."

"But I bet he'll be taller than you in no time." Trip twirled her again.

"You're a wonderful dancer, Mr. Andrews."

"Please, call me Trip."

"Given how we met, perhaps that should be my nick-name."

He grinned, and she longed to touch one of the deep dim-

89

ples adorning his cheeks. *Good grief. What am I thinking?* She tightened her grip on his hand, and her cheeks flamed.

"Calling any lady Trip would be a shame. Calling *you* Trip would be a crime."

"Well, I wouldn't want you to get in trouble with the law, so I suppose you'll just have to call me by my given name—Marguerite."

"French for 'daisy.'"

"You speak French?"

"No. I had an aunt named Marguerite. You're lucky I liked her."

Marguerite caught sight of Roger glaring at her through his wire-rimmed spectacles. She stiffened and clamped her lips together.

Trip's gaze swept her face. "I realize it's none of my business, but is there a problem?"

"You're right. It's none of your business."

Trip's eyebrows shot up two notches, but he didn't stop dancing. To her surprise, he pulled her a bit closer and spoke softly. "Remember, you said you needed a friend."

"You're right again. I apologize. My escort is a man I've been seeing socially for a while now, but tonight he's acting like a total stranger."

The last strains of the waltz came to a close, and Marguerite felt a tug of disappointment as Trip's hands slipped away.

"Maybe you never knew him at all." He glanced toward the glowering man. "Sometimes people aren't who we think they are."

Guilt stabbed at her heart. She thanked Trip for the dance, telling him she'd see him tomorrow.

"Miss Westing—Marguerite—if you need anything . . ." He tipped his head toward Roger, who was approaching.

"Thank you, but I'll be fine."

He nodded. "I won't be far."

She turned to Roger, only a few yards away, his wooly eyebrows pressed together in a deep frown.

Lord, boring I can handle, but this . . . what am I supposed to do?

Roger's face creased with a forced smile. He kissed her cheek and handed her the lemonade. "So did you enjoy your dance? I believe I will forgo my option of last dance and take you home."

"So soon?"

"Life isn't all fun and games, Marguerite. I have matters I wish to discuss with you."

Pressing his hand to the small of her back, he deftly moved her through the dancers and toward the exit. Once outside, he hooked her hand in the crook of his arm. "Now, as I was saying, my business venture with your father is quite complicated."

She sighed. Boring Roger was back.

This time, maybe that wasn't such a bad thing.

⁂

Thirty minutes of pillow punching left Marguerite's down-filled headrest lumpy and her thoughts reeling. Lilly's soft snores filled the tent, and every time Marguerite closed her eyes, Trip's words haunted her. "Sometimes people aren't who we think they are."

Why did he have to say that? She didn't want to deceive him, and she wasn't actually doing so. She did care about Mark's dreams, and she truly intended to see to it that her rambunctious brother stayed out of trouble when they got on the water.

Was it her fault if she accidentally learned his lessons alongside him? Besides, having to tell half-truths in order to learn to sail was Trip's fault—his and all the other men who thought women didn't belong in their sailing world.

He'd left her no alternative.

She flopped onto her back. The oppressive heat inside the tent made the sheets stick to her skin. Tossing them aside, Marguerite climbed out of bed, slid her feet into her shoes, and padded to the tent's opening. She untied the strings holding the canvas flaps closed and peeled one side back.

The cool evening air swept in, and the stars dotting the night sky beckoned her. Slipping out of the tent, she walked to the center of their camp and sat down on the wicker settee. She wrapped her arms around her knees and leaned her head back to view the open sky above. Orienting her position, she found the Big Dipper in Ursa Major. She moved on to identify the other constellations: Taurus, Leo, Virgo.

She knew each constellation like a botanist knows each plant, from the name of the brightest star to what season each star should be visible in Iowa. Calm soaked through her like a gentle rain. No matter how much the world closed in on her, the open expanse of the Milky Way made her feel free.

A rustling of canvas drew her attention. She spun toward her parents' tent in time to see her father slip out of the opening, slink around the tent, and head down the path leading to the lake.

What was he doing at this hour? Their privy was the other way, and she'd never known her father to take late-night strolls. She blinked at his disappearing figure. He appeared to be wearing street clothes rather than bed clothes. Twice he stopped and looked back as if to see if anyone followed him. Why was he sneaking around like a common thief?

Marguerite's pulse climbed as she sat outside for fifteen minutes, waiting for his return. When he didn't reappear, her concern mounted. Perhaps she should go after him.

No. He could take care of himself. He was probably just going to work early. She could ask him about it in the morning.

No, she couldn't.

At least not without revealing why she was awake.

Finally, deciding she needed to at least attempt getting some rest, she returned to her tent. Lilly mumbled something in her sleep and shifted. Marguerite kicked off her shoes and eased beneath the sheets. She stared at the pole holding the center of the tent and willed sleep to claim her.

Thoughts of Trip Andrews, Roger Gordon, and now her own father paraded through her mind like soldiers. She expelled a long sigh. Men made poor substitutes for sheep.

◈

No noxious glue or varnish fumes greeted Marguerite when she and her brother stepped inside the boat shop, but she thought she recognized the scent of fresh paint. They crossed through the office to the workshop.

Harry, paintbrush in hand, looked up. "Morning, Mark. Morning, Miss Westing." He pointed to Mark with his hammer and glanced toward Trip, who stood studying a half-completed vessel. "Trip, you planning on working the boy to death today?"

"Not to death. Just close to it."

A teasing grin didn't curl Trip's lips like it would have last night. What was he up to? Was he deliberately trying to make Mark nervous to scare his new pupil away? *Well, it won't work, Mr. Andrews. You're stuck with me. I mean us.*

93

Trip moved toward the mast they'd assembled yesterday. "I'll cut off the straps while you get the plane from the workbench."

She scanned the instruments hanging above the bench: hammers, saws, awls, and the like lined up like cornstalks along the back. Mark picked a plane and joined his instructor.

After cutting the leather bindings, Trip folded his pocket knife and ran his hand along the timber. "The mast has to be tapered on this end. Not too much, but enough. Like a candle."

"What if he makes a mistake?" Marguerite asked.

Mark glared at her. "I won't."

"You're right, because I won't let you. Go ahead. Make your first shaving."

Hands shaking, Mark laid the plane against the wood, grabbed the handle, and bore down while pushing it upward toward the top of the mast. The curled wood shaving fell to the floor.

"Good. Now do that about a hundred more times."

Thirty minutes later, after much grumbling, Mark wanted to give up, but Marguerite urged him on. After another thirty minutes, he stood up and showed her his blistered hands. "See, I can't do any more. It's stupid, and it's not teaching me to sail."

Glancing across the workshop, Marguerite found Trip absorbed in helping Harry on a different upturned boat. "Give me the plane."

"You?"

"Yes, hurry."

Mark handed it to her.

"Now stand so he can't see me."

94

Mark shifted positions. With a long stroke, she shaved off a thin wedge of the pine. Its woodsy scent filled the air. Over and over she drew the plane over the hard wood.

"What do you think you're doing?" Trip yanked the tool from her hands.

She jerked back. "Mark was getting tired. I gave him a break."

"I didn't tell you to give him a break."

"No, you wanted him to get exhausted, but that's no way to encourage a boy."

Trip pinned her with fiery eyes. "Mark, the sandpaper is on the workbench."

Mark paused. "But—"

"You heard me. Get busy." Trip pointed a finger at Marguerite. "You, come with me." He marched toward the massive doors in the back of the boat shop.

Marguerite didn't move. She swallowed hard and her stomach flip-flopped.

"I'm sorry, Marguerite," Mark said. "This is my fault."

"It's okay. I'll be fine." She patted the mast. "See how much you can get done before I get back."

Trip stood at the door, arms crossed over his chest, face stormy.

Lord, Trip Andrews could use a little attitude adjustment right now. Would You mind helping me out? Please?

Now her own anger grew. How dare he treat Mark so poorly? And she'd just been trying to help. If he wasn't so stuck on his almighty teaching abilities, he might have seen what was actually happening.

Determined to set Trip straight, she marched across the sawdust-covered floor of the workshop. Trip stepped outside as she approached, and she followed.

"Let's get one thing clear—" he began.

"Yes, let's." She squared her shoulders, refusing to shrink beneath his glare. "Mark is twelve. He's intelligent and he can do this, but he is still a boy. Working him like a man won't make him into one."

"And you would know this how? Last time I looked, you were a lady—at least I thought you were until I caught you using a man's tools to do a man's work. So exactly how do you know this won't make Mark into a man?"

"I . . . I . . . just do."

"Is that a fact? All right, here's a fact for you. If I catch you interfering with my lessons again, both of you will be out of here so fast it'll make the *Endeavor* look like a rowboat."

"Is this display because you think I undermined your authority as his teacher?"

Trip's silence answered her.

"Well, Mr. Teacher, your student's hands are covered in blisters. I was simply trying to help him out."

His brow furled in concern and his stern face softened. "They are?"

"He's never used a plane before. Actually, he's done very little manual labor. His hands aren't callused like yours. They're soft as a baby's."

Unconsciously she clenched her own fists and shoved them in the pockets of her pants. Her hands stung from the time she'd spent using the plane. He lowered his gaze to her pockets, eyes narrowed. "Let me see your hands. Hold them out."

"Ladies don't show their hands in public."

"You didn't seem worried about that in there." He took hold of her forearm and tugged her hand free. Lifting her wrist, he studied the angry red welts that had formed on her palms.

He dropped her hand. "Get your brother and meet me in the office."

His stony tone made her stomach quake. She watched him tramp away. She followed, her feet feeling like anchors.

In a few minutes, her dream would be shattered.

8

Roger loved it when each column in his ledger lined up perfectly and all the figures balanced to the penny. Unfortunately, that wasn't happening today. Glancing at his pocket watch, he noted the time and shoved the leather volume aside. As much as he longed to delve into the discrepancy, being tardy for lunch with Edward Westing simply wouldn't do. He needed Marguerite's father on his side.

But if he wasn't, Roger had that covered as well.

After descending the staircase of his three-story Queen Anne Victorian home, Roger stopped at the parlor's double doors when he spotted his mother. "What are you still doing here? I thought today was your day for charity work."

"Don't sound so disappointed." She tucked a rose in an amber-colored vase on the mantel. Its brilliant red exploded against the other paler blossoms. She turned to him. "I postponed that when Mrs. Baxter said you'd invited Edward Westing for lunch. It simply wouldn't do for me to be absent when someone so important to you visited our home."

His heart softened. He'd considered that it might be easier to direct the conversation without her attendance, but of course, she was right. Edward Westing should have the opportunity to visit with his dear mother. "I'm sorry. I was merely surprised."

She drew him down onto the sofa and straightened his tie. "Tell me, is Marguerite 'the one'?"

"Mother, Edward is coming to discuss business."

"I see. But that isn't all, is it?"

"You know me so well."

She patted his leg. "So, what about this young lady has captured your heart?"

"Marguerite is stunning." He stood and walked to the fireplace mantel. "You know how when you saw this John Walsh vase at the department store, you just had to have it? That's how she makes me feel."

The wrinkles around her mouth curved downward. "And how does she feel about you?"

"I'm not completely certain." That wasn't true. He didn't believe Marguerite shared his feelings, but the fact that he hadn't won her over made her all the more alluring.

"She must care a great deal for you if she has allowed your courtship to continue for so long. Three months is quite awhile."

The bell rang, and she rose from her seat. "I do believe our guest has arrived."

A minute later, the butler showed Edward Westing into the parlor.

"Mr. Westing, so nice of you to come." His mother nodded to the man. "I know you two men are having a business lunch, but I do hope you won't mind my presence for a wee bit. I'm anxious to learn more about this young lady with whom my son is so enamored."

Edward chuckled. "I'm not sure what I can tell you about Marguerite that Roger hasn't already shared."

She hooked her arm in Edward's, pulling him from the room. "Nonsense. Roger hasn't told me a thing."

Once they settled in the dining room, the cook served a light lunch of onion soup, cold pork sandwiches, pickles, and cucumber salad. Roger's mother and Edward Westing embarked on a discussion as if they'd been close friends rather than acquaintances for years.

Roger folded his arms and leaned back in his chair. Irritating idle chitchat. Talk of weather and news from the lake did little for his agenda.

Finally a lull in the conversation allowed him to slip in his foremost question. "So, what is my dear Marguerite doing this morning?"

Edward set down his fork. "I believe she and her brother went cycling. I tell you, buying the two of them bicycles for their birthdays was the best decision I've made in a long time. Pricey, but worth it."

Roger speared a cucumber. "They seem to be doing a lot of cycling at the lake."

"It does seem to be as popular a sport there as it is everywhere else in the country." Edward lifted his water goblet. "There's even a Manawa Cycling Club. Do you ride, Roger?"

Roger's mother twittered. "Roger? Heavens no. He says those machines are dangerous."

"I think they've proved quite beneficial to one's health, and women certainly seem to be enjoying the freedom they provide."

"That isn't necessarily a good thing," Roger mumbled.

Edward met Roger's eyes and held his gaze. "My daughter isn't one to be chained."

"So she's a forward thinker? That's delightful." Roger's mother passed Edward the plate of sandwiches. "I take it she and her brother are close. What else can you tell me about her? Is she quiet? Shy? I always pictured Roger with someone like that."

"Mother . . ."

"I don't think anyone would describe my daughter as either of those, Mrs. Gordon." Edward smiled. "She's quite . . . vivacious."

"Is that so? Now, that is a pleasant surprise." She called for dessert, and they were soon enjoying plates of cinnamon-laced fresh apple cake topped with a heaping mound of whipped cream. "Mr. Westing, you, your wife, and your lovely daughter must be our dinner guests soon."

"We'd be honored."

"Roger will speak with Mrs. Westing and Marguerite and arrange a date." She set her napkin beside her plate. "Now, if you men will excuse me, I have a copy of Mary Shelley's *Frankenstein* that simply begs to be read. Are you familiar with it, Mr. Westing?"

"I am. I hope it doesn't offend your sensibilities."

A light extinguished in her eyes. "Life has made me much stronger than I appear."

Roger shifted uncomfortably, stood, and pulled out her chair. "Enjoy the book, Mother."

"Be sure to get my son to show you his art collection, Mr. Westing. It is quite spectacular. If someone tells him it's impossible to acquire a certain piece, he always seems to find a way to obtain it."

As soon as she'd gone, Edward pushed back from the table. "Before we get down to business, I'd be interested in seeing that collection."

"It's just artwork I've gathered."

Edward stood. "I can use a little culture. Lead the way."

Marguerite stepped into the outer office, and Trip indicated two chairs. She settled and Mark sat beside her. The whole scene—the looming massive oak desk, the ramshackle piles of files and papers, and even the barren gray walls—reminded her of the headmaster's office from grade school.

Crossing the room, Trip perched on the corner of the desk, obviously prepared to mete out his unmitigated verdict. He set a canister on the desk. "Okay, who's first?"

Her eyes widened, and she scooted back in the chair. "For what?"

He held up the tin, which read Hoods Olive Ointment. "It's for your hands. Mark, stand up here like a man and show me the blisters your sister said you got."

Mark glanced at Marguerite and she nodded. He stood before Trip and held out his shaking right hand.

Wasting no time, Trip slathered liniment on it. When Mark winced, Trip apologized for hurting him, and before the boy could protest, he wrapped a fresh white bandage around Mark's blisters. He then repeated the process with Mark's other hand.

Marguerite marveled at his tender, efficient care. Gone was the anger she'd witnessed minutes before. The calm before another storm? She sighed. At least he was taking care of Mark before sending them away.

"Now, Mark, why don't you take a break before you start working again?" He squeezed his shoulder. "You deserve it. You did good work in there." He glanced at her. "You both did."

A little thrill took root in her heart at his compliment, and she couldn't keep a smile from bowing her lips. She dared not let hope take seed in her heart. Maybe he wasn't going to stop the lessons after all.

His dimples deepened. "Mark, you can go take a look at the boats while I tend to your sister's hands." As soon as Mark scampered from the room, Trip eyed her. "Okay, your turn."

"Really, that isn't necessary." She clasped her now gloved hands together. "But thank you for your considerate treatment of Mark."

"Marguerite, I'm the teacher, remember. I run the show." He raised one eyebrow ever so slightly as he tossed the canister back and forth in his hands.

So here it was. The moment she'd been dreading. Either she yielded to his direction or they'd be ousted. Her face warmed. He'd bested her, and what was worse, he was certain of it. Did he somehow see how much she wanted to learn to sail?

"As you wish." She tugged off one glove. "But I must insist on applying the liniment myself."

He shook his head and wrinkled his nose. "Too messy." Setting down the canister, he spun Mark's chair around and straddled it. He dipped a finger in the paste and held a dollop in front of her. "Ready?"

She held out her hand, mortified when it trembled.

Sliding his hand beneath hers, he clasped it, his touch warm and unyielding. "Relax. I won't hurt you." Using a feather-soft touch, he spread the oily medication over her tender palm.

With every circle of his thumb, the temperature of her face climbed. She shifted in her chair and licked her lips. Soon, to Marguerite's relief, he finished his ministrations. Before he could suggest bandaging it, she dropped her hand to her lap and tugged her glove back on.

Grinning, he motioned to the other one.

"Honestly, Mr. Andrews. That one is fine."

"Let me see it."

Rolling her eyes, she removed the cotton glove and held it out. "See?"

He slid his hand beneath hers and ran his thumb over the reddened area. His touch sent a ripple from her stomach to her toes and back again. She yanked her hand away. "As you can see, my left hand doesn't require your attention."

"So you say." He stood and stepped away, distancing himself from her.

She blinked. Had he been as unnerved by the contact as she had?

He cleared his throat. "Why don't you go see what kind of mischief your brother has gotten himself into? I need to go upstairs to the apartment and put this back. I'll be along in a minute."

Once outside the shop, Marguerite found Mark watching the other boaters.

"There you are." She placed a hand on his shoulder.

"Is he making us quit?"

She shook her head. "No. I think he feels bad about your hands."

"This isn't what I thought it would be." Mark leaned on the white railing with his sportsman's cap in his hands.

Marguerite stepped beside him. "I know, but hang in there. I think it will get better."

Sailboats with their sails lowered dotted the shore, waiting for their turn on the lake. Crewmen on the *Top Dog*, all dressed in matching jackets, prepared to take their boat out. They waited until the boat drifted free of the dock before they began to hoist the mainsail, and once raised, it instantly billowed but did not completely fill. The wind whipped the edge, making it flap.

"That's called luffing," Trip said from behind her.

She jumped.

He chuckled. "But we use the word luff for other situations too."

"Like?" Marguerite stared at the sailors moving about the *Top Dog*, each with obvious responsibilities.

"For one thing, the front edge of the sail is called the luff."

"What are they doing now?" Mark asked.

Trip propped his foot on one of the posts lining the deck. "Tacking. They have to zigzag their way across the lake, because they're going against the wind."

Mark's eyes widened. "When do I get to try?"

"Soon." Trip ruffled the boy's hair and handed him a pair of leather gloves. "Come on, Mark, let's get that mast finished."

Marguerite found a stool in the corner, settled on it, and picked up a neatly folded copy of the *Council Bluffs Daily Nonpareil* lying nearby on a barrel. A pencil line encircled an article about Captain Joshua Slocum embarking on a voyage, determined to be the first man to sail around the world alone. Slocum left Boston on April 24 in a sloop named *Spray*.

Sailing around the world. The adventure sounded marvelous. But who had circled the article? Trip? Harry?

Slocum, she read on, navigated without a chronometer. He simply planned to use a tin clock and the noon sun. It certainly didn't sound like a safe way to travel. He plotted a course using special lunar tables and tedious computations.

Marguerite tingled just thinking about it. She loved the challenge behind that kind of math. Her male teachers, however, had discouraged her, saying that the female mind wasn't designed to grasp the complexities of math or science. The memory still chafed.

Perhaps she and Trip could try celestial navigation one night.

Her face flushed hot. What was she thinking? There would be no nighttime excursions, even in the name of science, with Trip Andrews.

Raucous laughter drew her attention. Trip and Lloyd were ribbing Harry about taking more than his share of dances with Emily Graham at the ball the other night. She hadn't noticed, but then again, she'd been a bit preoccupied.

Trip tossed two more logs beneath the long steel troughs only a few feet from her perch on the stool. He turned to her. "You're dying to ask about the troughs, aren't you?"

"I admit I have an insatiable curiosity."

"We keep water in this lower trough. It steams the red cedar timbers in the trough above that we use for planking the hulls. The steam keeps them pliable."

He crossed the room into the office and returned bearing a large sheet of rolled paper under his arm. Moving to an empty table, he untied the string holding the sheet together and spread out the elaborate plans. He glanced at Marguerite. She knew immediately she'd been caught watching him. Warmth rose from her neck.

Trip motioned her over. "Might as well take care of some of that curiosity."

Marguerite grinned and hurried over. "What is this?"

"Plans for a round bilge sailboat hull." His hand swept over the complicated drawings where angles and lines crisscrossed the sheet.

"Which one is it for?"

"None of these. We haven't built it yet." His eyes sparkled mischievously. "But there's one here like it. Want to guess which one it is?"

Marguerite studied the plans, then shifted her eyes to the boats in the workshop area. "Is it the one Harry is working on?"

He grinned. "You've got a good eye. We haven't even put the sides on the hull yet."

"Where did these plans come from?"

"Dad drew the designs. I'm the loftsman."

Having not seen a loft anywhere, she glanced upward.

"The loftsman transfers the lines plan to a full-sized plan." He chuckled. "I'll transfer these plans first onto the floor and then onto the wood."

"You draw on wood?"

"Sure. I'll use a small nail and a batten to fair the boat lines too."

"You know, you sound like you're speaking Greek. Can you explain it to me? What's fairing?"

"Technically, it's joining the surfaces so they blend smoothly. Artistically, it's seeing a boat in your mind while it's still lines on the paper." He pointed to the drawing. "See here? These are three views of the same hull—the side view, the plan view, and the body plan."

"And you have to turn those three views into a boat." Her finger traced the intricate curves on the drawing. The math involved in the arcs had to be staggering. "Can you draw plans too?"

He nodded.

"Can I help you with the lofting? Numbers, lines, plot points—they all fascinate me."

After considering her request for a minute, he tapped the plans. "It's complex."

"And you don't think a woman can handle that?"

"No." He gave her a cockeyed grin. "I think you can handle

107

just about anything. But it takes a good teacher, and I'm not sure I'm patient enough."

Before he'd given a firm answer, Trip's father strode into the building. Within a fraction of a second, he'd sucked all the joy from the room. Mouths clamped shut, and the once jovial men cast glances at one another.

Captain Andrews scanned the room until his gaze settled on Trip and Marguerite. A deep scowl scrunched his weathered face. "Trip, why haven't you banked that fire?"

She flinched. Flames now licked at the long steel trough, making the water bubble. It was her fault. She'd distracted him with her questions. Not wanting the captain's wrath to turn on her, she hurried to join Mark on the other side of the workshop.

Trip crossed the area and shoveled ashes over the flames. "Harry, can you put some more water in the trough? I think I about boiled it dry."

"Phillip Sutton Andrews the Third," his father bellowed, "do you honestly think that at the rate you're going, you'll have the Lancasters' sailboat ready before the regatta?"

"Yes, Dad, I do." He accepted a canteen of water from Harry and took a long swig. "By the way, you know the doctor said you shouldn't be out here."

"He said I shouldn't be working. He didn't say a word about supervising."

Cocking an eyebrow, Trip crossed his arms over his chest. "Is that what you call it, Dad?"

"Don't get sassy with me. I was building boats when you were in diapers."

Shaking his head, Trip returned to working on the upside-down skeleton of a boat. When half of the boat's hull had been planked, Trip excused himself to check on his student's work. "Looks good, Mark. Smooth as a baby's bottom." He ran his hand over the surface. "Come on. Let's go."

Marguerite's eyebrows lifted. "Go?"

"Do you always ask so many questions?"

"I don't know, Phillip Sutton Andrews."

"The Third," he finished with a frown. "You were eavesdropping?"

"I wasn't trying." Her cheeks warmed as the truth registered. "Your father's voice carries."

"I suppose you're right."

"So your dad is Deuce because he's the second, and you're Trip because you're the third, the triple one."

"And Harry didn't think you had a brain under that pretty hat." He tapped the brim.

"Trip, you ready? The water's perfect." Lloyd stuck his head inside the boat shop.

"Are you taking us sailing?" Mark bounced beside him. "Am I going to start my lessons?"

"Sailing, yes. Lessons, no. My crew needs to practice for the regatta, and I decided we're going to let you tag along."

"Both of us?" Mark's eyes darted to Marguerite.

"That's the plan."

If it wasn't considered totally unacceptable, she'd have kissed Phillip Sutton Andrews the Third right then and there—on the cheek, of course.

❧

Despite the light breeze, Trip and his crew hoisted the sails and got the *Endeavor* to move along at a good clip. Marguerite sighed with contentment. Being on the swiftly moving sailboat felt so perfect.

The crew worked together like the insides of a clock, occasionally calling out to one another but mostly doing each task without a word. With her face to the wind, she didn't attempt to cover the excitement bubbling within her.

"Mark, isn't this amazing?"

He nodded. "I've never gone so fast."

Trip kept his hand on the tiller, glanced at Marguerite, and grinned. Her stomach flip-flopped. Did he have any idea how lethal that smile was? She looked away and out over the expanse of blue water. Across the lake, seas of white tents seemed to have sprung up overnight.

"Mark," Trip called, "sailing is a sport of perfection. A regatta is won by not making mistakes."

"And a good wind helps too." Harry chuckled. "Come here, boy. You can help me adjust the mainsail."

The crew laughed at Mark's wobbly attempt to cross the deck.

"You'll find your sea legs soon," Trip assured him.

Marguerite decided that this time she'd remain seated rather than follow her brother.

The boat tilted to the right, and Lloyd and Mel compensated by leaning farther out on the opposite side of the boat. Mark's face suddenly turned a sickly shade. He bolted for the rail of the ship, bent over it, and lost what little lunch he'd eaten.

"Mark!" Marguerite lurched in his direction, but Trip held up his hand to halt her.

Still holding the rail with one hand, Mark dropped to the deck. He accepted a canteen from Harry and sipped at its contents. "Some sailor I am."

"Oh, it'll get better, lad." Harry ruffled his hair. "The water is pretty choppy today."

Marguerite glanced at the barely rippling waves and smiled at Harry, touched by his thoughtfulness.

Mark lifted anguished eyes toward Marguerite. "Why is she fine?"

"Seasickness doesn't affect everyone the same." Trip pushed up the sleeves on his tan shirt.

"Figures."

Harry hoisted him up and returned him to his seat beside Marguerite. "Just take it easy. We'll be back on shore in no time."

"I think I'm going to hate sailing," he mumbled. "No one gets seasick exploring caves."

Marguerite patted his arm. "But you don't get to feel the wind on your face inside a musty old cave. Besides, you heard Harry. The seasickness will pass."

"It'd better, 'cause I ain't doing this every day."

"You *aren't* doing this every day," she corrected.

"You got that right."

She laughed, and then a bolt of fear shot through her. What if his condition didn't improve and he wanted to quit? Her sailing days would be over before they even started. She glanced at his pasty face and sighed.

Please, God, please let this pass. I'm so close.

Exhausted, Marguerite managed to kick off her boots before crawling into bed for a well-deserved nap. She didn't mind the stuffy tent today. Even the stifling afternoon heat didn't keep her body from relaxing into the tick of the feather bed. She moaned and shifted positions. The muscles in her arms knotted from working on the mast, but her pulse still pounded with wild abandon at each thought of the sailing excursion.

The lack of a good night's sleep began to overtake her. As her eyes drifted shut, she jolted. This morning her mother had told her that Roger would be joining them at their camp for dinner. Nothing like a little piece of nightmare to take the joy out of a good nap. She should get up and get ready, and she would if her eyes weren't so incredibly heavy.

Maybe a quick nap wouldn't hurt.

Just a little tiny one . . .

"Marguerite! What are you doing abed this late in the afternoon?"

Her mother's shrill voice sent her bolt upright. "I must have drifted off, but I only lay down for a minute."

"Are you ill?"

She covered her mouth and yawned. "If I say yes, can I be excused from dinner with Roger?"

"Marguerite. Please don't start." Her mother touched her forehead with a cool hand. "He's a fine, wealthy young man. You should be honored that he is so fond of you."

"But Mother, last night—"

"Did he bring up his uncle's carbuncle again? Sometimes, dear, you just have to tolerate a man's boorish behaviors. They simply aren't as refined as we are."

"No. It wasn't like that." Her stomach knotted in a familiar way. Her mother didn't understand and never would. She yawned again.

"Are you certain you aren't ill?"

"I just didn't sleep well last night."

"It's this heat. Your father should never have brought us out here to camp all summer. What was that man thinking? We are delicate women."

Marguerite swallowed a giggle. She could think of any number of words to describe her mother, but *delicate* was not one of them.

"Remember how your sister was overcome by the heat at

the county fair a few years ago? You know, ever since then she couldn't tolerate the heat."

And it got her out of going to the fair every year.

Her mother began to rifle through Marguerite's trunks. "You'd best hurry, dear. Roger will be here within the hour, and where is Lilly? I tell you, that girl is never around when you need her."

Whatever you pick, I'm not wearing it. I could almost guarantee you it was that horrid pink dress that made Roger act so strangely last night.

"Lilly is helping Alice with tonight's dinner." Marguerite swung her feet over the side of the bed and spotted the discarded boots on the floor. If her mother saw them, there would be no end to her questions. Jumping up, she deftly kicked them under the bed.

Camille straightened and held out a lavender dress that made Marguerite cringe. "This one will do nicely."

She started to protest, but stopped. She didn't want to impress Roger, and maybe if she wore the lavender dress, which made her appear pale and sickly, he'd be a gentleman and make it an early evening.

"That one will be perfect, Mother."

Her mother stared at her, eyebrows drawn together. "Marguerite, are you sure you aren't ill?"

❧

Back to his tediously dull self, Roger kept the dinner conversation fixated on the stock market while Marguerite struggled to stay awake. Certain the rattan furniture had left a waffle imprint on her behind by now, she shifted in her chair as she pushed the corn around on her plate, creating a tunnel for the gravy to escape its mashed potato crater.

"According to the *New York Times*, stock prices have more than doubled since the same time period last year." Roger forked a piece of fish.

Edward patted his mouth with his napkin and set it beside his plate. "And securities have reached a new high this month. Things are looking quite good for all of us."

Roger leaned back in his chair. "Marguerite, what is your opinion of the recent rise in stock prices?"

Her head jerked up. Did she hear the question correctly?

"Don't be ridiculous, Roger." Her mother sipped from her water goblet. "Marguerite doesn't have opinions in such matters."

"On the contrary. I believe your daughter has a great many secrets." He pinned her with his gaze.

She stiffened. What was he trying to prove? Did he know about the sailing? How could he?

Trying to remember the initial question, she took a deep breath. Stock prices. She had read about them. "I believe the Vanderbilts and the Grangers lead the improving market."

Roger shook his fork at her. "But what about prior losses in the market?" The dark eyes beneath his spectacles held no warmth. Was he toying with her?

"The recovery more than wiped out those losses," she said. "Foreign buyers have been active, and the forecast of good crops seems to indicate a bull market is at hand."

Roger threw his head back and let out a loud guffaw. "Who would have known our Marguerite had a mind for investments? You see, she is good at keeping secrets."

"Apparently not as good as you." Breaking a piece off her roll, Marguerite met his eyes.

Her mother let out a slight gasp. "Wall Street is hardly

an appropriate dinner topic. Perhaps we could talk of more pleasant things. I saw there is to be a regatta soon."

Marguerite choked on her roll.

"Sweetheart, are you all right?" Her father patted her back.

She gulped down a glass of water. "Yes, please pardon me. I must have swallowed wrong."

"Certainly." Roger dropped his arm around the back of her chair. "You seem in fine health now. Truly a vision."

The hollow compliment further confused her. She turned to him. "Thank you."

"As I said yesterday, you are like a painting—to be treasured."

And hung on a wall in your private museum?

"Marguerite, isn't that a lovely sentiment?" Her mother patted his arm.

"Yes, thank you." Marguerite pushed back from the table. "I'm afraid I'm developing quite a headache. Roger, if you'll forgive me, I believe I'll turn in for the night."

"I understand." He stood and held her chair. "You probably have a big day planned tomorrow. I'll walk you to your tent."

She avoided his accusing gaze and accepted his arm. "Indeed I do. Mark and I are going cycling."

"By the way, how did you injure your hand? I noticed you favoring it." He lifted her palm and examined the reddened marks with his finger.

She yanked her hand away. "Too much cycling, I guess."

"Then perhaps you should curtail your morning activities. On second thought, maybe I'll join you one day soon."

Swallowing hard, she forced a smile. "That would be a surprise."

Roger's mustache twitched. "Indeed it would."

Back in her tent, Marguerite tossed the lavender dress on the humpback trunk and slipped a lightweight nightgown over her head. She sank onto the edge of the bed. "Roger knows something, Lilly. I can feel it."

Lilly stopped brushing her chestnut tresses and gathered the discarded gown. "How could he? You think he was following you?"

Marguerite shrugged. "He knows a lot of people, and he's become so sneaky. Every minute with him is pure torture."

"You should tell him the truth, Miss Marguerite."

"What do I say? 'I'm sorry, Roger, but you bore me to tears'? Or perhaps I should send him a note. 'Dearest Roger, I find very little about you to which I am attracted.' Or maybe I should wait until he proposes and say, 'Roger, I can't stand to be in the same room as you, let alone share a bedroom with you.'"

Lilly scowled. "My mama would wash your mouth out with soap if she heard you say that. A lady doesn't talk about such things. I'm surprised at you."

"But don't you see? I can't tell him that."

"You don't have feelings for him, and he should know that. God would help you say it—properly."

Marguerite slid beneath the crisp cotton sheets. "Daddy will handle it."

"I don't understand you. You stand up for yourself in every other way, why not this one?"

She fluffed her pillow. "One word—my mother."

"That's two words."

Marguerite rolled her eyes.

Lilly folded the gown and opened the trunk. "Deep down, you know I'm right."

"Maybe. I'll pray about it."

"A you-telling-God-how-to-run-things prayer or a real Thy-will-be-done prayer?"

Marguerite opened her mouth to speak, but clamped it shut. If it was God's will that she marry Roger, could she do it? What was His plan for her? Had she even considered His will when she'd come up with the plan to learn to sail? The thought left her mouth dry.

Even though Lilly usually took care of Marguerite's evening toilet, tonight Marguerite sat in her bed and drew a brush through her own unpinned locks. Did she dare tell anyone the truth?

Trip's face came to mind. A few days ago, she'd thought of him as arrogant and rude, but now she found herself enjoying his presence. He was unlike anyone she'd ever met. If she told him the truth now and he dismissed her and Mark, she feared she would miss more than the sailing lessons.

Lilly laid the horrendous lavender dress in the trunk, then moved to put on her own nightgown. After she'd washed her face in the basin, she crawled beneath the thin sheet on her cot. "Good night, Miss Marguerite. Sleep well."

"You too, Lilly."

Marguerite set her brush on the washstand, then doused the lamp beside her bed. Darkness entombed her, pressing in on all sides. The suffocating heat, suddenly more unbearable, made taking a breath a chore. Lilly's steady breathing told Marguerite that slumber had already claimed her friend. Closing her eyes, she willed herself to sleep, trying to think of anything other than Trip, Roger, sailing, and lies.

But her thoughts refused to submit. *No, no, no. I cannot do this another night! I have to get some sleep.*

Marguerite stirred from the bed and pulled on a robe despite the heat. Stepping outside of the tent, she sought the comfort of her stars. *Sorry, Lord. I know they're really Yours. I don't mean to get into Your territory by claiming them as my own.*

Warmth flooded her. Two years ago, she hadn't even had an ongoing conversation with the Lord, her best friend. Back then, she hadn't even known Him—at least not personally. Sure, her parents attended obligatory services on holidays and enough Sundays to keep them from being considered heathens, but neither of them walked with the Lord like Alice and Lilly did. As Marguerite grew up, she'd wondered why God was so important to them. Then she'd found out.

Walking along the edge of their camp, she saw the lake glistening in the moon's pale light. Marguerite was transported to another lake, where her life had changed. Two summers ago, Aunt Carolyn had asked her to come stay with her in Chicago. Marguerite never dreamed she'd get the opportunity to go to Chicago, not to mention the added bonus of seeing the World's Fair.

Much like the Lake Manawa resort, the whole city had teemed with life that summer, and Aunt Carolyn and Uncle Mort took her to the Columbian Exposition soon after her arrival. The Ferris wheel left her breathless. The original copy of Charlotte Brontë's *Jane Eyre* brought tears to her eyes. The grand, gilded, arched entrance to the Transportation Building awed her. And the Yerkes Observatory telescope on display in the Manufactures and Liberal Arts Building ignited her dreams.

Yet it was a tent meeting outside the fairgrounds that changed her life. A friend of Uncle Mort's had spoken. A man named Brother Brumback.

Now, as the tangy breeze wafted off Lake Manawa, Marguerite could almost smell the lake where Brother Brumback had immersed her. She'd never felt so clean or free. Crowds on the bank had sung:

> What can wash away my sin?
> Nothing but the blood of Jesus.
> What can make me whole again?
> Nothing but the blood of Jesus.

Another wave of guilt washed over her as sure as the lake's tide. How long had it been since she felt whole? Her life had been split in half by lies—one lie with Roger and the other now with Trip.

That day in Chicago, she'd given control of her life to the Lord. Was she now trying to take it back? Do things her way?

She shook her head. *God understands. He knows I have to do this. He does.*

An owl hooted above her head and she jumped. Senses on alert, she heard the rustle of canvas, followed by heavy footsteps. She froze. The footfalls moved away from her. She spun silently in the dirt, and her heart sank like an anchor. Those broad, square shoulders and that deliberate gait could belong to only one man. A man who could fix anything, right every wrong, and make her believe she could do or be anything.

Her father.

Not once had she ever doubted him, but something felt wrong. Why was he sneaking away in the dead of the night—again?

9

To Marguerite's great relief, the noxious scent of glue and varnish no longer bothered her when she entered the boat shop. She pressed her hand against the stitch in her side. Once more, Mark's dawdling had forced the two of them to ride faster than she planned.

Mark tugged his cap into place as they crossed the threshold. "So what do you think Mr. Andrews will have for me to do today? Maybe shine his shoes? Walk his dog? Sew on a button?"

"Mark . . ." She attempted to sound stern, but inside she swallowed a giggle. "Be fair. A few days ago, he took us out on the *Endeavor*, and I think it was a reward for all your hard work."

"Some reward. I got sick."

"But that wasn't Mr. Andrews's fault."

Passing into the workshop, Harry told them they'd find Trip outside on the pier. She spotted him inside a small twelve-foot sailboat, big enough for a couple of passengers. What had he called it? A dinghy? The sound of the word made her want to giggle again.

Trip looked up from the rope he was winding and wiped his hands on his tan trousers. "Mark, I didn't think you'd be late on your first day to sail."

"Sorry, sir, I—did you say I get to sail?" Mark's eyes widened. "You're actually going to start teaching me?"

Trip chuckled. "I've been teaching you all along."

"I know. Just not . . ."

"Just not what you wanted to learn." He stood up in the center of the boat, one arm on the mast. "Let's get started."

Marguerite studied the precarious vessel. Would it hold all three of them?

Trip looked at her and laughed. "Yes, it's big enough for you too. Climb aboard."

"And how exactly am I supposed to do that?"

"One foot at a time."

Bracing her hand on a post, she lowered one boot into the flat-bottomed keelboat, glad she'd opted for the Turkish pants over the looser divided skirt.

"Don't worry. This isn't as tippy as you think." He took her other hand and held it firmly. "Now, let go of the post. Come on. Trust me."

Marguerite did and felt the boat tilt. She stumbled, falling into Trip.

He caught her waist. "No lively stepping in here, Marguerite. Just take your seat." He pointed behind her to a darkly varnished plank seat wedged in the front of the small boat.

She half sat, half fell into the seat in a most unladylike fashion.

A wide grin spread across Trip's face, but he didn't voice his thoughts. Instead he stepped over the middle seat and sat next to the tiller. He motioned Mark into the empty seat in the center.

"What do I do now?" Mark asked. "Untie the boat?"

"First we have to learn the parts of the boat." Trip explained that starboard was always the right side when looking toward the bow, and port was the left. He nodded toward the mainsail and showed Mark what knots he'd used to attach it to the mast and boom. The mainsheet, he patiently clarified, was the line that controlled the boom.

Marguerite soaked in each word and found Trip's explanations simple and thorough, but when he came to telling Mark that the leeward and windward sides depended on the direction of the wind, she shook her head. She would never get it all straight.

"Can you say that again?" she asked.

Trip cocked an eyebrow at her.

"I, uh, don't think Mark got that last part. Did you, brother?"

"To be honest, I don't think I got most of what you said, Mr. Andrews."

"You'll figure it out. Now, let's go over it again."

When Trip finished drilling him, Mark still understood only half of the terms. He tugged nervously on his plaid cap. "I'll never learn all this."

"Of course you will. It just takes time and practice."

"That's what Mrs. Johansen said about fractions, and I still haven't got those down."

"But I'm sure I'm a better teacher than Mrs. Johansen."

Mark rolled his eyes, and Marguerite shot him a look of warning.

"Listen up, Mark." Trip placed his hand on the mast. "This is important. If you hear 'Boom coming across,' duck."

"The boom's that arm thing coming from the mast with the sail attached, right?" He turned to his sister. "Marguerite, did you get that? Mr. Andrews, do girls duck too?"

"No, I believe my mother would insist I dip or bob." Marguerite feigned a curtsy from her seat.

Trip flashed her a dimpled grin. "Your sister can call it any-thing she likes as long as she does it," he said. "And another thing. Remember back in the shop what I told you about me doing the thinking? Out here that goes double. If you don't know something, ask. If you can't do it, say so."

She recalled his lessons in the workshop and smiled. Trip Andrews was a better teacher than she'd credited him for.

"Yes, sir." Mark nodded.

"Okay, untie that dock line from the cleat, and we'll cast off."

Trip kept the sail lowered until they'd cleared the other boats, then told Mark to hoist the mainsail. When its edge started to flap, Trip shouted for him to pull it a bit tighter. Immediately the sail billowed and the boat picked up speed. Soon it tilted to the starboard side, and Trip motioned for Mark to sit closer to the other side. "Do you recall on my boat how the guys positioned themselves on different sides to keep the boat from tipping too far? This one is so flat-bottomed that's not likely to be a problem, but you can shift to either side to balance it better."

Marguerite lifted her face to the wind. "This boat isn't as fast as yours."

"True. It's not meant to be. You have to learn to crawl before you can run." He turned the boat a bit to the right. "And mine better be fast if I'm going to win that regatta."

"I heard you and Harry talking about that the other day." She sent up a silent prayer that Trip wouldn't become angry with her for eavesdropping, but her curiosity burned. "Why is it so important to you?"

Mark frowned at her. "Why do you ask so many ques-tions?"

"Trip said if we wanted to know something to ask."

"He said if *I* want to know something. He didn't say anything about you."

"Know-it-all kid. Does he get that from you?" Trip chuckled, glancing at Marguerite. "Mark, treat your sister with respect, and what I said goes for her too. Now that I know you really are listening to me, Mark, switch places with me."

Marguerite's jaw dropped. "Already?"

"I can do it," Mark insisted.

"It's up to you since you're supervising his lessons," Trip said, his dimples deep as craters. "Do you want him to learn to sail or to be a passenger?"

"Go ahead, Mark. If Mr. Andrews thinks you're ready, then you must be."

Her heart took residence in her throat as she watched her brother gingerly exchange seats with Trip. Shifting to the right, she could barely see her brother over Trip's broad shoulders. Mark looked so small. What if he was too young to handle this? If he got hurt, she'd never forgive herself.

"Mark, take hold of the tiller. Get a feel for it. Turn a little to the right. That's it. Good job." Trip glanced at the sail. "We're sailing with the wind about thirty degrees off our backs. That's called sailing on a broad reach. It isn't as fast as running, but it's still a good clip."

The power of the wind filling the sail propelled them over the slightly choppy surface of the water. Closing her eyes, Marguerite tried to imagine the thrill that she'd feel if the dinghy responded to her touch with a charm all its own.

"You're hooked, aren't you, Marguerite?" Trip asked with a lilt in his voice.

Her eyes popped open. "Pardon me?"

"You've got a love affair with the water."

Warmth infused her cheeks.

Turning away quickly, he trimmed the sail and secured the line again. "I'm sorry. That's hardly an appropriate thing to say to a lady."

"No offense taken."

"It's just that I've seen it before. Be careful. You can end up doing anything to get in a boat. I just don't want you to get too attached to it—being a lady and all."

Marguerite stiffened. Trip had her pegged. Was he also trying to warn her?

"You know where you're headed?" Trip asked Mark. "You can't get anywhere in life if you don't know where you're going." Trip turned and pointed to the docks near the street-car turnabout. "Head that way."

Mark yanked the tiller toward the starboard side. The boat jerked in response.

Trip frowned and covered Mark's hand with his own. "Easy. Feel it in your hand through the tiller."

Mark lowered his head. "I don't know if I'll ever get this."

"You will. Give yourself some time. It just comes naturally to some folks, and others have to learn it. Hey, think about it this way—even Harry can sail." Trip laughed.

Marguerite grinned when she saw Mark's tense shoulders relax.

A few minutes later, the wind swept in, bending the trees on the shoreline. The boat leaned to one side. Mark groped for something to hold on to and, in the process, turned too quickly. Trip grabbed the tiller, put the boat back on course, and then sat on the far side of his seat. The craft righted itself.

Mark's eyes widened. "What happened?"

"When the boat leans, it's called heeling." Trip held out

his hand and tilted it sideways in explanation. "It's normal, remember? Sometimes a sailboat can be nearly lying sideways in the water."

Mark's face paled and he pressed his fist to his stomach. "The water isn't as calm as it was."

Trip's eyes searched him. "Mark, if you're going to be sick, you need to say something."

"I'm fine." He pulled his hand away and took a deep breath.

"Sure you are. Let's talk about something besides the water."

Grateful for Trip's attempt to distract him, Marguerite sat up and nodded. She considered repeating her question about the regatta's importance, but Trip spoke before she had the chance.

"So, I've met you two and your father." Trip swung around and straddled the middle seat. "Is your mother enjoying her summer at the lake?"

Marguerite and Mark shared a knowing look, and Marguerite giggled. "Not at all. You might say she's here despite the lake. What about your mother? Does she like it here?"

"Apparently she didn't." His face darkened. "She ran off on Dad and me when I was five."

"I'm so sorry." Marguerite swallowed the lump in her throat.

"It wasn't your fault. Dad said she could never be trusted. I'll tell you one thing, Mark, the woman who I'll take as a wife will be trustworthy in every sense of the word."

His words pricked her heart. She winced inwardly. If trust meant that much to him, how would he react if he ever discovered her subterfuge?

Too late now. What's done was done.

"You looking for a wife, Mr. Andrews?" Mark clenched his teeth and held his hand over his belly. "Or you got someone special already?"

"Why do you want to know?"

The dinghy bobbed in the increased wind, clearly doing nothing for her brother's turbulent stomach.

"I'm just trying to keep my mind off how awful I feel."

"Attaboy," Trip said. "Well, I'm not seeking the marrying kind of special."

Mark looked surprised. "You aren't?"

"Maybe someday. Right now, well, let's just say I've got more important things to do than worry about finding a woman I can trust." His hazel eyes glinted like hard mica.

Marguerite turned her face away as disappointment fluttered within her. Had his mother's desertion tainted his future that badly?

Trip leaned forward and took hold of the mainsail's rope. *Halyard*, Marguerite thought. *I have to remember the correct terms.*

As he lowered the sail, he explained that he was shortening it because the wind had picked up. He glanced at Mark. "We're not too far out. Another five minutes and we'll switch places."

"I see girls giving you that moony-eyed look all the time," Mark persisted. "Don't you like any of them?"

Marguerite cringed. Why couldn't Mark let this subject go? Couldn't he see Trip was trying to change the topic? *Sure, Mark, he'll tell you, a twelve-year-old boy, all about the women aching to cling to his arm. All he has to do is give them one of those charming dimpled grins, and they're putty in his hands.*

She dropped her head and studied the neatly coiled rope lying in the bottom of the boat.

Trip wound the halyard around a cleat. "I'm focusing on the regatta, but I do know some special ladies—one in particular."

"Who's that?" Mark asked.

Lord, this is Your idea, isn't it? You're putting all these ideas in Mark's head. Trip's going to say he likes some girl who's away for the season or, worse yet, Laura Thompson. I saw her making herself more than a little available the other night to be a dance partner.

Marguerite shook her head. *Good grief. What is wrong with me? Trip doesn't mean anything to me.*

"Well, as a matter of fact, I enjoyed dancing with your sister the other night." He gave Marguerite a rakish grin. "But she's already spoken for."

Marguerite choked. *Me?* Her hopes soared, then sank like a bobber with a fish on the line. He thought she was with Roger.

The sailboat rode another swell and plunged suddenly.

Mark covered his mouth with his hand. "I think I'm going to be sick."

Me too.

10

Roger carried his mother's parcels to store after store, telling her to buy anything she wanted. He enjoyed making her happy. His father certainly never had. For that reason, he always made time for his mother. So when she said she wanted to go shopping this morning, he cleared his calendar and ordered the carriage readied even though she insisted she could go shopping alone.

It would take time to make Marguerite as obedient as his mother, but he was certain a strong hand would help her learn her place. And once Marguerite learned to obey his wishes, she would discover just how doting and attentive he could be.

He fingered a silk scarf at the People's Department Store accessory counter while his mother pondered embroidered handkerchiefs.

"It's lovely." She touched his arm. "You should select something for Marguerite. A lady likes little trinkets and gifts. It would show you're thinking of her."

"But what would I purchase?"

"That scarf would do nicely. Or what activities does she like? If you can get her a gift that encourages one of her hobbies, it would be especially thoughtful. A gardening hat, a lovely bound journal, that kind of thing."

Hobbies? What did Marguerite like doing besides irritating him and doing things that no proper lady would? Still, she was beautiful, and the scarf in his hand would bring out the blue in her mesmerizing eyes. But was it the right gift to win her over? If he could win her heart, he could avoid the ugliness of his alternative plan.

The corners of his lips raised as an idea took shape. Perfect. He'd pretend to understand her unorthodox ways. His gift would say it all—how he planned to lavish gifts on her and how he couldn't wait until she belonged to him.

"Are you ready to go, Mother?"

"Yes, dear."

"Good. Then I'd like to make one more stop to purchase the kind of gift you suggested."

⁂

Dropping to his knees in the bottom of the boat, Mark managed to lean over the side before losing all of the breakfast he'd eaten.

Trip slipped into the vacated seat and took the tiller. He passed Mark a canteen. "Feel better?"

Mark nodded and took a swig from the canteen. "Some sailor I am."

"You'll get used to it. The water's a bit choppy this morning." Trip tugged at the line controlling the boom. "Ready? Boom coming across."

The warning registered, and Marguerite bobbed her head.

He grinned. "Good job. You remembered to duck."

"And if I hadn't?"

"You'd have had a nice swim. Wouldn't that be a surprise?"

More than you realize. The thought of being caught in her lie sent a bolt of fear through her. She cleared her throat. "What are we doing now?"

"We're heading back." He turned to Mark and gave him a hand up. "It's time to learn about tacking."

"Now?" Mark moaned, holding his head.

"Trip, he doesn't look well."

"We could dock, but it's a long walk back." He ruffled Mark's hair. "Thought you were tough. Sometimes a man's got to suffer a little to get a job done."

Her brother squared his shoulders. "I am tough."

"Good. Tacking." He turned into the wind. The edge of the sail began flapping wildly. "Mark, what's that called?"

"Fluffing."

"It starts with an *l*," Marguerite said, ignoring Trip's frown.

"Lifting? Loafing?"

Marguerite moaned. "Luffing, Mark."

"Well, at least one Westing remembered." Trip grinned. "Too bad it's the one who's supposed to be keeping her mouth closed. Mark, move on over here and take the tiller again."

Trip didn't take his eyes off Mark, but Marguerite felt comfortable in looking around the lake. As they neared the northeast shore, Colonel Reed's Grand Plaza and the splendid pavilion shone like a castle on the sand. The redbrick Yacht Club, farther down the beach, stood out as well. Beside it, she recognized the humble two-story boat shop where Trip and his father worked and lived.

Beyond the Yacht Club, set nearly a mile off to the side of the north shore, another building—a palatial, three-story, log cabin–looking structure—lay enshrined in a grove of trees.

"Trip, what's that building?" she asked.

Mark's eyes lit up. "The kind of place I'd like to explore."

"That is no place for boys." Trip's voice dropped in warning. "Stay away from there, do you hear?"

"Sure. No problem."

"I mean it, Mark. Don't go near that place."

❦

Homework.

When Trip sent Mark home with two ropes and eight different knots to master, Mark complained, but Marguerite was secretly thrilled. In case Mark needed help, Trip had chosen to teach her the knots as well.

Sitting in the rocking chair inside her tent, Marguerite twisted the ropes into one of the complex knots. She could still feel the warmth of Trip's hands on hers as he helped her shape the knots for the first time. He'd commented on how small her hands were as he explained in detail how each knot was used on a boat. Glad she'd buffed her nails to a shine that morning, she'd tried to focus on his words and not the frantic beating of her heart.

She wound the rope into a hopeless-looking fisherman's knot. Trip insisted it was the one a sailor would use most often. The two entwined cords in her hands resembled a pile of noodles a lot more than the tidy knot he'd produced with such ease.

The tent flap flew open, and Marguerite shoved the ropes under an adjacent chair. Her mother stepped inside and gave her a cursory examination. A scowl marred her mother's perfect complexion. "You are getting too much sun. Your cheeks are pink."

Marguerite lifted a hand to her face, surprised to find it

warm to the touch. She should have thought about sunburn and worn a wider-brimmed hat.

"It is a lovely day. What are you doing in this stuffy tent?"

"Keeping myself from getting too much sun." She couldn't keep a defiant grin from betraying her.

Her mother shook her head. "What am I going to do with you?"

"Did you come in here for something special, Mother?"

"Yes, in fact, I did." Her mother moved to one of Marguerite's trunks. "Where is your orange crepe gown?"

Marguerite wrinkled her nose. She hated that one more than both the lavender and the pink gowns. With its overly full skirt, it made her feel like a pumpkin. "Why? Do you want to borrow it?"

"I want you to look your best tonight. Roger is speaking to your father right now about some very important matters."

Marguerite sucked in her breath. Roger was speaking to Daddy? Now? Tonight?

"Why do you look so shocked? I've been trying to prepare you, dear, for the eventuality. You are ready to accept his offer of marriage, aren't you?"

"No!" The word erupted like a boiling pot of coffee under a hot flame.

Her mother's normally bright eyes turned icy, daring her to fight back. "You've had more than enough time to dissuade his attentions if you had wanted. You cannot turn him down at this point, or you'll be viewed as a tease."

"If I wanted to dissuade his attentions? I've done nothing to encourage them, and besides, since when has what I wanted mattered to you in the least? I've told you over and over I don't want to be with Roger."

"Then you are being foolish. He will make a wonderful husband. Steadfast, trustworthy, financially secure."

"But I don't love him." Marguerite stared at her mother. How could she listen and never hear a thing? Her heart thundered against her rib cage. "Father won't give him my hand."

"We'll see." A sanctimonious smile graced her mother's face. "Dear, put on the orange dress and your best smile. I believe you are about to marry one of the wealthiest men in the state."

❧

"What if he proposes, Lilly? I could never tell him yes. Not in a million, trillion years." Marguerite sat on the bed, clasping her Bible in her hands. "This can't be what God wants for me. You always say to delight myself in the Lord and He will give me the desires of my heart. Well, my heart has no desire for Roger whatsoever."

Lilly laughed as she slipped the Bible from her friend's hand and set it on the nightstand. "I know I've told you this before, but why don't you tell the man the truth?"

"I won't have to. My father won't let an engagement happen. I trust him. If I told Roger no, my mother would disown me."

"Nonsense. She's your mother."

"Are we talking about the same woman?" Marguerite raised her eyebrows. "Her heart is set on this marriage."

"But she isn't the one who'll be walking down the aisle to that man." Lilly walked to the trunk. "Speaking of your mother, she told me to have you wear the orange gown tonight."

"I'll take the gray one." She flopped back on the bed.

"Not very colorful for a celebration."

Marguerite drew a pillow over her face. "From this moment forward, I am officially in mourning."

⤜◈⤛

Dressed in a gray dotted skirt, solid gray vest, and red silk tie, Marguerite waited inside her tent for Roger to summon her, but he didn't call. She glanced at her watch. Almost 8:30. If she was lucky, her father had indeed turned him down and Mr. Boring had made a hasty exit.

She planted that hope in her heart but didn't dare let it grow. Not yet. Her stomach rumbled. At least she could ask Alice for something to eat. She exited her tent, relieved when she saw no sign of Roger or her mother.

She found Alice with Lilly, shelling peas at the wicker table. "Your mama told me to tell you she and Mark left for the Talbots' camp for dinner. Your daddy is to come when he's done talking to your fellow."

Marguerite's nose wrinkled. Hearing Roger called her "fellow" made her shiver. She glanced at Lilly, who giggled.

"So Roger's still here?"

Alice inclined her head toward her parents' tent. Roger's and her father's heated voices drifted from inside the tent. Marguerite scooted closer, and both Lilly and Alice scowled at her. She rolled her eyes.

"Edward, if you keep this up, there won't be a business deal." Roger's usually monotone voice escalated, taking on a hardness she hadn't heard before. "When it comes to business, I don't take chances on anyone, and right now you are a risk."

Her father? A risk? Before she could even consider the reasons why her tiresome suitor would say such a thing,

Roger stormed from the tent and plowed into her. He caught her roughly by the arms, keeping her from hitting the ground.

"Marguerite, what in heaven's name are you doing out here?"

She stepped free from his hold. "I thought we were going for dinner."

"Oh, of course."

His lack of apology staggered her. Where had Roger's impeccable manners gone? Maybe now was the time to do as Lilly suggested and tell him what she really thought of him, but not if her father's business dealings were in question. No, the timing simply wasn't right. She could endure Roger one more evening for her father's sake.

She tugged on her gloves and forced a smile. "So, where are we dining this evening?"

Taking her elbow, he led her away from the tent. "I'm afraid I'll have to postpone our dinner plans. I have business to attend to, but we can take a stroll, and I'll explain while we walk. I have something I want you to know."

How odd. He didn't seem put off, excited, or nervous. If anything, he still seemed irritated, and she guessed it might have something to do with the exchange with her father. Maybe he hadn't spoken to her father concerning her after all. "Of course we can walk. Just don't be surprised if I faint dead away from hunger."

"I'm sure you'll survive." He offered his arm and she reluctantly slipped her hand into the bend of his elbow. He covered her hand with his free one, and she cringed.

To Marguerite's surprise, they boarded the steamboat *Liberty* at the pavilion and crossed to the south side of the lake. Roger said he enjoyed the quiet offered there. As soon as they embarked, the tantalizing scents from Louie's French Restaurant made her stomach growl loudly.

Roger frowned. "Marguerite, that's hardly becoming."

And you think that hairy mustache is? She covered her mouth and coughed to cover her poorly timed giggle. "I guess you should have kept your word and fed me."

"You can't always have what you want."

"I was joking, Roger."

Marguerite chose to remain silent as they walked while Roger prattled on about his latest art acquisition. They approached the electric fountain, and Marguerite paused to watch the water dance in high arches and cascade back into the mosaic-tiled basin.

"Isn't it beautiful? In half an hour they'll turn on the colored lights. I haven't seen them yet, so can we stay?"

"I can't indulge your fancies this time. I told you I have to be going." He directed her to a bench without a view of the fountain. "You've been enjoying your time at the lake."

His matter-of-fact words made her nerves tingle. Did he know what she'd been doing? Nonsense. She was letting her imagination take hold. She stilled her hands by clasping them in her lap. "Yes, my days have been pleasant, and I've had a great deal of fun."

"Not too much, I hope."

"Can one ever have too much fun?" She forced a laugh, hoping to lighten his mood and dislodge the seriousness of his tone.

"I believe they can."

Of course you do. She rolled her eyes. If Roger wanted the discussion to be sober, she could lead it that direction. "Roger, what were you and my father discussing?"

"I don't think you need to trouble your pretty head with that." He captured her hand in his.

"You sounded upset with him. I heard you say something about a risk."

His Adam's apple bobbed, and he squeezed her hand hard. "You shouldn't be eavesdropping. It's rude."

"I wasn't doing so intentionally." She wiggled her fingers free from his beefy grasp and stood. Moving to the nearby rock planter filled with summer blossoms, she plucked a pink zinnia and fingered the blossom. She stared out at the inky, rippling lake lying beneath wrinkled ribbons of orange, yellow, and purple as the sun dipped behind a bluff.

The tension in Roger's rounded shoulders and the thin line of his lips told her he was clearly annoyed she'd heard the conversation. She rubbed her hand. How would he react if she pushed the topic further?

Taking a deep, solidifying breath, she turned to him. "Roger, did you really mean what you said? You know my father couldn't possibly be a risk in any way. He's an excellent businessman."

Roger got up and moved in front of her, impossibly close. "You don't know him as well as you think you do."

"What do you mean by that?" She took a step back, distancing herself from him. His piercing eyes made ice water flood her veins.

"Things aren't always what they seem to be, Marguerite." He closed the distance she'd created and loomed over her.

Please, Lord, make him go away. How about a nice meteor strike?

He took hold of her shoulders. "But I don't want to discuss that with you now. I have other things of pressing importance."

Her mouth went dry.

"I will be leaving the city on business for a couple weeks."

She fought the urge to smile and covered any traces by bringing the blossom to her lips. *Thank You, Lord! Talk about working fast.*

"Your presence will be missed, Roger."

It wasn't a lie. He might not be missed by her, but Marguerite felt certain her mother would notice his absence.

"That's kind of you to say." He stared into her eyes. "When I return, I intend to ask for your hand in marriage."

"Roger, I—"

"Don't say anything now." Before she could move away, he pulled her close and kissed her as if she belonged to him and him alone.

She yanked back, hating the feel of his whisker-covered mouth against hers. "Roger! What are you doing?"

His mustache twitched when he smirked. "I just wanted you to realize that you're already spoken for."

11

Too rattled to allow Roger to see her home, Marguerite insisted she could find her own way. Thankfully, he was in such a hurry he didn't argue with her.

She now wandered the boardwalk alone. Her stomach, soured by the news of Roger's intentions and his possessive kiss, left her without any hunger pangs. Even more nauseating was the knowledge that she had she let him leave without telling him the truth. God had given her the perfect opportunity, and she'd let it slip away.

She spotted a large tent pitched in a grove of oak trees that picnickers frequented. The tent was filled with individuals attending a revival, and rising strains of "The Old Rugged Cross" tugged at her turbulent heart. She crossed the lawn and settled in one of the wooden folding chairs near the back.

Kerosene lamps lit the tent, and within a few minutes of her arrival, a tall, angular man was introduced as Brother Davis. Given the late hour, Marguerite guessed he was probably the second speaker of the night. He paused at the podium and raked his gaze over the crowd. When he spoke, his baritone voice was as smooth as pulled taffy.

"God doesn't change, brothers and sisters," he began. "He's been the same from the beginning of time until today. And man hasn't changed much either. What was the fundamental issue underlying what happened in the Garden of Eden? It was truth. Who spoke the truth to Adam and Eve—God or Satan? Who were they going to believe? And what was the first sin? A lie."

The mere mention of the word renewed her guilt. Was the Lord spoon-feeding the preacher the words just for her? And why did it seem Brother Davis looked directly at her? She nervously glanced around at those gathered. They bobbed their heads, agreeing with his words.

"And since then, man hasn't stopped lying, and God hasn't stopped being God. Jesus describes Himself as the way, the truth, and the life. He is truth, and He values truth above all things."

Brother Davis went on to work the audience into a fever, telling them that God wants to be worshiped in spirit and in truth. "God is spirit. God is truth. He requires His worshipers to be compatible with His very nature. There it is, brothers and sisters. He tells us exactly how He wants us to love Him. How He wants us to worship Him daily, with every breath, without lying to ourselves in the process. We worship in spirit without worshiping in truth. But you can't do one without the other."

Guilt niggled at Marguerite like the mosquito that buzzed around her face. *But I wasn't really lying. Not saying anything isn't the same as lying, and the things I told Trip were just little fibs. They aren't going to cause the fall of man or anything.*

Brother Davis stepped down from the pulpit and stood directly in front of the crowd. His voice, deep and low, filled the tent. "Earlier I said God doesn't change and man hasn't changed. Guess who else hasn't changed? Satan. He's still trying to get folks to believe lies. And what are the biggest lies he wants us to believe? The ones we tell ourselves. 'I'm not that bad.' 'It's not that important.' 'It won't hurt anyone.'"

Marguerite touched her fingers to her lips, the words pricking her conscience. Her gaze landed on a man four rows in front of her. All afternoon she'd watched those broad shoulders pull lines and hoist sails. Even from the back she recognized him.

Trip Andrews.

"Truth and righteousness are intertwined. Since God is truth, pursuing God is pursuing truth. Satan wants you to believe lies because they bind you. They tangle you up and enslave you. And there's only one thing the Word says will set you free. The truth. It's your choice."

The group rose to sing, and tearful men and women made their way up the aisle during the altar call. Marguerite fought the urge to join them. Did she value truth? Of course she did.

She shoved the desire to confess aside. It wasn't needed. After all, she and God had an understanding about the whole sailing matter.

As the crowd dispersed, Trip appeared beside her. "Marguerite, what a pleasant surprise to see you here."

"I must admit I didn't expect to see you either."

"There's a tent meeting at least once a week, and I like to come to all of them that I can. Some speakers are better than others—Eli is one of my favorites."

"Eli?"

"Brother Davis." Trip motioned to the tall man who remained in the front, shaking hands. "I've known him most of my life. What did you think of the lesson?"

"To be honest"—she paused to giggle at her choice of words—"it was thought provoking."

"I imagine it was for all of us." A flash of lightning in the distance caught his eye. "Is your father's carriage outside?"

"No. I took the steamer across the lake."

"Alone?"

"I didn't plan on staying this long." She didn't want to disclose that she'd originally been out with Roger.

"In that case, let's get you home before you get soaked." Placing his hand on the small of her back, he directed her through the crowds. But instead of taking her onto the dock, he ushered her onto the sand. Harry and Mel waved from a large wooden rowboat as they approached.

"Look who I found inside," Trip called. "Thought we could drop her off on the way back."

They'd pulled the rowboat halfway onto the sandy shore. It lacked the grandeur of the sailboats or the assuring chug of a steamer. It also lacked a proper escort. Marguerite's nerves tingled. One woman with three men after dark? *Scandalous* hardly covered it.

Marguerite stepped back. "I don't want to trouble you."

"It's no trouble. Come on."

She hesitated. "Trip, it isn't . . . proper."

Another flash of lightning. Marguerite counted six seconds between the strike and the thunder.

"You won't get home on that little steamer." Trip nodded toward the boat. "Looks like they've already loaded as many passengers as they can hold. No one will know you're with us. We'll be discreet."

She glanced at the *Liberty* bulging with passengers.

"Marguerite, do I need to make this an order from the captain?"

"If I didn't know better, I'd think you enjoy telling me what to do."

"Somebody has to," he teased.

The steady *whop*, *whop*, *whop* of the steamboat told her that her options were now gone.

Trip touched her arm. "You were with me all morning in a boat. Think of it like another lesson."

She sighed and let him lead her down the sand until they were a few yards from the boat.

"Wait here," Trip told her. "I'm going to help the guys get the rowboat in the water."

"Shouldn't I get in first?"

"No, it's easier if you get in after she's out in the lake a bit."

"Do I need to take off my shoes?" She knotted her blowing skirt in her hand.

"No, I promise you won't get wet." He looked skyward and chuckled. "Well, at least not from the lake." After pausing to take off his shoes and socks and roll up his trousers, Trip jogged to the sturdy craft.

Thunder sounded in the distance. Thick clouds rapidly covered the stars. If they didn't hurry, she would most certainly get wet.

Trip returned. "Ready?"

She nodded.

Before she realized what he was doing, Trip scooped her into his arms. Instinctively she wrapped her hands around his neck. "Trip! Put me down!" Her heart fluttered as his whiskered cheek touched her own.

"Shhh, you'll have every man who didn't make it on that steamboat out here ready to hang me. Stop wiggling. We're almost there."

He sloshed into the knee-high water and stopped at the boat. "I'm going to put you down now. Don't try standing back up. The water's already rough." He deposited her on the seat in the stern. Harry and Mel had filled the last two seats, leaving Trip to take the one facing her.

The boat rocked as he climbed in, but the men held it steady. With practiced ease, the men attached the oars into the pegs and dipped them into the rough water.

Marguerite found herself mesmerized by the amount of distance the three oarsmen could cover. Still, they were only halfway across the lake when she turned her face toward the blackened sky and a plump raindrop landed squarely on her nose.

"It's starting to rain." Harry's oar slapped the water's surface.

Trip looked at the sky. "Lightning's still far off, so we're safe. Marguerite, you okay?"

"I won't melt in the rain."

"That's not what I meant. You're quiet."

"I was quiet today in the sailboat."

"But it about killed you."

"No it didn't."

"Remember tonight's lesson?"

"Okay, so maybe I was tempted to say something once or twice." She shivered as the sprinkles trailed down her neck. A gust of wind shook the boat, and she grabbed for the sides. "Right now I was thinking about what Brother Davis said."

Trip never stopped rowing. "What part?"

"I was wondering if Eve realized how much damage her one little lie did."

"No lies are little. Someone always gets hurt."

Lightning zigzagged across the sky above them. Thunder followed seconds later. As soon as the three men rowed next to the dock, Trip vaulted to the pier and secured the boat. Marguerite felt like a hot potato with Mel passing her to Harry, and Harry relinquishing his hold to Trip before she climbed onto the dock.

"Thank you." She held her hat in place against the wind. "If I hurry, I may manage to keep from getting doused. Thanks again."

She turned to leave, but Trip caught her elbow. "You don't think I'm going to let you walk home alone, do you? Especially in a storm?"

"My camp is less than ten minutes away."

Even shadowed by the stormy sky, his face creased with a scowl. "I'll walk you home, but I need to make sure all the boats are tied down for the storm first."

Harry clapped his back. "You go ahead. We'll handle the boats."

"Good. Just make sure—"

"He's as bad as his father," Mel joked. "Thinks we don't know what we're doing if he's not around."

Trip laughed. "Come on, Marguerite. Let's get you out of the rain."

Truth be told, other than the sprinkles while on the lake, the sky had yet to release its burden. As they walked briskly down the path toward her camp, they settled into pleasant conversation about the revival and their faith in the Lord. Trip told her how he'd come to know the Lord when he was fourteen.

"He's been the Captain of my boat ever since."

"And you're the first mate."

"No, I'm more like Mark—the bumbling student."

"Poor Mark. He's trying so hard."

"Sort of. He's young, and he's not used to working for what he wants. He'd rather let you do the work for him."

She stiffened. "Are you saying he's spoiled?"

"Probably."

"Just because my father has money doesn't mean he's spoiled."

"No, things don't spoil children, people do." He paused as they reached a long row of tented camps off to the side of the Grand Plaza. "Which one is yours?"

"Fifth one down. You can leave me now."

"I didn't mean to offend you, Marguerite."

"I guess the truth hurts sometimes." She shivered in a gust of wind.

Trip slipped off his striped jacket and draped it over her shoulders. The heat from the jacket, still warm from his body, seeped into her goose-pimpled flesh. A whiff of sandalwood and cedar made her inhale deeply. She had smelled that same woodsy scent when they'd danced.

"Trip, you're right. My mother does spoil Mark. She bails him out of things and doesn't make him finish what he's started. So if he comes to you and wants to quit, don't be surprised."

"If he wants to quit, I can't stop him."

"But you can encourage him to keep going. He needs that."

"I'll do my best." He stuffed his hands in his pockets. "You'd better go. Still don't want me to walk you the rest of the way? Don't want your daddy to see you come home with a man?"

"No, more like my mother."

"I'd think she'd simply be relieved you were back on a night like this, but I'll stop here and keep an eye on you till you get there."

"You know, you aren't at all like I originally thought."

"I hope that's a good thing."

"It is." Thunder cracked and lightning flashed across the sky. She grabbed his arm, her fingers digging into his shirt.

He patted her hand. "You surprise me too."

Before she could ask him to explain in what ways, the clouds burst. "Go!" He gave her a gentle push down the path.

Halfway down, she stopped and turned. "Your jacket."

"Keep it."

Hiking up her skirts, she dashed the rest of the way with a firm grip on the gift he'd given her.

She raced into her tent only to find another gift, tied in a bright red bow, sitting on her bed.

Lilly jumped to her feet. "Oh my goodness, look at you. Where have you been? I was afraid you might get caught in the storm."

Reluctant to remove the jacket, Marguerite stood dripping on the rug in the center of the tent. "I was at a tent revival on the other side of the lake when the storm rolled in."

"Looks more like it rolled over you." Lilly chuckled and handed her a towel. She lifted the coat from Marguerite's shoulders. "And who does this fine piece of tailoring belong to? I know Mr. Roger wasn't wearing that."

Marguerite's cheeks warmed. "I ran into Trip Andrews at the meeting. He and some friends saw me home." She quickly discarded her wet skirt, blouse, and underpinnings and then slipped into the warm gown Lilly offered.

"He brought you home in the dark?" Lilly laid Trip's coat across the brass footboard.

"In the rain." She eyed the long, narrow package on the bed. "Who's the present from? Daddy?"

"Nope. Your Mr. Roger."

"Oh." Disappointment washed over her like the cold, pounding rain.

"A messenger brought it all the way from town. He said Mr. Roger paid him double to make sure you got it tonight." Lilly picked up the discarded wet clothes and draped them over the trunk. "Well, aren't you going to open it? I've had to stare at it the last two hours, and I'm dying of curiosity."

Marguerite patted the bed beside her and waited for Lilly to join her before picking up the note tucked beneath the grosgrain ribbon. "It says, 'So my stargazer can think of me while I'm away.'"

"Isn't that sweet?"

The sentiment made Marguerite's empty stomach lurch, and she scrunched her nose.

"So I take it Mr. Roger is going somewhere?"

"He'll be gone for a couple weeks on business." Marguerite fingered the ribbon. The gesture was thoughtful, but she shouldn't accept it. Ladies accepted gifts only from their intended.

"If you don't open it, I will." Lilly chuckled again. Marguerite tugged the ribbon tails and the bow sagged. She lifted the lid to the wooden crate and pushed the straw inside away. She made contact with something smooth and withdrew a long, shiny tube.

Her heart skipped. Marguerite caressed the mahogany cylinder with its fine brass fittings. She extended its length and peered through one end. Lilly handed her two more lenses she'd found wrapped in the crate.

Tears sprang to Marguerite's eyes. She'd been hoping to have a telescope of her own someday, but even her father thought the cost exorbitant.

Knowing Roger had been listening the other night softened her ire toward him. Her heart warmed at his gesture, but she would have to give this gift back. It was simply too valuable, and keeping it would signify that she intended to accept Roger's proposal.

But she knew already that to return it would kill her—almost as much as saying yes to a marriage proposal from Roger.

Maybe she could simply use it until his return. She'd love to show Trip the stars and discuss the lunar navigation technique she'd read about in the newspaper article at the boat shop.

Lilly frowned. "What is that thing?"

"It's a telescope. For seeing the stars."

"Humph. I can see stars right here in this tent without that thing. Pretty ones in your blue eyes. Only they aren't for Mr. Roger, are they?" She cocked her head to the side. "It's your boat teacher who's putting the sparkle there, and poor Mr. Roger doesn't even know it."

"Mr. Andrews was simply being kind, and I admire him for his sailing abilities." Unconsciously she picked up Trip's jacket and caught a whiff of its woodsy, rain-fresh scent.

"Sure you do."

Marguerite looked at the two gifts before her. One planned. Intentional. Safe. Secure. Offering her the world.

The other offered on a whim. A dash in the rain. A risk. A chance. Offering her nothing but warmth.

She carefully set the telescope back in the crate and set it on the floor. Then, after one last whiff of the jacket, she hung it on the knob of the bedstead.

Two gifts.

She could keep only one.

❧

Since spending the last few days close to the boats, Marguerite found herself more in love with sailing than ever. Hoping Trip would declare today's weather perfect for sailing, she rose early and dressed in a brown divided skirt and an ivory shirtwaist. She topped that with a camel-colored linen jacket and black tie. If they hurried, perhaps they could catch Trip and his crew taking out the *Endeavor*. Yesterday Trip had told her they tried to get in one short practice run before breakfast and a longer one in the afternoon.

Just getting to watch Trip's regal sailboat race would be its own reward for missing breakfast. Her stomach rumbled in protest. Maybe she could grab a biscuit or two or three from Alice.

She glanced at Lilly's cot and was relieved to find it vacated. After slipping on her Wellington boots, Marguerite hurried next door to Mark's tent. Isaiah, who shared a tent with Mark, awoke with the roosters each morning, so she didn't have to worry about disturbing him.

"Mark? Wake up."

Rustling inside the tent told her Mark had heard her. He slapped the tent flaps open and stuck his head through the opening, hair sticking out like Medusa's. "Why are you here already? It's barely light."

"If we hurry, we can watch Trip taking the *Endeavor* out."

"You woke me up for that?" He rubbed his sleep-filled eyes and yawned. "Listen, Marguerite, I've been thinking. Maybe this sailing stuff isn't for me."

"Nonsense. You're a natural."

"Yeah, a natural at getting seasick, and it happens every time. You might as well face it—it's not for me."

"You can't quit now, Mark. You just learned all those knots."

"Mine look like lumps of coal. Yours were the ones that turned out."

"It takes some practice. Please, Mark, you can't quit now."

"I can quit anytime I want." He raked a hand through his rumpled hair. "Why don't you go watch without me? Maybe I'll come later."

Her mouth went dry. *Don't panic. Think this through.* "Mark, it's only polite to tell Mr. Andrews if you intend to discontinue lessons. He's been a good teacher. At the end of today's lesson, you can say something if you still want to."

"I guess you're right. I like Mr. Andrews, just not his bouncy boats."

"Now, go get dressed so we can get going."

"What about breakfast?"

"Let's try eating after you've gone sailing. Maybe that will help the seasickness."

Mark's lower lip jutted out. "No breakfast? I'm liking this sailing less and less."

"Okay, you go get dressed, and I'll get you some biscuits from Alice."

"Remember, I like—"

"Honey and lots of butter. I know."

Ten minutes later, Mark downed his biscuits in three bites each and washed them down with a glass of fresh milk Isaiah had procured from one of the local farmers. Marguerite took the time to dab the honey from her lips and finish her tea, then the two of them mounted their bicycles and rode from camp.

Marguerite turned an eye toward Mark. She didn't blame him for wanting to avoid becoming sick again, but Trip had assured him it would pass with time. What if he told Trip he wanted to quit today? She'd simply have to make sure he didn't have the chance. Maybe today would go well and he'd want to continue.

Lord, You can do anything You want to me. Please just don't let Mark get sick again. Shamed that she was thinking only of herself, Marguerite quickly added, *If he does, I won't make him keep taking the lessons.*

Dismounting quickly, they both laid their bicycles against the boat shop wall and hurried inside. No one was in the office or workshop, but the heavy doors in the back swung open toward the dock. Marguerite directed Mark outside and followed him. She paused when she caught sight of Trip on the deck of the *Endeavor*, his torso hard, wide, and masculine. Heat climbed her throat, and she touched her warm cheek.

Mark jogged to the boat and Harry waved at him. "Whoa, Mark. Where's the fire?"

"We didn't want to miss you all."

"And why might that be?"

Before he could respond, Trip shouted to Harry for a line. The curly-haired man snagged a coiled rope from a hook, and Marguerite hurried down to the dock to join them.

Harry handed Trip the line. "Look who I found."

"Good morning. You two are here early."

"Marguerite was hoping to watch you practice this morning."

"Was she now?" Trip straightened and grinned. He caught her gaze and her cheeks warmed even more. "I'll tell you what. Since we're one man short 'cause Max had a job to do, if you can tie these two lines in a fisherman's knot, you can come out with us."

Marguerite scrambled on board after her brother and followed him to the ropes Trip had indicated. Mark tried to make the knot but ended with a tangled mess.

Marguerite wiped her sweaty palms on her divided skirt. "Here, let me show you."

"Don't help him," Trip said. "Make him do it."

She sighed. The fisherman's knot was the easiest one. "Can I at least talk him through it?"

Trip chuckled. "I suppose."

While Marguerite coached, Mark looped the rope around. After a few false starts, he said, "I think I got it."

Trip stepped behind Marguerite. His skin-tingling breath on the back of her neck made her pulse drum.

"Then pull on it," he said.

In her head, she heard Trip's directions from yesterday. *If the knot "stops," then you did it right.*

Mark pulled both lines, and the knot tightened and finally stopped.

She released the breath she'd been holding and smiled.

"Good job, Mark." Trip slapped him solidly on the shoulder. He gave her a tilting grin. "You too, teacher. Now, go sit in the stern where you'll be safe. Mark, you can sit on the port side. Your job will be to help us keep the ship from heeling. Remember how we use our weight as a counterbalance?"

Her brother nodded and scampered into his assigned place. Marguerite hesitated for moment. If she asked, would Trip let her join Mark?

As if he knew what she was thinking, Trip pointed to the stern and waited until she moved that direction.

Mark grabbed hold of the safety line and a wave of fear rolled through her. Soon they'd be under way. How would his rebellious stomach fare? She'd almost forgotten how far the sailboats sometimes leaned, especially when racing. And today was so windy. If he got sick again, he would want to quit for sure.

154

Maybe his seasickness had passed, and if he got into trouble she could help him out. With everyone getting so busy, she doubted anyone would notice if she moved from her spot.

She looked up to see Trip standing before her. "I can trust you to stay here, right? I'm letting you on this boat now only because I believe you'll do what I say."

Great. He trusts me. Lord, don't You have any other believers You can make squirm this early in the morning?

"Now, I've got to go check all the knots 'cause—"

She grinned. "Because a bad knot is worse than a bad wind."

He tapped the top of her straw hat. "Ah, you were paying attention."

Let's just hope Mark was too.

Within ten minutes, Lloyd released the bow from the dock. Once the ship drifted clear, he tossed the second line to the deck and jumped on.

From her seat in the stern, Marguerite watched the four men move about with their tasks like a well-groomed team of horses as the *Endeavor* made sail. They ribbed one another and raucous laughter rent the air. But when the time came, they settled down to work. How differently Trip captained the *Endeavor* than his father had the *Argo*. High spirits and genuine respect for each other kept the top-notch crew performing each task with precision.

Harry swung into a seat near Trip. "Your dad seemed a smidgen impressed with our race times yesterday."

Marguerite strained to hear Trip's response over the flapping sails. He wiped a sheen of lake spray from his face. "Unfortunately, it'll take more than one good time to impress him."

"Like winning the regatta?" Harry leaned forward, his elbows on his knees. "Don't put so much pressure on yourself, Trip."

"He's working himself to death. You heard the doctor. If he doesn't let me take over soon, it's going to kill him. Before he'll let me do that, I have to prove myself."

Stunned by what Trip said, Marguerite thought about his father. Captain Andrews didn't look well, but if a person never cracked a smile, what did they expect?

"He's a proud man, and it's hard for him to trust anyone to do it like he would." Harry leaned against the mast and rubbed his temples.

Trip frowned. "Headache?"

"It's not what you think. I haven't been drinking."

"I didn't say anything." Trip turned the tiller into the wind.

"I didn't go anywhere near Stone's place. I swore to you I'm done with that, and I am."

Trip nodded. "I hope so. I just know there are a lot of temptations down there."

"There are a lot of temptations everywhere." Harry adjusted the mainsail. "Trust doesn't come easy to you either, my friend, but you're going to have to start giving me the benefit of the doubt. It's been a year, and I think I've earned it."

"You're right," Trip mumbled. "Sorry."

Trip turned and caught her eavesdropping. Marguerite averted her gaze, but it was too late. Anger flashed in his hazel eyes, and his lips turned downward. "Mark, go help Lloyd hoist the jib."

Even though the sailboat picked up speed once the second sail was unfurled, Trip told Harry to go ahead and put the spinnaker up as well. When it billowed under the headwind, the *Endeavor* flew across the water toward the buoy that marked their turning point.

Trip announced he was about to tack, and Marguerite prepared to duck when the boom came across. The ship heeled so far she had to reach for the lifeline. She fixed her eyes on Mark, who had turned positively puce. If he got sick now, the results could be disastrous. He could go overboard. With the others busy, no one seemed to notice him.

The ship evened a bit, and she made her move. Legs wobbling, she took a position beside him on the leeward side. Trip shouted. She grabbed the lifeline just before the ship dipped deeply to one side, setting the sailboat at a forty-five-degree angle to the water. Blood racing, she followed the others in holding the line.

If this wasn't flying, it had to be the next best thing.

Mark's face was now the color of the caps on the waves. She grabbed hold of his jacket with one hand. "Mark, hold on! Don't think about it."

Trip eased the turn and the boat leaned less, but Mark spun and got sick over the side. Marguerite helped him back, her heart plummeting with the water's dwindling swell.

"Trip, you might make a sailor out of her, but I don't know about the boy." Harry secured the jib sheet after the next crisscross in the water.

"I have to admit she seems more of a natural than he does." Trip turned toward her and raised his voice. "But she needs to stay where I tell her."

Pride swelled inside Marguerite like rising dough in a warm oven. She quickly punched it back down, recalling that "pride goeth before a fall."

Besides, today would be her last day. She'd already made a promise to God. After this last experience, Mark would want to quit, and she'd vowed to support his decision.

Her pulse thundered. *Lord, do I really have to give this up? I'm not sure that I can. It just keeps getting better.*

She pulled herself to her feet. The wind threatened to yank off her hat, and she caught it with her hand as she made her way back toward her seat in the stern.

"Tacking," Trip said.

Marguerite thought it odd that a week ago she wouldn't have known what tacking was, and now it seemed like a term she'd known her whole life.

"Boom coming across!"

She glanced at Trip. Why was he shouting?

Then she saw it. A gust of wind whipped the boom from Harry's hand and it swung wildly for her.

Her mind yelled, *Duck!*

But her body didn't listen.

At the last second, she lunged out of the way. The boat dipped and her footing on the deck slipped. Arms flailing, she fought to keep from falling. She lost the battle when the boom tapped her head and sent her flying over the lifeline, directly into the depths of Lake Manawa.

12 ⛵

"She can't swim!"

"What?" Fear wrenched Trip's gut at Mark's words. "But—"

"She can't swim. She lied to you. She doesn't know how to swim."

"We're losing her!" Harry shouted. "She can't reach the life preserver. It's too far away."

Mark hung over the edge. "Stop the boat and get her."

"Sailboats can't stop on a dime." Harry hauled him back by the waistband of his britches.

Trip shook off the shroud of panic threatening to consume him. His crew knew how to handle these emergencies. They'd practiced them dozens of times, and just as they'd trained, Harry refused to take his eyes off Marguerite since the moment the boom struck her. Lloyd tossed the cork life preserver overboard with a precise aim, only to have the waves carry it outward. As captain, Trip instinctively began a rescue turn.

"Mel, take the tiller. Bring her about on Marguerite's leeward side."

"She's got the preserver now," Harry said, "but she's having trouble holding on."

"That hit on the head must have dazed her. Get ready to haul her out." Trip's blood raced. He kicked off his boots, stood on the bow just long enough to sight her, and then dove into the lake. Keeping his head above water, he kept her in his view, making determined strokes through the choppy water. Pulse hammering, he prayed God would let him reach her in time.

She can't swim. She lied to me.

Still, guilt assaulted him. She was his responsibility and he'd failed. No novice could possibly have known that the boom could swing like that on a windy day if someone lost their hold on it.

The life preserver slipped from her grip. *Please, God, no!*

Muscles straining, he pushed harder. When he'd come close enough, he dove deep into the murky water. His eyes burned as he looked for her.

A dark object appeared a few yards below him. Lungs aflame, he pushed harder. His fingers wrapped around a piece of fabric, and he held it fast as he made strong scissor kicks with his legs until he broke through the surface. He drew the unconscious woman up beside him.

Fury and worry mixed in generous portions propelled Trip toward the sailboat. He ignored his burning muscles. Marguerite, breath shallow, awoke with a jerk, thrashing in his arms, and Trip nearly lost his grip on her. "Easy. I've got you."

She settled into him—he feared she was too weak to fight—and let him drag her along.

She couldn't swim.

She'd lied.

To him.

He'd been completely duped by her. His one stipulation he'd told her directly. No one got on his boat who couldn't swim. No one. Ever.

"Trip?" she croaked.

"Don't try to talk."

"I'm sorry."

She fell silent again and grew even more lax in his arms.

"Don't go back to sleep!" he shouted, wasting precious air. "Stay with me."

They reached the *Endeavor*. "Get that line down here," Trip yelled. "We're going to have to hoist her up."

Lloyd and Harry sent down the rope tied with a harness.

Trip caught it in his free hand. "Can you tread water so I can get this around you?"

"I . . . I can't swim."

"I know."

He drew the loop around both of them, and she put her arms through it.

"Listen. I'm going to let go of you and slide out of the harness."

She stiffened against him.

"You just make sure you have both arms through it. The guys will tighten it when I move. Whatever you do, don't panic. Understand?"

She nodded against his shoulder.

He slid away, ready to catch her. As soon as Harry saw she had both arms in, he yanked the line so hard Trip knew it would leave welts. Marguerite, shivering in the swells, clung to it.

He grabbed her chin and forced her to face him. His heart lurched at the sight of her eyes wild with fear. "Listen. I have to get on board to help hoist you up."

"You're leaving me?"

"Just for a minute. The boys won't let go. You're going to be fine."

Trip swam to the back and scrambled aboard. He sucked in

great gulps of air but allowed himself only seconds to catch his breath before joining his mates.

The *Endeavor* heeled so far now that Marguerite was only a yard beneath their reach.

"Bring her up." Trip stretched over the safety line.

She winced when the lifting began but didn't cry out. When they'd hoisted her to within reach, Trip snagged the collar of her jacket and hauled her aboard.

"Trip, I'm sorry. I didn't think it made a difference if—"

"Stop." Trip lowered her onto a seat at the stern. "Harry, get this boat moving. Miss Westing is going home."

⬥

Betrayal.

Marguerite saw it in Trip's eyes. Bitter, furious pain oozed from him like a festering wound. Worse than that, the deafening silence. He hadn't spoken another word to her. After feeling the goose egg–sized lump the boom left, he'd silently gone back to the helm, taking his position at the tiller and sending Harry to sit with her.

Harry eased into the seat beside her. "So, if you wanted to go for a swim, you should have said so."

Marguerite gave him a weak smile. Head throbbing, she pressed her hand to the back of her neck.

"Feeling woozy?"

She nodded. Immediately regretting the action, a moan escaped her lips. She glanced at Trip. Did she see concern, mixed in with all the other emotions, playing across his face?

"It'll pass," Harry assured her. "I been knocked on the head by more than one boom, and look at me. I'm fine. If you want, you can put your head on my shoulder."

Trip glared at him. "No. We don't want her going to sleep."

"Ah, Trip, she's going to be fine."

"We'll let a doctor decide that back on shore."

"I don't—"

Harry squeezed her hand. "Don't argue with him now. Trip and I have been friends for a long time, and that calm you're seeing is only about half a hair from becoming one hurricane of a storm."

When they docked, Marguerite listened to Trip bark orders at his crew. Anger seethed from him like a volcano on the verge of exploding. If he only knew how much like his father he sounded, he'd be ashamed.

She didn't argue when Trip ordered Lloyd to fetch a doctor or when he told Harry to take her up to his room on the upper level of the boat shop. But when he followed them into the room and told Harry he needed to go find her mother, she could no longer hold her tongue.

"No! You can't do that."

Trip arched a dare-me eyebrow at her. "And why not, Miss Westing?"

"Please, she thinks Mark and I are spending time with a friend today."

"So you lie to her too."

"No, that's the truth." She met his cold eyes. "I do consider you a friend." A wave of dizziness made her grab for the footboard on the bed.

Trip made no move to steady her. "Lie down."

"I'll get the bed wet."

"Don't you think I know that? Now lie down before you fall over. The doctor will be here soon."

She sank to the side of the bed, Trip's firm jaw warning

her she'd better follow through on the rest of his orders as well. Gingerly she lowered herself onto the thick pillow and glared back. *There, are you happy?*

Harry nodded toward her. "What do you want me to do about her mother?"

"Please, Trip." She tried to sit up but didn't quite make it. "You don't understand. My mother is just like your father."

A hint of compassion flashed across his face. "Well, she's going to need someone to look after her."

"I'll be fi—"

One stern look from Trip silenced her.

"If you have to fetch someone, you can get Lilly. She's my personal maid." Marguerite met Trip's unspoken accusation. "And before you ask, yes, she knows what I've been doing."

"Ah, your accomplice." Harry laughed.

Trip crossed his arms over his chest. "Harry, take Mark and go get her. Mel, go in the kitchen and put the kettle on. She's gonna need something warm to drink."

After they left, Trip sat down in a stiff-backed chair across the room and didn't take his eyes off her. She'd never been in a bedroom with a man before, and even though Harry had left the door wide open, Trip made the experience all the more uncomfortable with his penetrating eyes.

Her head throbbed, she was soaked through and through, and she smelled lakey. Guilt mixed with the pain, souring her stomach. She pulled the multicolored quilt up to her chin. "I truly am sorry."

"Sorry for what? Lying to me? Or getting caught?"

"Both, I guess."

"How could you sit at that tent meeting last night and still show up here today, knowing you'd lied like that?" The storm

164

broke loose and his voice rose. "You heard the preacher's words the same as I did. God values truth. What is it about a woman that just lets her lie to anyone she pleases? Why did you come to me? Did Mark even want the lessons?"

She couldn't look at him. His words stung, and hot tears pricked her eyes. Her head throbbed, and she pressed the palm of her hand to her forehead. "I had to do it. You wouldn't have taught me otherwise."

"I was teaching Mark."

"Then you'll still teach us?"

"You've got some nerve, Marguerite Westing." He shook his head, disdain marking his face. "I hear the doctor."

❧

Harry struggled to keep up with Mark as he tore along the back road to the Westing camp.

"Hey, speedy, take it easy on me."

The boy slowed to a jog. "I'm just worried about her."

"She'll be fine." Harry came alongside him. "It was just a bump on the head."

"Mr. Andrews is really mad."

"Trip gets like that sometimes."

Harry had seen Trip's fury before, but not since his own days of subterfuge. And Marguerite impressed the fire out of Harry, who knew a lot about keeping secrets. For that reason alone, he was determined to locate the maid and keep the truth from the poor girl's mother about what had happened.

As he reached the Westings' camp, the task before him proved to be difficult. A woman who resembled Marguerite, only much more severe, sat at a table issuing orders like a queen holding court. From his vantage point, he could see three servants: an older man and woman and a younger woman, nodding their "yes, ma'ams" and then going on with the work they were already engaged in. The two women bent over a washtub, picked up a bedsheet, and began to wring it out, each twisting an end. The water dripped onto the thick grass.

The younger woman, whom Mark identified as Lilly, hefted a basket filled with wrung sheets on her hip.

Harry saw his chance. "Where's the clothesline?"

"Behind the tents. It's strung between a couple of trees." Mark put his hand on Harry's arm. "But why don't I go?"

"If your mother sees you without your sister, she'll ask questions. You can follow me, but stay in the trees."

Harry snuck around to the back of the camp and waited while Lilly hung two pillowcases on the line. Whistling, she draped a sheet over the line and fished two clothespins from her apron pocket. Harry approached.

She eyed him warily as he neared. Fearing she'd call out for help, he pressed a finger to his lips.

"I don't want any trouble, mister," she hissed, backing away.

He stayed behind the wet sheet. "Please, hear me out. Are you Lilly?"

"Who wants to know?"

"My name is Harry, and I'm on Trip Andrews's crew."

Lilly's face paled. "And?"

"Your mistress, Marguerite, sent me to get you. Mark's with me." He pointed to the boy still hidden behind a sycamore. "Miss Westing's been hurt."

The older servant woman stepped around the side of the tent, and Harry ducked behind the sheet. "Who you talking to, Lil? I thought I heard voices."

166

"Just humming to myself, Mama."

"When you get those sheets hung, you should take a break and go for a walk. Pity to be cooped up on a nice day like this."

Lilly reached for another sheet. "Thanks, Mama. Maybe I will." When her mother left, Lilly leaned over the clothesline. "Is Marguerite okay?"

"Yes, but she got knocked in the lake."

"She can't swim."

"We know that now."

"So she got herself caught. I told her she would." Lilly lifted the last sheet. "I suspect you want me to fetch her some dry clothes and bring her home."

Harry took the other end and helped her hang it on the line. "If the doctor says she can travel."

"Is she hurt that bad?"

Harry shook his head. "Naw, I don't think so. More humiliated than hurt."

Once Lilly collected her hat and Marguerite's things, the threesome hurried along the lesser known but more direct path to the Yacht Club. Even though it consisted only of packed earth, it was faster.

"Tell me what happened," Lilly said.

Harry relayed the story of how the wind had torn the boom from his hand and knocked Marguerite overboard. "Trip's mad as a hornet right now. I think it hurt his pride a bit to know she duped him, but even more 'cause he hates dishonesty."

"I think she knew that. She's been up nearly every night fretting about it, but she just gets her heart set on something and wants it so bad that she'll do anything to get it."

"And this time she wanted to learn to sail?"

Lilly bobbed her head. "I've never seen her enjoy something more. You know she worked on those fool ropes for nearly three hours last night?"

"She's a natural on the water."

"Honest?"

He nodded. "Trip saw it too. He'd never let a woman on his *Endeavor* before, but now I'm afraid her sailing dreams have capsized."

Lilly lifted an eyebrow. "You think she's just going to give up?"

"You don't?"

"Let's just say it isn't usually her way of doing things."

⁂

Trip hated waiting. As a little boy he'd stood waiting at the door for days for his mom to come home, and she never did. And now he waited outside his bedroom for the doctor to emerge and update him on Marguerite's condition.

What had she been thinking? Why had he agreed to her foolhardy scheme? Women didn't have any business on a sailboat. Not that she hadn't done pretty well for a novice, but it was simply too dangerous.

Pretty good? What was he saying? She was the best beginner he'd seen in ages, and she wasn't even the student. He hadn't seen anyone take to sailing like she had since he first taught Harry.

But she'd lied to him. A straight-out, bold-faced, determined-to-do-it-my-way lie. And she couldn't swim.

Fresh anger burned in his chest. She could have gotten herself killed.

He rubbed his face with his hands. What was taking the doctor so long?

Finally the doctor stepped out of Trip's bedroom and closed the door behind him.

"How is she?" Even he could hear the nervous edge in his voice.

"She's got a nasty bump on her head, but I think she'll be fine. I told her maid to keep her in bed for the rest of the day, until the dizziness subsides."

"And the water?"

"Her lungs are clear. I don't think she swallowed much." The doctor stroked his bearded chin. "Might I ask what a young lady was doing on your sailboat?"

Trip moaned. "It's a long story, Doc."

"Then maybe you can tell me the next time I visit. Right now, I'd like to check on your father. Has he been taking it easy like I told him to?"

Rubbing the crick in his neck, Trip sighed. "Not really. He insisted on going to John Ratger's place today to do some repairs on his boat."

"Trip, he's got to slow down."

"I know. I'm just having a hard time convincing him." He took out his wallet and passed the doctor a couple of bills.

"Keep a close eye on the girl."

"I'll see that it's done."

❦

When Trip walked into the workshop, Lloyd and Harry looked up, concern written on their faces. He raked his hand through his hair. "The doc says she's going to be fine. Harry, can you get a rig so we can take her back to her camp? I don't think she should walk that far."

"Already done. I borrowed it from the Tanner place. If

we take her down the back road, her parents won't see her coming."

"Good. Take care of it."

"You aren't going to take her home yourself?"

Trip picked up a hammer and balanced it in his hand. "No. I've got work to do."

"Have you even been in to speak to her since the doctor came?" Harry shook his head. "Don't you have something to say to her?"

"I have a lot of things I'd like to say, only I don't think God would approve of most of them." He moved to the boat and began pounding in a brass nail with more force than necessary.

Harry pushed up from his stool. "So we just drop her off at her tent without so much as a 'been nice knowing you'?"

Trip shot him a glare. "Tell her whatever you want. Just get her home. I'm done with her. I don't care if I ever see Marguerite Westing again."

13

Unsure of what hurt most—her head or her heart—Marguerite lay in her own bed awash in guilt, anger, and disappointment. To her surprise, her mother believed Lilly when she explained Marguerite had taken ill with a bad headache.

Her mother entered her tent and placed a velvet-soft hand on her forehead. "No fever. It's probably this insipid heat. Perhaps I need to speak to your father about cutting our summer holiday short."

"Thank you for your concern, Mother, but I'm certain I'll be fine tomorrow."

At least on the outside. Tomorrow would come and there would be no more sailing lessons—and no more Trip Andrews.

Where did that come from? Trip? Well, of course she'd miss their time together. He'd been an excellent instructor—kind, encouraging, gentle—even if he was a bit cocky. The feelings wiggled their way into her heart like a fishhook refusing to let go.

No more lies, Marguerite.

While no one spoke, she felt the words impressed on her heart all the same. The words of the preacher the other night popped into her head. *What are the biggest lies Satan wants us to believe? The ones we tell ourselves.* Her stomach flip-

171

flopped and she swallowed hard. Was she lying to herself? Did she have feelings for Trip Andrews?

"Marguerite, darling, are you feeling worse?" her mother asked. "You look positively ghostly. Perhaps I should send for the doctor."

Lilly handed Marguerite a cup of tea. "I don't think that'll be necessary, ma'am. You know how Miss Marguerite gets. She just needs some sleep. I'll keep an eye on her."

"Make sure you get her a cool cloth for her head. On second thought, I'll send Isaiah for ice. That will be even better."

"Really, Mother. I'll be fine." She sipped the hot liquid, tasting the bitter willow bark infused in the brew Alice had made for her.

"In that case, I'll leave you. Lilly, keep these flaps open to let in the breeze. It's positively stifling in here."

"Yes, ma'am."

They watched her go, then Lilly perched on the foot of the bed. "Okay, spit it out."

"What?"

"Whatever has you looking so spooked."

Marguerite picked at the lace trim on the sheet. Tears rimmed her eyes, and she blinked them away. "I won't lie to you."

"Now there's a first." Lilly smiled.

"So much has happened." How could she even explain everything going through her mind right now? "I feel guilty and disappointed and angry with myself. I guess I need some time to work through it."

Lilly nodded and stood up. "I hope you know that God forgives you."

Marguerite released a long, shaky breath, her body surrendering to the soft feather mattress. "I know, but I don't think Trip Andrews will."

Bending the last piece of cedar planking around the frame, Trip held it in place with his knee and pounded in the brass nails. He stepped back and surveyed his work. His father would be impressed when he returned. He and Lloyd had made good progress this afternoon. The Robertses should have a new sailboat by the end of next week, complete with a mast shaped by the hands of Mark and Marguerite Westing.

Why hadn't he seen through her lies? She'd used him to get what she wanted, plain and simple. And she'd used her sweetheart smile and those powder blue eyes to win him over.

"Wonder what's taking Harry so long." Trip wiped his hands on a towel. "He should've been back by now."

Lloyd nodded. "You know Harry."

He did. Maybe he should have taken the girl and the maid home himself. After all, she was his responsibility.

Stop thinking about her.

Harry sauntered in, whistling a tune, and immediately set to work putting a finish on the mast.

"Well?"

"What?"

"Did you get Marguerite home okay?"

Harry dipped a brush in the varnish and then laid a thin strip of it along the length of the mast. "Of course I did. Stubborn woman made me stop two camps away, though, and let her walk the rest of the way."

"You let her walk?"

"It was that or carry her. I figured she had her maid and Mark to help her." He looked up from his work and grinned. "Thought you were done with her."

Trip crossed his arms over his chest. "I am."

"Good, because I'd enjoy getting to know a spirited girl like her. I like a little spunk in my ladies. Even sopping wet, she sure was something to look at."

"Stay away from her, Harry."

"Why?"

"Because I said so." Trip turned back to the workbench and sighed. Why did Marguerite always make him sound like his father?

That was one good thing—she wouldn't be able to do that anymore.

❧

After sleeping all afternoon and into the evening, Marguerite found herself wide awake when everyone else had long since gone to bed. Lilly must not have wanted to wake her to change into her bed clothes. She snored softly from her cot in the corner.

Marguerite checked the alarm clock on the nightstand but couldn't make out the hands in the dark. She scooted out of bed and stuffed her feet into her boys' boots. Some fresh air would clear the cobwebs taking residence in her throbbing head. Easing from the tent, she gathered her skirt in one hand. In the stillness of the night, the skirt whispered against the grass as she crossed to the wicker table at the heart of their camp.

Stars speckled the ebony sky, and she lowered herself into a chair to bask in their glory. It felt silly, but she spoke the childhood poem all the same. "Star light, star bright, the first star I see tonight . . ."

Only her wish wasn't one made by little girls.

Muffled voices rose from her parents' tent. She froze. She

174

couldn't make out the words, but she recognized her mother's angry voice all too well. In a tone usually reserved for Marguerite, she spat something at her father.

"Stay out of it, Camille!" Her father threw back the tent flap. "What I do is none of your business."

"It is when you risk everything."

Everything? What did she mean? Did this have something to do with Roger? Marguerite held her breath and watched her father head for the packed dirt road on which Harry had brought her home this morning. Questions filled her mind. Where was he going at night, and what had upset her mother so? She could count on one hand the number of times she'd heard the two of them argue. Generally, if her father actually put his foot down, her mother would reluctantly give in, but this wasn't like either of them.

Marguerite shouldn't be surprised. Her father hadn't been himself lately, and she suspected the answers she sought could be found at the end of that road. Biting her lip, she made a decision to follow him.

Moonlight filtered through the trees, casting ethereal shadows on the road. Heart pounding, Marguerite followed her father, keeping to the side, cloaked beneath the canopy. Her father must have known the path well, because he traveled fast and soon was only a dark blotch in the distance.

Marguerite, on the other hand, strained to see the ruts in the road. Twice she nearly tumbled when she misstepped. An owl hooted and she jumped. Maybe she should go back. Her father could take care of himself.

But something was wrong. She had to know what was going on.

She lost sight of her father as he continued on the path toward the only well-lit building set beyond the Yacht Club—

the one Trip warned her wasn't a place for boys. She gathered that went for women as well. Still, she needed to know if her father was at risk. He might be in some kind of trouble, and if he was, he needed her help.

Glancing at the boat shop, she noticed a light still burned in the workshop. Maybe Trip couldn't sleep either. Pious, self-righteous, unforgiving man.

Good. It served him right.

⌘

Ever since Harry had suffered with gambling problems last year, Trip made it a practice of checking things out one last time after everyone else retired for the evening. Tonight he knew sleep would be a long time in coming, so he took his time latching all the doors of the boat shop.

He stopped short when a lone figure walking along the road caught his eye. Harry? No, he was asleep upstairs. He'd already checked. Besides, Harry didn't wear a skirt. Perhaps she was some lost lady or sleepwalker.

Twisting the key in the lock, he opened the door and stepped into the night. Jogging down the path, he slowed before he could startle the woman. He'd heard a sleepwalker could die if you startled them, and he'd had enough near-death experiences for one day.

She looked young from the back, her waist and hips narrow. Light hair, hanging loose, was gilded by the moonlight. Where had she come from? The hotel was across the lake, and the only other place to stay was the camps. She seemed intent on something down the road.

With whisper-soft steps, he drew close. "Ma'am, do you need some help?"

The lady whirled and let out a strangled cry. He caught her by the arms before she could strike him.

Wait. He knew that face.

"Marguerite Westing, what on earth are you doing out here?"

14

"Unhand me." Marguerite twisted from the viselike grip wrapped around her arm.

Trip released her and crossed his arms over his chest. "Now, tell me what you're up to. Going to sneak in the Yacht Club and steal a boat? Take a little midnight dip in the lake?"

Her eyes darted toward the building down the road, and he followed the direction of her gaze. Even in the dark, she saw his nostrils flare.

"You were going there?"

"No . . . I . . . What is that place?"

He shook his head. "It isn't something you need to worry about. Come on. I'll see you back to your camp."

When he took hold of her elbow, Marguerite refused to budge. "I can't leave. I have to know what goes on in that place."

Trip's eyes narrowed. "Why?"

"It's none of your business."

"I'm making it my business. What's going on?"

Her heart thundered, but she didn't answer.

"So? Why do you want to go there?" He paused and then tossed his head back. "I know why. It's because it's off limits. That's the kind of girl you are. You have to push boundaries and make waves. Draw a line and you just itch to stick a toe over it every time."

"No . . . yes . . . ooooh, you've got me making as much sense as a mynah bird. I'm following my father. He keeps sneaking off in the night to go there."

His brows shot up. "And you decided to take it upon yourself to follow him to Lord knows where without a second thought as to the danger involved?"

"I thought about it. I just decided the risk happened to be worth it. And if you aren't going to tell me what that building is . . ." She turned on her heel and started down the road.

Trip caught her arm. "Over my dead body are you going there."

She turned and raised an eyebrow. "I could arrange that."

"Marguerite, that's a gambling hall, a den of iniquity. The only women there are *working*."

"Working? Oh." Her cheeks burned as the meaning of his words registered, and she prayed the darkness hid them. The throbbing in her head intensified and she rubbed her forehead. "I have to know if my father is . . . well, you know."

"Let's go sit down, and you can tell me the whole story." His voice softened, and he led her to a bench outside the Yacht Club. "How's your head?"

"We're talking about my father, not me. My mother said he was at risk."

He tipped her chin toward him and studied her face. She blinked as the moon's light reached her eyes, and he frowned. "Your head hurts, doesn't it?"

"I've had worse."

"I don't doubt it. Still, you should be resting, not wandering the road alone at night."

"I'm not alone, now am I? And you said we could talk about my father."

He sighed. "Your mother told you he's in trouble?"

"No, I overheard them arguing."

Trip frowned. "You never learn."

"Now, don't go judging me. I accidentally overheard them. I had too much on my mind and couldn't sleep, so I went outside. They were fighting in their tent. My father has never acted like this before, and I just know something is wrong. Maybe someone is forcing him to go to that awful place, and he's in some kind of trouble."

"I doubt it, but anything is possible."

"Trip, my daddy is the most wonderful man on earth. He's good and kind and tolerant."

"To put up with your shenanigans he'd have to be."

She frowned. "I'm serious. I can't imagine any reason he'd do this other than him being forced into something against his nature. Now do you understand why I have to go check it out?"

Trip could. When Clyde Stone's Gambling Den lured Harry into its clutches, he'd watched the damage a few innocent games of chance could do to someone in a remarkably short time. But he didn't want to share those suspicions with Marguerite.

"Why don't you just ask him what he's up to?"

"I don't think he'd tell me the truth."

"So lying runs in the family." He wished the words back immediately.

She stiffened and rose to her feet. "I'm going to find my father."

Trip stepped into her path. "No, you're not."

He expected her to argue, fight him—anything but cry.

She seemed as angry about the tear that slithered down her cheek as she was about being stopped by him.

"Don't you understand?" She swiped the tear away. "I have to know what's going on."

"I do understand." He placed his hand on her forearm. "That's why I'll go after I take you home."

She opened her mouth to argue.

He held up his hand. "You wouldn't find out what you wanted to know if you were to go there anyway. Your father would see you and promptly tan your hide. I'll go. No one will notice me."

"How will I know what you found out?"

"Well, seeing as I don't have a student in the morning . . ." He paused to gauge her reaction. She frowned and looked away. "I'll meet you for breakfast at the pavilion and tell you all about what I've found out."

Blinking, she stared at him. "The whole truth? You won't try to sugarcoat it?"

"Unlike some people, I always tell the truth."

She winced at his words and lowered her chin.

Good. You should feel guilty.

Kicking a stone with the toe of her boot, she turned to him. "Trip, I said I'm sorry."

"I know you did." He drew his hand through his rumpled hair. "But that doesn't make it all right. Don't you realize how close you came to dying today? You scared ten years off my life."

"Only ten?"

A throaty chuckle escaped his mouth. "Come on. I'll take you home."

When he offered her his arm, she tentatively accepted, and they started to retrace her earlier steps. He heard her sniff and spotted her dabbing her eyes with her free hand.

Compassion shook him, but he wanted to stay angry. After this morning, she certainly deserved it. And if what she did hadn't been foolhardy and irresponsible enough, she had honestly planned on going to the gambling hall.

He looked at her again—strong yet vulnerable—and his heart softened. He considered the horrible day she'd endured, and this situation concerning her father could only get worse.

He was no stranger to the feelings she stirred in him, but he didn't plan to act on them, especially with the race only a few days away. Besides, he couldn't trust her. He'd help her out because it was the Christian thing to do, but he'd guard his heart.

"So, Marguerite, what did you name your camp?" he finally asked.

"Camp Andromeda."

"Isn't that the maiden who was chained to a rock as a sacrifice to a sea monster because of her mother's bragging? Your mother let you name your camp that?"

"You know mythology?" Marguerite laughed. "Suffice it to say my mother doesn't."

"And are you chained to a rock with a sea monster hovering at your door?"

"You might say that."

He raised an eyebrow but didn't pry.

She stopped in the road and turned her head toward the sky. "Do you know where Andromeda is?"

"The constellation?"

"Yes. It's visible only in the fall and winter. Do you know any constellations?"

"The Big Dipper."

She smiled, her face bathed in moonlight. "That really isn't a constellation. It's an asterism."

"A what?"

"A pattern in the sky that isn't an official constellation." She lifted her hand and pointed at a cluster of stars. "Tonight you can see Hercules and Scorpius quite well."

"You're a stargazer." He couldn't keep the surprise from his voice.

"Amateur astronomer." She tucked her hand back into the bend in his arm. "I know. It's a strange hobby for a girl."

He chuckled, patting her hand. "Maybe for some young ladies, but not for you. It fits."

They walked in silence the rest of the way, listening to the wind in the cottonwoods, frogs croaking by the water, the chorus of chirping insects, and the occasional wail of a coyote in the distance.

Marguerite's concern for her father was palpable. Who was this woman on his arm? Would-be sailor, protector of her family, and now an astronomer? What other secrets did she hold? The desire to discover each of them threatened to surface, but he pushed it back down. *Don't even go there. You can't trust her*. He shook his head. Even if she hadn't lied to him, he didn't need the distraction. Too much was at stake, and he had his own family to protect.

She stopped beneath a sign with "Camp Andromeda" neatly carved in arching letters across its surface. "Thank you for checking my father's situation out for me."

"You aren't going to follow me, are you?"

She bit her lip. "I thought about it, but I decided you're right. Unfortunately, you'll have a better chance of finding out what's going on there than I ever would."

He nodded and flashed an encouraging smile. "Try to get some rest. I'll see you in the morning."

Knots of men gathered around the gaming tables in the gambling hall, intent, absorbed, obsessed. Rows of polished glasses and glistening bottles beckoned thirsty gamblers, while scantily clad scarlet women slipped between the men, offering their own form of entertainment. Trip stole to the corner to take in the action.

A wide mirror behind the bar provided a better look at the patrons of Clyde Stone's Gambling Den. Trip saw many familiar faces. These frock-coated men, a far cry from what one would expect at such an establishment, represented bank presidents, company owners, railroad executives, and other men of significant means.

Trip casually leaned against the wall, a sick feeling pooling in his stomach. How well he remembered coming to this gambling den, attempting to haul Harry away. Between the liquor and the lure of Lady Luck, his best friend since childhood had quickly become someone he barely recognized. But even then he couldn't abandon him.

Night after night he'd followed Harry to this very spot and watched him toss his inheritance down on the tables. Then, on the one night Trip hadn't followed, Harry's debts surpassed his abilities to pay them. The club's goons hauled him from the gambling hall, beat him senseless, and tossed him in the ditch.

Later, Harry described it as the longest night of his life. Too weak to move, he'd lain in the mud, thinking about how he'd gone from being a wealthy dandy to a penniless gambler. After that night, Harry insisted he'd changed and rededicated his life to the Lord, but Trip still found it difficult to trust him completely. The brazen lure of this place, with its glitzy gas lamps, brass trimmings, and party atmosphere, had a strong pull. Even the mightiest fell under its spell.

And tonight the mightiest appeared to be Edward West-ing.

Trip shifted so he could see and hear Marguerite's father eagerly exchanging a wad of bills at the faro bank for a stack of blue twenty-dollar double eagle chips. A portrait of a fierce tiger hung above the table, a common marker for those who enjoyed "twisting the tiger's tail" at the faro table. From his vantage point, Trip could see the table with its cards, from ace to king, printed in red and black on the cards' faces.

Clyde Stone, the finely dressed club owner, greeted Mr. Westing by name, slapping him on the back in welcome. He then nodded toward the dealer.

"Punters, place your bets." The dealer pinched his handle-bar mustache between his fingers and waited for the crowd of drink-sodden men to set down their colored chips.

Mr. Westing placed three blue chips on the queen.

The man next to him removed his bowler and ran his hand over his bald head. "Edward, you sure you want to back the queen?"

Leaning forward, Mr. Westing also set chips between the five and six and the ace and king. "What do you think if I split those too?"

The acquaintance nodded, placing his own bets on the table. Other patrons laid various-colored chips on the table as well.

Finally the dealer seemed satisfied that all bets had been placed. "Discarding the soda card." He withdrew the top card from the dealing box and set it aside.

Moans went out as the losing card of an ace was revealed. The dealer quickly scooped up all bets placed on the ace. Then the dealer displayed the winning card—a king. Only one man bet that, and the dealer quickly paid him.

Shaking his head, Trip studied Mr. Westing's reaction. He'd lost close to two hundred dollars, but his wild eyes focused only on the next hand. Before a half hour passed, Trip had watched Edward Westing lose close to a thousand dollars and win less than a hundred.

Trip clenched his fists as Mr. Westing placed another large bet. Even when the man he was with suggested they head home for the night, Marguerite's father insisted on laying down a pile of chips on a queen.

"Hello, sugar."

Trip turned to find one of the painted ladies standing next to him with a tray bearing a bottle of whiskey and two glasses.

"Buy a lady a drink?"

"No thanks. I'm about to leave."

"What's your hurry?" she purred. "You been watching that faro table all evening. Are you interested in the game or in someone at it?"

Trying to focus only on her face and not her scanty costume, Trip glanced from the raven-haired lady to Mr. Westing but didn't say anything.

"Oh, don't look so shocked, sugar. I make my living reading men. Buy me a drink and I'll tell you all about him."

"I don't drink."

"But I do." She moved to the table nearest them, beckoning him to follow.

Against his better judgment, Trip took a seat across from her.

She popped the crystal stopper on the bottle and filled one of the shot glasses with amber liquid. "Sure you don't want some?"

"Yes, ma'am."

"You don't have to look like it's painful to be here with me. I don't bite, sugar."

"Sorry, ma'am. I don't mean any disrespect."

She laughed. "Ma'am? I haven't heard that in a while. My name is Rosey. What's yours?"

"Trip. Now, about him." He inclined his head toward Mr. Westing. "How often is he here?"

"Ed? Guess he's at that faro table most nights, plunking down his money like there's no tomorrow." She downed the glass of whiskey.

"Just this week?"

She raised an eyebrow. "For at least a month. I heard he likes to bet the foot and horse races too."

Trip frowned. Things were worse than he thought.

"Why are you interested? Does he owe you money?"

He cleared his throat. "No. Someone is concerned about him."

"And you fancy that someone."

Trip stiffened. How could she see something that even he wasn't sure about?

"I told you I'm good at reading men," she said. "If you get tired of her, sugar, you know where I am."

Pushing back from the table, Trip stood and reached into his pocket. He withdrew a couple of coins and dropped them on the table. "If you ever want out of here, I'll help—"

She held up her hand. "No preaching. I've heard it all before. Who knows? Maybe someday."

He tipped his head toward her and smiled. "Thanks for the information, Rosey."

Slipping out of the establishment, Trip drew in a lungful of night air. Though the breath helped clear the stench of tobacco smoke from his nostrils, it did little to clear the dread from his heart. It wasn't fair. How dare Edward Westing do this to his family. Anger flaring, Trip picked up a stone on the path and hurled it into the trees.

Lord, help me find the words to tell Marguerite that the father she worships has fallen from his pedestal.

15

The lake glimmered in the morning sun like a beaded sapphire ball gown. From her window seat in the pavilion's restaurant, Marguerite studied the sailboats, large and small, dotting the lake, all training for the upcoming regatta. The *Endeavor* wasn't among them, so she prayed that meant Trip was already on his way to the restaurant to meet her.

She tapped her fingers on the table and eyed the door for any sign of the tardy sailing instructor. Where was he? What if he didn't show? This could be his way of getting back at her. Maybe he thought he'd give her a taste of her own medicine. Tell the fibber you'll meet her for breakfast and let her feel what it's like to be lied to.

"Miss, are you sure you don't want to place an order?" the waiter asked, his white jacket buttoned smartly up to the collar.

"Thank you, but I'll give him a few more minutes."

"Yes, miss." He nodded, filling her coffee cup. "I'll be back when he arrives."

After pouring a generous amount of cream and adding two sugars, Marguerite took a sip of the brew and glanced out over the water. The cloudless sky promised another hot day. Already the humid temperature had her blotting her upper lip. An ache formed in her chest when she thought about how much cooler it would be on the water. But there would be no sailing today.

"I'm sorry I'm late."

She startled, jostling coffee from her cup. "Trip, you scared me!" She blotted the spill while he sat across from her. "I was beginning to think you weren't coming. You did say 9:00, right?"

"Unlike you, I prefer not to run when I'm late." He flashed a dimpled grin. "Oh, wait, you don't run—you step lively."

The corners of her mouth lifted. At least he didn't appear to still be angry with her.

"Besides, the guys and I had to make a practice run early this morning. With the regatta only two days away, we can't miss even one." He spoke casually, but a bitter edge seemed to find its way back into his voice.

"Like yesterday's?" Marguerite glared. "Trip, I've apologized. I can't undo what I did, but I also don't intend to be reminded of it day and night. So if you'll kindly tell me what you found out, I'll be on my way."

He touched her arm. "I'm the one who should apologize. That was uncalled for. Have you ordered?"

She shook her head and he signaled the waiter. They placed their orders, and Trip skillfully skirted around the subject at hand. He questioned her about what things she had seen and done since her arrival at the lake. Reluctantly, Marguerite admitted that her experiences so far had mostly been limited to his boat shop and the Yacht Club beside it.

Trip frowned. "But there are so many more approp—so many more things for a young lady to do."

"You were going to say 'appropriate' things." She wrinkled her nose.

"That doesn't make them automatically distasteful."

"Would you like to sit in a sewing circle all morning?"

He laughed. "You don't fancy that kind of excitement?"

The waiter arrived and deposited a plate of biscuits and gravy in front of each of them. Without a second thought, Trip offered grace for the food.

Warmth ignited inside Marguerite like a kindled fire. In all the times she'd been with Roger, he'd never offered any kind of thanks to the Lord.

"What are you thinking?" Trip asked between bites.

She shook her head. "Nothing."

"Lying comes easy to you, doesn't it?"

Her temper flared a bit, but then she realized he was attempting to rile her. "I wasn't completely lying. What I should have said was, I wasn't thinking anything that I cared to share with you. Do you like that better?"

"Not really." He lifted his hazel eyes to hers. "I'd rather know what put that sweet smile on your face."

Her cheeks burned and she reached for her glass of water. "I know you've been avoiding the subject, but what did you find out about my father? Is he going there under duress?"

"Let's talk about it after breakfast."

"Don't you dare coddle me, Trip Andrews."

He scowled. "I was simply hoping to put off that part of the conversation until you'd finished eating."

A chill coursed through her, and she gripped her fork, her knuckles whitening. "Just tell me."

"Marguerite, I can't know anything for certain—"

"What did you find?"

He drew in a long breath. "It looks like he's gambling heavily and he has been for some time."

Tears pooled in her eyes, and she tried in vain to blink them away. "Are you certain?"

Trip pushed back from the table. He pulled out his wallet and dropped a dollar near his plate. "Come on. Let's get out of here."

The touch of his hand on her elbow anchored her while her emotions churned like the lake on a stormy day. She let him propel her out of the restaurant, down the pavilion stairs, and toward a bench in one of the flower gardens.

"Trip, how certain are you?" Her voice cracked. "Maybe he's there to get someone else to leave. He'd do that for someone, you know. Try to protect them. Get them out of a bad situation."

He pinched the bridge of his nose. "I don't think that's the case. Some of the workers said they've seen him there every day for over a month."

"A month? He was gambling even before he brought us here?"

"Apparently." With the toe of his boot, Trip nudged at a weed wedged in a crack between the sidewalk's bricks.

"But why would he do this?" Marguerite fought to keep the moisture from gathering in her eyes. "We don't need the money."

"It isn't about money."

She stood and tugged her jacket into place. "Well, I need to go talk to him. I'll straighten this out. He'll listen to me. If he's going down this wicked path, I'll stop him. Would he be at that den of iniquity now?"

"No, it's too early. It isn't even open." Trip moved to face her. "And there are two things wrong with your plan, Marguerite. One, remember, that is no place for a lady, and two, you can't stop him."

"Why not?" She marched off in the direction of the gambling den. "Are you changing your story now? Afraid for me to confront him because I'll find out the truth?"

Trip fell in step beside her. "You know that what I'm saying is true. Deep down inside, you know."

Roger's words now mocked her. *You don't know him as well as you think you do.* So Roger knew. That was what his fight with her father had been about. He said her father was a liability.

"Doesn't Daddy know how wrong this is?" She ignored the quiver in her voice.

"He probably does, but he has to be the one to choose to stop it."

She whirled toward him. "I'll go there and drag him out if I have to!"

"Marguerite." His eyes sparked with flecks of gold. He took a deep breath, and when he spoke again, his voice was as soft as a purr. "Have you listened to anything I've been saying? No one's there now, and even if they were, I don't want you going there. It isn't safe, and no respectable woman would ever be seen near that place."

Hot, angry, traitorous tears broke through and trailed down her cheeks. "But I have to do something. This isn't at all like him—he's got to stop going there!"

Trip fished a handkerchief from his pocket. "I know how you feel."

"You can't know how I feel."

"You're wrong." His voice echoed of a story she had yet to hear.

"How?"

"I'll tell you later. I promise." They walked in silence for a few more minutes.

Never had Marguerite felt so powerless. She knew a lot of men dabbled in games of chance and had heard of a few who gambled professionally. Once, she'd overheard some ladies at one of her mother's teas talking about the poor Winchells losing their home and business because of Mr. Winchell's fondness for dice. Her father would die if he lost everything.

She stopped on the path and turned to Trip. "I have to do something."

"Then pray. It's a lot safer, and it'll do more good." He placed his hand on her arm and squeezed it. "You need to get your mind off this. Hey, how about this afternoon I show you some of the sites that the lake has to offer?"

"I'd rather go sailing." She released a long sigh.

"Not going to happen." He chuckled. "What do you say? You can spend the morning praying, and then you and Mark can meet me at the fountain at 1:00."

"You just want to keep an eye on me."

"Someone has to."

"Trip, I shouldn't. Not right now."

"Yes, you should. Come on. It'll be fun."

"I guess I would like to see more of the lake."

"Good. Bring your bathing costume."

"We're going in the water?"

"You said you wanted to see more of the lake, and what better way to do it than to get in it? Besides, that's what one does at Lake Manawa—especially if they can't sail." He grinned, his dimples deepening. "Don't worry. I won't let you drown, and I've already had plenty of experience pulling you out of the water."

❧

Another potential sailboat buyer came into the boat shop, and Trip and Deuce spent most of the morning talking to the man about the exact specifications for his order. After he agreed to a spring delivery date, he left the office and Trip joined his crewmates in the workshop.

Lloyd looked up from sanding a mast. "So, how did your breakfast with Miss Westing go? It's good to see you didn't hold her little escapade against her."

"Don't give him a hard time." Harry cuffed Lloyd on the head. "It's hard to stay angry at a girl as pretty as her."

Lloyd ran his hand along the wood. "But we have a regatta to win, and the last thing we need is for Trip to get distracted."

"Don't worry. I am completely focused on the race. What's more, I'm still mad at her." Trip dipped his cotton cloth in a can of wax. "But she's got a lot going on in her life. I'm just trying to help get her mind off some of it."

Ignoring the laughter between his friends, Trip ran his rag in circles along the outer hull of the most recently finished boat, buffing it to a shine. Who was he kidding? He knew his anger had ebbed since yesterday, but if he gave any thought to Marguerite's lies, it still burned him. She could have gotten herself killed, and because of her they'd lost a half day of racing practice too.

Deep inside, though, he admired her fierce determination and her unwavering family loyalty. That fact scared him almost as much as yesterday's near disaster. She would clearly do anything for her father.

The memory of her on the deck of the *Argo* that first day, soaking up the experience like a sponge, took shape in his mind like a painting on the wall. With her blue eyes alight and her skirt dancing in the breeze, he'd never seen anyone take to sailing more. Too bad she'd had to quit. If she'd told him the truth from the start, maybe things could have been different.

And he didn't mean with sailing.

No. He wasn't allowing himself to go there. Any feelings he had for her consisted of a misplaced sense of responsibility. *She isn't my problem. After today, I'm done looking after Marguerite. Spending time with her is simply too dangerous.*

"Hey, Trip, didn't you say you were supposed to meet her at 1:00?" Mel called across the workshop. "You'd better hurry. You've only got thirty minutes to get there."

Ready in fifteen, he easily beat her to the park's fountain. He spotted Mark and Marguerite and waved them over. Marguerite, face still etched with worry, carried a rubber swim bag in her hand. Mark already wore his bathing suit.

"Is that your bathing costume?" Trip pointed to the bag.

Marguerite nodded and her cheeks pinked.

Mark spotted some friends and asked Trip if it would be okay if he swam with them.

"Can you really swim?" Trip asked.

The boy rolled his eyes. "Of course I can. You think I'm a girl?"

Trip laughed. Since he couldn't very well tell Mark that the more time he spent alone with his sister, the more he felt like a boy at his first dance, he sent the youth on his way. "Make sure you stay where Marguerite can find you."

As soon as Mark left, Trip swept his arm toward the bathhouse. "Well, don't just stand there holding your costume. Go put it on."

"Now? I thought we could talk about you-know-who for a while since Mark's gone. I saw him this morning and he acted like his old self."

He gave her a gentle shove toward the changing area. "Play

first. Talk later." After checking on Mark, he hurried to the men's bathhouse to change into his own suit.

Trip's breath hitched as Marguerite emerged from the bathhouse in a sailor-collared bathing costume. She jogged across the sand toward him, her knee-length light blue skirt bouncing with each step. A red sash accentuated her narrow waist, and even though she wore black stockings, he had no trouble envisioning the shapely calves and ankles hidden beneath them.

An appreciative smile played across his lips. If he wasn't careful, he might forget all the reasons he had for not courting Miss Marguerite Westing.

No, no, no. Don't even go there. He steeled himself with a deep breath. If he could sail a schooner single-handedly, he certainly had the fortitude to spend one afternoon with Marguerite without being drawn in by her feminine wiles. After all, he was a disciplined sailor and a Christian. He simply needed to remind himself that the only reason he'd asked her to do this was to help get her mind off her father. One afternoon of fun.

One.

No strings. No commitments. No tomorrows.

She stopped in front of him, cast an embarrassed glance at his Union-style suit and bare legs, and giggled. Her cheeks bloomed. "Sorry. I've never seen a man in a bathing suit before. I mean, I have—out there—but not someone I know. Not that I actually know you. I mean I do, but I don't too."

He laughed. Why did the fact that he followed her ramblings scare the daylights out of him? "Ready?"

She looked around. "Where's Mark?"

"Over there. We can spot him if need be."

"Oh." She pressed a hand to her exposed neck. "What are we going to do?"

"It depends. How's your head?" With her hair tucked beneath her bathing cap, a purplish bruise on her temple was visible.

"I feel perfectly fine."

"I thought you said you were done with lying."

"Okay, very dull ache. Sleep did wonders."

"If you're up to it, I thought we'd go down the toboggan slide."

She whipped around to see the thirty-foot-high toboggan ramp standing about twenty yards off the Manhattan Beach shore. Using curved wood sleds, whooping bathers rolled down the slatted logs into a shallow area of the lake. With a bathhouse attached to it, the toboggan run was one of Lake Manawa's crown jewels.

"We're going on that?" A broad grin spread across her face, and she bounced on her toes as if the excitement would carry her away. "Where do we get the toboggan?"

He snagged her rubber knapsack and slung it over his shoulder along with his own before heading toward the water. "We rent them inside the bathhouse. They even sell refreshments there."

The waist-deep water made swimming unnecessary. Although Trip preferred the much larger toboggan slide out in the deeper water, this one would be better today. Even at the base of the slide, Marguerite would be able to stand up in the shallow water after their ride down.

After wading through the tepid water out to the slide, he offered her his hand, then pulled her onto the narrow dock surrounding the bathhouse. Inside the building, they rented a toboggan and stashed their knapsacks in one of the bathhouse cubby holes. Trip led her down the dark, damp hallway until they joined a long line of swimmers bearing sleds at the base of the stairs. Only the daylight coming from the platform on top lit the stairwell.

"Looks like we'll have to wait our turn." He noticed her worrying her lip. "What's wrong? Are you scared? We don't have to do this if you don't want to."

"No. I want to." She offered a halfhearted smile. "Truly."

The longer they stayed in line, however, the more shallow her breaths became. She grew quiet and pensive. Why was she suddenly so nervous? Where had the adventurous woman gone? She could travel a road in the dark but couldn't go down a slide? Maybe heights scared her. He'd heard of that before.

He placed his hand against the rough wall. "Hey, are you sure you're okay? Why don't I just take the sled back? We can do this another time."

"No! Please don't. I'll be fine as soon as we're back outside again." Gooseflesh pimpled her skin, and she rubbed her arms. "I'm just a bit cold."

The line moved forward. They'd be up next, but perhaps he should still insist they leave. "If you're chilled . . ."

She tugged at the ends of the tie on her sailor collar. The line moved forward. "Look! It's our turn." Without waiting for him, she bounded up the stairs. She paused at the top with her hands on her hips and a cocky expression on her face. "What's taking you so long?"

"Someone had to lug the toboggan up the stairs, Miss Sassy." He grinned, glad to see a rose-tinted glow on her cheeks. He set the toboggan on the platform and directed her to get on first. "I'll sit behind you, like on a sled. Then I'll push us off."

Sitting with her knees raised, Marguerite hugged them tightly. Trip started to climb on behind her and paused. He'd gone on the toboggan slide before with Harry and Lloyd, but this was the first time with a lady. Why hadn't he thought about how close they'd have to sit?

"Trip?"

"Just waiting for you to get settled."

"I am."

"Oh yeah, I guess you are." He slid in behind her.

She sat bolt upright when their bathing suits made contact.

"Relax. It's going to be fun."

"I'll admit I'm a little scared. What if I can't swim at the bottom?"

He chuckled. "Just stand up. Remember, it's shallow."

"Right." She shuddered.

"And don't worry, I've got you." Wrapping one hand around her waist, he drew her against him, her cold suit pressing against his own. Her breath caught beneath his grasp. With a mighty push, he sent the toboggan careening down the ramp.

16

Marguerite squealed at the stomach-lurching thrill of the descent down the toboggan slide. The trees on the shore blurred as they flew by. She and Trip collided with the water with a colossal splash, and instantly she sank under the water.

She jumped up sputtering and laughing. "That was amazing!"

Trip laughed, then dragged the toboggan up from the water and flipped his wet hair out of his face. "Better than sailing?"

"No, but pretty close. Can we go again? Please?"

"You going to haul the toboggan up those stairs?"

"Certainly, if you aren't strong enough." She grinned at him over her shoulder.

"For that, you're going under." Laughing, he flung the sled aside. His eyes twinkled mischievously.

She backed away. "Trip Andrews, I don't like that look on your face." Giggling, she bolted, water sloshing behind her.

He gave chase, launched forward, and caught her with ease. Swinging her by the waist, he tossed her into the air and she landed in the water with a splash.

She came up coughing. Her bun undone, she pushed damp curls from her face. "I can't believe you did that!"

He roared with laughter. "Now, what were you saying about my strength?"

"I will get you back for this."

"So you say, but we all know how good your word is."

The smile slid from her face.

"Marguerite, I'm sorry. I shouldn't have said that."

"It's okay. I guess I'd better get used to it. Apparently forgiveness isn't your strong suit."

He snagged the toboggan, took her elbow, and flashed an impish grin. "Let's go for another ride, okay?"

Together they made their way to the dock. Trip suggested they sit for a minute to catch their breath before making the steep climb again. While Marguerite sat on the dock's edge, dangling her feet in the water, Trip went inside to get them a soda.

After he'd departed, she spotted Mark taking a turn on the toboggan run and waved. She attempted to wind her hair into some semblance of a bun but found it hopeless. What would Roger think of her now? Dripping like a sponge. Hair let down. If she was a reflection of him, as he so often said, he wasn't looking very good right now. She giggled. Not that he ever did.

How different Trip was from humdrum Roger. She tried to picture Roger's stocky body in Trip's Union-style suit with its horizontal lines, topped off by the caterpillar mustache and wire-rimmed glasses. A far cry from the way the suit accentuated Trip's broad shoulders. If the two men stood side by side, it would be like comparing an earthworm and an eagle.

They were different in other ways too. When she'd panicked inside, Trip's concern was genuine. Roger would have been aggravated by her inability to control her emotions. And then the toboggan ride. Roger wouldn't dream of doing anything like that, but Trip knew how to have fun. Even Trip's chase after the ride had been delightful despite her drenching.

She pressed her hand to her rib cage where he'd held her on the ride. His touch only compounded the strange mixture of excitement and terror. Her face warmed at the thought. She dipped her hand in the water and rubbed it on her cheeks. Never had Roger's touch made the heat pool inside her like Trip's had.

With a long sigh, she tipped her head back. She was no schoolgirl, and she didn't need to give in to these mindless fantasies. Trip hadn't meant to stir anything in her. This was a mercy excursion, not a romantic one.

Casting her gaze toward the slide, she watched other couples, even brothers and sisters, travel down the slide in the same fashion. The truth was right before her. Trip had held her because there was simply no other place to put his hands.

Drawing a circle in the water with her toes, she longed for something that would never be. She could dream all she wanted, but the facts remained. Roger wanted to marry her, and her parents expected her to comply. Worst of all, her father was wrapped in a vice that threatened to consume him. Her moment of escape wouldn't make any of it go away.

"Hey, why the long face? I thought we were having fun." Trip sat down beside her and passed her a bottle of Coca-Cola with a straw extending from its top.

"Thank you. Where's yours?"

He held out a second straw. "I thought we'd share. One soda now. One later."

Pushing her dark thoughts aside, Marguerite allowed a smile to crease her face. There would be time enough for worries later. She held the bottle between them and he dropped in his straw. Heads nearly touching, they sipped the soda.

He sat back. "Before we go inside, you want to tell me what got you as skittish as a new colt in there?"

"A new colt? What do you know about horses?"

"Okay, how about as skittish as a rookie on a skiff?"

She smiled and took a long drink. "That's much more sailorly."

He chuckled and waited until she looked up before speaking. "Fess up, Marguerite."

"It's nothing important." She shrugged and climbed to her feet. "I just don't like cold, dark, enclosed places."

Scrambling up beside her, he picked up the toboggan. "Why?"

"It's silly."

"Not to me."

"Laura Thompson locked me in an icehouse when I was in grade school."

"The redhead at the dance the other day?"

Who was hanging all over you? "Yes, one and the same. By the time my father found me and got me out, I had nearly frozen to death."

"You must have been scared out of your wits. I'm glad your dad found you. Did he always come to your rescue?"

I thought he would. She dropped her gaze, then lifted her face with a forced bright smile in place. "I promise that I won't get as skittish as a rookie on a skiff this time."

"If you do, I understand. Maybe we'll get lucky and there won't be much of a line."

He touched her back, indicating they should go inside.

She stopped suddenly. "Wait! I owe you something."

Without warning, she shoved Trip's shoulders, sending him flailing backward into the lake. She wiped her hands together in glee. "I told you I'd get you back."

Trip climbed back on the dock and shook his head, water droplets showering them both. "Life is never boring with you around, is it?"

"Not if I can help it."

⤜∽⤛

It was simply too good to be true. Following their afternoon of fun with no fewer than ten trips down the toboggan slide, Marguerite couldn't believe Trip suggested the three of them change back into their day clothes and go for ice cream. The soda fountain, located in the middle of the pavilion, sported everything from phosphates at five cents a glass to expensive lemonades for fifteen. When she asked why the pint glass cost more, Trip explained that lemons came all the way from California but milk cows were local. With pride, he pointed out the exclusive Waterlogged ice cream and declared it to be the best on the lake. Then, to Marguerite's delight, he asked her what kind of sundae she wanted.

Asked!

"Can I have one with crushed strawberries on top?" Marguerite licked her lips at the thought.

"Sure." He turned to the clerk. "Make that two strawberry sundaes. What about you, Mark?"

"Can I have a butterscotch one?"

"Sure, sport." Trip paid for the treats, and after the clerk presented them, they took them outside to eat in front of the bandstand. Mark joined a friend on a different park bench while Trip led Marguerite to one in the center.

A few minutes after their arrival, the Chicago Ladies Military Band began to warm up. Trip dove into his sundae and scooped up a syrupy spoonful.

Marguerite let hers melt slowly in her mouth. "This ice cream is delicious."

"The best."

"Did you know there was a concert this afternoon?"

He nodded but waited until he'd swallowed to answer. "They do one every afternoon and evening. One of the ladies plays the cornet and piano at the same time. See, there is a lot more to do at the lake than sail."

"What else?" She spoke loudly over the din of the tuning woodwinds.

"There's swimming." His dimples deepened with a grin. "Oh, wait. We know how good you are at that."

She rolled her eyes at him.

"And, of course, you already know about the dances." His eyes darkened.

For a moment Marguerite feared he would ask about Roger. She dipped her spoon into the ice cream. "And?"

"There are attractions to see. The Tyrolean Warblers will be here soon, according to Colonel Reed."

"He manages Manhattan Beach, correct?"

Trip nodded. "There's always croquet, horseshoes, yard tennis—"

"Really? Where?" She twisted in her seat to find the courts, balancing her glass dish in her hand. "Do you play?"

He laughed. "Not much."

"I could teach you." The words escaped before she could suck them back in. Mortified, she covered her mouth with her hand. "I apologize. Please forgive me."

"I'll make you a deal. Tomorrow afternoon, you can teach me to play yard tennis if I can teach you to swim."

The heat infusing her cheeks could melt the ice cream remaining in her dish. "Y-y-you want to teach me to swim? Is that proper?"

"Bring Mark along as a chaperone."

"I guess that would work." She slipped the last strawberry into her mouth, closing her eyes at its succulent sweetness. When she opened them, she found Trip staring at her. "What's wrong? Do I have ice cream on my cheek?"

"No. You're perfect."

She only wished he meant it. Yesterday he never wanted to see her again, and today he was buying her ice cream, holding her on the toboggan run, and offering to teach her to swim.

He took the empty dish from her hand and set it aside on the park bench. When the band director stepped up to the podium, Trip chastely slipped his arm onto the back of the bench, careful not to let it brush her shoulders.

As strains of "The Band Played On" filled the air, Trip leaned over and crooned the words in her ear.

> Casey would waltz with a strawberry blonde
> As the band played on;
> He'd glide 'cross the floor with the girl he adored
> As the band played on;
> Well, his head was so loaded
> It nearly exploded.
> The poor girl would shake with alarm;
> He'd ne'er leave the girl with the strawberry curl
> As the band played on.

He brushed the loose tendrils at the nape of her neck. A shiver rose from within her, prickling her flesh. Did he realize what he was doing to her? More importantly, why wasn't she running the other direction? She didn't dare hope he had feelings for her.

Even if he did, her mother would never condone a courtship with Trip Andrews—especially with Roger Gordon ready to whisk her away to a lackluster life.

Dear God, how can I live a vanilla life when I'm a strawberry girl?

As if he could hear her thoughts, he suddenly stiffened and drew his arm away. "We'd better get going. Your parents will be wondering where you've been off to."

17 ⛵

"Dad! What do you think you're doing?" Trip rushed to his father's side and lifted the load of planks from his arms. "Didn't you hear a word of what the doctor said? You have to take it easy. Do you want to have another heart attack?"

"Well, somebody has to work around here."

Trip heaved an exasperated sigh. "We needed to let the varnish dry on the Simpson boat, so we couldn't sand the new mast. You knew that."

"You think you're ready to take over this place, but you go off and play willy-nilly whenever you get the chance."

"There's nothing wrong with having fun." Trip dropped the boards into the corner. He opened his mouth to argue more but clamped his lips shut, remembering the doctor's warning not to upset his father.

His dad hadn't always been like this. Before his mother deserted them, he could vaguely recall the sound of his father's unencumbered laughter. When she left them, she'd stolen that as well.

"So, Dad, since you're here, do you want to watch us practice for the regatta? It's a great night. We might even let you ride along."

Deuce harrumphed. "You'd think if you wanted to win

that regatta, you'd have been out practicing this afternoon instead of gallivanting around with that girl."

"I said we're practicing this evening." Trip tried to keep his voice calm. "Do you want to come with us or not?"

His father reached for the broom. "I'll sweep up around here. Someone has to keep the place in order."

Trip blocked his path and took the broom from his hands. "You can sail with us or go upstairs and read or something, but I'm the one who will be closing up the shop for the night. That's my job, and it has been since I was ten years old."

A hint of a smile creased Deuce's wrinkled face. "I remember when I first gave you that task. You hated it because you didn't like coming down here alone."

"A lot of kids are scared of the dark."

"But I didn't let you stay that way." He squeezed Trip's shoulder. "I didn't want you to be afraid of anything."

Only of you. Trip felt a prick in his heart.

Deuce headed toward the steps. "You're going to have to work a lot harder to beat those rich boys from Spirit Lake. That skipper runs his boat like the insides of a clock. You could learn a thing or two just watching him."

"Sure, Dad." A lump formed beneath Trip's Adam's apple, and he swallowed. "I take it you aren't coming with me."

"Not tonight. Maybe another day. I'll save you some supper."

Trip leaned against the workbench. "Thanks. See you later."

❦

Perched on the deck rail like crows on a fence, Lloyd, Mel, Max, and Harry jumped up when Trip arrived. It would have made him laugh if he wasn't still so irritated with his father.

"What are you all doing just standing there?" he barked, swinging onto the deck of the *Endeavor*. "Let's get this boat in the water."

His crew cast knowing glances at one another. Making his way to the mainsail, he kicked a bucket out of his way. It hit the starboard side with a clunk.

Harry swung under the boom. "Okay, out with it. Is it the girl or your dad? Something's got you all hot and bothered."

"I don't want to talk about it."

Sure, his father had let him down once again, but he was used to that. He laid that particular burden at Jesus's feet so often he wondered if the Lord got tired of hearing from him. The niggling feeling that his father had a point irritated him more. He'd been an idiot today. He didn't have time to court a lady, entertain one, or even console one, and with the race days away, he certainly couldn't afford the undeniable distraction Marguerite Westing posed.

"I bet she looked pretty in her swim costume." Harry checked the halyard. "What color was it? Red or blue?"

"I don't know."

"Now who's lying?"

Trip scowled at his best friend. "Blue."

"And?"

"And she did look pretty." What was he saying? She'd looked spectacular. Her hair, the color of straw in the sunlight with red streaked through it, had been done up with little ringlets around her face and down her neck. And her eyes. How had she found a costume that matched them so perfectly? But all that was nothing compared to the way she ate her sundae. Did she have to do everything with so much passion?

Trip ordered Mel to cast them off, and soon they sailed under full sail at a good clip.

"So did you take her on the toboggan slide?" Harry asked.

"Do you ever stop?" Trip pressed the tiller to port. "You're as bad as a gossipy old lady."

Lloyd adjusted the jib. "Why don't you make it easier on yourself and just tell him what he wants to know?"

Trip sighed. "After we went on the toboggan slide, we got ice cream. We listened to the band play a song or two, and I took her back to her camp."

"Did you meet her parents?" Mel grabbed hold of the lifeline and leaned outward to counterbalance the heeling ship.

"Did she like the toboggans?" Max joined his brother.

"No to you, Mel, and yes to Max." Trip pushed up his shirtsleeves. "Lloyd, don't you have a question?"

Lloyd tugged on his navy cap. "What kind of ice cream?"

"Are you kidding? Why do you want to know that?"

He shrugged. "Why don't you want to tell me?"

"Good grief. We each had a strawberry sundae." He turned toward Harry. "Okay, is everyone done with their interrogation?"

"Almost." Harry shifted positions to be closer to the others. "Are you going to see her again?"

Trip turned the boat but didn't announce that they were tacking.

Harry ducked when the boom suddenly came across. "What do you think you're doing?" He quickly secured the swinging arm.

"Sorry, I forgot the warning." A stupid, mindless, rookie mistake that he couldn't afford to make. The main reason he shouldn't have even gone today. Too much was at stake.

"All you had to do was say you didn't want to answer instead of sending me into the drink. You may be falling for her, but I'd prefer not to fall off the boat because of her."

"I'm not falling for her."

Harry chuckled. "Hey, Lloyd, you think lying can be contagious?"

"Methinks he doth protest too much," Max teased.

Trip silenced them with an angry stare he'd learned from his father. "All this talk is distracting. We've got a race to win."

The crew grew quiet for a while, but gradually conversation resumed. He didn't mind as long as he and Marguerite weren't the main topic of discussion.

Harry plopped down beside him. "Listen, mate, you deserve to win the regatta, and you deserve to win the girl."

"I don't want to win the girl."

"Whatever you say." Harry pushed up his shirtsleeves. "But take it from a gambler. There are more important games in life to win than that regatta."

"I don't play games with a lady's affections. You know that."

"I know, but sometimes it's hard not to."

Trip wiped his brow with his sleeve. Was he playing a game with Marguerite? He didn't want to hurt her any more than she already had been. If she hadn't lied to him, maybe he'd take a chance on her. But she had, and that made just one more reason he shouldn't see her again.

"I can't be distracted right now with the race coming up. I'm supposed to see her tomorrow, but I'm going to send word in the morning that I can't make it. You saw what just happened. I almost got you knocked off the boat."

"It's your choice." Harry stood up. "Just remember you don't have to lose one to win the other. Your father's voice is in that head of yours so bad you don't even realize that you deserve to win both."

Deserve Marguerite? He could take that either way. Maybe God was smiling on him, or maybe He was having a good laugh at his expense. Whichever it was, finding out would have to wait until after the regatta—if even then.

Right now, the regatta was everything, and he refused to let his father down. Not this time.

⬥

After locking up the club, Trip tried to sleep. Juggling thoughts of Marguerite and the regatta, he attempted to lay them at the Lord's feet, but somehow he kept picking them back up. Marguerite had gotten to him like a bad case of poison ivy. And the rash was spreading. He could feel the itch creeping into his heart. This morning, when he'd told Marguerite about her father's gambling, she'd looked so devastated that he ached for her. How well he remembered the desire to do something to stop Harry from his downward spiral, but being paralyzed to do so. Was she sleeping any better tonight than he was?

Suddenly he shot out of bed. What if . . .

He scrambled back into his clothes and jammed his feet into his boots. Not bothering with a hat, he hurried outside. On the dirt road behind the boat shop, he perched on an enormous log in a grove of trees and waited. Bats circled above him, screeching eerily, searching for their nightly dinner. A bright, moonlit night made it easy to recognize the men who passed on their way to the gambling den, including her father, but thankfully there was no sign of Marguerite.

Maybe he'd been wrong. She was a smart woman. He'd made it clear just how dangerous Clyde Stone's gambling parlor was. Besides, what could she accomplish by following her father?

Just as he was about to return home, he spotted her. Dressed in a dark shirtwaist and skirt, she'd obviously planned this little venture. She kept to the side, probably hoping the trees would hide her.

He shook his head in disbelief. She actually planned to go exactly where he'd told her she shouldn't. What if he hadn't come out tonight and spotted her? Fear gripped him with a raw terror that turbulent lake waters never produced.

His emotions somersaulting from fear to anger, he crossed his arms over his chest. When she neared, he'd grab her.

It would scare her senseless, but she deserved it.

18

Shifting shadows made Marguerite's nerves tingle. Moonbeams bathed the path. Cicadas whirred and crickets chirped. She stifled a shriek when a raccoon darted across the road in front of her. Maybe she should return home. Now that she knew where her father was headed, the drive to solve the mystery was gone.

Still, loyalty drew her down the lane. If she could just reach him, talk to him, he would stop this insanity.

As she glanced at the boat shop, guilt washed over her. Even though she hadn't promised Trip to stay away from the gambling hall, she felt deceitful all the same. She dismissed the thought. Trip had no claims on her. He'd been kind enough to help her keep her mind off this ordeal, but it didn't mean he had any intentions toward her personally. The decision to follow her father was between her and God.

She jumped at a cracking branch and placed her hand to her heaving chest. Her heart thundered beneath it. She took a deep breath and whispered, "Even though I walk through the valley of the shadow of death, I will fear no evil."

A hand shot out from a clump of trees and clamped over her mouth. Pulled against a solid chest, she fought and kicked. One of her blows landed solidly on her capturer's shin. The man grunted but didn't release her.

"Marguerite, it's me," he hissed in her ear. "Trip."

He held her until he felt her relax, then let her go. She whirled to face him and fired a booted foot at the other shin.

Yelping, he grabbed the injured leg. "What was that for?"

"For scaring the wits out of me."

"You? How do you think I felt when I saw you walking up the road, going to the place where I specifically warned you not to go? What do you think you're doing?"

His anger, laced with concern, warmed her in a strange way. "Why are you here?"

"I had a sneaking suspicion you'd try to do exactly what you're doing. And now you're going back to where you came from." He grabbed her arm and pushed her forward.

She dug her heels into the earth. "No, I'm not! I'm going to stop my father."

"Don't you understand?" His voice softened, but he didn't release his hold. "You can't stop him. He has to do that for himself. And Marguerite, I'll throw you over my shoulder and haul you home before I let you go there."

"You wouldn't dare."

"You think so?"

She didn't have to see his face to know he was glaring at her. He would do exactly what he'd said, and he'd enjoy humiliating her the entire way. How could she make him see that her father needed her?

She blinked back the burning tears in her eyes and twisted her arm free. "What difference does it make to you what I do? Why do you care?"

"I just do." He took a step closer. "I don't want to care, but I do."

Heart flapping like the wings of a bird, Marguerite tipped her face up to him. "But he's my father."

"And you don't want to see him hurt." He cupped her cheek. "I know."

A single tear slid down her cheek onto his callused hand.

He nudged her chin up with the pad of his thumb. "But Marguerite, I don't want to see you hurt either."

He bent, so close they seemed to breathe together.

Time froze. Then he brushed her lips with a feather-soft kiss.

Chaste, quick, but oh so sweet.

He pulled back but still held her face. "So now will you let me take you back to your camp?"

Before she could answer, he yanked her into the cover of the trees and pulled her down into the brush. Trip touched his lips to her ear. "Shhh, someone's coming."

The approaching form ran past them in seconds, pumping his spindly arms hard and covering the distance in remarkable time.

Marguerite grabbed Trip's arm. "That was Mark!"

"The boy's fast." Trip paused. "You're going to want to follow him now, aren't you?"

She could hear the scowl in his voice. "If you let me go with you, I promise to do exactly what you say." She felt Trip stiffen. "Please, don't make me go back to camp. You know I can't. I'd just have to lie and promise to stay put, then sneak off after you left."

Releasing a long breath, he studied her face. "Why is it so hard for me to tell you no?"

She nibbled on her lower lip. "I've heard I have that effect on people."

"I know I may regret this, but if we're going to catch him, we'd better hurry."

❦

Clyde Stone's Gambling Den, the three-story log cabin mansion, sat on a small hill about a mile from the lake. Lights filled all of the windows on the first floor and a few on the second.

"What's that smell?" Marguerite wrinkled her nose at the rank ammonia scent filling the air.

"Hogs," Trip whispered. "This is a working farm too."

The outbuildings came into view, and Marguerite saw the shape of a barn rise against the starlit backdrop.

Trip captured her hand in his and pulled her around the outskirts of the farm. Reaching the barn, he eased the door open and pressed a hand to her back. Marguerite slipped inside and he followed. The barn was dark as tar, so she waited until her eyes adjusted before moving.

Questions pummeled her mind, but she dared not ask them. Trip hadn't made a sound since they'd reached the buildings. He tugged her hand, and she followed him to the ladder leading to the loft. With her skirt gathered in one hand, she made her ascent with Trip close behind. When she slipped, he caught her waist.

"Careful," he whispered.

Up top, she fell into the sweet-scented hay and waited for him to join her. He dropped down beside her. "See that window over there? We can probably see the gambling parlor's front door from there."

They moved to the window and poked their heads out. Beneath them, a group of five men stood outside the door—and one boy.

"There's Mark!"

Trip put a restraining arm around her. She elbowed his

side. Did he think she'd jump out the window to get her brother?

A tall, heavily bearded man stepped out of the house, and the others parted.

"That's Clyde Stone," Trip said.

"Why's he talking to Mark?"

Trip held a finger to his lips. In the stillness of the night, a few words carried to their ears: "footrace," "bets," "make us a fortune." Mark shook Stone's hand and ran back down the road toward camp.

"Great. Just great." Trip fell back against the barn wall and slid down the rough boards.

Marguerite turned to him and stared. "What did that mean? What is Mark doing? I don't understand."

"The gambling hall is only one form of gambling Stone has his hand in." He met her gaze. "There's also horse and footraces."

"Footraces. They gamble on the runners?" The realization made her dizzy, and she slid to the hay beside him. "Mark is going to be in one of their footraces."

"Apparently."

She buried her face in her hands, grateful for the darkness. Her voice hitched. "What am I going to do now?"

Trip draped his arm around her shoulders and pulled her toward him. "I promise, we'll think of something."

Shouts from below made her jerk away from him.

"Stay down!" He moved toward the window and peeked out.

"What is it?"

"A raid."

She inched beside him and he didn't stop her. From their view, she witnessed the sheriff and his deputies pouring inside the gambling hall.

"Get to the other side, Mr. Westing," Trip breathed. "Get to the other side."

"What are you talking about?"

"The gambling den straddles the Mills County–Pottawattamie County line. Most of the regulars know to go through this special set of doors to the opposite side of the place when there's a raid. These are Pott County authorities. If your dad goes to the Mills side, they can't arrest him."

She held her breath and prayed. Did God hear prayers for a sinner to not get caught in the act?

After what seemed like an eternity, the deputies escorted a handful of men out of the building. Marguerite scanned their faces, but the height of the window prevented any recognition. A rooster crowed, and one man lifted his face and looked directly at the barn. He spotted her in the window, and she locked eyes with him.

Her father.

Shock and guilt showed on his face as he was bound and arrested. Marguerite watched in horror, unable to come to his aid.

They loaded the prisoners into a horse-drawn paneled wagon.

She turned to Trip. "Where are they taking him?"

"Jail." His voice, soft and kind, didn't ease the harshness of the word.

"He can't stay there."

"He'll have to unless someone posts his bail."

She spun, ready to scramble down the ladder and find a way to get to the jail, but Trip caught her arm.

"Marguerite, I know what you're thinking, but you can't go there."

She opened her mouth to protest, but Trip held up his

hand. "Your father would be mortified. I'll go bail him out after I take you home." When she didn't immediately agree, he added, "You can talk to Mark and see what's going on there."

Her heart felt as heavy as an anchor. What had happened to her family? All these lies consumed them.

She blinked back tears. "You'll bring him home?"

"Before breakfast." He kissed her forehead. "I promise."

19

It was 2:00 in the morning before Trip could get to the jail across the lake. After gathering up all the cash they kept at the boat shop, he took the little skiff across the choppy waters since no steamers traveled at this time of night, and walked the remaining distance to the jail.

"Trip, I didn't expect to see you." Mel, who served as a part-time deputy, ambled to his feet when Trip walked in the jail.

"Got the night shift?"

"Yeah, but at least we had us a little excitement. We raided Stone's place, but you already know that, don't you? Harry isn't here, if that's why you came."

"I know. He's at home sleeping." Trip reached in his pocket and drew out his wallet. "I'm here to bail out Edward Westing. How much is it?"

"No bail, just a hundred-dollar fine. So we were right about you and Miss Westing sparking. Trying to get on the old man's good side?"

Too tired to argue, Trip shot his crewman a glare and forked over the cash. He hoped Marguerite's father still had enough money on him to pay him back. He certainly didn't relish the idea of having to explain the missing funds to his father. "Listen, Mel, it's late and I'm tired." He raked his hand through his hair. "You mind getting him before it's time for the sun to come up?"

Mel chuckled and exited the room. Through the door, Trip could see him unlock one of the four cells and heard him call for Westing, who gathered his jacket and followed the deputy out.

The first time Trip had seen Marguerite's father was when he brought her aboard the *Argo*. Both of them dressed to the nines, he seemed to take as much pleasure in seeing Marguerite happy as in the trip itself. But today deep, dark circles rimmed his bloodshot eyes. Lack of sleep lined his skin.

He looked at Trip and his brows scrunched together. "Mr. Andrews?"

"Yes, sir. Are you ready to go home?"

He cocked his head to the side in question, but Trip merely held the door for him, tipped his navy skipper's hat to Mel, and followed the older man outside. "My boat's at the dock."

When they'd settled in the skiff, Trip pushed off and raised the sail.

Mr. Westing looked out over the lake. "She saw me tonight, didn't she?"

"Yes."

After a long silence, Mr. Westing turned toward him, his voice low. "I have only two questions: what was Marguerite doing there, and what were you doing out with my daughter alone, after dark?"

"Trying to keep her from following you." Trip laughed at the irony. "I stopped her the first time—"

"You should have stopped her this time too."

"Me? Why should I have to protect her from her own father?" Trip took a deep breath. *Lord, help me say the right thing.* "Do you realize how much you've hurt her? How disappointed she is in you?"

Mr. Westing pulled off his hat and drew his hand through his hair. "I know. I know. I'm going to stop."

"Sure you are." Trip sighed. He'd heard that before. "Do you even know that your son is going to be in one of Stone's footraces?"

"It's just one time. He's helping me out. It'll cover a debt I owe."

Trip shook his head. "Listen to yourself. You've broken your daughter's heart, and you're sending your son like a lamb to the slaughter. Those races are rough. Who knows what the promoters will do with a boy with Mark's speed? What if he gets wrapped up with them?"

"And how is this any business of yours? Last time I looked, you were my son's sailing instructor, not my family's guardian angel."

"When I paid that fine tonight, this became my business."

"And just why did you do that?"

"I promised Marguerite. You remember her. Beautiful girl. Takes lots of risks. Undying love for her father."

"I know my daughter, but just how well do you know her?"

Mr. Westing's tone dared him to say something he shouldn't.

"Not as well as I'd prefer. I'd like to court her."

Now where did that come from? So much for guarding his heart. Trip shook his head. What a way to ask a girl's father for permission to see his daughter.

"Don't hurt her."

"No, you've got that covered fine." Bitterness seeped into his voice.

Mr. Westing grew quiet. An owl swooped to the lake, scooping a fish in its talons and carrying it away. "You don't understand. I want to stop, I do, but it's hard."

No sympathy stirred. "A lot of things in life are hard."

"Besides, even if I stop today, she could never forgive me."

"You're wrong. I think Marguerite knows a thing or two about needing someone's forgiveness." As they neared the shore, he dropped the sail, rolled it, and secured it. They drifted the rest of the way in.

Trip prayed for the right words. When he spoke this time, the edge in his voice had vanished. "Mr. Westing, you don't need Marguerite's forgiveness nearly as much as you need God's. If you really want to change, only He can give you the strength to do it."

"I've never been much into looking for God." He clasped his hands in front of him.

"That doesn't make a difference. God has always been trying to get your attention." Trip looped a rope over the post and quickly tied off the skiff. He assisted Mr. Westing out of the boat, and the older man withdrew his wallet.

"Mr. Andrews, how much was the fine?"

"A hundred dollars."

"Then I'm afraid you have me at a disadvantage. I have only forty left tonight." He passed the bills to Trip. "I'll get you the rest tomorrow."

Trip nodded. "Fine. Tell Marguerite good night for me. I'm sure she's still awake."

"You really like her, son, don't you?"

"She's a hard person not to like."

"At least we agree on that." He shook Trip's hand. "Thank you for coming for me. It won't happen again."

Trip watched the proud man walk away slowly, shoulders slumped, chin pressed against his chest. How many times had he seen Harry look that way before the Lord finally opened his eyes? Words had come so easily to his friend. Not until he'd lost it all had Harry worked at making a real change.

For Marguerite's sake, he prayed that Edward Westing wouldn't have to lose it all to do the same.

～⌘～

Marguerite awoke with a start before she vaguely recalled her father's kiss on her forehead sometime before dawn. Stretching like a cat that had spent the afternoon in a window seat, she tossed the sheets away and swung her feet out of bed.

Lilly breezed inside. "Morning, sunshine."

"Good morning. My father's home, right? I wasn't just dreaming it?"

"Yes, but home from where?" Lilly's eyes narrowed.

"I don't think I can tell you."

"More secrets?"

"No. It's complicated. Is he here?"

Lighting a lamp, Lilly set Marguerite's curling iron in the flame to heat. "He was gone before breakfast. He got up early, unlike you. But I guess that's what happens when you're out half the night."

"You knew?"

"I heard you come in." Lilly set a fresh towel on the washstand. She turned, her lips drawn in a thin line. "And I heard you crying." Her right eyebrow arched. "That Mr. Andrews try something he oughtn't?"

"No. Absolutely not. Trip was a perfect gentleman." A soft smile lifted the corners of her mouth. "But a lot more

227

than that is going on." She patted the bed beside her and sighed. "I might as well tell you it all, but you'd better be sitting down for this one."

To Marguerite's surprise, when she told Lilly about her father's visits to Clyde Stone's gambling hall, her friend wasn't shocked. She said Isaiah had noticed Mr. Westing's odd nightly activities weeks ago, and she and her mother had been praying for him every day since. Only when Marguerite mentioned Mark's involvement did Lilly get upset.

"Your mama's been paying so much attention to marrying you off, she isn't noticing that boy is getting into all kinds of mischief."

"Then I'll have to keep a close eye on him myself."

"You're already too late. He took off this morning."

"He did?" Marguerite dipped the washcloth in the basin, wrung it out, and scrubbed her face. "Trip and I were going to take him with us when we went to play tennis and go swimming."

"Hard to do if you don't know where he is." Lilly removed Marguerite's tennis outfit from the trunk and shook it.

"I've got an idea where he might be."

"Why do I sense a 'but' coming?"

"Because it isn't someplace ladies generally go."

"But it's exactly where you're headed anyway."

"You don't have to go with me." She quickly donned her tennis outfit—a narrow bell-shaped white skirt and white shirtwaist. Topping it with a plaid vest, she turned to Lilly, who added the stiff collar and cuffs.

"Oh, I'll go." Lilly slipped a silk black tie around her neck and tied it. "Someone needs to keep you out of trouble."

Marguerite sat at her dressing table and picked up her brush. "Why does everyone always say that?"

Lilly chuckled. "I have no idea."

After Lilly twisted Marguerite's hair in a chignon, she curled the wisps on her forehead. Marguerite then pinned her soft tweed sports cap in place and packed her bathing suit in the rubber bag. She devoured a waffle drenched in maple syrup as quickly as she dared, then she and Lilly headed toward the lake.

Calm, glassy water meant only a few sailboats stippled the lake, but the steamy, humid weather had filled the steamboats with city patrons anxious to escape the heat by swimming at Manhattan Beach.

Marguerite scanned the crowds for Mark.

"He's hiding good." Lilly shielded her eyes from the sun. "I don't see any sign of him. Maybe we should ask Mr. Andrews if he's seen him."

"I've got two hours before I'm to meet him. If we don't find Mark by then, I'll ask for his help as soon as I see him." She squeezed the bunching muscles in her neck. Trip wouldn't approve of where she intended to look next. Starting down the dirt road leading to the hog barn, she resisted the urge to look back over her shoulder.

"You're mighty familiar with him."

"Mr. Andrews?"

Lilly cast a sidelong glance at her, a teasing glint in her eye. "I believe you referred to him as Trip."

A giggle tickled the back of Marguerite's throat. "I'm going to 'trip' you if you keep this up."

"You know, you still haven't told me about the kiss."

"How did you know?"

"So I'm right!" She clucked. "I was just guessing."

Marguerite's cheeks burned hot. She still felt the softness of his lips pressed against hers. "I think it surprised us both. Lilly, Trip's so different, so exciting."

"Then I take it that Mr. Roger is yesterday's news?"

"I don't think Roger has ever been interesting enough to even be news."

As they walked, Marguerite explained that Trip said the footraces were usually held somewhere on Clyde Stone's property, but never near the buildings, as it would implicate Stone in the illegal activity. She instructed Lilly to keep an eye out.

"And what do you intend to do if we find these races?"

"Whatever it takes to get Mark to go home."

Ten minutes later, the sound of men shouting drew their attention. They followed the noise down a narrow path. Off in a clearing they saw a crowd of men—and then they saw the runners. Three of them. Two young men and one boy—Mark. At one end of the race strip, a barrel-chested, bald fellow accepted bets.

At least her father wasn't there.

But his absence brought an unexplained ache. Hadn't Trip talked to him about Mark? Why hadn't he come to intervene?

Lilly touched her arm. "We should go back. This is no place for ladies."

"I can't."

She inched closer, unsure of whether to march up and claim her brother or wait until the racers crossed the finish line and the crowd dispersed. A gun sounded. The racers shot forward. Legs and arms pumping, Mark surged ahead of the two men and the crowd cheered.

More men waved bets at the bald man.

Marguerite and Lilly emerged from the cover of the trees, but no one noticed. Lilly squeezed her hand. "Wait back here. It's almost over."

Suddenly Mark grabbed his stomach and doubled over. Crumpling to the track, he vomited blood.

Marguerite gasped and let out a strangled cry.

No one came to his aid. Instead, the men ran off in all directions, clambering into their fancy rigs or taking to the paths.

Fisting her skirt in her hand, Marguerite ran through the tall grass. The man taking bets walked slowly toward the fallen runner, but Marguerite beat him there, dropping down beside him. "Mark." She ran her hand through his sandy hair. "Don't try to get up. Just stay right there and tell me where it hurts."

Mark raised his head and glanced back toward the burly man. A crooked smile creased his face as he sat up. "How'd I do, Mr. McDonough?"

"Great, kid." With a massive hand, he hauled her brother to his feet.

Marguerite looked from the man to Mark. "What's going on? Why do you look fine now? What about the blood?"

"Lady, who are you, and what are you doing here?"

Mark rolled his eyes. "Mr. McDonough, this is my sister. Marguerite, this is Mr. McDonough."

The man raked his eyes over her. "She need a job? We could use another pretty thing at the gambling hall."

Marguerite stepped back.

"Naw, Mr. Gordon's her beau, and he wouldn't like that much."

"Roger Gordon?"

"Yes, sir. Can I tell her how I bit that chicken liver to make it look like I was bleeding inside?"

McDonough narrowed his eyes. "That's supposed to be our secret."

"You sure were right, though. The men scattered like flies shooed off a piece of pie. Why?"

He rumpled Mark's hair. "They were afraid they'd get arrested if you died. They'd have a part in causing your death."

"So they just left their bets?" Marguerite asked.

"Better 'n being charged as an accessory to murder." McDonough hooked his thumbs in his suspenders. "I came up with that plan myself."

Marguerite took hold of Mark's arm and cleared her throat. "If you'll excuse us, Mr. McDonough, I'll be taking my brother home now."

"He's got another race to run this afternoon."

"No, he doesn't." She shoved Mark toward the trees. "Speak to my father if you have any questions."

"Lady, that's who arranged the race."

She stopped short, directed Lilly to take Mark, and then marched back to the man. "Sir, I'm sure there's been some error."

"Lady, I'm telling you, if that boy don't race today, your daddy is going to be in a world of hurt."

"I'll speak to my father, but don't expect my brother back—today or at any time in the future."

❧

"You went there alone!" Trip stopped in the middle of the grass tennis court and let the ball sail by.

Marguerite winced. Did she dare tell him she'd just gotten the point?

He approached the net. "How do you manage to make me so furious with you every time we're together?"

Marguerite shrugged. "Natural talent?" She stepped back

to the corner of the court and waited for Trip to take his place.

Chest heaving, he finally moved to the center of the court.

"Trip, I couldn't just leave him there." She tossed the ball in the air and lobbed it over the net.

"Fault!"

"It wasn't my fault," she protested. "Besides, I wasn't alone. Lilly's gone back to camp now, but she was with me."

"Not that kind of fault. The ball was out, Marguerite."

"Oh." She served again. Hard.

Reaching the volley, Trip fired it back. "And you having Lilly along is supposed to make me feel better?"

She strained to reach the ball and fell short. "To tell you the truth, I wasn't thinking about your feelings. I do appreciate your concern, but clearly you realize I wasn't trying to be foolhardy. I just wanted to get Mark away from those awful men. Then when he fell and I saw all the blood, I had to do something."

Trip's face paled. "Blood? Do I even want to know?"

She quickly explained how McDonough told Mark to bite a chicken liver toward the end of the race. Retrieving the ball, she tossed it back to him. "You don't need to clobber this thing. Lobbing it will do just fine."

"It would be easier to hit it more lightly if someone wasn't upsetting me during the game." He stepped back to the line, bounced the ball, and hit it with the wooden racquet.

The powerful serve landed to her right, and she easily returned it. The two of them continued the volley in silence for several minutes. A close shot to the net by Marguerite earned her the point. She shot him a cocky grin and stooped near the net to retrieve the ball from Trip's side.

He caught her wrist. "Marguerite, those men are dangerous."

"I know. That's why I needed to get Mark away from there." He let go of her hand and she tugged her vest back into place. "But they wouldn't hurt a woman."

"If they thought you endangered their business, you could be the queen of England and they wouldn't care."

She pointed at Trip with her tennis racket. "He isn't going back there today."

Trip glanced at Mark bouncing a tennis ball on a racquet in an open area and sighed. "At least we agree on that." He aced a serve that left little opportunity for her to return. "I believe that means I won."

"You said you didn't play. Did you lie to me?" She paused to study him. Blue-striped tennis jacket, straw hat, bow tie. He knew all the tennis terms and he knew how to play the game. If she wasn't mistaken, Trip had fooled her about playing the game before. If she'd any doubts, the way he held his Horseman wooden tennis racquet and stood on the balls of his feet when he volleyed confirmed her suspicions.

His dimples deepened, a piratelike grin marking his face. "How does it feel?"

"That isn't nice, Trip Andrews."

"I didn't say I didn't play. I said I didn't play much." He took her racquet, brushing her hand in the process. "Besides, you know what they say. 'Love means nothing in tennis.'"

⬡

Trip watched Marguerite sashay to the bathhouse, her skirts swishing about her ankles. What had he just quipped? "Love means nothing in tennis"? Where did that come from? Love? It didn't even make any sense.

If I had any brains, I would be running as fast as I can right now. Then again, as Dad has always been quick to point out, I'm lacking in the brain department.

He stowed the racquets in his canvas bag, called to Mark, and led him to the men's bathhouse so they could change as well.

"You beat her!" Mark shook his hand. "No one beats Marguerite. I bet she's fuming."

"She didn't seem upset." At least not from losing. His words, however, left her rosy-cheeked and speechless. A look he certainly could get used to.

Trip pushed open the door of the bathhouse. "Why can't Marguerite swim?"

"Mother never let her learn. Alice, Lilly's mom, snuck her to the pond a few times, but not enough so that she could practice."

"But you can?"

"I'm a boy. Mom says I can do anything I want."

So that was the injustice that ignited Marguerite's fire. He tried to imagine what life would be like if he'd been constantly told he couldn't do something. He'd never considered that. Thanks to his father, he understood being reminded of inadequacies, but his father had never stopped him from trying something new. In fact, if his father did anything right, it was encouraging him to face challenges head-on.

No wonder Marguerite dared to go anywhere forbidden to women. Some ladies wouldn't think twice about such confines, but not Marguerite. Her adventurer's heart wouldn't allow that. Maybe that's what drew him to her.

Fifteen minutes later, the trio entered the water. Trip ushered them away from the crush of swimmers to a more isolated area near Turtle Island. Mark dove in and swam away, leaving Trip and Marguerite staring at one another, waist-deep in the water.

"I really don't need to swim," Marguerite said. "You can go enjoy yourself. I'll just sit on the beach and watch." She dropped her gaze and made wide circles in the water with her hands.

"If you're going to sail, you have to be able to swim."

Snapping her head up, wide-eyed, she gaped at him. "Sail? You're going to let me?"

"I think we can arrange it if—and I mean if—you learn to swim." His lips curled into a grin, but he crossed his arms over his chest to appear stern. "Like I told you from the beginning, no one goes on my boat if they can't swim."

Her face lit up as if he'd just given her a Christmas present. "I'll learn fast. I promise."

"There's no hurry." He chuckled. "The longer it takes, the better."

She splashed him. "What do we do first?"

"Learn to float." He demonstrated the buoyant position in the water. "Your turn."

Slowly she lay back in the water, but immediately she sank and came up sputtering.

"Take a deep breath before you lie back, and relax. Pretend you're rolling over a barrel."

For a brief second she remained afloat. When she started to sink, he reached beneath her, placing his palm against her back and supporting her.

Jolts shot through him, not unwelcomed. Her eyes grew wide.

"Relax. I've got you." He stepped closer, and his hip brushed against hers.

"I hope," she breathed. It took her a few minutes, but finally she was able to let the water buoy her body.

He smiled in encouragement. "You can do this now. Take a deep breath. I'm going to let go."

Cornflower blue eyes, filled with trust, locked on his own. He let his hand slip away. Arched in the water, she floated for nearly a minute. When she started to go under, he grabbed her hand and pulled her up.

"I did it!" She threw her arms around his neck.

He returned the embrace. "You sure did. Ready for the deep water?"

"Sure." She started out and he caught her arm.

"I was teasing you."

She turned and gave him a cheeky grin. "I know. Scared you, didn't I?"

He shook his head. How could he tell her that everything about her scared him, and like watching a sinking boat, he was powerless to stop it?

⌘

Much to Marguerite's disappointment, Mark announced he wanted to go back to camp. Trip planned to practice for the regatta one more time before tomorrow's race and she wanted to watch, but no amount of cajoling could change the boy's mind. Trip reminded her that Mark had endured quite a day. He asked her and Lilly to meet him at the tent revival that night, and afterward he wanted to show her something special.

"Ask your father to the revival too," Trip suggested as they approached the boat shop.

"My father? He isn't much for church attendance, Trip."

"We talked about that last night. I'm hoping it'll change." Trip placed a hand on Mark's shoulder. "See to it your sister gets back to camp without any side trips."

Mark beamed. "Yes, sir."

She rolled her eyes.

"Come on, Marguerite," Mark said. "Hurry up. I'm hungry."

"We can't have that. Marguerite, you better go feed this growing boy." Trip flashed a mind-numbing grin. "See you later, and remember, ask your father to join us tonight."

The closer Marguerite got to Camp Andromeda, the more she began to think about her father's after-dark activities. She still hadn't had the chance to speak with him about the gambling and wasn't sure what she'd say when the situation presented itself.

Lord, guide my words. Give me courage to face this and courage for Daddy to change.

Now, where should she start? Trip wanted her to invite her father to the revival. Maybe that was as good a place as any.

When she and Mark reached the camp, she sought out her father. She found him sitting on the wicker settee while her mother prepared for dinner. She slid in place beside him. To her surprise, he didn't seem shocked by her request to join her at the revival, but he politely declined, saying that her mother had arranged a dinner engagement with the Prestons.

She studied him for a moment. He'd lost weight in the last month, but he didn't seem to be harboring some dark secret. Perhaps Trip was wrong. Maybe her father's involvement in gambling was merely sport. But either way, it was still wrong.

A familiar knot wedged in her throat. In her heart, she knew the truth.

"Daddy, about yesterday—"

His voice deepened. "If you'll forget you saw me, I'll forget I saw you."

"I'm worried about you."

"Don't be." He smiled but it didn't reach his eyes. "You've been out in the sun, Maggie dear. Your cheeks are pink. What will your mother say?"

"That I'll freckle." The familiar nickname warmed her. Only he called her Maggie, and it seemed like weeks since he'd done so. "I played tennis and went swimming."

He lifted an eyebrow. "With Trip Andrews?"

"And Mark," she hurried to add.

He tapped her nose, and his lips bowed. "The color suits you." With that, he stood. "I'd best go get ready before your mother comes calling. Enjoy your evening, sweetheart."

She considered telling him to do likewise but figured he'd had enough enjoyable evenings lately.

"Why the frown, Maggie?"

"I'm afraid."

"Sweetheart, I would never let anything hurt you. You know that. Don't you trust me?"

The sadness that shadowed his eyes tore at her heart. "I do, Daddy, but . . ."

"No buts." He pulled her into his arms. "I love you. Just remember that." He released her at the shrill sound of her mother's voice calling him to leave. "We'll talk later tonight. Now, you go and have a good time with Mr. Andrews."

Back in her tent, Marguerite and Lilly prepared for the revival. Marguerite's thoughts kept turning to her father. Of course she trusted him not to hurt her. She wanted to tell him that she wasn't afraid for herself but for him. And how did he know Trip had asked her to the revival? He seemed to be giving her permission to see him. But surely he knew of Roger's intentions. She shook her head. Nothing her father did right now made sense.

She sighed and drew the brush through her wavy tresses. Roger would be back soon. What would she tell him? How would she explain Trip? What's more, how would she explain what her father had been involved in? If Roger didn't already know about it, he would never understand. He couldn't tolerate weakness in others.

And she couldn't tolerate him. She wrinkled her nose in the mirror. The scrunched face brought a slant to her lips. She set the brush aside and wound her hair on top of her head.

Lilly moved behind her, pinned it in place, and patted her shoulder. "Mr. Andrews won't be able to focus on the sermon tonight if you get any prettier."

"I think he'll manage." Marguerite held out her wrist and waited while Lilly secured the stiff cuffs. With its tailored fit and large leg-of-mutton sleeves, the purple walking suit she'd chosen for the evening was one of her favorites. She picked up the matching summer hat, hoping Trip wouldn't think the abundance of lavender, pink, and white silk flowers, the trailing silk ribbon, and the small ostrich plume was too much for the casual evening.

"You're quiet tonight. Have a lot on your mind?" Lilly secured her own much more modest bonnet.

"Just thinking about some different things." Marguerite pinned the hat in place and tucked her watch beneath her belt. "I've decided to tell Roger the truth—I don't have feelings for him, I never will, and I can't accept his proposal."

Lilly picked up her Bible and a smile lit her face. "About time."

❧

The tent revival left them all stirred. The preacher delivered a powerful sermon on the dangers of gambling. Marguerite wished her father were in attendance, and when she saw Trip speaking to the minister, she wondered if he'd already contacted Brother Davis concerning her father.

Before she could ask, he whisked her and Lilly away, explaining they'd better hurry if they wanted a good view of the attraction at the beach. With the setting sun, Marguerite expected the patrons to begin boarding the steamboats to take them back to the streetcar terminal. Instead, a crush of people gathered in front of the pavilion, pressed against the rail.

Harry waved them over as they approached. "I thought you weren't going to make it."

"Were you at the tent meeting?" Trip asked.

"Of course. I just snuck out early." He patted the railing and winked at Marguerite. "Wanted to save our girl a good spot."

Trip shot his friend a glare, and Marguerite giggled. He pressed his hand to her back, urging her to the rail. When Lilly didn't follow, he motioned her forward as well.

"There she is!" Harry pointed to a tower set beyond the docks in the lake.

Marguerite couldn't believe her eyes. "Is that a woman climbing that ladder?"

"Not just any woman," Trip said. "That's Miss Fishbaugh."

He said the name with a sense of awe in his voice, and Marguerite leaned over the railing. "But that tower's at least two stories high."

"It's thirty feet, but who's counting?" Harry chuckled.

Miss Fishbaugh reached the diving platform, and Trip leaned close to Marguerite's ear. "Now watch."

The female diver lifted a metal can and doused her bathing suit with liquid. She then attached a large, cone-shaped collar around her neck. Marguerite tipped her head toward Trip. "What did she pour on herself?"

"Gasoline."

"Why on earth did she do a fool thing like that?" Lilly asked.

Before anyone could answer, Miss Fishbaugh struck a match and her suit burst into flames. Marguerite gasped along with the hundreds gathered to watch the spectacle. A few women in the crowd screeched. Then, like a bird, Miss Fishbaugh dove into Lake Manawa. She surfaced a moment later and pulled herself onto the dock. She waved at the crowds and the people cheered.

"That's amazing!" Marguerite pressed her hand to her chest, attempting to quell her racing heart.

"I knew you'd like it." Trip offered Marguerite his arm. "What did you think, Miss Lilly?"

"I think you'd better be careful giving Miss Marguerite any ideas."

Trip laughed. "I hadn't thought of that."

The foursome headed down the boardwalk. Harry paired up with Lilly in polite conversation, allowing Trip and Marguerite to dally behind alone.

"How does she keep from catching afire?" Marguerite touched the back of her upswept hair.

"Her suit is made of asbestos. It's a fabric that doesn't burn. I think that collar protects her hair. But I can't imagine what possesses her to do something so dangerous."

"I can."

He shook his head. "That doesn't surprise me."

The teasing lilt in his voice made her smile. "Oh, I wouldn't want to do that, but I understand wanting to try the impossible."

Trip glanced at the night sky. "To reach for the stars?"

"Yes. Or at least enjoy trying."

"Marguerite, I need to ask you something." Levity now gone, his voice dropped lower.

"All right."

"That man who came for you the night you fell in the lake and took you to the dance . . ."

"Roger Gordon."

"I haven't seen him around."

"He's been out of town recently."

He stopped on the path and waited until she turned toward him. "What does he mean to you?"

Trip's face, awash in dusk's pale light, showed tiny worry lines around his eyes and, if she had to guess, a spark of jealousy. She smiled. "He means less to me than he thinks he does."

"I don't understand."

"Roger is my mother's answer to my lack of marital bliss."

His scowl deepened. "You're going to marry him?"

"Heavens no! But if my mother had her way, I would." She squeezed his arm with her gloved hand. "Trip, you have nothing to worry about. Let me put it this way. You're like the dive tower, and Roger is like a beach chair. Who do you think I'd choose?"

He raised an eyebrow and his dimples cratered his cheeks. "So you're willing to take a chance on me?"

"Maybe." She eyed him with a smirk. "Since you have a sailboat and all."

❧

If it were possible to float to her tent, Marguerite was certain she could. The taste of Trip's lips still lingered on

243

her own. He'd asked for one kiss for luck tomorrow, and she'd willingly provided it despite Lilly's attempt to shoo him away.

Now, when Lilly suggested they get to bed early before the big day, she deferred, saying she just wanted to sit under the stars for a few minutes.

"More like get the stars out of your eyes," her friend teased. "Just don't expect me to stay up and wait for you."

After assuring Lilly that she wouldn't wake her, Marguerite walked to the sitting area in the center of the camp.

A lamp on the table illuminated her father. He held his head in his hands.

Heart thundering, she stopped short. "Daddy? What's wrong? Has something happened to Mother or Mark?"

He glanced up, his eyes glistening with tears, his face pale and drawn. "Maggie dear, come sit down."

20

Fearing her knees would give way, Marguerite grabbed for the back of the wicker chair before lowering herself onto its cushion.

Her father reached across the table and captured her hands. "Your mother is fine—for now."

"Daddy, you're scaring me. What's wrong?"

He released his hold and drew his hand through his hair. "I've made a horrible mistake, sweetheart."

"I know about the gambling, Daddy, but I forgive you. God will forgive you too. Just ask Him."

He held out his hands, palms up, and spread them wide. "It's all gone. The money. The business. I've lost it all. We're penniless. Not even enough to pay Trip Andrews back for bailing me out."

Her mouth went dry and the words came out in a hoarse whisper. "Because I wouldn't let Mark race?"

"No, that was merely to buy me more time." He leaned back in the chair.

"There's nothing left?" she squeaked. "You gambled it all away?"

"I had one more business deal, but . . ."

"But what?"

"It's with Roger Gordon."

"Oh."

"He'll be home soon."

"I guess that's good." She unpinned her hat with trembling hands and set it on the table. "You can focus on your business with him. I'm certain he'll give you a loan until the situation improves."

Her father leaned forward, steepled his hands in front of him on the tabletop, and released a long sigh. "Marguerite, don't be naive. He arranged this business deal in hopes that it would soften me toward giving him your hand in marriage."

"You'd do that? Agree to me marrying him?" Her hand shot to her mouth and her stomach clenched.

His silence answered her.

She blinked. "And if I don't accept his proposal?"

Still no answer.

"Daddy?"

"He will most likely withdraw his offer of partnership in the new business venture."

"And we'll have nothing," she croaked. "Is there any other way?"

He laid a hand on her arm. "I'm sorry, Marguerite. I can't think of anything else."

Mind spinning, Marguerite looked into his eyes. What did she see in their tear-filled depths? Fear? Desperation?

She must have misunderstood him. Her father wouldn't allow this. No. Not him. Not her hero. He loved her. He saved her from life's injustices. He didn't feed her to the monsters. Not him.

"Daddy?"

He stood, kissed the top of her head, and departed, leaving her alone in the darkness.

Oh, Lord, this can't be happening.

A shudder shook her frame, the pain splintering her heart. She felt so raw even tears didn't come. How could she say yes to Roger? Not now. Especially not now.

My father can't ask this of me. He'll think of something. He can't ask me to make a sacrifice like this.

But he had.

If she didn't accept Roger's proposal, what would happen to her family? To Mark? To Lilly? Could she watch them suffer because of her selfishness?

Lord, help. I can't do this.

❦

Try as she might, Marguerite couldn't force her feet to go faster even though it was the morning of the regatta. Tugging on the puffy sleeve of her tailored jacket, Mark dragged Marguerite toward the *Endeavor*, still docked behind the boat shop.

Marguerite's feet felt tangled in a net. A net of lies. At least this time they belonged to her father and not her.

Now I know where I learned to lie so well.

"Come on! We're going to miss seeing him before they shove off!"

Plastering on her best smile, she let Mark haul her behind the building and onto the dock. Would Trip see through a fake veneer of excitement? She didn't want to upset him before the big race. This day was too important to him.

Mark hailed the *Endeavor*'s skipper. Trip looked up from his preparations and beamed at Marguerite. He was dressed in a white shirt with the sleeves rolled to the elbows and a pair of tan creased trousers, and his tousled sandy hair peeked out from beneath a flat straw hat. He hopped over the side of the boat and jogged to meet her.

"You look beautiful—and tired. I thought you'd have sweet dreams last night." He flashed a smile with dimples so deep she ached to touch them.

"Ew." Mark stuck out his tongue. "She ain't beautiful. She's just Marguerite."

Marguerite frowned. "*Isn't* beautiful."

"See, she knows it too."

Trip chuckled and laid a hand on Mark's shoulder. "Hey, sport, why don't you go save your sister a spot to watch the race?"

After Mark trotted off, Trip turned back to Marguerite. "Why couldn't you sleep?"

"I guess I was simply too excited about the regatta." She glanced around. The bright sky and gentle breeze didn't mirror the storm in her heart. "The weather seems perfect."

"Perfect for leaving those pretty boys and their fancy boat in our wake." He pointed to one of the other crews, all wearing matching jackets, and chuckled.

"You really don't like them, do you?"

"Let's just say we have a history, and Dane likes to throw his past victories in my face." Trip glanced at his crew readying the boat. "Listen, I've got to go, but I want to ask you something first. The Yacht Club is sponsoring a ball tonight to celebrate the regatta, and I would be honored if you'd allow me to escort you to it."

Her heart lurched. One more night with him. Dancing in his arms. Laughing with him. Sharing dreams. Pure heaven or pure torture?

She should say no and end this once and for all. She really should. It wasn't right to pretend they could have more. Still, she couldn't make her mouth form the word, especially not today with the impending regatta. This was the most important day of Trip's life, and she wanted to be there for him.

She forced a smile. "I'd love to go with you."

"I'll call for you at 7:00." He kissed her cheek. "For luck."

"For God's blessing." She pressed her handkerchief in his hand, then watched him trot back to the sailboat and hop lithely aboard. With a commanding voice filled with respect for his crew, he barked orders and they jumped to fulfill them.

Everyone loved Trip.

Do I love him?

Taking a step back, she pressed a hand to her wildly beating heart pounding a rhythm of truth.

Trip gathered his crew. They removed their hats and bowed their heads in prayer.

Her heart shattered. It wasn't fair. Trip was everything Roger was not. Didn't God want her with a man who loved Him?

He stood in the bow and waved to her. "Marguerite, meet me in the winner's circle!"

She blew a kiss back to him and whispered, "God bless you, Phillip Sutton Andrews the Third."

⊗

Enthusiasm buzzing amid his crew, Trip surveyed their work one final time as they prepared to float away from the docks. With hearty approval, he declared everything in order.

Then Trip saw him—his father, standing on the dock, critically assessing every detail. Trip hopped off the *Endeavor* and hurried over to meet him. "Here to wish us luck?"

"No."

Trip's heart sank.

"You don't need luck. You have skill."

Mouth dry, Trip swallowed the lump in his throat. "Thanks, Dad. I . . . uh . . . better go. The race will be starting soon."

"Just remember to take your lead early, so you can keep away from all those idiots who don't have a clue what they're doing."

Trip nodded. "Yes, sir."

The *Endeavor* glided to the starting line at the sound of the five-minute warning gun. Glancing back at the shore, Trip shook his head. He'd never expected to hear those words from his father. Almost a compliment.

Trip surveyed the triangle-shaped course marked by flagged cork buoys. The wind—he guessed at fourteen to fifteen knots—was true, and they should make top speed.

"What do you think of our competition?" Harry stepped beside him.

"The *Antilles* always does pretty well, and the *Ranger* looked sharp yesterday."

"Ahoy there, *Endeavor*!"

Trip lifted his gaze to see the captain of the *Viking*, Dane Henderson from Spirit Lake, waving. Trip nodded in greeting.

"You don't really think you have a chance, do you, Andrews?" Dane tugged at the lapels of his striped jacket.

Trip shook his head. "Well, let's just say I'll see you at the finish line—coming up behind us."

"The nerve of those pretty boys!" Harry readied the mainsail.

"Too bad there's no photographers around. They make a good picture in their matching jackets."

Harry laughed. "And too bad we're going to trounce them."

"Absolutely." Trip spotted the racing official step onto the main dock. He raised a pistol in the air and fired the one-minute warning.

Adrenaline surged through Trip's veins. He waved his navy skipper's hat in the air, the gold cord flashing in the sunlight. "Places!"

The crew tightened the sails, and Trip turned the ship into the wind. When the starting gun sounded, the *Endeavor* took the lead, crossing the starting line well before the others.

This was going to be a good day.

A fantastic, marvelous, amazingly good day from start to finish.

◈

"Look at her go!" Marguerite jumped up and down beside Mark. She leaned over the railing, trying to catch every moment of the race. With the rippling water, clear skies, and gusty breeze, she could almost picture herself aboard the *Endeavor*, flying through the water and feeling the spray on her face.

She gasped as the *Viking* neared. Oh, how Trip disliked that crew. Anyone other than Dane Henderson could beat him and he'd handle it fine. She could see Harry, Lloyd, Mel, and Max all leaning far out of the ship's windward side to balance the heeling vessel.

The *Endeavor* neared the first buoy and made its turn. The *Viking* followed a length behind. She bit her knuckle, and Mark jumped up and down, cheering. Masterfully tacking their way along the second leg, the *Endeavor*'s crew maintained their lead. Finally they reached the second turn. Dane cut off the *Endeavor* so he could turn closer to the buoy. Ignoring safety concerns for both vessels, Dane forced Trip to make a wider turn.

"Did you see that?" Mark shouted. "What an underhanded move! If Trip hadn't given him the right of way, the *Viking* would have tipped. That isn't fair."

Marguerite clenched the railing but cheered when the spinnaker sail on the front of the *Endeavor* filled and puffed like a proud man's chest as the ship sailed the final leg of the triangle. The *Viking* followed moments later, and the two ships raced neck and neck for the finish line.

The men in the crowd shouted, and the women fanned themselves furiously, overcome by the excitement. Marguerite stood on her tiptoes to see who crossed the line first.

"It's a tie!" Mark shouted.

His words, echoed throughout the crowd, were confirmed by an announcement from the official, Colonel Reed.

"What happens now?" Mark asked.

"I don't know."

Trip hadn't spoken of this eventuality. They watched the other ships come in, but neither the *Endeavor* nor the *Viking* neared the pier where the winners were to be announced.

Both boats lowered their sails and pulled near the dock. Trip and Dane met the official, and soon the crews on both ships disembarked—all except for the two captains.

"They're going to do a single-handed race," a man in the crowd shouted.

Marguerite racked her mind for the term. She remembered Trip telling her that it was possible to man the *Endeavor* by himself—single-handedly—but it was difficult. Could that be the way they planned to break the tie?

Colonel Reed announced the tiebreaker would be a cannon

race, out and back, with only the skippers of each sailboat at the helm.

Marguerite's chest tightened. *Lord, please help him. He can't lose this race. It's too important.*

A five-minute shot went off. Under half sail, Trip and Dane negotiated their ships back into position to start. Alone on his boat, Trip managed to hoist the mainsail before the one-minute shot was fired. When the signal sounded, the *Viking* surged forward. Dane got the jump on Trip, who struggled with the jib sail. Once Trip raised both sails, the *Endeavor* flew across the water and made up the distance separating the two vessels.

Heeling so far to the right she feared the boat might capsize, the *Endeavor* surged onward. Marguerite pressed a knuckle to her lips. She knew Trip needed to use each gust of headwind.

"A race is won and lost on the turns," she remembered Trip saying. Was that still true when he was manning the thirty-two-foot vessel alone?

As Dane had done before, he hugged the buoy on his turn, forcing Trip to go wide. But this time the tactic backfired, and the *Viking* tilted so far it took on water. Dane used precious seconds to tack out of the turn.

Trip hoisted the spinnaker and the crowd cheered. Marguerite held her breath as he covered the last leg with the smaller *Viking* gaining on him every second. She squeezed her eyes shut. She couldn't watch.

But she had to. She peeled her eyes open.

Time suspended. The two boats flew between the buoys. Her heart came to a halt.

He'd lost. At the last second, the *Viking* had nosed past him.

Phillip Sutton Andrews the Third, her Trip, lost the Manawa Regatta and the hopes of gaining his father's trust.

Her heart shattered along with his dream.

⚘

Stepping on the dock, Trip watched Dane Henderson be whisked away to the podium. He went through the motions, extending his hand in congratulations to Dane when the other skipper passed. Trip's crew and other spectators gathered around and praised his efforts, but he found their words hollow. He'd lost. Failed.

How had he let this happen? One minute he could taste victory, and the next it was ripped from his grasp.

Lord, why? You know I needed this.

He spotted his father, whose wrinkled face registered disappointment.

Trip had failed him.

The crowd crushed in, rehashing the race minute by minute. The stifling air closed in.

"I still think we deserve a congratulatory dinner, don't you, Captain?" Harry clapped him on the shoulder. "Second place is nothing to sneeze at. There's always next year."

Next year? How was he going to keep his father from working himself to death for a year? He had to get away. He had to think.

"Later, Harry." Nudging his friend aside, he raced off the dock.

⚘

Even though she'd tried for more than an hour to find Trip, Marguerite couldn't locate him anywhere. Harry insisted Trip needed a little time. He walked her and Mark home,

254

assuring her that Trip would be back to his old self by this evening's ball.

"At least he has you. That means a lot to him." Harry removed his hat and ran a hand through his curly hair. "He's used to other people disappointing him, but he isn't used to disappointing himself."

She prepared for the evening with a heavy heart. After donning one of her favorites, a blush pink sleeveless moiré gown, she dusted her neck and shoulders with talcum powder.

"You want to talk about it?" Lilly placed a set of pearl earrings in Marguerite's hand.

Marguerite slid the wires of her earrings through her pierced ears. "The race? I already told you all about it."

"No, about whatever has you looking so lost." Lilly swept Marguerite's hair into a wavy pompadour and secured a bun at the crown.

Marguerite spilled the story to her dearest friend as Lilly listened patiently.

"You can't marry that dreadful man." Lilly used the hot curling iron to form a perfect ringlet beside Marguerite's ear. "What did Mr. Trip say?"

"I haven't told him. There wasn't an opportunity." Marguerite drew on her long kidskin gloves. "How will I tell him what I have to do? Especially now? I'm sure he's devastated about losing the race."

Lilly straightened the lace flounces on the dress's bodice. "You don't have to do anything, and if your daddy was thinking straight, that's exactly what he'd tell you."

"I wish that were true." Marguerite squeezed Lilly's hand. "Thank you, Lilly. You're a good friend."

Outside the tent, her mother met her. "You look lovely

tonight, dear. I thought you'd want to see this before you go." She passed a telegram to her.

Marguerite quickly read it and her throat tightened. "Roger will be home tomorrow."

"Indeed."

"Mother . . ."

Camille stood in front of her and took both of Marguerite's hands in her own. "Enjoy tonight, dear. Every minute of it."

Because it's the last night you'll have. Marguerite heard the warning in her mother's words silently as if her mother had spoken them aloud.

Tears pricked her eyes, and she squeezed them shut. "I will, Mother."

❦

A pirate dance? Trip had neglected to disclose to Marguerite that this was a themed ball, but when he arrived at the camp dressed in swashbuckler's knickers, a billowing white shirt, a dark leather eye patch, and a white plumed black tricorne, she easily guessed. To her relief, he said all the ladies still wore ball gowns.

Removing his hat, he took her hand and bowed over it. "You look stunning, Lady Marguerite."

Even her ears grew hot under his gaze. "Why, thank you, Captain Andrews, but where's your peg leg?"

"I left it at home. It makes dancing mighty difficult."

Arm in arm, they walked to the Yacht Club. She stopped on the veranda. "Trip, are you truly all right?"

"I will be."

"Earlier today, I wish I could've told you how proud I was of you."

"Glad someone is."

"Trip, your dad is too." She licked her lips. "What did he say?"

"Not much afterward, but before the race he said I didn't need luck, that I had skill."

"That had to feel good."

"It did." He released a long sigh. "But then I let him down."

"No, you didn't. Maybe you weren't the winner today, but you raced exactly how he taught you to—with honor and fairness."

"Thanks." He paused at the base of the Yacht Club's stairs and turned to her with a roguish grin. "But no more regatta talk. Tonight belongs to you."

Glistening beneath gaslight chandeliers, the Yacht Club's ballroom robbed Marguerite of breath. A stringed quartet played a waltz in one corner, and a bountiful refreshment table had been set up across the room. In keeping with the pirate theme, men of all ages and sizes danced in costume.

Trip led her toward the refreshment table. When they ran into Harry, who was escorting Emily Graham, Trip left Marguerite to speak with her friend while he got them both something to drink. He returned with two frosty lemon ices. They said their goodbyes and found a secluded spot.

"I may not have won the regatta, but at least I'm going to the ball with the prettiest lady on the lake." He winked at her and the plume on his hat bobbed. "So, what did your father say about the other night?"

She swallowed hard. "Can we talk about that later? Tonight I simply want to enjoy the evening."

And she did. Every dance in his arms. Every look on his

face. Every brush of his hand. Every stolen glance. Every word whispered in her ear.

But it was all over much too soon.

She cherished each moment and hid them away like a buried treasure. When the stringed quartet announced their last set of songs, her heart lurched.

Trip grabbed Marguerite's hand and pulled her toward him. He leaned close to her ear and whispered, "All the rest of your dances are mine."

"Trip, we can't dance them all. What will people think?"

He ignored her protests and led her to the center of the dance floor. "Considering all that is going on in your life, sharing more than one dance in a row with a handsome man should be the least of your worries." He paused when she giggled. "Let's enjoy ourselves and dance."

They stayed on the dance floor during the last four songs. Once, she spotted a disapproving glare from a young lady who'd set her eyes on Trip, but Trip spun her away. As the final waltz played, Trip twirled her in a wide circle, making her the center of attention on the dance floor. Her gown rippled around her ankles with every turn.

His eyes locked with hers. "You may have literally fallen for me first, but I believe I've fallen for you now. Marguerite, I think I'm falling in love with you."

Her eyes brimmed with tears. "Trip, please."

"Why are you crying? Don't you feel the same way?"

"I do, but there's something you don't understand."

He pulled her from the dance floor and out to the veranda. "You're upset. What is it? Is it your father? I'll speak to him."

"Tomorrow Roger returns."

"But you said you didn't want him."

"I don't."

"So? I won't let him bother you, if that's what you're worried about."

"Before he left he told me he plans to propose when he comes back."

"Oh, I understand. You don't want to hurt him. I'm sure he'll be upset, but he'll get over it."

"Trip," she croaked, "I plan to accept."

"You what?" His nostrils flared and a tick throbbed beneath his eye patch. "Do you love him?"

"I don't have a choice."

"What do you mean you don't have a choice?" His voice rose. "Of course you do. No one can force you to accept a marriage proposal." He tore off the eye patch, revealing swirls of emotion. "Do you love him?"

She dropped her gaze. "It doesn't make a difference. I have to do it."

"What's going on?" His tone icy, he glared at her. "And don't lie to me. Remember, I know that's one of your specialties."

"That isn't fair."

"Why? Hasn't this all been an act? Another lie?"

"No!"

"But you're willing to marry a man you don't love."

"My father is broke. We have nothing. My father said that if I don't accept Roger's marriage proposal, Roger will withdraw his business deal and we'll be penniless. I can't do that to my family." Energy drained, she slid onto the bench. "So you see, that's why I can't see you anymore. I have to do this to save my family. It's the way it has to be."

Trip clenched the railing, his chest heaving. "What happened is your father's problem, not yours. I told you before he has to get himself out of it."

259

"Wouldn't you do anything for your father?"

"I wouldn't lie for him."

"But that's where we're different, as you've so aptly told me. I would lie for mine."

He spun toward her, eyes flashing. "You're going to get caught in your web of lies like my mother did hers."

"Trip, try to understand."

"I understand perfectly. You're just like her. You say you love me, but then you leave."

21

With eyes puffy from a day's worth of crying, Marguerite slipped into the horrid purple dress with the tight-fitting high collar, anticipating Roger's return at any minute.

Trip had brought her home the previous night in complete silence. The stony look in his eyes made her heart ache, and his words haunted her dreams. *You're just like my mother. You say you love me, but then you leave.* They sliced at her resolve, and the wound had festered during the night.

Why couldn't he see she didn't have a choice? Did he think she desired to marry a man who brought her no joy? She didn't want this any more than he did, but it simply had to be.

Roger stepped into the open area, and she forced herself to rise from her seat in the wicker rocker. She swallowed hard. "Roger, welcome back."

"It's good to be home." His eyes raked her hungrily. "I've missed you. You look lovely."

She shivered despite the heat of the evening.

"I've reserved a table for us at the Pelican Bay restaurant." The caterpillar mustache wiggled under his nose. "Are you ready?"

No, I'll never be ready. She glanced at the sky rapidly filling with clouds. *God, don't You think this is a good time for a lightning strike? I'll be happy to move out of the way.*

He moved closer and kissed her cheek. Then, without offering his arm, he grabbed her hand and stuffed it in the crook of his elbow. He covered it with his own and held it fast. "I spoke to your father." His voice was laced with arrogance, as if he'd won a game.

She tugged at the itchy lace collar strangling her neck. "I'm sure that was an enlightening experience."

"It was."

Roger had a one-sided discussion about the state of affairs in the economy on their walk to the restaurant inside the pavilion. Once there, he ordered for them.

Shoving the oysters around on her plate, Marguerite sighed. She hated oysters. Slimy things. Like swallowing chunks of worms.

"You don't care for oysters?" Roger slurped one from its shell.

"Not really."

"You should have said something."

"I don't believe I was given the chance."

He frowned, his bushy eyebrows bunching over his nose.

Then, after polishing off a bowl of egg custard, he asked her to become his wife.

No flowery expressions. No words of love. Not a single touch of elegance. He spoke matter-of-factly, like he was talking about the weather, but with a presumptuous assurance that she'd accept.

Her stomach roiled, and she balled her napkin in her lap. If she answered no right now, this misery would end, but thoughts of her parents, Mark, and Lilly flashed through her mind. She squeezed her eyes shut.

Lord, help me do what I have to do.

With granite resolve, she steeled herself with a deep breath and whispered the words that would seal her fate. "Yes, Roger, I'll marry you."

❦

"I don't think I've seen you looking this bad since you had to haul me out of Stone's ditch." Harry handed Trip a handful of copper nails. "It's been three days since you lost the regatta, and you haven't said boo since the ball. If I had to venture a guess, which apparently I do, I'd say you and Marguerite had a falling out."

Pocketing most of the nails, Trip slipped a few between his teeth. Of all the days he should have taken off, today would have been it. When Harry sensed a newsworthy occurrence, he was like a dog with its teeth sunk into a ham bone. Trip braced the cedar plank with his knee and bent it around the new boat's skeletal frame. Striking the nail full force, Trip hammered it in place in one swing.

"Impressive. Maybe we should get you angry more often. We'd get a lot more done."

Trip glared at his friend, then removed another nail from between his teeth and pounded it in the same way.

Lifting a board from the corner pile, Harry brought it over to where the two of them worked. "Okay, if you aren't going to tell me, I'll be forced to guess." Harry passed the board to Trip.

Trip aligned it with the last board and used a pencil to mark the places that needed to be shaved to make it fit perfectly. Moving to the workbench, he began to chisel the marked area.

How could Marguerite do this?

His anger surged and he gouged the wood. He tossed the worthless piece of lumber in the corner. Worthless. Like her. "Get me another one."

Harry chuckled and retrieved one. "Here you go—seeing as you asked so nicely. Okay, I know you're mad as a hornet, so I'm guessing she probably lied to you again."

"I don't want to talk about it," Trip growled.

Relax. It's not Harry's fault. He remeasured the plank. Why didn't the physical exertion quell the fury he felt, as it usually did? How could he explain what he was feeling even to his best friend? *Well, Harry, she said she loved me, but she didn't mean it any more that my own mother did.* It sounded childish and much too simplified for the situation.

The more he thought about it, the more enraged he became with her, her father, and the whole mess. He'd been a fool to let himself get involved with the whole lot of them. After the boating accident, he should have listened to that inner voice that said he should have nothing to do with her.

He took a deep, steadying breath. He needed to give Harry something or he'd keep on for days. "She just didn't turn out to be who I thought she was."

Harry took the chiseled board, placed the new board against the hull, and nailed his end in place. "You know, Trip, someday you're going to have to realize that we're all just human." He stood and scratched his cheek. "If we're lucky, God blesses us with a few folks who are willing to look beyond the flaws and see the person we try so hard to hide. And if we're blessed, we find someone who'll love us anyway."

Before Trip could argue, Harry walked away. Scooping up his canteen, Trip downed a good half, tasting the slightly acrid influence of the metal. He screwed the lid back in place. Did Harry think Trip's expectations of Marguerite ruined everything? He wanted to shout, "She chose to marry another man!"

Trip threw the half-filled canteen toward the workbench. It hit the edge and clattered to the floor. Everyone in the shop turned to stare.

"What are you looking at?" He glowered at all of them. "It's over, and I don't want to hear another word."

Chest constricting, he strode through the workshop's back doors. He kicked an empty pail on the dock, and it clattered across the boards before splashing into the lake. He climbed aboard the *Endeavor*. With a sigh, he sank down on one of the seats and held his head in his hands. He was done with her. Finished.

I survived without my mother, and I'll do just fine without Marguerite Westing.

Besides, by now she belonged to another man.

⌗

Riding in the open-air streetcar back into the city, Marguerite bit her lip to keep the tears from escaping. The streetcar neared her stop, and she and her father stood. He cupped her elbow and lifted her overstuffed carpetbag, which held her unmentionables, two shirtwaists, a skirt, and Trip's jacket she had yet to return.

"A couple of days with your sister will do you wonders, Maggie," he said as they stepped onto the cobblestone street.

And so would a one-way ticket to the West Indies, but that would take money we don't have anymore. Right, Daddy? Her heart squeezed and a tear fell from her eye. The past few days she'd lived in a fog. Her mother had been thrilled by the engagement and insisted on telling everyone, and each time she did, Marguerite's hopes that something would save her died a little more.

Maybe a few days away from the lake would help—not seeing the boats, not seeing her father, and definitely not seeing Roger.

Or Trip. She missed him more than she thought possible. If she went to him, maybe . . .

265

But he must hate her now.

She let her father lead her up the familiar streets toward her sister's home. He huffed as they made their way along Broadway and then up the hill on Willow.

He stopped halfway up on Mary's porch steps and kissed her cheek. "I'll say my goodbyes here."

"Aren't you coming in for a moment? Mary will want to see you."

"Not today." He wiped his sweaty brow with a handkerchief. "Enjoy your time, but remember, Marguerite, you don't need to tell her everything."

She nodded. Earlier he'd made it clear that her sister knew nothing of the events at the lake, and he expected her to keep it that way.

"Yes, Father, I know all about keeping secrets."

She watched him leave before she knocked on the door.

Mary opened it and gathered her into her arms. "I'm so glad you've come." She linked Marguerite's arm and led her inside. "Nellie can't wait to see you. I've missed you so much this summer."

Marguerite set down her carpetbag. "Thank you for letting me come visit on such short notice. I hope it isn't an imposition to you."

"Nonsense." Mary held her at arm's length. "Let me look at you. I can't believe my little sister is an engaged woman. The summer sun has lightened your hair." She paused and her brows drew together. "And apparently it's stolen the shine from your eyes. Oh dear, this is worse than I thought."

As tempted as she was to lie and say nothing, Marguerite couldn't do that anymore. "Can we talk about it later?"

Her sister seemed to study her for a second, as if deciding whether she wanted to press the point. "Later then. For now, let's get you settled and then have lemonade on the veranda."

Marguerite glanced around in search of her four-year-old niece. "Where's Nellie?"

"Napping. She'll be awake in an hour or so. Actually, why don't you go lie down too? You look like you could use a little extra rest."

A yawn escaped and Marguerite smiled. "I think you're right."

"Older sisters generally are." She motioned toward the winding staircase. "We set up the pink toile room for you. It has the nicest breeze at night. Go on up and make yourself at home."

"Thank you." Marguerite climbed the stairs, found the room, and set down her carpetbag.

Days of overtaxed emotions had left her drained, and it didn't take long for sleep to claim her in the soft feather bed. She awoke with a start to a dim room and a gnawing stomach. She checked her watch and was surprised to see it read 7:00. Why hadn't Mary wakened her?

After a quick check of her hair, Marguerite hurried down the stairs and made her way through Mary's well-furnished parlor. She followed the sounds of her niece's giggles to the veranda.

As soon as she spotted her aunt, Nellie scampered away from the ever-patient black Labrador, Hero.

Marguerite squatted and gathered the toddler in her arms. "How's my princess?"

Nellie giggled. "Auntie Margweet, you wanna play hide-and-seek?"

"Nellie, let Aunt Marguerite have her supper," Mary said.

"Why don't you go inside and ask Miss Beulah to bring out your aunt's plate?"

With a skip in her step, Nellie hurried inside.

"You should have woken me."

"I didn't for selfish reasons. I want you to be rested so we can sit up all night and talk."

Tall, slender Beulah returned with Marguerite's niece in tow. She carried a heaping plate of food in one hand and a pitcher of lemonade in the other. Beside her, Nellie precariously carried two tumblers. Beulah set the plate in front of Marguerite, then filled the two glasses. Marguerite thanked her and told her the food smelled delicious. The aging cook left with a smile on her wrinkled face.

"It's so hot this evening it's like living in an oven." Mary fanned her face and sipped the lemonade. "I know it's better at the lake. I tried to convince Thomas to set up a tent for at least one week, but he's afraid to have Nellie so close to the water. I suppose he has a point."

Marguerite immediately thought of her own experiences, and Trip hauling her out. "It can be a dangerous place."

"I wanna play." Nellie tugged on Marguerite's skirt.

Marguerite scooped her up and blew raspberries on her tummy. When her niece's giggles subsided, she righted her. "Why don't you go get your doll and we'll play hospital? I'll show you how to be a nurse and take care of your sick patient."

Nellie scampered inside and returned a few minutes later carrying her German-made bisque baby doll and two bandage rolls.

"Where did you get the bandages?" Mary cupped her daughter's chin.

"Miss Boolah gave them to me to play with."

"Miss Beulah is very kind." Marguerite smoothed the doll's dark, spiraling curls. "Why don't you put your patient to bed in that wicker chair? Would you like that?"

Blonde curls bobbed when Nellie nodded enthusiastically.

"And here's a blanket for your doll." She handed the girl a linen napkin from the table. "What's her name?"

"Patience. Mommy named her. She said I needed patience."

Marguerite raised an eyebrow at Mary. "Patience?"

"What can I say?" Mary refilled her lemonade glass from the flowered pitcher. "She's definitely your niece."

With her doll tucked beneath her arm, Nellie moved to the other chair. She crooned singsong lullabies as she rocked her baby. Then she swathed the doll's head in bandages until the poor thing looked more like a mummy than a plaything.

Marguerite sipped the tart beverage and sighed. When had her problems stopped being about playing house and started being about building one with a man she couldn't stand?

Holding up the pitcher, Mary waited until Marguerite set down her glass to refill it. "Marguerite, I love when you visit—but why are you here?" She covered her mouth with her hand and giggled. "That sounded bad, didn't it? What I meant to say was, I'm thrilled you're visiting, but I can see something is troubling you and I'd like to help. You just got engaged, but you are far from ecstatic."

"Look, Mama, a black squirrel." Nellie dropped her doll on the chair and tore through the yard after the little creature.

The two ladies paused to watch her race to the oak only to lose her prey up the tree.

"Marguerite, what can I do to ease your burden? Is it Mother? Is she pressuring you into this marriage?"

"No, Mother isn't pressuring me."

"You mean to tell me that you agreed to marry Roger Gordon of your own volition?"

"Yes."

"I don't understand. You've never even liked him. I know. You've told me that at least a hundred times."

"I can't explain it."

"You mean you won't."

"Either way the answer is the same."

Mary took a deep breath. "You're serious?"

Marguerite nodded, the tightness in her throat keeping her from saying more.

A frown tipped Mary's lips, and for a minute Marguerite feared her sister might force the matter. Finally Mary released an exasperated sigh. "All right then, I'll let it go for now."

"Thank you."

"Don't get too excited. I have something else to ask you about. Have you noticed how stressed Father appears?"

"Yes."

"I would have thought summering at Manawa would have helped, but when I saw him the other day for lunch, he didn't seem himself at all." Mary set her glass down and leaned forward in her chair. "What have you heard? Is business going poorly for him?"

"I wouldn't know."

"Marguerite Westing, if I didn't know you better, I'd say you were being deliberately evasive."

"Maybe." She forked the last bite of her pork chop. "Anything else bothering you?"

"Changing subjects? You are good." Mary checked Nellie's location with a quick glance and then leaned close. "As a matter of fact, I have a secret, and you must promise not to breathe it to a soul."

Secrets. The word soured Marguerite's stomach. Secrets surrounded her. She pinched the bridge of her nose. "What is it?"

"I'm expecting." A smile set Mary's face aglow. "Nellie is going to have a little brother or sister by Valentine's Day."

Marguerite squealed and squeezed her sister's hand. "That's wonderful. How have you been feeling?"

Mary wrinkled her nose. "In the mornings I've felt horrible. Thomas was so worried about me yesterday morning that before his business trip he almost sent for the doctor. But he calmed down when I told him the peaches we had for supper didn't agree with me."

"Why didn't you tell him the truth? That it was the baby?"

The smile slid from her face. "I haven't told him about being in the family way."

"Why not?"

"He wanted only one child. Since it's been four years, I thought he'd gotten his wish."

"So you aren't going to tell him? Won't the truth be obvious soon?"

"Probably." Mary pressed a hand to her stomach. "But I'm hoping I'll find the right words before then. And praying that God will help him come to terms with it." She paled. "I'm afraid dinner isn't settling well. Would you mind terribly tucking Nellie in for me?"

"Not at all." As if on cue, Nellie ran up beside them. Marguerite pulled the girl onto her lap. "Would that be okay with you, Nellie-pooh?"

"Will you read me a story?"

"Better than that," her mother answered. "Marguerite will

tell you all about the stars." She kissed the top of her daughter's head and turned to leave. She stopped in the doorway. "And Marguerite, you're right. When you love someone, they deserve to know the truth. I'll tell Thomas tomorrow when he gets back from his trip."

❦

Two hours, three books, and a set of paper dolls later, Marguerite slipped Nellie's nightgown over her head.

"Did you like the stars?"

Nellie nodded. "And the story of your Camp An . . . an . . ."

"Andromeda." Instantly Marguerite was transported to the night she'd told Trip about their camp's name. He'd rightly guessed that she felt like the chained maiden about to be devoured by a monster. Except she'd thought it was her mother who'd chained her, not her father.

Marguerite blinked back the tears that flooded her eyes, drew back the covers, and watched her niece slide beneath them.

"Aunt Margweet?"

"Yes, sweetie?"

"Why do you look so sad?"

"My heart is broken."

"I have a bandage. I can fix it."

Marguerite fingered a curl. "I wish you could, little one. I wish you could."

22

Adjusting her flower-bedecked straw hat, Marguerite took a deep breath and braced herself before entering the Yacht Club. After returning from the stay at her sister's, she'd spotted a notice posted at the pavilion that said volunteers were needed to assist in planning the Water Carnival. Right away she knew she'd found the answer to her prayers. She simply had to escape her mother's engagement party preparations. She didn't want the party, and she certainly didn't want the fiancé who came with it. What she needed right now was something to take her mind off the whole nightmare.

Mary had tried to, and her joyous news helped. An added blessing had come when Mary told Thomas about the baby and he'd been elated. Mary explained that he'd kept telling her how happy he was with only one child because he didn't want her to feel bad about not conceiving for so many years.

Maybe the truth wasn't always painful.

Climbing the steps to the front door of the Yacht Club, Marguerite entered, and a pinch-faced man motioned her to the back. There she found the office door marked "Water Carnival." She knocked and received a gruff "Come in." She nudged the door open and stepped inside. A man with salt-and-pepper hair shooting from beneath a wide-brimmed straw hat bent over an oak desk. He muttered, "Just a minute."

"Captain Andrews?"

His head lifted. "Well, if it isn't the girl who broke my son's heart."

"He told you that?"

"He didn't have to."

Marguerite looked at the floor. "It's complicated."

"And it's none of my business." He motioned for her to have a seat. "So, you want to volunteer to help an old man organize the Water Carnival?" He rubbed his whiskered chin. "Well, seeing as how I don't have anyone else beating down the door, I suppose you'll do. You got any ideas?"

"Can you tell me about the event first, sir?"

A frown cratered the wrinkles in his weathered face. "Because I'm president of the Yacht Club, the task of putting this whole shebang together falls on my shoulders. With Trip getting second in the regatta, we got a whole slew of new boat orders, so I'll tell you right now that I won't have time to hold your hand."

"I understand, sir."

"Good. You'll need to organize a committee of other women to help. The Water Carnival is to be the climax of the summer for all the visiting patrons. It needs to be spectacular."

"And who is footing the bill, sir?"

The corners of his mouth lifted. "Practical. I like it. I have a commitment of funds from Colonel Reed, the Manhattan Beach Company, and the Electric Motor Company to purchase decorations and such."

"And would the 'such' possibly contain fireworks?"

"You have an idea, don't you?"

"Sir, I always have ideas." *Except one to get me out of marrying Mr. Boring.* "I attended the World's Fair in Chicago two years ago. I think we could almost duplicate the Water Carnival I saw at the Jackson Park Lagoon right here at Lake Manawa. May I tell you about it and see what you think?"

To her surprise, Captain Andrews listened intently while she described the magnificent event she'd witnessed. More than once she caught him smiling, revealing dimples similar to Trip's. But his eyes, a sea-foam green, spoke a shocking difference.

Yet it was the baritone timbre of his voice that shook her most. When Captain Andrews wasn't grousing or growling at someone, he sounded exactly like his son.

A lump the size of the boat shop formed in her throat as he spoke. Spending time with Captain Andrews made her feel closer to Trip. He was an extension of the man she loved, and despite his gruff exterior, she could sense the heart of a good man.

Inhaling deeply, he leaned back in his chair. "This would be a massive undertaking."

"I know, but—"

He held up his hand to silence her. "I'm not against big jobs. I like hard work and I like the idea. Tell you what. You get me a committee together by tomorrow afternoon, and we'll move ahead with this."

"How large a committee?"

"Say, twenty women. I know if you get the wives involved, the husbands will follow."

Twenty? She didn't know twenty women at Lake Manawa. Maybe she could find ten to help, but twenty?

He rose from his desk and pushed back his chair dismissively. "They can meet in the Yacht Club's parlor. If it's not large enough, get a room at the pavilion. Tell them I sent you."

She stood. "Yes, sir. I won't let you down."

"See to it that you don't."

On the way back to camp, Marguerite pondered how to find twenty women willing to join the Water Carnival committee. She'd start contacting potential committee members after lunch.

When she arrived at Camp Andromeda, the scent of fried ham wafting from the camp's gasoline stove told her lunch would soon be forthcoming. She headed to the table and found her mother surrounded by papers.

The engagement party. How could she forget? If she snuck away before her mother spotted her . . .

"Marguerite. Good. You're home." Camille shifted a pile of paper to make room for her daughter. "I wanted to go over the guest list with you."

"Mother, can we eat? Wait. Did you say guest list?" Marguerite snatched the paper from her mother's hand. Scanning the sheet, she saw at least fifty names in her mother's familiar elaborate script. "Are all these people vacationing here this summer?"

"Of course, darling. Some are staying and some are commuting. We can't possibly invite everyone at the lake, but we can't leave out anyone important either." She held up a second sheet of paper. "See, these are the questionables."

"Can I see that too?"

"Yes, dear. I'm so happy to see that you're taking an interest in this." Her mother handed the paper to her. "I knew you'd come around. As you can see, I think I've included everyone."

Marguerite read the list of names, remembering her mother

once telling her that the secret to getting socialites to participate in something was recruiting someone at the top of the social ladder first. Who could be better to recruit than her own future mother-in-law? This list contained an entire committee's worth and then some.

"Can I borrow this for a while?"

"Oh, I understand. You want to go over it with Roger. Yes, that's fine."

Marguerite stood up. "Thank you, Mother. I'll bring this back."

"But what about lunch?"

"I'm not hungry."

"But you haven't eaten well since your engagement."

Lilly suddenly appeared and thrust a bun with a piece of ham tucked inside it into Marguerite's hand. "Your mama's right. You need to eat. That ought to tide you over."

She smiled at her friend and kissed her mother on the cheek. "I'll see you both at dinner."

⚜

Setting out the cookies and the punch Alice had made for her, Marguerite readied the large, open parlor of the Yacht Club for her committee guests. Yesterday it had taken her all afternoon to get the first five women to commit, but after she had their word, including that of Roger's mother, the remaining slots filled quickly. Even her own mother offered to help, but Marguerite wasn't sure if that was a good thing or not.

After setting up a few extra wooden folding chairs, Marguerite tugged her businesslike taupe vest into place, then stepped back to examine her handiwork. A gavel lay on the table, tablets beside it. Chairs, punch, cookies—check.

The door opened, and she drew in a steadying breath. Ready or not, her guests were here.

Welcoming each lady, she encouraged them to find a seat. When she was sure most had arrived, she tapped the gavel on the table. "Ladies, may I welcome you to the organizational meeting for the Lake Manawa Water Carnival Ladies Auxiliary."

Following a vote of officers, of which she became president, the meeting proceeded with Marguerite filling them in on her idea. She explained that the program would be a reenactment of a naval battle, replete with an abundance of fireworks.

Excited chatter filled the room. She tapped her gavel again. "Ladies, I'm glad to hear you like the proposal. Now, how shall we encourage the boat owners to embellish the boats the way we need them to?"

Emily Graham raised her hand. "Prizes would work. We could offer one for the best-decorated boat."

"Excellent idea. And we'll need men to construct the two forts."

Mrs. Whitson lifted her fan. "I believe my husband would enjoy doing that. He doesn't own a boat, but he'd love the reenactment of a battle and I'm sure he'd want to do his part."

"Perfect. Are there others who would like to help him?"

Within minutes, Marguerite had divided the committee into four groups that would be needed for the carnival: decorations, refreshments, fort construction, and fireworks.

She cleared her throat, but the ladies kept chatting. "Ladies. Ladies!" They quieted. "We'll also still need to recruit boat participants."

"I think I can help with that," Captain Andrews announced

as he entered the room. "The Yacht Club is one of the sponsors, after all. How many boats would you need?"

"I believe there were about forty boats in the Chicago exhibition."

Captain Andrews rubbed his right arm. "That shouldn't be much of a problem." He tugged at his collar.

"Thank you, sir."

The captain's face paled and scrunched in pain.

Concern shook Marguerite. She moved to his side. "Sir, are you all right? Here, sit down."

He didn't argue, which shot even more shards of fear through her. His breath came in short gasps. "Heart."

Marguerite turned to the anxious women around her. "Emily, get the doctor. Laura, go next door and get his son." She undid the buttons on his shirt collar. "Captain, try to relax. Breathe. Nice and slow."

Minutes later Trip and Harry burst through the door. Trip paused when he saw her kneeling beside his father.

"It's his heart. I sent for the doctor." She gently stroked the captain's arm. "He needs to be in bed."

"There's a stretcher in the back. Harry—"

Trip's curly-haired friend was already halfway down the hall.

Standing over her squatting frame, Trip crossed his arms over his chest. "How did this happen? Did you upset him?"

"No! We were just finishing up our meeting."

"What meeting? He's supposed to be resting."

"Don't," Captain Andrews gasped. "Not . . . her . . . fault."

Harry sped in with the stretcher tucked beneath his arm. Marguerite cleared the ladies out while Trip and Harry loaded the captain onto it. On instinct she followed them into the boat shop, but stopped inside at the foot of the stairs that led to the second-floor apartment. She didn't belong there, and she definitely wasn't wanted.

Trip glanced at her for a brief second before disappearing down the hallway, his face a hurricane of emotions. He'd lost his mother. He'd lost her. What would he do now if he lost his father?

Sinking to a stool, Marguerite buried her face in her hands and begged God to spare the captain's life. Guilt heaped on her like too many quilts in the summer heat. Why did it feel like this was her fault?

She waited and prayed and prayed some more. Harry had promised to come fill her in, and that had been nearly half an hour ago.

Finally she heard a noise and lifted her head. She climbed to her feet as soon as she heard heavy footfalls on the stairs. Instead of Harry, Trip appeared, shoulders sagging, worry etched on his face.

"How is he?"

"The doctor says it's another heart attack and his chances are less than fifty percent." Trip dropped onto the last step and rubbed his forehead. Voice cold, he asked, "Why are you still here?"

She dabbed at her eyes, aching to wrap Trip in her arms and ease his burden.

"I wanted . . . I needed to know how your father was."

"Now you know."

"Trip, I'm so sorry. One minute he was fine, and the next the pain started. I didn't mean to upset him."

"But you just have that effect on people, don't you?" He shook his head and his lips narrowed to a tight line.

"This is not about you or your need to assuage your guilt, Marguerite."

Harry called down the staircase and told him that his father wanted to talk to him. Trip stood. "Go back to your fiancé. We'll be just fine without you."

Marching from the boat shop, Marguerite allowed the door to slam behind her. Fury propelled her down the walk. How dare he? Fine without her? Not about her? Of course it wasn't. None of this was about her. She didn't have a choice in this matter. Hadn't Trip come to an understanding of that by now?

She smirked. No, the only thing high and mighty, perfect Trip Andrews knew was that the rest of the world failed to meet his expectations. Everyone everywhere let him down.

A thread of guilt pulled at her heart, but she refused to unravel it. Even if Trip's father was seriously ill, she didn't deserve that kind of treatment. If this was how Trip wanted it, she didn't care if she ever saw him again.

∽⌽∾

Leaning against the door frame, Trip watched Harry leave and then paused before entering the room. *Lord, don't take him. He may be a pain sometimes, but he's my pain.*

He entered and sat down beside his father.

"He's been asking for you." The doctor squeezed Trip's shoulder. "Don't tire him. He needs all the rest he can get. Each hour he survives, he gets stronger and his chances improve."

Trip nodded, taking his father's hand in his own. "Thanks, Doc."

After the doctor quietly closed the door, Deuce opened his eyes. "Where is she?"

"Who? Marguerite?"

He nodded.

"I sent her home."

"She's good for you."

"She's a liar, just like Mom." He brushed a wisp of wiry white hair off his father's forehead.

Deuce coughed weakly. "No, son."

"You don't know what she did."

"Son, listen. I'm the liar."

He held a cup of water to his father's lips. "Shhh, it's okay." The poor man didn't even realize what he was saying. "Whatever you have to say can wait till later. Just take it easy."

"Don't hush me," Deuce said forcefully, trying to sit up. "You need to hear this. You need to know the truth. In case . . ."

Trip pressed him back against the pillow. What was his father rambling about? Should he try to keep him quiet when trying to silence his father only seemed to stress him more?

Finally Trip nodded. "Okay, okay, I'm listening."

"I lied to you about your mother. She didn't leave us . . . She died."

Trip's brows drew together. "What? No, I was five, and she left."

"You were five and scared to death of the water." He coughed again.

Trip leaned closer to hear his father's hoarse whisper.

"Just when you were getting over your fears, she drowned. You saw it, you just don't remember." His father's eyes drifted shut, but his chest continued to rise and fall.

Mouth dry, Trip tried to speak but no words came out. All this time he'd thought his mother had deserted him. Left him. He'd loved her so much. He remembered telling her so all the time, bringing her bouquets of dandelions, kissing her petal-soft cheek, wrapping his arms around her neck. She smelled of ginger cookies, spice, and vanilla.

Did he remember the incident? He'd had nightmares his whole life of a woman thrashing in the water and a man trying to save her, but he'd never considered it could be a memory. Is that why Marguerite's lie about being able to swim had made him so furious? His own mother had drowned.

"Why?" he croaked. "Dad, why didn't you tell me the truth?"

Deuce lifted heavy-laden lids. "You gotta understand. I couldn't have a boy afraid of the water. The water was all I knew. All I had left. I had to build boats for you and me."

"So you told me she left us."

"Thought it would hurt less." His breath came in short gasps.

"That's enough talk for now, Dad. We can discuss this later."

Deuce's eyes widened, a fierceness in them that Trip hadn't seen before. "You have to know. She didn't choose to leave you."

But Marguerite had.

His father squeezed his hand. "You need to take over the Water Carnival for me—and you'll have to work with Marguerite."

"Dad . . ."

"Promise me." He fought to keep his eyes open. "Promise—"

"I promise."

"Good."

23

With papers splayed across one of the desks in the Yacht Club's office, Marguerite tapped the tip of her pencil against her mouth. She had arrived at the Yacht Club early, figuring the best way she knew to help Captain Andrews recover was to organize the Water Carnival. Her thoughts kept drifting to Trip's face awash with anguish. But from the bitterness in his voice, he'd made it obvious she was the last person he wanted comfort from.

Sighing, she picked up the list she'd made at the meeting yesterday: decorations, forts, fireworks, and food. So many details to oversee. Recruiting the boat skippers, advertising the event, and securing the necessary supplies to transform the boats into battleships. She pinched the bridge of her nose. What had she gotten herself into?

Footsteps in the hall alerted her to someone's approach. Wanting to at least appear like she had a handle on the situation, she quickly set her pencil to her tablet. Someone entered the room, but she kept writing. "I'll be with you in a minute."

"You'll be with me now."

Roger. Her heart sank to the pit of her stomach with a sick thud. She looked up and forced a smile. "What are you doing here?"

"Shouldn't that be my question to you?" He pushed up his spectacles. "You have a wedding to plan. You don't have time to waste putting on water shows."

"Water Carnival, and I do have the time." *Because I'm going to make this engagement last forever.* "Besides, Mother is working on the wedding plans."

"I don't like this." Roger tapped the tablet in front of her with his index finger. His bushy mustache twitched over his pouty lips. "You shouldn't be working in an office like some common clerk. You should be parading the boardwalk on my arm, where everyone can see the beautiful catch I've made."

Does he think I'm a fish? A giggle tickled her throat, and she swallowed to keep it from erupting. *If I was, I guess I'd be a largemouth bass.*

"I'm sorry, I simply can't stop now. This is much too important, and Captain Andrews has taken ill. Did you know your mother is on the planning committee? What would she think of me if I should quit?"

"My mother?" His chest puffed at the mention, and he tucked his hand in the gap between the shiny buttons on his vest. "She's helping?"

Marguerite nodded. "And I think she's very excited about the whole event. She has wonderful ideas."

"I suppose, then, I will just have to make do with seeing you for lunch and dinner."

Both? Last night, after the captain's heart attack, she'd endured a mind-numbing evening discussing his business trip. How could she stand two dreary meals a day?

Lord, if I have to marry Roger, can You please give his character a boost? I wonder if any doctors make a personality tonic.

285

"Roger." Marguerite clasped her hands in front of her, hoping to show a patience she didn't feel. "I will be meeting with the various women on the committees during lunch most days. Perhaps we should simply count on having dinner together."

"Ladies? Are you certain that's who you'll be meeting?"

"Who else would there be?"

"Why don't you tell me?"

She shifted a stack of papers on her desk. "I need to get to work. If there's nothing else, perhaps you should leave."

He sat down across from her in a straight-backed chair. "I'm in no hurry. Why don't you let me help?"

"Roger! Please, just go. You're distracting me."

Snickering, he stood up. "As I told you before, you do seem prone to being easily distracted."

Something in his tone, bathed in a fake lightness, made her skin crawl. How could someone seem so bland one minute and so threatening the next?

After he left, she returned to her notes. But Roger's visit had unnerved her, and she found it difficult to focus. What had he meant by his last statement?

She put the final star on her doodle of the constellation Orion.

"Working hard?"

She jumped. "Trip?"

"Miss Westing." Voice cold, he turned the paper so he could see her work. "Which one is this?"

"Orion."

His finger traced an imaginary line between the stars. "The most handsome of the earthborn and killed by the goddess of love."

"Actually, I believe it was Artemis who killed him—the goddess of the hunt."

"Oh, how could I have forgotten?"

Was this stab-Marguerite-to-death-slowly day? She sighed. "What can I do for you, Trip? I have work to do."

"Correction. We have work to do." He pulled his chair up to the desk. "I'm taking over for my dad."

"I . . . I can handle this. You need to tend to his health."

"You'd deny his dying request?"

"Trip, I'm so sorry. I didn't realize he—"

Trip laughed. "No, he's alive. In fact, Doc says he's much better today, but he did make me promise to take his place working on this brouhaha."

"It's the Water Carnival, and if that's his wish, I'll gather my things." She stood up and collected her papers. "I'm sure you don't want me around."

"I don't, but he does. He says you're part of the deal. I won't say I'm happy about it, but I'll do it for him. The last thing I want to do right now is upset him. This is business, not personal. Can we be civil to one another for a few weeks?"

She nodded.

"Good. Sit back down and show me what needs to be done."

Summer at Lake Manawa was always balmy, even with the breeze off the water, but in the last few days, Trip had found that being in the same room with Marguerite raised the humid summer temperatures to an unbearable degree. Everywhere he turned in the small office, she was there. Did she have any idea what the brush of her shoulder or accidental touch of their hands did to him? Didn't she feel the undercurrent that still surged between them?

And if her physical presence wasn't enough, wherever she

moved, she left a rose-scented path in her wake. His irritation grew each time his nerves tingled, and the fact that his empty stomach now growled at the late afternoon hour didn't help.

He rubbed the crick in the back of his neck. "Are we about done?"

Marguerite waved a paper fan in front of her face. "Almost, but I still have a few things on my list."

"Like?"

She held up a sheet of paper. "How did the work on the floating fort go yesterday?"

"Well, it sure isn't floating yet."

"That isn't what I asked and you know it."

He leaned back in his chair and chuckled. "It's as hot as a piece of coal in a tinder box in here. Why don't we go for a walk and you can take a look for yourself?"

"I'd better not."

The light extinguished from her eyes, and he felt a twinge of concern. "Why?"

"It's just best if Roger doesn't see us together."

An uneasy feeling took root that Trip couldn't shake. His memory shot back to the dance when Roger Gordon had appeared less than gentlemanly. "He's not giving you any trouble, is he?"

"Nothing I can't handle." Forcing a smile, she stood from the desk and began to gather her things. "Did you look at the time? If I don't hurry, I'll be late for my own birthday dinner."

"It's your birthday?"

She covered her lips with her hand. "I didn't mean to let that slip."

"Is Roger taking you to Louie's?"

"No, I don't think he even knows it's a special day."

"Your fiancé doesn't know your birthday? Why not?"

She shrugged. "He never asked."

If he hadn't already loathed the man, he did now. What kind of suitor didn't find out important things like that?

Trip studied Marguerite for a minute. Beneath the silk roses adorning her straw hat, a vulnerable, pale-faced woman stared back at him. Good. She should be miserable.

His heart pinched. He couldn't think about her that way no matter how hard he tried. He rose to his feet and offered her a lopsided grin. "We could go get some ice cream in honor of the special occasion. I know how much you like it."

The corners of her mouth lifted slightly, and for a moment he saw a familiar twinkle in her cornflower blue eyes. Then she blinked and it was gone. She tucked her lower lip between her teeth. "Thank you, Trip. Truly. But I'd better go."

Then, before he could stop himself, he brushed her creamy cheek with a kiss. "Happy birthday, Marguerite."

⁕

Touching her cheek with her hand, Marguerite fought the powerful sadness building inside. With Camp Andromeda only a few yards away, she prayed she could make it to her tent before any tears fell from her misty eyes. Coming in the back way, she was sure to avoid her mother's questions about her tardiness. Today of all days she should be allowed to be a tad sneaky.

Why did it have to be so hard? She was trying to do the right thing, and she was doing this for her family. Why had God put Trip back in her life to face every day? A tear escaped and she batted it away. *Happy birthday to me.*

She shook her head. She mustn't dwell on the emptiness

in her heart. Maybe if she thought of something besides how right Trip's kiss had felt, she could silence the deafening sadness. But what?

Almond cake. Alice always made it for her birthday, and it was her favorite as well as her father's. Another thing the two of them shared.

Presents? Since her father had gambled the family's money away, she didn't expect any of those.

A special evening? Not if Roger was involved.

She neared her parents' tent and heard voices coming from within. Immediately she recognized Roger's deep intonation.

"I don't like her working on that Water Carnival, and I want to make something clear to you, Edward." Roger's voice held a hint of a threat. "If Marguerite changes her mind about our engagement, then the business deal is off. It's your responsibility to see that this marriage occurs."

Now was her father's chance. He could end this whole charade. He could set her free.

Edward cleared his throat. "She won't change her mind. I'll make sure of that."

Stomach wadding into a ball, Marguerite fought the lump in her throat. *I won't scream. I won't cry.*

She had to escape. Scurrying back down the path, she ran in the direction of the gambling den—the place that had ruined everything, poisoned her father, corrupted his heart, and made him a slave to cards. He'd sell anything for the money now. Even her.

Sinking onto a log, she shook with sobs. All those times he'd been her hero . . . When awful Laura Thompson had locked her in the icehouse, he'd come to the rescue. After her mother had told her that science was for men, her father gave her books about the stars and told her she should dream big. He'd even saved Lilly's position when her mother wanted to send her away.

Memories flooded her thoughts, one after another. *Things aren't always what they seem to be*. Roger's words haunted her. Had Roger known the truth about her father all along?

"Miss Marguerite." Alice lowered her ample body onto the log beside her. "I thought I saw you running off." She draped a heavy arm around Marguerite's shaking shoulders, pulled her against her, and held her while she sobbed.

After a minute, Marguerite raised her head, and Alice dried her tears with the hem of her apron.

"D-d-did you hear Daddy and Roger?"

"Hard not to."

"Daddy had his chance. All he had to do was tell Roger no. He could have saved me."

Alice passed her a hanky from the pocket of her apron. "He isn't your savior, child."

"Well, it doesn't look like my heavenly Father is any more reliable in getting me out of this than my earthly father has been." She sniffled and blew into the handkerchief.

Alice sighed. "Miss Marguerite, I love you like my own, but you are one stubborn girl. You know, you could've gotten yourself out of this a long time ago. You just didn't want to tell Mr. Gordon the truth."

"So you think this is my fault because I didn't turn Roger down in the beginning?" She felt another stab of betrayal, and she couldn't keep the edge from creeping into her tone. "I didn't ask to be forced to marry Roger Gordon to save our family."

"Now, don't get yourself in a dither. Hear me out. When you said yes to Mr. Gordon's proposal, it was because you felt trapped. You were doing what you thought you had to do. But deep down, you didn't intend to go through with it. In a way, I think you've been countin' on your daddy coming to your rescue all along." The wind blew and a shadow drifted across Alice's face.

"No, I haven't," Marguerite snapped. Alice didn't flinch. After a few moments, Marguerite released a long breath. "I don't know, maybe you're right. I just thought he'd find another way. I didn't think he'd sell me." A pain the size of a comet shot through her heart, and fresh tears moistened her lashes. "I thought he loved me more than he did his money."

Alice took her hand and squeezed it. "Child, I think he does. He just doesn't remember that right now. Satan's got a foothold."

"And I still have to go through with this . . . this marriage."

"No, you don't."

"I love my family, Alice. I can't see them penniless. And what would happen to you and Lilly?"

"God took care of us when I lost my Peter, and He brought us to your family. He'll do it again if need be." Alice laughed. "Besides, my Lilly says she could always work for you and Mr. Boring."

Marguerite moaned. "I'm trapped. Totally and completely hemmed in. What am I going to do?"

Standing, Alice shook out her skirt. "I don't know the answer, but I know Who does, and you do too. Why don't you go back to your tent and pray about it? Besides, it's your birthday, and Lilly's got a present for you."

"She made me a gift?"

"I didn't say that."

"She bought one?"

"No, didn't say that either."

"What is it?"

"You'll just have to go ask her."

Marguerite found Lilly inside their tent. After sharing with her friend what she'd heard, the two of them prayed for answers. When Marguerite could hold her tongue no longer, she mentioned what Alice had said about a gift.

Lilly laughed. "I reckon you're dying to know what it is, aren't you? My present is that I'm going to teach you to swim. I found us a nice, quiet place where we can practice in the afternoons."

"Oh, Lilly, how can I thank you?"

Lilly grinned, revealing her stunning smile. "By being a good student and doing what I tell you."

Marguerite hugged her friend. What would she do without dear, constant, devoted, and honest Lilly?

I'd be no better than my father if I let something happen to her. To any of them. Marrying Roger isn't about me.

It seemed God had given her an answer.

24

All the committee members and volunteers loved Marguerite. Over the next couple of weeks, Trip noticed how they responded to her, listened to her suggestions, respected her ideas, and followed her directions. Generously bestowing compliments on all of the volunteers, she fostered an esprit de corps among them.

Every carefree giggle, tender touch, or kind word had hammered his pain deeper. How had she broken down his walls and wormed her way back inside his heart?

The birthday kiss had been a foolish move on his part. Ever since then, the tension between them had been taut as a bowstring. He'd come today with the sole intention of making sure Marguerite knew even though he could be civil to her, he refused to give in to the feelings that kept drawing them together.

He pulled himself from his reverie when he heard John Nelson, a former schoolmate, speak to her.

"Miss Westing, how do you want me to decorate my *Windy Sue*?"

Trip scowled. Nelson stood much too close to Marguerite for his liking.

Marguerite pulled a sheet from the stack and smiled at

the boat owner. "Why, Mr. Nelson, I happened to just be thinking of you."

"I like the sound of that."

What was Nelson doing flirting with Marguerite? He knew she was an engaged woman.

Jealousy poked Trip solidly in the chest. Engaged, yes, and not to him. Still, Nelson didn't need to fawn over her like a lovesick dandy.

She laughed and handed Nelson the sheet of paper. "Think you can make your sweet *Windy Sue* look like this warship?"

"You planning to help me?"

"Sorry, Mr. Nelson. I have too much to do to decorate boats, but I'm sure I could get a few of the other girls to help. How about Emily Graham and Sally Voght? They've volunteered, and I think they'd make excellent assistants for someone such as yourself."

He grinned. "Sure. That'd be great."

Trip waited until Nelson left before he approached Marguerite. "What's on the agenda for the rest of our day?"

"I thought we could spend the afternoon working on the *Endeavor*'s decorations."

"My boat? But I just heard you tell John—"

A smile bloomed across her face. "You were eavesdropping on my conversation. Shame on you. Now, about your boat . . ."

"I wasn't sure I was going to enter her yet."

"Trip, you have to. You're in charge, and I planned to make yours the most spectacular ship in the armada. I even drew up plans. Look." She flipped through her stack of papers and handed him an elaborate drawing of the *Endeavor* decorated to look like an ironclad warship. "See the powder guns and smokestacks? There's even a howitzer on the bow."

"And how exactly are we going to change my thirty-two-foot sailboat into a warship?"

"Come on. I'll show you." She jumped up from the desk, grabbed her rubber bag and tablet, and headed for the door. She reached it before she realized he wasn't following. "Come on, Mr. Andrews. We don't have all day."

Too bad. Suddenly he wished they did.

To Trip's surprise, Marguerite had already arranged the supplies needed to decorate the *Endeavor* to be delivered to the boat shop. He scanned the roll of chicken wire, sacks of flour, and bolt of gauzy cheesecloth as she proclaimed the boat would make an excellent battleship.

"We need the flour first." She reached for a large bag and struggled to drag it.

He nudged her out of the way and hefted it onto his shoulder. "Where do you want this?"

"On the dock." She pulled an apron from her bag and slipped it over her head, then scooped up two tin buckets. He followed her out with the flour.

After dropping the flour sack onto the pier with a thud, he turned to see her precariously leaning over the edge of the dock, filling one of the buckets with water. One slip and he'd be pulling her out of the lake once again. Quickly he dropped beside her and took the bucket, brushing her hand in the process. She met his eyes. Clearly she'd felt it too. The tiny current that had passed between them.

He cleared his throat. "Okay. Before we go any further, you have to tell me what you're planning to do, because I highly doubt you're making bread with lake water, flour, and a stick."

"How about pancakes?" she teased. "I like mine with a lot of maple syrup."

"That doesn't surprise me. Fine, you get the first bite."

She giggled. "Actually, we're making papier-mâché."

Had he heard her right? "You aren't putting flour and water on my boat."

"Of course not." She yanked on the string sealing the burlap flour sack and it gave way. "At least not until it dries." She glanced at the water crock just inside the doorway. "Can you hand me that tin cup?"

"For what?"

"Making the paste." Dipping the cup into the flour, she began to fill the empty bucket.

"It would work faster if you had a milk pitcher."

She added some water to the flour, picked up a scrap piece of board, and stirred the mixture until it made a watery paste. She lifted the board and let it drizzle from the end. "Too thin."

Trip cleared his throat and shifted uneasily. "Now, about what you're doing with this paste . . ."

Alternately adding water and flour, she continued, "We make a frame for the ship out of the chicken wire, and then we cut the gauze into strips, dip it in this, and put it on the frame. It will take a few layers, but when it dries, we'll paint it and mount the frame on the *Endeavor*."

"It'll never work." He shook his head in disbelief.

She rolled her eyes at him. "They've been making Mardi Gras masks like this for years. Floats too. Even some of the floats at the Independence Day parade in town were made of papier-mâché. Remember the giant rooster?"

He nodded. Who could forget the cock mounted on the hayrack with a sign proudly advertising Red Rooster Coffee? "Then I'm guessing I get to make the frame."

"And Emily Graham didn't think you had a brain inside that handsome head of yours."

When she tilted her face and giggled, the sunlight kissed her honey-colored hair bound in a bun on top of her head. He ached to see it free, touch it, feel its silkiness slip between his fingers.

He took a step back. "Uh, I'll just go get started inside."

"The plan's in my satchel. I'll bring this in when it's ready."

"Marguerite, don't you dare try to lift that. I'll come get it." He flashed a smile. "Just try not to fall in the lake while I'm gone."

⁂

Today was a mistake and Marguerite knew it. But try as she might, she couldn't bring herself to feel guilty about relishing her time in Trip's company. He'd even started calling her Marguerite again instead of the formal-sounding Miss Westing. Surely it wouldn't hurt if they remained friends. Couldn't they at least be that?

As soon as Trip went back inside, she removed her celluloid cuffs, stuffed them in the pocket of her apron, and rolled up her sleeves. If she got paste on her clothes, she'd receive a lecture from Alice.

She finished mixing a second bucket of paste just as Trip appeared. Straightening, she pressed her hands to the small of her back, which ached from being hunched over. "You're finished already?"

"With one section, but I just didn't want you trying to haul those pails in." A dimpled grin erupted on his face. He stepped forward and brushed his callused fingertips across her cheek. "Flour."

"Oh."

Taking one pail in each of his large hands, he carried them

inside and deposited them near the chicken-wire frame he'd created. Like his boats, he'd created a piece of art.

"What do you think?"

"Trip, it's perfect."

He beamed. "It's chicken wire."

"It won't be for much longer." She crossed the workshop and brought the bolt of cloth over. "We need to cut this into two-foot lengths. Do you have a knife?"

Trip produced one from his pocket, and together they commenced making a pile of cheesecloth rags.

"Now for the fun part." Marguerite sank the first strip of cheesecloth into the paste, withdrew it, and ran her hand along its slippery sides to remove part of the glue. "Do you want to do the honors and put the first one on?"

Bending at the waist, he swept his arm in front of his body. "I believe it's customary for a woman to do the christening honors."

She grinned and draped the soggy piece over the chicken-wire stern. "I christen you the battleship . . ." She glanced at him to fill in the blank.

"*Marguerite.*"

"You want to name a battleship after me?"

He chuckled. "Seems appropriate."

She rolled her eyes. "I christen you the *USS Marguerite.* May she fight as well as I do."

"I should've expected that." A teasing glint sparked in his hazel eyes. "Do I get to help too?"

"Absolutely." She took a strip and lowered it into the mixture.

"Now what?"

"Just watch again. First you take your hand and run it down the strip to take some of the paste off. Like this." She demonstrated, and the slurry oozed between her fingers. She laid the cloth across the wire frame. "Then you have to smooth it out."

He ran his hands along the slippery surface beside hers. When their hands touched, he cleared his throat. "I think I've got it now."

She swallowed hard and pulled her hands away, willing her frantic heart to still. Her eyes darted to Trip. Only the pulse ticking beneath his eye gave notice that the encounter had jarred him.

We can do this. We can at least be friends.

Marguerite cautioned Trip that they shouldn't make the first layer too thick or it wouldn't dry. When they finished with the frame an hour later, Marguerite attempted to wipe the paste from her caked arms with a piece of wood. "Look at me. I'm a mess."

She glanced at Trip. With his face dotted and his well-defined arms coated, he resembled some sort of specter.

He wiped the worst of it off his hands with a rag. "This is useless. Let's go for a swim."

"Excuse me?"

"I saw you carrying your swim bag. Isn't your suit inside?"

"Yes, Lilly and I are going for a dip later, but—"

"Good, you can show me how well you're doing on learning to swim." He didn't let her protest. Instead he snagged her bag from the workbench and thrust it into her hand. "You can change upstairs in my room. I believe you know where it is."

"But Trip, what will people say if they see us?"

"We'll swim here—out back. No one is around this time of the day besides Dad and me. If it'll make you feel better, it's time for him to come down for some fresh air. He can come out and sit on the dock while we swim."

Marguerite hesitated. That should be fine. No one would question Captain Deuce Andrews as a chaperone, and with his father watching, Trip would do nothing that might get either of them in trouble. Besides, she did need to wash up, and a dip in the lake would feel divine.

Before she could change her mind, she hurried up the stairs.

⚬⚬⚬

By the time Trip emerged with his father, Marguerite was sitting on the dock, her black-stocking-clad feet dangling in the water. Immediately Trip's eyes traveled to her shapely calves and ankles. Maybe this wasn't such a good idea.

"She looks good in a bathing suit, huh?" his father whispered as Trip settled him in a deck chair.

"Dad, she's engaged."

"Haven't you fixed that yet?"

"It's complicated."

"Whatever you say, son."

Marguerite turned and waved to them. "Hello, Captain. You're looking much better."

"Thanks, Miss Westing. You look pretty good yourself."

"Dad!" Trip whispered.

"Oh, go on and enjoy yourselves. See if you can change her mind about you-know-who."

"I don't know if I can. She thinks she has to marry Roger Gordon or her family will go broke. Her dad has a gambling problem and lost everything."

"So she doesn't love this Gordon?"

"I don't think she even likes him."

His father frowned, deepening the wrinkles on his weathered face. "I may not be the best father in the world, but there's no way on God's green earth that I'd let you suffer the rest of your life because of my mistakes."

"I know you wouldn't." Trip glanced at her. She'd removed her hair pins, and her long gilded locks reached past her waist. He swallowed hard. "But it has to be her decision."

"Can't you at least do a little persuading?"

"Dad, believe me, I'm going to try."

❦

Marguerite watched Trip jog down the pier, dive off the end, and glide into the water without a splash. Surfacing, he tossed his head back. "Why are you still sitting there?"

She wrinkled her nose. "How deep is the water?"

"At the end, it'll be up to that pretty little sailor collar, but you'll do fine." Moving closer, he held out his arms. "Jump."

Marguerite did. Trip caught her in his arms, lowered her feet until they touched the silt-covered bottom, and then released her. The moment his hands left her waist, she wished them back. So much of the last few weeks had been tumultuous, filled with threats and fears. But when Trip held her, she felt secure and safe.

You're engaged. Stop daydreaming about Trip like a schoolgirl.

He motioned to the open water. "Show me what you can do."

"You want me to swim?"

"You said you've been practicing." He grinned, his eyes daring her. "Or was that a lie too?"

Marguerite frowned. "Lilly's been teaching me."

"Good. Then let's see it."

She took a deep breath and awkwardly propelled herself forward. Lilly's admonitions rang in her ears. *Reach with your arms in big circles in front of you. Kick with your legs like scissors.* After covering about six yards, she stood up. "Well?"

"She taught you the rescue stroke. Good work. Can you do the crawl too? The one I showed you."

"Sort of, but I have to get my face in the water for that." She wrinkled her nose again.

"You don't have to, but it's a lot easier if you do. As a matter of fact, Miss Flour Freckle, I'm thinking that getting your face wet is a good idea."

She wiped a remaining smudge of flour from his forehead. "That's the pot calling the kettle black."

"Okay, I'll race you back to the dock."

"I can't beat you."

"Not up to a challenge?"

Hoping to gain an edge, she catapulted forward. Despite her rapid departure, she knew he'd still overtake her, but at least it gave her a modicum of a chance. When she reached the pier, she found him waiting. She held onto its edge and tossed her head back. "That isn't fair."

"Life isn't fair, Marguerite."

"You're telling me." Her words came out laced with bitterness. What was she doing? Being with Trip made her say things she shouldn't, feel things she'd given up, and think about things she'd already put to rest. She quickly swam away as fast and as far as she could.

"Hey, Marguerite, catch!"

She whirled and a ball landed directly in front of her, splashing her face. Using both hands, she swiped away the water. "This means war, Trip Andrews." She yanked up the ball and headed for him.

Just friends.

Remember that.

Spiking the ball in front of him caused a fountain of water to hit him squarely in the face, giving him the perfect reason to retaliate. She knew he would. Maybe that's what she wanted.

She shouldn't want it. But she did.

❧

After an enjoyable afternoon of working and then swimming with Trip, the evening with Roger seemed even more tedious. As a belated birthday gift, he insisted on taking her into the city for dinner at his home, followed by a performance at the Dohany Opera House.

His mother had their cook prepare a special dinner. Even though she and Mrs. Gordon tried to discuss the Water Carnival plans, Roger monopolized the conversation and insisted on her complete attention. To her surprise, Mrs. Gordon accompanied them to the performance of the play *Alabama* in the newly restored theater, and introduced her to many acquaintances as her son's fiancée. A few offered the couple congratulations, and Roger's chest puffed with pride.

The play, a Civil War story, transported Marguerite to another place and time. However, all too soon it was over, and once again she found herself on the arm of dreary Roger Gordon. After escorting his mother home, they took the streetcar back to Lake Manawa.

When Marguerite made a genuine attempt to engage Roger in a conversation about the moving play, he brushed her off, saying the play was a melodramatic waste of time.

Marguerite tried again. "Your mother is delightful."

"She approves of you." The streetcar halted and he pulled her to her feet. "She means the world to me. If anyone ever disappoints her, I'll . . ."

He let his words die like the setting sun. Did she sense another threat? Just how far would Roger go to get what he wanted?

He walked her back to her camp and leaned in for a less than chaste kiss. Marguerite squirmed free of his embrace and distanced herself.

"We're engaged, Marguerite. You can kiss me with a little more passion than that."

She clenched her hands together. *If I felt any passion for you, then I might be able to.* "I'm sorry, Roger, my thoughts are elsewhere this evening."

"With that ridiculous Water Carnival."

"Yes, of course I'm thinking about it. It's only a few days away, and I have a lot of responsibilities. But I'm enjoying the planning a great deal. I'd like to do more of these events in the future." She stopped when Roger's eyes darkened, hooded with a desire that made her shiver. "Roger, are you listening to me?"

Without warning, he grabbed her face in both hands. "You are so beautiful. I can't believe you belong to me."

She tried to pull back, but he held fast. "Belong to you?"

Crushing her lips, he kissed her again, the feel of his shaggy mustache making her nauseous. She brought her hands up between them and pushed him away. "Roger, you will refrain from that kind of indulgence until we are married. Is that clear?"

He snickered. "Sure, Marguerite. Until then."

For Marguerite, the next three days were a blur of activity. Each morning, she worked on various aspects of the Water Carnival. The shipment of fireworks arrived, and Trip and some of the men began planning out the pyrotechnic display, which would imitate the naval battle firing between the boats and forts. Phyllis Dodge, the supervisor for those making Chinese paper lanterns, bedecked every nook and cranny of the Yacht Club with one of her elaborate creations. Marguerite flitted from one area to the next, checking on the progress of the committee assigned there. Excitement coursed through them all like the electricity that powered the streetcars.

But it was the afternoons Marguerite relished. Two blessed hours spent with Trip, and often the rest of the crew, painting the papier-mâché pieces for the *USS Marguerite*. Thankfully she'd persuaded Trip to call it simply the *USS Maggie*. Since only her father called her that, it couldn't possibly upset Roger.

Marguerite hurried to gather her things inside the Yacht Club. Today she and Trip would be putting the final touches on the boat, and she couldn't wait.

Stepping outside the crowded Yacht Club into the warm afternoon, she paused and took a deep breath. Even the lake air seemed laced with anticipation.

"Hello, Marguerite."

She jolted. "Roger, what are you doing here?"

He rose from the park bench and faced her. "Can't I come to see my fiancée?"

"Yes, of course, but you know how busy I am." She attempted to step around him, but he caught her arm.

"Perhaps I could help."

"Do you paint?"

He chuckled. "No, I can't say that I do."

"Then perhaps you can go inside and help the men plan

the fireworks display. A group of them are gathered in the parlor."

"And where are you headed?"

"To the boat shop. There's a boat there that needs a few last-minute touches."

"That only you can provide."

"As a matter of fact, yes." She attempted to step around him.

He caught her shoulders, pulled her close, and kissed her lips.

When he released her, she covered her lips with her hand. "What do you think you're doing? We're in public!"

Roger looked over her shoulder, his lips curling in a triumphant smirk.

She turned to see who or what had his attention. Trip. Hurt flickered in his eyes, and his roguish pirate smile melted from his face like candle wax.

Roger tapped her nose. "I guess my work here is done."

Whirling away from both of them, Marguerite held her hand flat against her roiling stomach. The acidic taste in her mouth foretold the future—what she'd face day after day with Roger.

Run. Somewhere. Anywhere.

She raced around one of the many ice sheds to be alone and propped her hand against the rough wall. Taking great gulps of air, she tried to quell her churning stomach and whirlwind of emotions.

A man's hand on her shoulder made her spin around, much too quickly. The face before her rippled, and she swayed.

"Whoa." Trip steadied her. "You okay?"

She nodded but didn't pull free from his hand. "I just got dizzy."

"Are you ill? You look pale." Genuine concern etched his amber-streaked eyes.

"Not the way you think."

His expression said he wanted to ask questions, but instead he took hold of her elbow. "Let's get you out of the sun and someplace cooler."

To her great relief, he didn't take her back to the boardwalk. Rather, he followed the worn path that led to the back of the boat house. Inside, he helped her into a chair.

"Why does she look like a haint?" Harry asked as soon as they came into the shop. "She okay?"

"Can you get her a glass of cold water? With some ice? I think all of the excitement and the heat is getting to her."

"Sure, Trip. You sit tight with Marguerite. I'll be right back."

She pulled a handkerchief from her pocket and dabbed at the moisture forming on her upper lip. "Really, Trip, I'm fine now."

His brow knit together in a deep frown, making him look a great deal like his father. After fetching a cloth from the workbench, he dipped it in a water bucket and wrung it out. He drew up a stool and sat facing her. "I hate seeing you like this."

"I'm sorry, but it hasn't happened often."

"That isn't what I meant." He touched the cloth to her cheek.

Marguerite leaned into his hand and prayed the cool rag would settle her churning stomach.

"Marguerite, you can't keep lying."

"I haven't lied to you."

"I saw him kiss you."

"I know. I'm sorry." She lifted her face, and he set the

damp cloth aside. "Trip, I never meant for that to happen, but I haven't lied to you about him."

"The only person you're lying to is yourself. You don't love that man, and being with him is making you sick inside and out. You can't keep living a lie."

"But my family—"

"Lord knows I understand that, but there's got to be another way. Your father made money before, and he can find a way to do it again. God will provide."

If he'd yelled at her, she would have been able to fight back, but when he picked up both of her hands in his own, all her resolve vanished like the fluff on a dandelion.

He searched her face. "Please, don't marry him."

"Trip, I . . ."

He squeezed her hands and let them go. Slowly he stood. The stool grated on the floor of the workshop. "It's your decision, Marguerite. More than anything, I want you to be happy. I won't push you or tell you what to do, but I also can't do this anymore." He looked around the workshop and sighed.

Noticing the name *USS Maggie* had been outlined on the boat, she knew exactly what he meant. This had been their secret place for the last week—a place where they could pretend no Rogers, engagements, gambling debts, or lies existed.

"If you stay with him, I can't simply be your friend." His voice broke when he spoke. "I love you. I hate the thought of that man holding you and calling you his. I can't pretend this is enough anymore. Actually, Marguerite, I just won't."

What could she say? He was absolutely right. She pushed herself to her trembling legs and left the boat shop in silence. At the door she met Harry bearing the glass of ice water. She waved him off, tears brimming on her lashes, and pushed past him.

Her heart pounded with each step she took away from Trip. It was over. This time for good. Her fate had been sealed.

At least God had let her feel truly loved.

But would the pain of having lost that ever go away?

❧

He wasn't there.

Marguerite had arrived at the Yacht Club before breakfast and scanned the committee members for Trip's presence. His absence underscored what he'd said yesterday, and the emptiness ripped through her.

She forced herself to focus on the task at hand. With the Water Carnival only a day away, the men and women present were hard at work. A group of ladies chatted and giggled as they slid red, orange, yellow, and blue Chinese lanterns onto a rope. Another group continued to craft more elaborate lanterns to hang from the trees.

The clang of metal outside led her to investigate. She followed the sound to the back of the Yacht Club, where a couple of men were constructing a small platform.

"Grab that other pipe." Harry motioned to his fellow crewmate Mel to bring him another short length of lead pipe. He screwed it in place next to the other foot cylinders, then looked up from his work. "Mornin', Marguerite. Feeling better?"

"Much, thank you."

"Trip said he'd be working on the island all day, arranging the fireworks there. I'm rowing this mortarboard over as soon as we've finished. Want to come?"

"No, I'm afraid I have a lot to do here."

"Don't work too hard." He adjusted his sailor's cap and resumed threading the next pipe in place.

Marguerite recalled Trip explaining how the fireworks would have to be shot off from the shore. The pipes, or mortars, attached to boards would be set along the shore and inside the "forts." She smiled, thinking about the elaborate plans he'd drawn up with his strong, angular script noting each detail. Timing, he insisted, was everything.

And that was true about more than fireworks. She swallowed the watermelon-sized lump in her throat. Why couldn't she have met Trip before Roger Gordon entered her life? Or before her father had started gambling . . .

But she hadn't.

And today Trip Andrews was as scarce as a snowflake in July.

The cavernous hole in her heart widened. If she could just see him, talk to him, even for a minute . . .

Emily Graham shouted her name and Marguerite acknowledged her with a limp wave.

"Do you think this flower garland is long enough?" Emily called over the din of the workers.

No time for self-pity. Marguerite took a deep, fortifying breath and hiked up her navy work skirt to cross the lawn.

Emily and her decorating committee had strewn mounds of blossoms across the picnic table and arranged them in piles—multicolored zinnias, magenta coneflowers, yellow marigolds, a mix of sweet peas, pale blue cornflowers, and a collection of roses.

Thick-waisted Rose Doughman held up the newly completed garland with a variety of flowers secured to the string of lush ivy and ferns. "So, what do you think?"

"It's perfect. The flowers will be the crowning glory of the boats."

"Warships with flowers still sound odd to me." Hannah Townsend grunted. "But I suppose this is a carnival."

Emily seemed to drink in the beehive of activity and practically glowed. "It certainly is. I can just feel the excitement in the air. Can't you, Marguerite?"

"Yes, of course." Marguerite forced a smile. "You ladies keep up the good work."

Taking out her notepaper, Marguerite studied the to-do list she'd made for herself this morning. The letters blurred on the page and a tear splashed on the ink. The letter *t* magnified beneath the perfect half circle.

She shook the paper and the tear ran off the side, smearing the word. There wasn't any time for this. What was wrong with her? She'd made her decision. Marrying Roger would assure that her parents and brother would be cared for. There wasn't a choice. What kind of person would she be if she allowed them to become destitute because of her selfishness? And what would happen to Lilly and Alice?

A man cleared his throat behind her, and she spun, hopes soaring for a brief second. Her heart plummeted at the sight of Harry, his mop of curls wiggling in the wind.

"Marguerite, you got a minute? I've been meaning to talk to you."

"If there's a problem with the mortars, I'm afraid I can't help you."

"No, the mortars are all set." He removed his cap and held it in his hands. "This isn't easy, so I'm just going to say it. I know something's been going on between you and Trip and that other fellow. I can't for the life of me figure out why you chose that other guy when there's no finer man in the whole state than Trip Andrews."

312

Her lips thinned to a tight line. Trip had told Harry about Roger.

"Trip's my best mate, and I haven't seen him hurt this bad since . . . well, never."

"I don't think it's proper for us to be discussing this."

"Probably not, but I don't stand on ceremony. I have only one more thing to tell you. You're a great girl, Marguerite, but for his sake, I hope that after tomorrow he never has to see you again."

She stepped back as if she'd been slapped. "I didn't mean to hurt him."

"Intentions rarely mean much." He glowered. "You're making a big mistake. Anyone who has eyes can look at the two of you and see you have something special. What does that other fellow have? Money? Prestige? Power? I know you didn't tell us the truth about wanting to learn to sail, but I never took you for the kind of girl who'd betray Trip for all that."

"That's enough, Harry."

Trip's smooth baritone voice made her heart whirl like a windmill. She spun toward him and met his gaze. The warm golden flecks that had welcomed her yesterday had been replaced with hardened dark ones.

"Miss Westing." He nodded. "We're heading over to practice with the boats for tomorrow. I thought you might want to preview the show."

"Thank you. That's very thoughtful."

"I wasn't doing it to be thoughtful, just thorough." Without so much as a goodbye, he turned on his heel and strode away.

Instantly she felt the sting of a hundred bees in her heart.

Harry shot her one more hard glare and walked off after him, muttering a string of insults referring to her as a money-grabbing, coldhearted . . .

Liar.

Wrapping her arms around her middle, she leaned against a tree and slid down its length in a sliver of shade.

Lord, give me the courage to do what I need to do.

❦

Half an hour later, Marguerite sufficiently gathered herself to walk north past the boat shop. She spotted the square fort erected on Coney Island for tomorrow's show. It stood on four poles at least six feet in the air. Two more "buildings" were on the ground and a makeshift fence surrounded them. Pride swelled in her chest at how hard the men had worked to make the naval battle appear authentic.

She moved to the end of the dock. The smooth water amplified the voices on the boats, and she was surprised at how clearly she could hear.

On the lake, Trip stood in the bow of the *Endeavor*—now temporarily bearing the name *USS Maggie*—shouting orders to the smaller boats. The larger ones, like his father's *Argo*, represented the battleships and remained anchored. Complete with freshly painted papier-mâché turrets and Dahlgren howitzers, it wasn't hard for her to picture them engaged in the heated battle with fireworks blazing. The smaller rowboats, which acted as gunboats, wove between the larger ones under Trip's carefully orchestrated direction.

Not once did he appear to grow flustered or weary. Not once did he bellow or become ill-tempered. He simply told the boats where to go and on what signal. How did he do it? Stepping into his father's shoes had been easy. Filling them was something altogether different. He probably hadn't noticed how the others accepted his leadership without question, or how much trust he garnered from both young and old.

After they'd gone through the entire program once, he made them repeat it two more times. Even then, despite a bit of grumbling, they complied. Finally he told all the ships to dock and then meet him.

Marguerite moved a few yards off as she listened to Trip's final warnings regarding safety.

"Each of the fireworks on the floating fort and at the stationary fort are positioned so that they won't harm anything on your own boat. However, it's your job to make sure you don't direct anything at anyone else's boat either. It'll be dark, so you'll have to remember where you're supposed to be and when you're supposed to shoot off your rockets. And remember, timing is everything."

Timing! Marguerite opened her watch pinned to her bodice—12:30. Half an hour late for lunch with Roger. Great. Fisting her skirts, she hiked them up and darted between the strolling couples on the Grand Plaza. She raced up the stairs of the pavilion in a most unladylike fashion. Stepping inside the open-air pavilion, she scanned the area for Roger, pausing only to straighten her hat and shake out her skirt. If she was lucky, perhaps Roger had been held up as well. *Held up by a robber with a very large gun.*

She giggled. Even Roger didn't deserve that. She arranged the tails of the ascot-like bow at her neck, smoothed her hair, and placed her hand on the door latch leading to the restaurant.

Roger's thick hand clamped on her wrist and yanked it back. "Where have you been?" he hissed, pulling her against his chest.

"You know where I've been."

"With him."

"Working on the carnival." She fought to wrench her wrist

free, but his fingers dug into her tender flesh. "Roger, let go of me."

"I have no intention of ever letting you go." He squeezed harder, pressed her against the wall, and let the threat beneath his words sink in.

Icy fear seeped into every pore of her body. "Roger, you're making a scene."

His mustache twitched with amusement. "No one notices a little lover's spat, darling."

"They will if I scream."

"You wouldn't."

She cocked an eyebrow. Did he really believe she wouldn't? His hot breath against her cheek tempted her to spit in his face. Before she could get the courage to do so, he removed his hand from her wrist, one finger at a time.

Sidestepping him, she rubbed the chafed wrist, willing her heart to settle its relentless chugging. *Relax, you're free.* But she didn't feel free. She felt trapped. Penned. Caged.

How had her father described Roger? That he liked the sound of his own voice far more than he could ever like anyone else? That same day, he'd also said he wanted her to marry a man who held her heart. And what Roger wanted was to possess her. To have her.

What am I supposed to do, Lord?

The truth will set you free.

The words struck her so hard her breath caught. The truth. Trip said she was lying to herself. Was he right? How would she ever be able to make a vow to God, promising to love, honor, and obey this man? If she did, it would be a lie.

She couldn't do it. Not anymore. She couldn't make promises to Roger that she had no intention of keeping. It was as simple as that. And she could never promise God she'd love this horrible man when her heart belonged to another.

If I tell the truth, then I'll be free.

Yanking off the engagement ring before her courage could wane, she held it out in the center of her open palm.

"What are you doing?" Roger glowered. "Don't be foolish."

"I can't marry you. I don't love you."

"I never thought you did, but I want you anyway."

"Take the ring, Roger."

"You can't be serious. Remember the situation? Your family will lose everything."

"God will help me find a way to support my family without living a lie with you."

"It's him, isn't it?"

"The truth? I do love Trip Andrews, but it's you who drove me away." She rubbed her aching wrist. "At first I thought you were boring, but now I know you're also cruel. Maybe your parents never told you no, Roger, but I most certainly can. I'll have my father return the telescope you gave me by the end of the week."

She started to leave and he grabbed her elbow. "You'll regret this."

"No, Roger, I don't think I will."

25

Workers paraded around the decorated boats lining the piers, adding finishing touches for tomorrow's festivities. Marguerite searched for Trip among the many volunteers but couldn't find him. Then she spotted Lilly, paintbrush in hand, adding a flourish of gold to the lettering on John Nelson's *Windy Sue*.

Marguerite approached the boat, and John assisted her in boarding his vessel. He showed her around as he touted the sailboat's specifications and explained how he'd elaborated on the plans she'd given him.

"It's turned out beautifully, Mr. Nelson. Now, if you'll excuse me, I'd like to go speak to Lilly." She pointed to her maid. "I believe I'll be requiring her assistance later."

"Just don't take her until she puts the final letters on my boat. I can't have it saying *USS Fear* instead of *Fearless*."

"I see your point." She smiled. "I'll make sure she has the time to finish it."

Even though she wanted to rush to her friend and share her news, Marguerite practiced restraint and remained a few feet back, watching as Lilly stuck the tip of her tongue out while she painted the letter *l* with a flourish. Her face was only inches from the papier-mâché turret.

Lilly stepped back. "Perfect."

"I couldn't agree more."

Lilly turned. "When did you get here, Miss Marguerite?"

"A minute ago. Have you seen Trip?"

The maid-turned-artist set her paintbrush in a water-filled canning jar. "He's made himself scarce today. What's got you looking all glowy like a lightning bug in June?"

Marguerite raised her bare hand and wiggled the fingers.

"You did it! You broke off the engagement!"

Lifting her finger to her lips, Marguerite hushed her friend. "I want to tell Trip myself."

"What did your parents say?"

Marguerite's stomach cinched as if someone had lassoed her and pulled the rope taut. How had she forgotten about telling them? The exhilaration of finally being free of that officious man had made her forget how much her decision was going to hurt them all. What would Lilly do if they had to let their servants go?

"I . . . haven't told them. Lilly, what if I've made a terrible mistake?"

"The only mistake you made was putting up with him as long as you did." Lilly wiped her hands on a rag. "God's going to take care of all of us. Why don't you sit down here and tell me what happened?"

"Would you mind terribly if we talked later? I suppose I should explain things to my parents before Roger shows up and tells them his version."

"True." A broad smile bloomed on Lilly's face. "Just remember, you'll still be able to look forward to telling Mr. Trip your news."

"I only hope I'm not too late."

Like a sacrificial lamb, Marguerite stood before her parents.

Somehow her father appeared to know what she'd done the moment she stepped into the center of their camp, and disappointment flooded his face. Still, he didn't say a word.

"I need to speak with you both." Her voice sounded foreign even to her own ears.

Her mother set her teacup on its saucer. "Your timing couldn't be better. Your father and I were just going over the guest list for the engagement party next week."

"Mother, there won't be a party."

"Nonsense, dear. It's all arranged." She tapped the list. "We weren't certain about inviting the Sheratons because you know how Edith can gab, but your father has persuaded me to be solicitous. Edith would be greatly wounded if she was omitted, and Mr. Sheraton is considering investing in the new business."

Her father placed his hand on his wife's arm. "Let Marguerite speak."

Marguerite's mouth felt as if she'd swallowed a handful of milkweed down. She licked her parched lips. "Mother, there won't be an engagement party because I'm no longer engaged."

Her mother's face paled to the color of the moon. "What have you done?"

"I told Roger I couldn't marry him."

"Oh, Marguerite, perhaps if you hurry and go find him, I'm sure he'll still forgive you. After all, brides-to-be often get cold feet."

"No, Mother. He knows it was no such thing." She stared

at her father, waiting for his reaction, wishing he'd say something, anything. Even suffering his wrath would be better than enduring his silence.

Her mother turned to her husband. "Edward, you go to him. He'll listen to you. You can explain things. You can make him understand that Marguerite is impulsive at times."

Marguerite held her father's gaze. Did she see a flicker of fear? Not her father.

The realization shook her. Perhaps the situation was worse than she'd imagined. Had his physical safety been threatened as well as the family's finances?

A fraction of a second later, whatever she'd seen on his face passed like a fleeting shadow. Her father drew in a long, ragged breath and released it slowly. "I don't think I need to explain anything to him." He met her gaze. "Do I, Maggie?"

His familiar term of endearment poured like a balm over her fearful heart, and she shook her head.

"Marguerite, how could you? Do you realize what you've done?" Tears wetted her mother's cheeks, and she turned to her husband, pleading for him to do something.

"I'm sorry, Mother, but I just couldn't promise to love him."

"But you could send us all to the poorhouse," her mother spat. "You selfish little—"

Her father struck the table with a clenched fist. "Camille, that's enough."

"She's thinking only of herself, Edward."

"Is she?" He drew his hand down the length of his peppered beard. "I think it's we who've been thinking only of ourselves. I've always known Roger Gordon wasn't the man for her, and I believe you only hoped he would be."

Her mother sucked in a trembling lip.

"I'm so sorry, Daddy. I'll get a job. I'll do anything. Just don't make me marry him. It's not just that he's boring, he's . . ." Marguerite rubbed her wrist.

Her father looked at the injured spot. "Why are you doing that? Did he hurt you?"

"Daddy, it's nothing, really."

Her mother captured her hand. "You're hurt? Let me see it." Her cool fingers brushed the slightly swollen, reddened flesh, and her eyes filled with fresh tears. "He did this?"

Marguerite nodded.

"Was it the first time he's manhandled you?" her father demanded.

"He didn't do anything serious."

"I had no idea." Her mother pressed a hand to her dampened cheek. "Why didn't you say anything?"

"Camille." Her father laid a hand on his wife's arm.

Marguerite pulled her hand away, and her mother faced her husband, pain etching her delicate features. "What have we done?"

"We gave our daughter to a monster." Chest heaving, he pulled his wife's head against his chest. "This is my fault."

Showered in fresh guilt, Marguerite slid into the empty chair at the table. She clenched her hands in front of her, praying she could make her parents understand. "I'm sorry. I'm so sorry. I wanted to fix it all, but I just can't do it."

"Marguerite, look at me." Her father stroked her hair until she turned to him. His pain-filled voice broke. "I did this to you and to this family. I created the problem. I should never have told you to marry him. I should have forbid it. I don't know who I am anymore, but I know one thing." He squeezed her hand. "You have nothing to be sorry for. If anyone has failed, it's me. I know you must hate me, but someday I hope you can forgive me."

She looked into his care-worn eyes brimming with tears. "Daddy, I could never hate you."

Silence hung in the air until her mother broke it. "And I'm sorry too. I've just been so afraid. I didn't want you—or any of us—to have to be without."

"I know, Mother."

The corners of her father's mouth lifted slightly as he brushed a tear from Marguerite's cheek. "Now it's time for you to dry your tears. I do believe you have a certain gentleman who deserves to know about this turn of events."

"But don't we need to figure out what to do now?" Marguerite's eyes darted between them. "If I don't marry Roger, then—"

"No." Her mother shook her head, looking to her husband for confirmation.

"No," her father echoed. He took his wife's delicate hand and pressed it to his lips. "Your mother and I have much to discuss, but you don't. This is our fight. We were wrong to let it become yours."

❧

Persuading Mark to join her in searching for Trip after supper wasn't difficult. Even though Mark didn't enjoy sailing, the starry-eyed look in his eyes told her he idolized Trip Andrews. And the promise of ice cream along the way didn't hurt either.

She could have gone alone. After all, tomorrow was the big day, and she had numerous responsibilities she shared with Trip. She doubted even busybody Ruth Ellen Hutton would be surprised to see her out and about unchaperoned this evening. However, Mark's attendance would eliminate any questions, and the truth was, she knew her parents didn't need her little brother underfoot during their important discussion.

Her heart grabbed. She knew she'd done the right thing, but seeing the pain in her parents' eyes still haunted her. She prayed for peace, and her father's words came to mind. *This is our fight. We were wrong to let it become yours.* Was God trying to help her understand she was now truly free? That the burden of her family's well-being belonged with her parents?

Mark picked up a stick and bashed it against the bushes as they walked. "Where do you think Trip is now? How many more places do we have to look?"

They'd already checked the boat shop, the *Endeavor*, and the restaurant inside the pavilion. Perhaps there was another tent meeting on the other side of the lake, or maybe he'd gone for a late swim. She scanned the crowded Grand Plaza for any sign of him or one of his crewmates.

"Hey, do I get a prize?" Mark pointed to a park bench near the ice cream parlor. "I found him."

Marguerite froze. Trip wasn't alone. Laura Thompson sat next to him on the narrow bench. How could he be socializing with her, of all people? That girl had tormented her practically every day of grade school. She was the one who'd locked her in the icehouse, and he knew it.

Laura giggled and laid her hand on Trip's arm.

"That little imp!"

Mark grabbed her sleeve. "You aren't going over there. What if he's courting her?"

Trip shifted farther away and frowned. If he was courting Laura, he wasn't doing a very good job of it.

Marguerite took a step forward and stopped. "Wait a minute. What am I doing?"

"What?"

Fresh fear mushroomed inside her. "Maybe you're right, and he is courting her."

"Looks to me like she's the one trying to woo him. Besides, she isn't nearly as pretty as you."

"Thanks, Mark." She gave him a brief side hug.

He shrugged her arm off. "Don't go getting all sappy on me. Go find out already."

"I can't very well march right up and ask him if he's courting her!"

Laura covered her mouth and appeared to twitter at something Trip said. Marguerite's stomach churned. What if Trip had changed his mind and moved on? She could easily understand if he'd finally had enough of her. Yesterday his goodbye had been permanent, as witnessed by his absence since then. She'd hurt him too many times by lying to him and, most of all, to herself.

She didn't blame him, but she needed to know if there was an inkling of a chance. Marguerite took her writing tablet from her pocket, tore a strip of paper from it, and penciled a message. "Mark, I have an idea, and I need your help."

A few minutes later, with her plan in place, she stepped into the ice cream parlor, took a seat in one of the darkened booths with her back to the door, and prayed that it wasn't too late.

❧

The ring in his fist dug into Roger's palm. Jaw clenched, he jammed the ring in his suit coat pocket. He found an empty park bench and sank to its hard surface. He should have anticipated this setback. Marguerite's unpredictability was the one thing he could count on.

Foolish woman thought this was over. But she couldn't be more wrong. He'd do whatever he needed to make sure she was his. He knew how to up the stakes. Every person had their price, and Marguerite's was her undying love for her family and friends. If destroying her family's financial safety wasn't enough to make her agree to marry him, threatening their physical safety would have her begging to become his wife.

A fresh idea brought a grin to his face. He hurried down the boardwalk. Once he found his partner, he could arrange everything.

❧

Extricating himself from the present situation seemed impossible. Trip sighed, mentally kicking himself. How had he allowed Laura Thompson, of all people, to latch on to him this evening?

"Do you like sweets, Mr. Andrews?" The curly-haired redhead batted pale eyelashes at him over a generous sprinkling of freckles. "Of course you do. Who ever heard of a man who didn't like his sweets? Our cook makes the most delicious gingerbread cookies, and I'll have extras packed in my picnic basket tomorrow after the display."

"Is that a fact?" He sighed. What else could he say? He had no intention of sharing a picnic with the young woman, tomorrow or ever. He'd only come to the Grand Plaza in hopes of catching a glimpse of Marguerite as she made the final preparations for tomorrow's big event. Is this how trapped she felt when she was with that Gordon fellow?

A familiar face appeared in the crowd, and Trip's pulse quickened. He jumped to his feet when Mark neared.

"Mark, what are you doing here? Is everything all right?"

The boy glanced at Laura and frowned. "I brought you a note from my sister, but if I'm interrupting something . . ."

"No!" He glanced at Laura, whose lower lip jutted out in a well-rehearsed pout. "I mean, Miss Thompson and I were talking, but I can still read the note. Where is it?"

Mark tugged it from his pocket, and Trip snatched it from his hand. He read it quickly, the words sending a jolt through him.

I said goodbye to a vanilla life. I'll be in the ice cream parlor if . . .

If what? If he still wanted her? Of course he did. He loved her. Did she think he'd change his mind overnight?

"Mr. Andrews," Laura whined, "we hadn't made plans yet. Who is this boy?"

He'd almost forgotten about the high-pitched woman on the bench. Had Marguerite seen them together? The disapproving scowl etched on Mark's face answered that question.

Trip stuffed the slip of paper into his jacket pocket. He turned to Laura. "If you'll excuse me, I have something to attend to."

"Don't you mean some*one*?" she said cattily.

Trip grinned. "You're right, and I believe you know her—a Miss Marguerite Westing."

"Her?" Laura gaped at him.

"Be careful, Miss Thompson. I wouldn't leave my mouth open like that. The mosquitoes are thick tonight."

Mark's chuckles gave way to a full-bellied laugh by the time the two of them reached the ice cream parlor. Trip paused at the door. "Listen, buddy. I sort of need to speak to your sister alone."

"I thought maybe you did." Mark gave him a lopsided grin. "But it'll cost you."

"It will, huh?"

"I can make myself scarce for, say, a cherry soda."

Trip's mouth bowed. "Well, isn't that convenient. I was just about to purchase some ice cream myself." He placed a hand on the boy's shoulder and directed him inside. "And Mark, has anyone ever told you you're a lot like your sister?"

Five minutes later, Mark left the parlor with a couple of friends, and Trip scanned the room, holding a creamy confection in his hands. He found Marguerite sitting in a corner booth with her back to him, her hands clasped tightly in front of her. He stepped to the end of the table with the treat hidden behind his back and cleared his throat.

Marguerite's cornflower blue eyes locked with his. "Did you get my message?"

"I did."

"Oh." She dropped her gaze to her hands. "I understand."

He removed the fruit-topped ice cream sundae from behind his back and set it in front of her. "This is for my strawberry girl."

Tears laced Marguerite's lashes as Trip slid into the booth across from her. He scooped up a spoonful of strawberry-topped ice cream and held it to her lips. "It's melting."

"So am I." She licked the treat from the tip of the spoon and swiped the tears from her eyes.

He watched the strange mixture of emotions play across her face. "You did the right thing."

"I know, but it's still hard."

He took her hand in his. Spotting an angry red welt on her wrist, his jaw clenched. "Did he do this to you?"

Marguerite pulled her hand away and buried it in her lap. "It looks worse than it is."

"I doubt it." He took a deep breath. "Eat your sundae, then tell me what happened—and Marguerite, I mean everything."

She held up a spoonful to him. "I'll share."

"The ice cream or the truth?"

She licked her lips. "Yes—to both."

26

Crowds numbering into the thousands gathered early along Manhattan Beach facing Coney Island. Marguerite, dressed in a striped silk promenade dress with a solid blue sash, stood on the edge of the dock with her tablet in hand, checking off completed tasks.

The refreshment committee's tables groaned beneath the delicacies of the season. A performer called Du Shea, "the upside-down wonder," mesmerized the crowd while standing on his head in midair on a half-inch iron bar and performing feats of gymnastic daring. And the Ladies' Military Band again proved to be a tremendous success, as was the rowing competition earlier in the afternoon. But with the sun now setting, anticipation sparked like the hundreds of colorful Chinese lanterns that decorated the trees and boats. More people arrived to watch the armada prepare for the Water Carnival.

Marguerite checked her watch. Less than forty-five minutes until the show began.

Cheers went up as Miss Fishbaugh dove from the thirty-foot tower into the shallow water. Marguerite smiled. The spectators never tired of the woman's act. If something ever happened to the entertainer, maybe Marguerite could take her place and bail her family out by setting herself on fire each evening. Wouldn't that make Trip happy?

Marguerite glanced at her list and saw that each item had been checked off. Wanting to wish Trip Godspeed before the show, she wiggled her way through the crowd and paused at the rope cordoning off the area. The former rowboats and sailboats, now bedecked as battleships, lined the pier as crews readied them for the big show.

"They're something, aren't they?"

Marguerite turned toward the man beside her and tried not to stare at his bulbous nose. "Yes, they certainly are."

"Do you have a favorite?"

"I do." She pointed to the *Endeavor*, temporarily named *USS Maggie* in her honor. "That one." Floral swags draped the boat's stern, but no lanterns sparkled on the empty deck. Trip was nowhere in sight. She sighed. He and the rest of his crew were probably readying for the fireworks displays.

"She's a beauty. Is that man her captain?"

Craning her neck, she shifted so she could see the round-shouldered figure the man referred to standing on the dock beside the *Endeavor*. Her breath caught. What was Roger doing in that area? It was roped off for the participants only. She should march right over there and tell him to leave.

With my luck, he'd toss me in the lake and hold me under just for the fun of it. Then again, I could always catch him off guard. Maybe a nice dip in the lake is exactly what Roger needs.

Before she could decide if she should act on her thoughts, Roger made his way to the rope and slipped back under it without noticing her.

"Excuse me." She turned to man beside her. "I need to go tell my friend to be careful before the show begins."

She hurried away from Roger down the north end to where the floating battery was moored.

Trip hopped off it when he spotted her approaching. He kissed her cheek and held out his hand. She accepted his offer and he grinned. "I was afraid I wouldn't get to see you before the show."

She glanced at the large raft, otherwise known as Manhattan Fort, which the men had constructed and loaded with mortars. "Is everything set?"

"These fireworks here are, and so are the ones on the island. I checked them myself."

"Grand Plaza Fort." She smiled. His name for it had stuck, but he seldom used it, as if doing so gave him too much honor. "And the *Endeavor*?"

"You mean the *Maggie*." A roguish grin deepened his dimples. "She's set."

Marguerite's cheeks warmed. "Trip, Roger is here. I saw him."

His face darkened. "Did he bother you?"

"No. I avoided him."

"Good. Stay away from him. I don't trust him."

"That makes two of us." She sighed, glancing at the bluffs with the last vestiges of sun dipping beneath their rounded tops. "But this is a day of celebration, and since it's almost time to start, I'd better get back to the pavilion."

Instead of releasing her hand, Trip drew her closer. "I believe you promised me a kiss for good luck."

She stood on tiptoe and kissed his cheek.

He chuckled. "Not much luck in that little kiss."

"I don't believe in luck. I believe in God."

Placing a finger under her chin, he tipped her head up. "And you know what the Bible says. 'Greet one another with a holy kiss.'" He dipped his head and brushed the sweetest kiss across her lips—warm, soft, reverent.

"I like your interpretation of the Scriptures, Trip Andrews."

"And that was just a taste."

Her cheeks suddenly burned hot as a new thought popped in her head. What could he do with the Song of Solomon?

She stepped back and cleared her throat. "We have a show to put on."

"I'll meet you at Louie's after the display."

"Be careful."

He tapped her nose. "And you stay out of trouble and away from Roger."

❧

Taking her place on the porch of the pavilion beside Captain Andrews and Colonel Reed, Lake Manawa's chief proprietor, Marguerite adjusted her new wide-brimmed straw hat. Lilly insisted only her best would do for such a special occasion. Marguerite just hoped the plume, the lacy ribbon, and the clusters of silk flowers didn't block anyone's view, as Mark claimed it would.

From her vantage point, Marguerite surveyed the spectators. Thousands lined the shore. In the last rays of sunlight, she spotted her parents and Mark a few yards from the base of the stairs.

"Excited?" Captain Andrews asked.

"I'm about to burst." She clasped her hands together to still them.

He grinned, his dimples matching his son's. "Trip said the two of you worked things out."

"We did."

"Good. My son was so grumpy he made me look like a circus clown. You're good for him."

"I think I'm the one who's been blessed."

"Deuce," Colonel Reed interrupted, "I think it's time to begin."

Captain Andrews patted her arm and stepped closer to the porch railing to address the crowd. "Ladies and gentlemen!" he bellowed into a megaphone. The crowd quieted. "On behalf of the Yacht Club Association, welcome to the 1895 Water Carnival."

His voice rose over the din. "This event couldn't have occurred without the financial contributions of Colonel Reed, the Manhattan Beach Company, and the Electric Motor Company." He waited until the applause died down to continue. "In addition to these fine benefactors, I personally wish to thank my son Trip Andrews for spearheading this event, and Marguerite Westing for assisting him. They make a good team." He nodded toward her. "And now, ladies and gentlemen, boys and girls, we give you the crowning glory of the Water Carnival. We hope it will both thrill and delight you. Please enjoy."

The crowd erupted in cheers. Colonel Reed raised a pistol in the air and fired three shots, signaling the start. One by one, the forty participating boats, which had taken their positions on the lake between the beach and Coney Island, began to sparkle on the dark water. A hush fell over the crowd as the Chinese lanterns on each boat were ignited in turn.

The report of firecrackers shattered the silence and echoed over the surface of the lake. Marguerite gasped as Roman candles shot into the air and exploded in brilliant arrays of red, blue, yellow, and green in the ebony sky. Back and forth, the two forts "fired" their weapons. The choreographed boats moved in the water, shooting off their own Catherine wheel fireworks at precise moments, creating spiraling displays against the jet-black sky.

Marguerite clapped her hands in delight. She turned to Captain Andrews. "You must be very proud of Trip."

"You and I both know I could never have masterminded this display. And he couldn't have done it without you."

"It's so spectacular I can hardly breathe."

Suddenly a rocket shot from the north end of the lake directly toward the *Endeavor*. The rocket hit the half-raised sail and the cloth burst into flames.

Terror gripped Marguerite's heart, and a strangled cry escaped her lips. She pressed her fist to her mouth. "Lord, please no. Not Trip's boat."

❧

"Cut the sail away!" Heart thundering, Trip scrambled toward the mast, hung on to it with one hand, and started slicing the ropes holding it in place with his other. Harry whacked at the other end. The flaming fabric broke loose. "Swing the boom out over the water!"

Harry released the halyard and gave the boom a solid kick. The fully engulfed sail slipped from the mast and fell half onto the boat's rope safety line and half into the water. Lloyd and Max kicked it the rest of the way. The piece of silk sank silently into the lake.

"Trip!" Harry shouted.

He jerked around to see flames shooting from the boom. Fear pumped through Trip's veins. In minutes his ship would be ablaze.

"Here!" Harry tossed Trip the axe.

Trip caught the center of the handle. Then, balanced precariously, he began chopping at the solid pine. The others attempted to douse the flames with buckets of water hauled from the lake. Perspiration trailed down Trip's back, trickling beneath the waistband of his pants. He paused to wipe the sweat stinging his eyes with the back of his arm. The rockets continued to flare around them.

Flames licked at his targeted chopping area. Seconds mattered. Lungs burning, he raised the axe and sent it crashing down.

The boom cracked. Harry yanked the mainsheet free and the engulfed piece of timber dropped into the lake with a horrendous hiss.

27 ⛵

Despite Captain Andrews's firm grip on her elbow, Marguerite found her legs so rubbery they threatened to give way. She released the breath she'd been holding as the boom fell into the water.

"What happened?" Marguerite asked Trip's father.

"He had to cut the boom away or the ship would've burned."

She grabbed hold of the porch rail. The climax of the program—the exploding of both forts in a spectacular array of fireworks—occurred, but she could scarcely look at them. The crowd erupted in thunderous applause and zealous cheers. They believed the burning boat was part of the show!

"How did that happen?" Marguerite gasped. "The rocket. Where did it come from?"

The older man glanced down the beach and rubbed a hand over his chin. "From the shore, I think."

"There weren't supposed to be any mortars on the shore." Marguerite recalled the diagram of the placements just as clearly as she would a chart of the constellations. Mortars were set at the two forts—the stationary one on Coney Island and the floating battery. A few were on each of the large ships, but she recalled that Trip insisted none come from the shore because of the danger involved to both the crowd and the boats.

She tried to remember the trajectory. Doing a quick bit of geometry, she figured that from the angle at which the rocket struck, it had to have been shot from shore, most likely from the icehouse area.

Where she'd last seen Roger heading.

Her breath caught.

Roger's threats replayed in her mind. Surely even he wouldn't go as far as to try to destroy Trip's ship.

Or would he?

With the carnival over, Marguerite accepted the thanks and congratulations from those around her and slipped away. If she hurried, she'd be able to check out her theory and be back at Louie's in time to meet Trip for a celebratory dinner.

Moving through the dispersing crowd, she followed the boardwalk past the Yacht Club and boat shop to the end. She snagged a Chinese lantern from one of the trees and slipped the paper covering off the small kerosene lamp contained inside. With the aid of its thin light, she found the footpath winding through the trees toward the icehouses.

Dew-dampened grass clung to her silk skirt. This area lacked a sandy beach, so she walked along the edge of the lake, searching for any sign of a rocket having been shot off. The smell of gunpowder, heavy in the humid night air, kept her from following the scent of anything set off in the immediate area.

Approaching the pair of large icehouses, she turned the lantern's wick up. Trip had told her that tons of ice blocks were harvested in the winter and stored in the two structures for use by the lake's restaurants and saloons as well as the surrounding community. Nothing seemed amiss around the first icehouse, but in the narrow alley between the two, a box caught her eye when she held her lantern aloft.

Steeling herself, she ventured between the buildings, knelt by the wooden crate, and set her lantern down. Prying off the loose lid with a stick, she found the box filled with Roman candles. A discarded mortar remained stuck in the ground beside it. She yanked the tube free and held it to her nose. The unmistakable scent of gunpowder, which Mark always claimed smelled like a mix of chalk and burnt paper, wafted toward her.

Oars slapped the water at the beach. She startled and dropped the metal tube into the crate. After turning down the lamp's wick as far as she dared, she hid it behind the crate's lid. Who was out there? Besides the floating battery the men had kept there for the carnival, the only vessel that used this dock was the barge that delivered ice around the lake. Perhaps one of the participants had decided to moor his boat there.

She pressed herself against an icehouse wall. Was the boat coming or going? She heard two distinct voices. The rowboat scraped as they hauled it onto the rocky shore.

"Too bad Andrews's boat didn't sink. Are you going to try again?" a man asked in a thick Southern accent.

"I think I made my point."

The second voice hit her like a medicine ball to the stomach. Roger! She sucked in her breath.

"No one steals something that belongs to me, Clyde."

She nearly bolted. He was talking about her! She racked her brain for a Southerner named Clyde at the lake. Clyde Stone? The gambling hall owner? He was friends with Roger?

Clyde chuckled. "Are you still going to try to get that girl to marry you?"

"She will. I guarantee it. I'm a man who always gets what he wants. Just because my first plan didn't work doesn't mean this second one won't. I think Andrews got the picture of what's at stake."

Two plans? Roger had shot off the rocket at Trip's boat, but what other plan had been thwarted?

"As long as my name stays out of it," Clyde growled. "I have to admit that first idea of yours was a stroke of genius. We made a formidable team taking her old man's money."

She gasped.

"Only because your gaming establishment is so reputable." Roger laughed. "All I had to do was introduce Westing to the delights of the faro table. When I saw how easily he got hooked, I decided to use it to my advantage. I still can't believe that he kept going there night after night."

"Like taking candy from a baby."

"But you were the one who made sure he lost. How'd you manage it?"

"Faro's harder to rig than the roulette wheels." His boots scuffed against one of the rocks leading to the icehouses. "But crooked faro banks look just like legit ones. Helps to have a good dealer too, but it cost me to keep him on the sly. Remember our deal. I keep all the winnings. You aren't going back on that even though you didn't get the girl, are you?"

"I haven't gotten her *yet*."

"By the way," Clyde drawled, "what happened with her? I thought you said she'd have to accept your proposal if her father was penniless."

"Trip Andrews happened." Roger's voice sounded mere yards away. "And after tonight, he'll get the idea she isn't worth it. He won't risk his precious sailboat again—even for her. When he's gone, she'll need my strong arms to comfort her."

340

"And if he doesn't take this warning to back away?"

"That nice boat of his will be missing more than a sail."

Bile rose in Marguerite's throat and her stomach roiled. Roger had stolen her father's money to get her, and now he intended to hurt Trip's *Endeavor*. She covered her pounding heart with her hand.

A rodent scurried over her shoe. She jumped and clamped her hand over her mouth to keep from crying out.

"Did you hear that?" Clyde asked, stepping closer. "I heard something in the alley."

"Probably a coon."

"Either way, why don't you grab that box of fireworks you left in there so we can leave? The last thing I need is to get caught. The sheriff is breathing down my neck as it is."

"Good idea." A branch cracked under Roger's foot. He was close. Much too close.

She inched down the alley, wiggling down the length of the wall of the icehouse. Like the lapping waves, two thoughts pounded over and over in her head. *Escape. Warn Trip. Escape. Warn Trip.*

Roger stepped into the alley with the box of fireworks in hand, his rounded shoulders still noticeable against the moonlit sky.

Her heart hammered so loudly in her ears she was certain he could hear it. A few more yards and she could run for the trees.

A twig snapped beneath the heel of her shoe.

He set down the box and looked up. "Who's there?"

She bolted for cover in the wooded area.

～∞～

In stoic silence, Trip and his crew brought the crippled *Endeavor* back to the boat shop's dock. He glanced at his vessel and relief washed over him. A new boom and fresh sail and she'd be good as new. An expensive accident, but at least no one was harmed and his ship remained intact.

Harry hopped off the boat first and began the process of tying her down for the night. The others followed suit in silence. Lloyd carried the unfired Catherine wheels off the boat, Mel doused all of the Chinese lanterns, and Max gathered the ax and buckets they'd used in dealing with the fire. The *Endeavor* might be Trip's boat, but she belonged to all of them.

Trip scrubbed his face with his hands and sank beside the tiller. How had this happened? He'd checked and rechecked all of the rocket positions himself. Nothing should have come close to any of the boats, especially not his.

A few of the men had chosen to let their wives ride with them on the lake. He shuddered. What if he'd let Marguerite join them?

Mel, the deputy, sat down across from him. "She's all set. Are you planning on joining us at Louie's? The steamer's still going."

"You guys go ahead. I need a few minutes alone first."

Harry dropped from the side down to the deck in front of him. "Marguerite will be worried."

"Tell her I'll be along shortly."

Squeezing his shoulder, Max sighed. "This wasn't your fault, Trip. That rocket came out of nowhere."

The four men trickled off the boat and, he guessed, out of the boat shop as well. Trip lifted his face to the stars and smiled. Marguerite's stars.

"Lord, that was a close one." He prayed aloud as he often did when he was alone. "Since she came into my life, it's been one close call after another. Are You trying to tell me something?" He rubbed the kink in his neck. "I blew it tonight. Somehow, Lord, I messed up, and I could have gotten someone killed."

"Nonsense." The unmistakable deep voice of his father made Trip startle. "That was the finest piece of orchestration I've ever seen."

Trip scrambled off the boat, landing on the dock in front of his father. "Thank you, Dad, but—"

"But what? Some boy must have shot that one off. It sure didn't come from any of your batteries. I saw it." He handed Trip a canteen and waited for him to drink his fill. "Son, Marguerite saw it too."

Trip nodded. "I should probably get cleaned up. I'm supposed to meet her at Louie's."

"She isn't there."

"What?"

"I saw her head down the beach. I think she wanted to check where the stray rocket came from. She seemed . . . intent."

"And you didn't stop her?"

"I'd have better luck stopping a comet." He chuckled. "Go on. Go get her."

❦

Three more steps and she'd be free of the alleyway. Though he'd tried, Roger hadn't gained on her. With her skirts hiked to her knees, she raced through the opening.

Strong arms caught her and violently swung her around. "Whoa, there, little filly. What's got you so spooked?"

Kicking, clawing, and scratching, she fought to break free, but the man held her fast.

"Let go of me!"

"Marguerite?"

Roger's voice stopped her cold. An icy hand tickled her spine. She stilled.

"This is your girl?" the casino owner asked.

"Yes."

"Absolutely not." Bringing her heel down hard on her captor's foot, she broke free when he yelped.

Roger caught her wrist and, in one swift move, twisted it painfully behind her.

"Let me go!" She squirmed. "You won't get away with this. I heard what you did to steal my daddy's money, and I know you shot that rocket at Trip's boat."

He forced her to turn so she could see his face. "Like my father said, 'Survival of the fittest.' Marguerite, only the strong survive. I intend not only to survive but to thrive with you by my side."

"I'll never marry you."

"Never?" He laughed. "We'll see. So after Trip, who do you want me to destroy next? Your brother's future? Your sister's home?"

"You wouldn't."

He yanked her arm harder. "Oh, but I would."

"Just let me go. I won't tell anyone. I'm good at keeping secrets."

"You certainly are. Do you honestly believe I didn't know about your little forays with Trip Andrews?"

"I don't like it," Clyde growled. "She knows too much. Let's just drown her. No one will be a bit surprised if a young woman whose engagement had recently fallen apart killed herself."

"No." Roger ran his free hand along her cheek. "I'll take her with me."

"Don't be a fool. If she talks, we'll both end up in jail."

Marguerite struggled to break free, kicking and clawing, ignoring the pain streaking up her twisted arm.

"Besides, you can't take her anywhere like that. She'll have every man in the Grand Plaza after you. Let's put her in the icehouse until she learns to cool her hot head."

"I don't know about this, Clyde."

The gambler moved to open the door and swung it wide. "I didn't get to where I am by being soft. I know a bad risk when I see one, and letting her go with you right now is a chance I'm not willing to take. Either you let me put her in here or I'll take care of her my way." He grabbed Marguerite's other arm and yanked her from Roger.

"Roger, please, you can't put me in there! I hate closed spaces. I won't be able to breathe!"

"Isn't that too bad?" Clyde shoved her inside with more force than necessary.

Landing on the edge of a block of ice, she cried out.

Clyde laughed and slammed the door.

Running back to it, she clawed around the edges. No handle. No latch. No knob. "Roger! Roger, please, get me out of here!" Gasping, she slid to the sawdust-covered floor. She couldn't breathe, she couldn't think, and she couldn't stop Roger from damaging Trip's *Endeavor* again.

28

Trip reached the Grand Plaza in record time. He took the steps of the pavilion two at a time to gain some height and get a good view of the crowd. In the darkness, the task was nearly impossible.

Frustrated, he hurried into the throng. He felt a tug on his arm.

"Mr. Andrews, how's your boat?"

Trip turned and found Mark beside him. "Have you seen your sister?"

Mark shrugged. "About an hour ago I saw her making her way down the boardwalk. I thought she was going to meet you, but by the look on your face, I guess I was wrong."

"Which way did she go?"

He pointed to the northwest. "Toward the icehouses."

"Thanks." Trip turned and dashed off.

Mark ran up beside him.

"Hey, where do you think you're going? Go on back. I'll find her and bring her home."

"She's my sister." The youth pulled ahead.

Trip didn't have time to stop and escort the boy back. He regained his position beside him. "Just do what I say, and don't go leaving me in the dust, speedy."

⁓

With the icehouse walls measuring at least eight inches thick, no one on the lake or even passing by on the way to their campsite would hear Marguerite's cries from inside the structure. Still, she called out until her voice grew hoarse.

At first, the reprieve from the stifling heat of the August day was welcome, but now the water trickling off the melting ice soaked the hem of her silk gown, and the chilly air made her skin pimple in the darkness. She shivered uncontrollably, muscles convulsing.

She sat down on a sawdust-covered chunk of ice. She was so cold.

Perhaps she could tunnel out. She toed the loose planks and one slid sideways. Dropping down, she slipped her hand between the boards. Gravel. As deep as her hand.

She tucked her frigid fingers beneath her arms, hugging herself tightly. How had this happened? How had she missed Roger's desire to own her at all costs? She'd been such a fool. If she'd only told Roger the truth from the beginning, maybe his feelings for her wouldn't have taken root. Now everyone she cared about was in danger and she was a prisoner once again.

More violent shivers took hold. Desperate for a way to get out, she ran her hands along the rough walls, ignoring the splinters that dug into her fingers. Her pulse raced. *Lord, forgive me. Please don't make Trip suffer for my cowardice. Help me find a way out of here.*

Nothing.

Not a lamp.

Not a match.

Not a set of ice tongs.

The room closed in around her, its darkness sucking the air from her lungs.

Lord, I'm so cold. I can't breathe in here. I have to get out.

⤝⤞

Directing Mark around the outside of the buildings, Trip watched the two figures in the pale moonlight. In a few seconds he recognized both voices.

"I want her out of there now, Stone. This wasn't part of our deal."

"Our deal changed when she followed us. Leave her in that icehouse for another couple of hours, and she won't give you a bit of trouble."

Fury surged through Trip, constricting his chest. How long had she been in there?

"And you can come to her rescue, and she and her family will be eternally grateful." Clyde Stone tugged at the lapels of his jacket as if he were conducting a business transaction. "Bet her hot head's cooled down a few degrees by now."

"I want her out, now," Roger demanded.

"I don't think an hour in there has really taught her a lesson. You can go. You've got business to attend to. I'll stay and keep an eye on your pet icicle."

"What if she freezes to death?"

Clyde chuckled. "I don't know her as well as you, but I'm thinking she'll be fine."

Trip's fists clenched at his sides. Locked up for an hour? Marguerite would be frantic.

"What are we waiting for?" Mark hissed.

"For Roger to leave. It looks like Stone's calling the shots now. One against one is better odds than fighting them both."

348

"You're forgetting me."

Trip leaned closer to the boy's ear. "No, you're going to get your sister out of that icehouse while I deal with Stone."

"What if he has a gun?"

"Just get Marguerite out and get her somewhere safe."

Roger stood up. "I'll walk back to the pavilion and rent a rig. When I get back, I'm taking her with me."

"No, I don't think you will."

"What do you mean?"

"Gordon, don't be a fool. The more I think about it, it's too much of a gamble. That girl talks and we're both ruined. Time to cut your losses."

"But I want her."

"And I'm telling you . . ." Clyde pointed his finger at Roger's chest. "I'll deal with this."

Roger stared at his partner for a moment, his silence indicating he was calculating the decision. "I don't like this."

"Don't take it personally." He shook Roger's hand. "It's been a pleasure doing business with you.

Trip stiffened. Roger doing business with Stone couldn't be a good sign, but at least Marguerite's suitor was leaving. Every nerve tensed as Trip watched Roger walk away. Fighting the urge to move too fast, he held on to Mark's arm until he was certain Roger was completely out of earshot. Then he leaned close to Mark's ear. "Get ready."

Mark must have misunderstood. Before Trip could stop him, he bolted from the trees toward the icehouse.

With no other choice, Trip launched from his hiding place. Running full speed, he tackled Clyde Stone's midsection and sent the man sprawling.

Stone, seasoned in fighting, recovered quickly and jumped to his feet. "You just made a big mistake, mister!"

Trip easily sidestepped the uppercut. He danced around Stone, testing the man's strength and agility. Stone was much faster on his feet than he expected. With his weight placed on his back foot, Trip prepared to deliver a strong punch.

One powerful blow and this could all be over. He heard the icehouse door opening and the sound of Mark calling for Marguerite. Being distracted cost him the first blow and allowed Clyde the opportunity to land a right that caught him in the ribs and left him slightly winded.

Trip circled his opponent, jabbing and ducking. *Attaboy, Clyde. Just keep swinging. Wear yourself out.* All the years he and his crewmates had spent sparring one another was paying off.

Blood spurted from Clyde's lip when Trip delivered a lightning-fast fist to his chin. Stone's head snapped back. He added a hook to the gambler's kidneys. He didn't care if it was too hard. This man was ready to kill Marguerite.

Thinking of her, he glanced toward the icehouse. Again the distraction cost him dearly. Stone landed a blow to Trip's right eye, yielding a fresh cut, and followed it with a lip-splitting jab.

Stepping back, Trip saw the perfect opportunity to end it all. Stone left his midsection open. Lightning fast, Trip delivered a thundering right to Stone's left side with bone-crunching accuracy. The gambler spun, fell against the bushes, and landed on the damp earth. Trip leaned forward, hands on his knees, trying to catch his breath.

"Trip! Look out!" Marguerite shouted.

Before Trip could react, Stone came up swinging a log.

Blinding pain suddenly came crashing down on Trip's skull. He dropped to his knees. The shoreline blurred in his vision.

Then the moonlight slipped away and the darkness swallowed him completely.

⚜

Marguerite was too late. The log hit Trip squarely on the side of his head, and he crumpled to the ground like a rag doll.

Stone spun toward her.

"M-M-Mark, get out of here."

"I can't leave you. Trip told me to get you out of here."

"Please, Mark, I can't outrun him. I still can't feel my toes. G-g-go. Get help."

He hesitated and she gave him a shove. Then, without looking back, he sprinted from their hiding place.

Stone started toward her but suddenly stopped. Marguerite watched in horror as he returned to an unconscious Trip and dragged him down to the dock.

Marguerite tried to stand, but her burning legs wouldn't hold her. Under the cover of the alley between the two buildings, she trembled uncontrollably.

Her gaze fell to the lantern she'd hid earlier. It still cast a faint glow not far from the box of fireworks.

Marguerite fought her numb fingers and turned up the wick.

Stone now had Trip on the end of the dock.

Realization froze her more than the ice ever had. He was going to toss Trip in the water. Unconscious, Trip would drown. But in her own condition, she'd never make it there in time.

Please, Lord, help me!

The fireworks.

Jamming one of the Roman candles into the mortar, she

fumbled with the flue on the lantern, her cold fingers refusing to work. *Now would be a good time for that blessing, Lord.* Feeling returned enough for her to manage to touch the flame to the wick. The rocket shot into the air and burst open like an exploding blossom.

She fired another and another. The rockets would bring the men on the Grand Plaza running.

Stone heaved Trip into the water. He turned toward her.

She lit yet another rocket, aiming it directly at him. He dove out of the way. Rolling to his side, he jumped up and ran away into the night.

Struggling to her feet, she ignored the knifing pain and stumbled down to the water. The shore's water, like boiling tea against her flesh, forced the feeling back into her muscles. "Trip!" She searched the dark water for his body. She'd seen where Stone had tossed him, but where was he now? Driven to find him, she dove into the water.

Lord, where is he?

Frantic, she moved deeper until she had to swim. Her arm struck his solid form. Straining with his weight, she dragged him back toward the shore. Finally her feet touched the slushy mud and rocks, and with strength only God could provide, she dragged him onto the shore.

Placing her mouth over his, she breathed air into his lungs. *Breathe, Trip. Breathe.*

He coughed and opened his eyes.

Tears seeped down her cheeks, falling onto his wet face along with her kisses.

Thank You, Lord. Thank You. Thank You. Thank You.

29

Crowds dispersed quickly once Trip told them the rockets had gone off by accident. Only he, Deuce, Mark, and Marguerite knew differently. Deuce left first, telling them he'd meet them back at the boat shop. Marguerite prayed that the night hadn't been too much for Trip's father.

Now drenched, Marguerite couldn't stop shivering in the night air.

"I'm taking you back to my place," Trip said.

"I'm fine. I just can't get warm."

"That isn't fine." He draped his arm over her shoulders and pulled her close to his side. "Mark, go home, tell your parents what happened, and fetch her a change of clothes from Lilly. Bring them to the boat shop."

Seeming glad to have a job, Mark sped away.

Marguerite leaned into Trip's side. "Shouldn't I be fussing over you? You're the one who almost drowned. How's your head?"

"Not as hard as yours." His voice held a warm lilt. "How'd you get me out?"

"I swam."

"Remind me to thank Lilly." He chuckled and kissed the top of her head.

She stopped and held the lantern up to his face. Gingerly

she brushed her fingers over the gash above his eye. "I'm so sorry about all of this. If I would have just told Roger the truth in the beginning—"

"Shhh. It's over."

"No, it's not. Trip, they stole my father's money."

"What do you mean?"

"Stone said something about rigging the faro bank. They were in it together. I'm not excusing my father's choices, but . . ."

"I know." He pulled her into a tight embrace.

She shivered again. "I just want it to all go away."

"It will. I promise."

Reaching the boat shop, Trip held the door for her. "If we go into the workshop, the embers should already be glowing beneath the troughs. I'll throw on another log and that ought to warm you up."

They crossed through the office, Trip snagging a jacket from a hook on the way through. He stirred the embers and wrapped her in the navy wool coat. How could she be cold when it was at least eighty degrees tonight?

Trip stood behind her, wrapping his arms around her waist. "Better?"

"Much." She leaned into his solid chest, letting the warmth in her heart fill her.

"Get your hands off her." Roger stepped in through the open back door.

Trip moved between Marguerite and the man who'd made her life miserable. "What are you doing here?"

"I came to take what's mine." He pulled out a small pistol from his pocket.

Marguerite gasped.

Roger's lips curled and he raised his bushy eyebrows. "When

I saw you at the icehouse, I figured if you won, you'd bring her here. If you didn't, Stone would have taken care of you, and I'd still be able to have her. Either way, she's mine."

"She isn't yours." He took a step forward. "She belongs to God, and there's no way you're taking her anywhere."

Marguerite turned when she heard someone in the office doorway. Captain Andrews nodded toward her. Then she saw the rifle resting in his hand, aimed directly at Roger.

"Trip," he said, "I thought you'd like to know I already sent Harry for the sheriff. And mister, I'd set down that little gun if I were you. I'm not exactly feeling friendly toward you right now."

Roger paused, but when Captain Andrews didn't flinch, he laid the pistol on the floor. He held his arms out. "So it's come to this, Marguerite. Who's going to believe you? The sheriff knows who I am. It'll be your word against mine, and you're going to look like a fool. Why don't you let this go?"

She stepped beside Trip. "You tried to force me to marry you by stealing my father's money, your partner almost killed Trip, and you nearly froze me to death."

"I didn't steal it. He gambled it away."

"With help from your partner."

"All right, I'm a businessman, so I'll make you a deal." He pushed up his spectacles. "I'll repay all of your father's losses if you keep this from the authorities. Your family will have their money, and you can go have a happily ever after with sailor boy."

"Let you go free and you'll repay his losses? All of it?" It was almost too good to be true. She turned to Trip. "What do you think I should do?"

He didn't take his eyes from Roger. "It's your decision."

Telling the sheriff that the whole incident was a misunderstanding would be such a simple thing to do. But she was so tired of the lies and so tired of not trusting the Lord.

The truth will set you free.

She licked her lips. "I won't lie anymore. If my family has to suffer the consequences for my father's choices, then so be it. I have to trust God to take care of us."

Last night seemed like a lifetime ago. When the sheriff had arrived, he'd arrested Roger and said he'd also arrest Clyde Stone before morning. He'd warned Marguerite that Stone was a slippery character, but he still thought he might be able to get her father's money from the gambling hall owner. Stone had too much to lose if he didn't cooperate.

Now tonight, Marguerite was free. No lies weighed her down. A lightness filled her as she went about preparing for the Water Carnival ball, the conclusion of the festivities.

Lilly held out a sapphire blue moiré and cream-colored damask gown. "I been savin' this one for a special night 'cause I know it's your favorite."

"Thank you, Lilly." Tears pricked her eyes.

"Now, don't go gettin' all misty. You'll mess up that pretty face of yours."

"You are the best friend I could have ever hoped for, and I don't know what's going to happen to us—to you."

"God'll take care of me, Miss Marguerite." She touched a handkerchief to Marguerite's tear-streaked cheeks. "He always does. Don't you fret. Now let's get you dressed for that dance."

Marguerite took Trip's breath away. From the envious expressions of the other men at the ball, he could tell they

356

found her fascinating. She moved with a rare grace and fire. They couldn't help but watch her.

His chest swelled as he took her into his arms. She was remarkable. Nothing kept her down. Nothing stopped her. Even tonight, she had overcome the discouraging events and now danced as if her only thought was of him.

Although she couldn't possibly look lovelier, it wasn't the elegant gown, the upsweep of her honeyed hair, or the sparkle in her powder blue eyes that drew him to her like a moth to a flame. Tonight it was a heart at peace with the Lord.

The music died away from the waltz and she mentioned the heat of the room.

He chuckled. "Yesterday you couldn't get warm and today you're too hot. Just like a woman. Can't make up your mind."

She swatted his arm.

He flashed a grin and dropped a kiss on her cheek. "Let's go outside for a breath of fresh air."

They migrated to an empty area in the club's veranda. Stopping by the rail, she turned to face him, gently brushing her finger over his bruised lip. Her heart swelled. "I'm sorry you got hurt because of me."

"It's nothing."

"I'm sure your head doesn't agree." She placed her hand on his heart, a rush of feelings engulfing her. "But I hurt you more here."

He covered her hand with his own. "The truth is painful sometimes. We both had a lot to learn about it."

"Your mother's death?"

"Was tragic, but it's good to know she didn't leave me."

Pain flashed in his eyes. He looked upward. "She's up there—in your stars—watching over us."

"My stars?" She stepped away from him, but kept hold of his hand and tipped her head to the sky. "Do you know why I like them so much?"

"Because it drives your mother crazy?"

She giggled. He knew her so well. "That too. But it's because they always remind me of how great, how vast, God is. Nothing I do or don't do can take away God's love. For someone like me, that's important."

He kissed her gloved fingertips.

"Look! A shooting star." She pointed at the sky.

"Make a wish." He moved behind her and wrapped his arms around her waist.

She closed her eyes, let her head fall back against his shoulder, and made her silent request. "Did you see the comet last November?"

"I think the whole city saw it."

"It scared my mother. Especially the earth tremors afterward. She thought the world was coming to an end."

"I'm glad she was wrong, because then I wouldn't have met you." He hugged her tighter. "What did you do?"

"I made a wish on it."

"Why doesn't that surprise me?" Laughter filled his voice. "Let me guess, big comet, big wish. Same one or different from tonight's?"

"Same."

"You're not going to tell me?"

"Then it wouldn't come true." She turned in his arms. "Tell me yours."

"That hardly seems fair. Besides, how do you know I made a wish?"

"I just do."

"Well . . ." He paused, and the look in his eyes made her shiver in anticipation. "Since I don't believe in wishes, I'll tell you I've been praying I could spend the rest of my life pulling you out of the water."

"Wait a minute, mister. I pulled you out this time." She stopped and her eyes grew wide. Her heart hiccuped. What was he saying?

He grinned, dimples deepening like craters. "I do believe I rendered you speechless. I think I'll take this rare opportunity to ask you to marry me." He cupped her face. "I love you, Marguerite Westing. I love how you make me laugh. I love your determination, and I love your spirit. I love how you make waves wherever you go. Will you fill all my days with strawberry sundaes and stars and surprises? Will you do me the honor of becoming my wife?"

She blinked. He meant it. He loved her. Her heart felt like it would burst.

She cocked her head to the side and bit her lip. "On one condition."

"Oh?"

"You let me sail with you wherever you go."

"I think that could be arranged."

His head dipped, and his lips, soft and gentle, grazed her own. Then, cradling her head, he deepened the kiss, filling it with passion and promise.

Her wish and her prayer had come true.

Author's Note

Having lived in Council Bluffs all my life, I grew up hearing about Lake Manawa and its heyday as a resort from my dad, Lester Kinney, who lived near the lake as a boy. As I researched this area, I discovered that much of the rich history would have been lost if Frank Smetana, author of *A History of Lake Manawa*, had not interviewed those who lived or worked at Lake Manawa during the resort period. His compilation of the history was invaluable.

Many people have asked me how much of *Making Waves* is true. I explain that the characters and plot are fictional, but the setting, which is almost a character itself, was very real. Miss Fishbaugh did light herself on fire and jump from the tower into the water every night. The rich camped in tents at the lake, there was a hog farm gambling establishment that sat on the county line, and there was a Water Carnival copied after one seen at the World's Fair.

By the late 1920s, the resort had fallen out of popularity with the elite, due in part to the clientele and workers the Midway attracted. Attendance at the park declined, and several buildings were destroyed by a series of fires and tornadoes.

In 1927, the park was closed and the last of the remaining

buildings auctioned off. My grandfather purchased one of the bathhouses for three hundred dollars and moved it to a lot on what was once part of the Midway. My father and his two brothers grew up in the long, narrow bathhouse-turned-home. It was torn down only a few years ago.

Today Lake Manawa is a beautiful state park, but sadly, nothing remains of the grand pavilions, the Midway, or the boardwalk.

Acknowledgments

God has blessed me immeasurably more than all I could ask or imagine, and I am deeply grateful for the people He has placed in my life. Before any pages were filled, He gave me a risk-taking husband, David, who wouldn't let my dream die. He then blessed us with three children, Parker, Caroline, and Emma, who understood why their mother spent hours on her computer in the freezing basement.

I also want to extend my heartfelt thanks to:

Andrea Doering for her willingness to take a chance on this story and for her belief in this series.

Judy Miller, my dear friend and mentor.

Shannon Vannatter, Brenda Anderson, Marlene Garand, and Dawn Ford for their wonderful critiques and precious friendship.

My agent Wendy Lawton for cheering me on.

Deb Garland for her sailing expertise.

My church and extended family for their prayers and support.

The Scribblers. Write or wrong, we write.

And thank you, dear reader, for taking this journey with me. May you always worship the Lord in spirit and in truth.

Lorna Seilstad is a history buff, antique collector, and freelance graphic designer. A former high school English and journalism teacher, she has won several online writing awards and is a member of American Christian Fiction Writers. She lives in and draws her setting from Iowa. This is her first novel.

"If you're looking for an awesome writer and a story charged with romance, you don't want to miss *A Hope Undaunted*."

—JUDITH MILLER, author of *Somewhere to Belong*, Daughters of Amana series

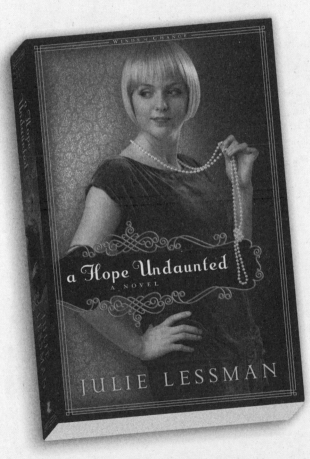

The delightful story of Kate O'Connor, a smart and sassy woman who has her goals laid out for the future—including the perfect husband and career. Will she follow her plans or her heart?

Revell
a division of Baker Publishing Group
www.RevellBooks.com

Available Wherever Books Are Sold

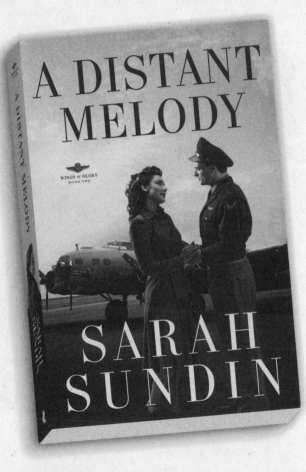

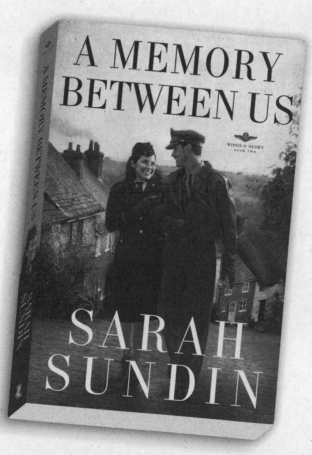